PRAISE

"Jeneva Rose is the queen of twists."
—Colleen Hoover, #1 *New York Times* bestselling author

"Rose demonstrates a formidable command of character . . . Fans will enjoy the ride."
—*Publishers Weekly*

"Jeneva Rose is a powerhouse of an author, and an exceptionally talented writer. Sign me up for whatever she comes up with next!"
—Hannah Mary McKinnon, bestselling author of *The Revenge List*

"Rose's deep insight into the complexities of human nature and her gorgeous prose carried me along in a single breathless read."
—Karen Dionne, bestselling author of *The Marsh King's Daughter* and *The Wicked Sister*

"Suspense at its finest: original, emotional, and a twist for the ages. Jeneva Rose is a force to be reckoned with."
—Alex Finlay, bestselling author of *The Night Shift*

DATING AFTER THE END OF THE WORLD

OTHER TITLES BY JENEVA ROSE

STAND-ALONE NOVELS

Home Is Where the Bodies Are

It's a Date (Again)

You Shouldn't Have Come Here

One of Us Is Dead

The Girl I Was

#CrimeTime (with Drew Pyne)

THE PERFECT SERIES

The ~~Perfect~~ Marriage

The ~~Perfect~~ Divorce

THE DETECTIVE KIMBERLEY KING BOOKS

Dead Woman Crossing

Last Day Alive

DATING AFTER THE END OF THE WORLD

JENEVA ROSE

This is a work of fiction. Names, characters, organizations, places, events, and incidents are either products of the author's imagination or are used fictitiously. Otherwise, any resemblance to actual persons, living or dead, is purely coincidental.

Text copyright © 2025 by Jeneva Rose
All rights reserved.

No part of this book may be reproduced, or stored in a retrieval system, or transmitted in any form or by any means, electronic, mechanical, photocopying, recording, or otherwise, without express written permission of the publisher.

Published by Montlake, Seattle
www.apub.com

Amazon, the Amazon logo, and Montlake are trademarks of Amazon.com, Inc., or its affiliates.

EU product safety contact:
Amazon Media EU S. à r.l.
38, avenue John F. Kennedy, L-1855 Luxembourg
amazonpublishing-gpsr@amazon.com

ISBN-13: 9781662520204 (paperback)
ISBN-13: 9781662520211 (digital)

Cover design by Jarrod Taylor
Cover image: © KingVector, © YummyBuum, © MPrapat Aowsakorn, © PreciousArt / Shutterstock

Printed in the United States of America

This one's for the man who attended my book event back in 2022 and held up a sign he wrote on the back of a Cheerios box that said "Jeneva Rose, please write a zombie suspense murder thriller killer."
I don't think this is exactly what you had in mind—specifically, the enemies-to-lovers storyline—but I've taken it upon myself to redact portions of your copy.
So, request granted.
Here's your zombie book, Dad.

Chapter 1

2009

My dad says the world's going to end, and we'll be the only ones ready for it. That's why he's got me out here on a Saturday afternoon digging holes for a perimeter fence and a barricade, whatever that means. The kids at school get to have fun on the weekends, but not me, because my dad's a prepper. And apparently, that makes me one too. At least until I turn eighteen and can get the hell out of here. Only five more years, but who's counting?

It's nearly the end of September and fall should be approaching, but that wet Wisconsin-summer heat still lingers in the air. It's sweltering, having overstayed its welcome. Most people don't think of heat when it comes to the Dairy State, but our summers are hot and sticky, or maybe they just feel that way because of how brutally cold and long our winters are.

The sun's rays beat down on my skin, making every pore on my body ooze sweat. My arms ache and the palms of my hands sting, thanks to a spatter of blisters. Some are freshly formed bubbles, ready to pop. Others are torn open, exposing the raw, tender skin beneath. I'd wear the pair of work gloves tucked in the back pocket of my overalls, but they're too big and they slow me down, which is the last thing I need. I just want to be done for the day, and I know that's not possible until the work is finished—as my dad always says, *Pearsons don't quit until the job is done.*

I pause, let out a heavy sigh, and glance over at Dad. He sports a damp white T-shirt and an old pair of ripped jeans, complete with a focused gaze and a firm-set mouth. That's how he always appears: determined. I'd find it admirable if it weren't so annoying. Gripping both handles of the post digger, he plunges it into a hole I previously started, stamping it into the soil a few times before clamping it closed and excavating a hefty scoop of dirt. I lean against my shovel and wipe my arm across my sweaty forehead while my dad continues to work. Obviously, I don't have the stamina or strength he has. I'm a hundred pounds soaking wet, whereas Dad is at least 6'3" and built like a brick shithouse. His words, not mine. To me, he looks more like a lumberjack, thanks to his thick beard and burly frame.

"Are we almost done?" I place a hand over my eyes, shielding them from the sun so I can see his facial expression.

Dad drops the post digger into the hole and uses the bottom of his shirt to soak up the sweat that's amassed on his face and neck.

He looks over at me, his mouth still set in a hard line. "It's not even noon yet, Casey."

That doesn't answer my question.

I tighten my ponytail and push back several baby hairs clinging to my forehead. "But we started at seven."

"Yeah, an hour later than I wanted to," he says, raising a brow.

I roll my eyes and groan, throwing my head back dramatically. "Why are we even doing this?"

"To keep us safe."

I mouth the words at the exact same time he utters them and then snap my head forward, glowering. "That's all you ever say, Father."

"Because it's all I ever mean, daughter." The corner of his lip perks up in amusement.

"Can't we ever do anything fun? Most dads take their kids to the park or to the movies or out to ice cream. You just make me work."

"It's not work. It's prep for the end—"

"Of the world," I cut him off, mockingly reciting what he's repeated to me every day for the past three years. When he first told me we had to prep for the end of the world, I thought it was exciting, like we were embarking on our own supersecret, fun adventure. But after a couple of years, that excitement wore off, and now I'm just tired, longing for a normal life . . . not whatever this is.

I toss my shovel in the grass and put my hands on my hips. "What if it never ends, Dad? Then what? We just wasted all this time prepping for nothing."

He scratches at his beard. "Well, I really hope it doesn't . . . but it's going to because everything eventually ends, and that includes the world."

I know you're supposed to believe your parents, trust what they're saying, and I have. I've believed every word my dad has uttered since I learned what words meant, but now I'm not so sure anymore. I stopped believing in Santa when I was nine years old, and I feel like I'm gonna stop believing in my dad one day too. Maybe I already have.

"If it does, why would I wanna stick around? I'd rather die along with it." I raise my chin defiantly.

"No, you wouldn't, Casey."

"Yes, I would. I hate it here."

Dad lets out a heavy sigh. "Let's just get the rest of these holes dug, and then I'll make us some sandwiches, and we can enjoy them under the apple tree." He seals his offer with a smile and goes back to work, plunging the post digger into the ground.

"And then what?" I practically yell.

He glances at me while excavating a scoop of dirt. "Then we'll install the posts, the fencing, and the barbwire. You know that, Casey."

My bottom lip trembles and tears well up in the corners of my eyes. I turn away to hide my frustration and kick the handle of the shovel before plopping down in the grass. Pulling my knees into my chest, I try to make myself as small as possible. The post digger thuds against the hard soil, followed by Dad's work boots crunching over dried grass. He kneels in front of me, lifting my chin with his thumb and index finger, forcing me to meet his gaze. I'm not one to cry, and he knows that. But it's all too much.

"Sweetheart, what's wrong?"

"I don't wanna do this anymore," I say, jerking away.

"Why not?"

"Because I wanna be normal."

"Who says we're not normal?" Dad cracks a small smile.

I pull a piece of skin from an open blister on my dirty, inflamed hand and flick it into the grass.

"The kids at school." I briefly look up at him. "They say you're a freak and a kook who wears a tinfoil hat."

"Well, I don't care what people say about me, Case, so I wouldn't let it bother you." He ruffles my hair.

I smack his hand away. "They say I'm a weirdo too! They call me Crazy Pearson." A tear breaks past my lower lashes, spilling out. "And they filled my locker with canned goods yesterday."

Dad's brows shove together with concern. "What? When did this all start?"

"Two weeks ago. We had to write a short paper on what we did over the summer and present it to the class. I wrote about all the work we did, the trench we dug for fresh water, the bunker excavation, the gardening, combat training, installing solar panels, everything. And now . . . all they do is make fun of me, except Tessa. She's my only friend."

Dad's arms engulf me as he pulls me in for a tight hug, my face smushing against his brawny chest. I want to shove him away, but I need the embrace more than I need to be obstinate in this moment.

"I'm sorry, sweetie. I didn't realize you were having such a hard time at school."

"I wasn't. Everything was fine until stupid Blake came along . . ." The words come out muffled, and the strength I was trying to display fades away. I sob, unable to speak.

"Who's Blake?" he asks, rubbing my back to comfort me.

"A new boy at my school." I pull away and meet his gaze. "He's the one that got everyone to make fun of me."

Dad arches a brow. "That's probably because he likes you. Boys always pick on the girls they like."

I scrunch up my face. "Well, I don't like him at all. He's an asshole."

"Casey!" Dad warns, but he's unable to hide the small, amused smile on his face.

"Sorry . . . but he is, though."

"I don't doubt that. Do you want me to talk to his parents?"

"No, Dad. Then I'll be a freak and a tattletale. It'll be way worse."

"Okay, do you want me to scare him, maybe rough him up a little?" He pretends to box with closed fists.

"Dad, no!" I say, slapping his hands.

He puts his punching paws away and chuckles. "Then what would you like me to do, Case?"

"Nothing," I huff. "I'll just . . . I'll just ignore him."

Dad pats me on the shoulder. "I think that's a good idea, sweetheart."

"But I'm gonna picture Blake's stupid face every time I spike that shovel into the dirt," I say with a firm nod as I wipe away the tears with the back of my hand.

"And every time you hit the boxing bag too."

"And every time I wield my throwing stars."

Dad grins. "And when the world ends, we won't let Blake in here."

"That's right. He'll be crying down at the road begging me to save him, and I'll be like, 'You should have been nice to me, Blake, because now you're going to die.'" I put on a huge smile.

A look of concern flashes across Dad's face.

"What?" I shrug. "He's a rotten, terrible, stupid boy."

"I know, but just because he's terrible doesn't mean you need to be."

I let out a heavy sigh and nod. Dad gets to his feet and reaches his hand out for mine. In one fell swoop, he yanks me up into a standing position.

"Let's finish up here. I've got ice cream Drumsticks in the freezer with our names on them." He smiles.

"Deal," I say. The sun set high in the sky illuminates his head, making it look as though he's wearing a crown. We shake on it and get back to work.

I grip the handle with two hands and raise the shovel, glowering at the partially dug hole while picturing Blake's stupid face in the dirt. If I squint, I can even see his bright-green irises. The other girls at school think he's hot because his eyes are the color of summertime grass, but I think they look more like vomit. I plunge the blade down, spiking it as hard as I can into the soil, and then I smile.

Chapter 2

Sixteen years later

The toe of my shoe taps quickly against the tiled floor while I wait for a pot of coffee to finish brewing. I only have a few minutes before a nurse or an attending physician comes looking for me, abruptly ending my reprieve. As a doctor in residency, my breaks are short and few and far between. *Come on, come on,* I silently plead, willing the process to speed up. A news bulletin flashes across the television screen hanging in the corner of the break room, snapping me out of my daze.

"Tonight's top story, a mysterious illness that popped up seemingly overnight is sending people to area hospitals in droves. Patients are reporting flu-like symptoms, such as nausea, brain fog, and debilitating headaches. Top health officials are unsure as to what caused the sudden outbreak, but their top priorities are to treat the symptoms and slow the spread."

Every year, we go through something like this. A new illness. A new outbreak. The news hypes it up for ratings. Crowds of fearful people show up at their local hospitals, complaining of sniffles and runny noses. And those prepping for the end of the world sit back, thinking this is it, this is the end. It never is, though. Modern medicine always prevails.

The door swings open and I sigh, realizing my break is finished before it even started. I glance over my shoulder, ready to address whoever is about to request my time and energy, but instead, I find Nate strolling in with no urgency whatsoever. He's got it all—looks, height, brains, a great job, and a full head of hair—so I'm not exactly sure what it is he sees in me.

"Nate," I say with a small smile.

His hand cups the back of my head, pulling me into him. Nate presses his lips hard into mine, and my cheeks immediately feel warm.

"It's Dr. Warner," he teases. "I'd hate to have to report you to HR."

"I'd hate that too, Doctor," I say before kissing him again. We both work long hours, our shifts overlapping here and there, so the moments we have together are fleeting. We try to make the most of them.

"Dr. Warner?" a voice calls out, interrupting us.

We quickly pull apart. Turning away from him, I wipe my mouth, straighten my top, and try to look as nonchalant as possible. Nurse Garcia stands in the doorway, a clipboard in hand. She saw what we were doing, but she pretends not to have noticed.

"Yes, Nurse Garcia, what is it?" Nate says, brushing his white coat flat and running a hand through his perfectly coiffed blond hair. Even though he's my fiancé, I still don't know how he maintains the shine and volume throughout a full fourteen-hour shift.

"Emergency waiting room is backed up due to that virus outbreak, and we're out of room, so we can't check any more people in. I contacted other area hospitals, and they're in the same boat as we are, so what do you suggest we do?"

"Start discharging patients, then," Nate says.

"No can do." She shakes her head. "There aren't any to discharge."

Nate sighs heavily, scratching his brow. "Do we have more beds?"

Nurse Garcia nods.

I pour myself a cup of coffee and impatiently take a small sip, burning my tongue and upper lip in the process. I need the caffeine to get through the rest of my shift. I should be halfway done at this point, but given the state of the hospital, it's most likely just starting.

"Have a few orderlies start lining the hallway closest to the emergency room with beds on either side. Space them six feet apart from one another, check in any patients reporting symptoms related to that unknown illness, and assign them to a hallway bed. Just mark them with numbers if you need to keep track. Bed one, bed two, et cetera... Dr. Pearson and I"—he throws me a quick, flirty smile—"will process all the 'flu,' or whatever it is, patients and hopefully get them in and out quickly. Most of them are just looking for medication to manage their symptoms, right?"

"For the most part, yes, but we're starting to see repeat patients, ones that came in yesterday. I recognized at least eight when I did a quick scan of the waiting room," she says.

Nate furrows his brow for a moment but then relaxes it. "Get the repeat patients checked in first. Hopefully, it'll give us an idea of what's not working. That way we can make adjustments for any new ones coming in with similar symptoms."

"Yes, Dr. Warner," Nurse Garcia says, before making a quick exit.

I blow on my hot coffee and look to Nate with a coy smile. "Wonder if there's a spare bed for you and me."

He snaps his fingers and points one in my direction. "That reminds me. My parents are coming into town in a few weeks."

"The mention of us in bed together reminded you of your parents?" I cock my head.

Nate chuckles. "No, *spare* and *bed*." He flicks a hand at me. "Anyway, they want to meet your dad, and I'd like too as well. I don't want to meet him for the first time at our wedding. So, is there any chance he can come into town? Even just for dinner."

I take a long sip of my coffee. It's still too hot, but I need time to come up with an excuse while also going through the Rolodex of reasons I've already given him for why he can't meet my dad. *Let's see. There's the farm that doesn't exist that he has to take care of. He's had every doctor's appointment under the sun. Jury duty. Can't use that again. His truck's in the shop. He's on medication that he's not supposed to drive on. He caught the flu again. He's got an old army friend staying with him. Hmmm.*

"I'll ask him," I say, knowing full well that I won't, and ultimately, I'll tell Nate that he can't come for one reason or another, once I think of one I haven't already used. It's been nearly two years since Nate and I started dating, and a month ago, he slipped this sparkly rock on my finger and asked me to marry him. It's too big for my taste, but I told him I loved it, and I said yes. Afterward, Nate wanted me to call my dad to tell him the news, but I claimed it went to voicemail and that I'd call him back. I never did.

"Your dad can stay with us too, and if driving in the city is a problem, he could take the train down from Harvard, and I'll pick him up."

"I'll let him know." *Another lie.*

The truth is, I haven't really spoken to my dad in nine years—I mean, aside from occasional short replies to his lengthy texts, letting him know I'm still alive. But I can't tell Nate that, because if I did, I'd have to explain to him why I don't really have a relationship with my dad. That's not something I ever intend to revisit. I left that part of my life behind, and that's where I want it to stay.

"I'd really like to meet him, Casey."

"I know, and he wants to meet you too," I say. It's not a total lie. If my dad knew Nate existed, he'd want to more than meet him. He'd welcome Nate with open arms and treat him like the son he never had.

Nate nods, accepting my answer again. I'm not sure how much longer I can keep up this charade. We've already agreed on a two-year engagement so I can finish my residency before I have to start thinking about planning a wedding. Plus, Nate and I haven't been able to get out of the city for even a night, due to one of us always being on call. That's the only reason I've been able to keep my past separated from my present. If I had known when Nate and I first started dating that our relationship would last longer than a few months, I would have told him my dad lived on the other side of the country, rather than up in Wisconsin.

"Dr. Warner to the hallway waiting area. Dr. Warner to the hallway waiting area," a voice calls through the hospital PA system.

"Ready?" Nate asks, tossing me a charming smile.

Grinning back, I plant a kiss on his lips. "Always."

By *always*, I mean from the age of fourteen—that's when I knew I wanted to be a doctor. My father's impractical way of protecting people never made sense to me, so I sought out a realistic way of actually doing some good. An ideal I still cling to in the early stages of my career, despite complaints from the other, more jaded doctors, who now seem only to enjoy the paycheck, Nate included.

Nate and I walk side by side through the long corridor, the walls a sterile mix of white and light blue, not shades you would ever pick for a room in your home.

Hospital beds line either side of the hall, spaced six feet apart, just as he requested. Half are still empty, but a dozen plus, set closest to the waiting room, are already occupied with newly checked-in patients. I recognize several from yesterday, but from their pale faces and sunken eyes, it's clear their conditions have worsened.

A middle-aged woman presses her palms against her temples and lets out a moan. She rocks back and forth, trying to alleviate the pain. A thin man squeezes his eyes shut and winces. Nate and I pull apart to make way for a nurse pushing an ailing patient in a wheelchair. Nods and tight smiles are exchanged, our way of saying, *This is totally fucked*, without actually saying it, because it's our job to stay calm.

We reach the first set of beds and do an about-face, surveying the work ahead of us. It's madness, with hospital staff moving quickly and a couple dozen confused and sick patients waiting to be seen. Some sit calmly, coughing and sneezing, while a few writhe in pain.

"You take the left, and I'll take the right," Nate says. "Report anything out of the ordinary, and let me know if you have any questions, okay?"

"Sounds good." I nod.

He reaches for my hand and squeezes it once before beelining to the bed located on the right side of the hall. My first patient is an older woman. She's lying on her back with her eyes closed. Her breaths are slow and deep, and she must have dozed off between when she was assigned to the bed and now. I review her chart, picking out key details. Repeat patient from around ten hours ago. Symptoms started about twelve hours ago. Fever increased to 102.4 degrees. Headache reported as an eight out of ten on the pain scale. Experiencing confusion, brain fog, and extreme fatigue.

I touch her shoulder lightly. "Ms. Klein, how're we doing?" My voice is soft to ensure I don't startle her. She doesn't stir, but her breathing remains steady. After ten seconds and a few more light touches, I decide to let her rest with the plan to circle back. She seems to be well enough, and there are too many patients to tend to. I approach a thin middle-aged man with a shiny goatee, either from good grooming or spittle and tears. He writhes in pain, begging for pain meds. I grab his clipboard, reviewing the notes: Repeat patient from yesterday. Symptoms started around twenty-four hours ago.

Just as I'm about to greet him, a confused voice calls from behind me, "Where am I?"

I turn, finding Ms. Klein seated in her bed, her mouth agape, while her eyes frantically scan the hall.

"Hi, Ms. Klein," I say, quickly returning to her side. "You're at the hospital. How are you feeling?"

Her skin has paled to the color of the crisp white sheets she's sitting on, and there's an emptiness to her expression, like she's looking through me rather than at me.

"Who are you?" she asks.

"I'm Dr. Pearson," I say, touching the name badge clipped to the front pocket of my white coat. "Can you tell me how you're feeling?" I try to meet her gaze, but her eyes won't settle and are constantly on the move.

"Where am I?"

"You're at the hospital, Ms. Klein," I tell her again.

"Ms. Klein?"

I tilt my head, unsure if she's repeating my words or asking a question. "Yes, Ms. Klein," I confirm.

"Who's that?" she asks.

I find her response perplexing to say the least, and my first thought is that it must be the result of a head injury. I retrieve a penlight from my pocket and click it on. "Ms. Klein, can you look straight ahead?" She squints and looks away as I shine the light in her eyes, trying to examine her pupil dilation.

"What's going on?" she asks. "Where am I?"

I don't answer her this time because she's clearly not retaining anything. Something is very wrong.

I repocket my penlight and flip through her chart again, double-checking to make sure I didn't miss anything.

"Hey," I say to Nurse Garcia as she passes by, hustling back to the waiting room.

"Yes, Dr. Pearson." She stops in her tracks, exhaling sharply, like she's grateful for the brief pause.

I step toward her. "Did Ms. Klein report a fall or an accident of some sort?"

"No, why?" she says, wiping her glistening forehead with the back of her arm.

"Because she doesn't know who she is or where she is." I keep my voice low. "Are there any other patients experiencing confusion or memory loss?"

Nurse Garcia shakes her head. "Not that I've seen. But maybe Ms. Klein did experience a fall or have an accident."

"That's what I was thinking, but her pupils responded normally to a light test." I scratch the side of my neck, mulling it over. "I'm ordering a CT scan to rule out a head injury," I say, noting it on Ms. Klein's medical chart before handing it over.

"I'll get that in the system right away, Dr. Pearson."

"Thanks. How's the waiting room looking?"

She sighs heavily. "It's packed. If this continues, we're gonna look like a nightclub with a line out the door."

"Not possible. Nightclubs have closing hours," I say with a smirk. She stifles a laugh and smiles at me, before heading back out to the waiting room.

"And I want those CT results as soon as they're in," I add.

"You got it," Nurse Garcia calls over her shoulder.

Nate appears at my side. "You're ordering a CT scan?" he asks, his eyes meeting mine.

"Yeah, for Ms. Klein, to rule out a head injury," I whisper.

"She came in for the flu, though."

"I know, but I think she's lost her memory."

"What?" Nate pulls his head back.

"She doesn't know her own name."

He raises a brow and glances over at Ms. Klein. Her eyes are searching the hallway for recognition or familiarity.

"Is she shaking?" Nate squints.

I notice it too, a slight tremble, and I'm immediately at her bedside. "Ms. Klein, are you okay?"

Her teeth chatter, and her body quakes.

"Where's her medical chart?" Nate asks.

"I gave it to Nurse Garcia, so she could set up a CT scan," I explain.

Ms. Klein shakes even harder. Instinctively, I press the back of my hand against her forehead. It's cold, like the metal railings outside the hospital on a winter night. "Her fever broke." I pull my hand away and look to Nate, cocking my head in confusion.

"That's good."

"No, Garcia took her temperature maybe fifteen minutes ago. It was 102.4. This . . . isn't possible." I grab a thermometer and a disposable guard from a box set beneath her bed.

I tell Ms. Klein that I'm going to take her temperature, but she doesn't seem to register my words. Maybe her chattering teeth are too loud for her to hear me.

Swiping the thermometer across her forehead, I bring the screen to my line of sight, waiting for it to beep and a number to appear. When it does, my mouth drops open.

"What is it?" Nate asks, grabbing my elbow to steady me.

"89.8."

"What? That's . . ."

"Impossible," I say, finishing his sentence.

"Yeah, unless we were pulling her out of Lake Michigan or a meat locker."

"He needs help," a woman yells, stealing our attention.

She wears a look of horror as she points at the bed one down from Ms. Klein's—where the man with the shiny goatee was writhing in pain just a few moments ago. He now lies completely still. I run to him and immediately check for a pulse. It's faint, but it's there beneath his cold skin. His mouth is parted, but his eyes remain closed.

"Pulse?" Nate calls out, still tending to Ms. Klein. He helps her lie back and covers her with blankets.

"Barely, and he's cold too," I say.

Nate's eyes widen with fear or surprise—I'm not sure which. "Watch out!"

Just as I turn my head, the man with the shiny goatee lunges up at me and sinks his teeth into my flesh. It happens in a flash, giving me no time to react. The first thought that goes through my head is that I should have seen it coming. The pain is instant and excruciating. He clamps down harder, ripping through skin and sinew. I howl in agony and try to pull away, but his bite is too strong. I ball up my free hand and thrust it into the side of his head. The two-carat diamond on my ring finger slices at his flesh, but does nothing to stop him from gnawing on my arm.

Nate pins him down by his shoulders, yelling for security.

Screams and cries fill the hall, my own and others.

Fed up, Nate punches the man in the side of the head as hard as he can, over and over, until his jaw goes lax. I jerk away, falling back and landing on my ass.

"We need security!" Nate shouts again, still pinning the crazed man down as he thrashes and growls, snapping his teeth. I scramble to my feet, grabbing a hospital gown and wrapping it around my wound.

A piercing scream cuts through all the chaos. Four beds down, a nurse tumbles to the floor, blood pooling from her torn-open cheek. The patient she was tending to staggers toward the downed nurse, his mouth and teeth stained red. There's another scream, and another, each one more earsplitting than the last. Several of the repeat patients have become feral, attacking anyone in sight, their nails and teeth tearing into flesh, painting the once sterile hall red. It's complete madness, and as much as I want to help, I already know it's a lost cause.

"Nate, we have to get out of here!"

He's still trying to restrain the man, but the scene unfolding around him is far more dangerous. A security guard bursts through the emergency waiting room doors, his gun already drawn. Nate releases the guy and rushes to my side. We back up behind security as the man swings his legs out of bed and lurches forward, snarling and grunting, his lips and teeth coated with my blood.

The security guard shakily points his gun, telling the man to stop, but he doesn't.

"I'm warning you. Stop or I'll shoot." His voice has very little conviction in it, so I'm not even sure he's capable of pulling the trigger. I consider taking it from him and doing it myself, but his gun only holds ten bullets max, and I know he's gonna need a hell of a lot more than that. Nate and I continue backing away, watching in horror as patients and staff are ripped and torn apart by other sickly patients. This isn't some flu-like virus.

The security guard finally fires a shot, piercing the man in the shoulder. It does nothing to slow him down. Another shot rings out. This time it strikes him in the other shoulder, but he continues staggering toward him. Two more shots. One in the upper arm, the other in the thigh. Those don't stop him either.

"What's going on? Where am I?" Ms. Klein says, rising from her bed.

Several more shots ring out before the gun clicks over and over, signaling that it's out of ammunition. Panicked, he scrambles to reload. But it's too late. The man riddled with bullets lurches at the security guard, puncturing his neck. Blood squirts everywhere, having clearly ruptured the carotid artery. The guard screams as he's yanked to the ground.

"What do we do?" Nate looks to me with wide eyes full of fear.

"We have to get out of here."

"What about our patients?" he asks. It's a silly question, given the scene before us. Maybe Nate just needs a second opinion that fleeing is the right thing to do. We took an oath to do everything in our power to save them, but that's not happening tonight.

"Those aren't our patients anymore," I say, reaching for his hand.

Nate leads the way, pulling me with him through the doors behind us that lead to the emergency waiting room. I press my wounded arm against my chest to ensure the hospital gown stays tightly wrapped around it. It's full-on panic—most likely from the gunshots, because the horror we just witnessed hasn't made its way out here yet. They have no idea what's coming. But even so, people shove and trample one another, fight or flight taking over.

"Dr. Warner," the front desk receptionist calls out. "Police are on their way."

It's too late for that. Whatever's happening is just the beginning. A thought creeps into the back of my mind, one that I try to suppress immediately, but it won't stop clawing at me, scratching and scratching relentlessly. *He was right about everything.*

"Get out of the hospital!" I yell.

Her face crumples with confusion like she can't believe what she's hearing. "What?" she says just as the doors behind us burst open with those things that used to be our patients spilling out, like hell just threw up. Their arms are stretched out in front of them, already clawing the air, mouths agape, snarling and snapping. They're caked in gore, with bits of human tissue stuck to their clothes and skin, some even wedged between their teeth. The hallway behind them is a bloodbath. People who were walking and talking just a few minutes ago lie still on the floor, torn and ripped to shreds, crimson liquid pooling around them. They're not people anymore, though. They're bodies.

"Let's go," Nate says, leading us toward the exit doors.

Normally, the hospital is a place you go when you need help, but not today. We weave through the clusterfuck of fleeing people, a blur of screams and carnage. I'm nearly knocked over by a woman slamming into my side, but Nate keeps me upright, keeps me going, and never lets go of my hand. Unfortunately for the woman, there's no one holding hers, so she crashes to the ground face-first. A heavyset man tramples over her, his boot stomping her head. I look away, focusing on the exit sign up ahead. The glowing red letters blur together as I fight to push through the crowd. We just have to make it through those doors. Because I know if we do, we can survive this.

Chapter 3

Six weeks later

Roaring sirens, beeping horns, and the rumble of traffic are no longer the sounds of the city. It's mostly quiet these days, and when it's not, you know something's amiss—like right now.

I push the drapes aside only a sliver or so and peer out the living room window. Across the street, a woman stumbles along the sidewalk, yelling, "Hello? Is anyone there? I need help. Where am I? What's going on?"

Her cries of confusion echo, bouncing off the rows of townhomes lined up one right after another. In a different life, I would have helped her. But in this one, I know she's merely being used as bait to draw out someone like me, someone who hasn't been affected by the virus—or whatever it is.

I look down at the raised skin on my forearm—a pale purplish scar shaped like a set of human teeth. After I was bitten by an infected, I thought for sure I was a goner, but somehow, I was one of the lucky ones. I started getting really sick twelve hours after I was bitten. It felt like my brain was on fire. I was sweating buckets. My vision blurred. My head felt like it was in a vise, ready to pop. But at the twenty-four-hour mark, my fever broke, and I felt fine again.

I've learned the virus affects each person differently. I'm not sure why, but I know it does. Some, like the woman roaming the street or Ms. Klein, my patient at the hospital that night, lose all their memories, a total brain wipe. About twelve hours after infection, they become a shell of a person, a body with no sense of purpose or belonging. I call them *Nomes*—stands for *no memories*. I don't know what other people call them, because it's just been Nate and me since it all started. Actually, he calls them *Losers* because they lost their memories, but we're not on the same page with that name.

"What's going on out there?" Nate whispers from the kitchen.

"It's a Nome," I say, briefly looking at him. He stands in front of the stove watching a pot of water, waiting for it to boil. His shaggy hair is slicked back, and he sports a beard that he somehow manages to keep trimmed despite the world having ended—the one we knew, at least. As soon as the water begins to gurgle, bubbles bursting into plumes of steam, he pours two cups of rice into the pot and covers it with a lid.

My gaze returns to the poor, confused soul roaming outside our building. She stops suddenly, staggering in place as a pack of biters emerges from a courtyard through a broken gate. Their skin is covered in rashes and lesions, making them appear almost like burn victims. Their clothing is frayed and dirty, covered in blood and human remains. They don't speak. The only sounds they make are a mix of labored breaths, raspy grunts, growls, and snarls.

"Hello?!" she says, unsure of who or what is approaching her.

The creatures plod toward her, some faster than others. If this woman had the foresight, she could run, but she doesn't know who she is, what they are, or what's happened to this world. As soon as they reach her, they claw and bite at her flesh, shredding it with ease. She barely gets out a scream as she's dragged to the asphalt. Four of them dive headfirst into her stomach, like it's a trough set out especially for them, unraveling her intestines from her center. A deep-crimson pool seeps into the cracked pavement. I carefully slip my hand from the curtain, letting it close and settle back into place.

"This area is getting worse," Nate says, watching the pot on the stove. He doesn't have to see what just happened to know what happened. It's a common occurrence these days. "We can't stay here," he adds.

Here is Nate's apartment, nestled in a four-story building in the Lincoln Park neighborhood of Chicago. Even before everything happened, I hadn't lived with him long enough to feel like it was mine too. The top two floors are his, and so far, we've been able to go undetected. The skylights in the living room and kitchen provide light during the day, so we keep the shades drawn, further concealing our existence. It's better that no one knows we're here, because the only ones we can trust are ourselves. At night, we're careful, sticking to the rooms without windows and only using a single flashlight or a candle. We keep quiet too. Nate's downstairs neighbor fled, so between her food supply and the one I kept stocked (just in case), we've been able to survive thus far without venturing outside. But we won't be able to keep that up for much longer. The flat-screen TV hung above the fireplace and all the lamps and fixtures around the living room and kitchen are just that, lifeless fixtures. The power stopped working about a week after everything happened. I was surprised it lasted that long. The smell of rot from the refrigerator and freezer took days to get used to, but we did—because apparently, you can get used to anything.

"Casey! Did you hear me? We have to go." Nate is now right in front of my face, gripping both of my shoulders, his eyes darting back and forth, searching mine for a response.

"I know we do. But where?"

"What about your dad's place? Didn't you say he—"

"No," I cut him off before he even begins down that path.

"But you said he has like a compound, some sort of bunker. You two prepped for something like this."

I regret telling Nate about my dad and his compound. It was day twenty of us being locked in silent isolation. I was going stir crazy, and I'd gotten into a bottle of whiskey—well, more than gotten into it. And then I told Nate everything, everything I had been hiding from him about my past and my upbringing. He hasn't dropped it since I brought it up. For him, it's salvation. For me . . . I don't know what it is. I'm not even sure my dad is still alive and well. I know he prepared for the end of times, but was he really prepared for whatever this is? I'd call it a zombie apocalypse if it weren't for the Nomes. Those I can't make sense of.

"We're running low on food, and it's too dangerous here. Your dad will have supplies, right? And you said he lives in the middle of nowhere, Wisconsin. Less people means less danger."

"But it's not safe to leave," I say, shaking my head. "And it's too far away. We don't know the conditions of the roads or what the outside world is like. We'd probably die trying to get to my dad's place. Plus, I don't even know if he made it. You remember how confusing it was when this all started. It's not worth the risk . . . at least not until it's our last resort."

"Look around, Casey." He pulls away and gestures to the dimly lit living room. It looks like we're just having a quiet night in, but it's been forty-two days of quiet nights in. "This *is* our last resort. We're sitting ducks, and eventually someone will find us, someone we don't want to find us." Nate lets out a heavy sigh.

He's right. It's not a matter of if; it's a matter of when. But right now, we have enough supplies to last us three weeks, four if we ration. That's a long time to survive in an apocalypse. I can't guarantee we'd survive another day if we ventured outside.

"Casey," Nate says.

I look up at him, meeting his gaze. I know why he wants to leave. He's scared. And when you're scared, you run. Or in my case, you hide.

"We really need to consider leaving."

"Okay."

He tilts his head, squinting at me. "'Okay,' we'll leave?"

"No, we'll consider it."

The water boils over, sizzling against the hot stove. It's too loud. Nate dashes to the pot and removes it from the flame, muffling a cry of pain as he drops the pot, the handles having gotten far too hot.

My body tenses up, and I sit still for a moment, listening, making sure the noise didn't draw any unwanted attention. Satisfied with the quiet, I stand from the couch and tell Nate I'm going to use the restroom, hoping that will table the "let's leave the city" conversation for the time being. He's preoccupied with cleaning up the mess, so he doesn't acknowledge me.

In the bathroom, I reflexively flick the light switch, but nothing turns on. I still haven't gotten used to that. A flashlight lies on its side, wedged between the wall and the faucet. I click the on button and a beam of light bursts out of it, illuminating most of the room. After peeing, I empty a container of rainwater collected from the rooftop into the toilet tank and yank up on the chain. Gravity forces the urine to flush. Too bad it can't do the same for what the world has become.

As I stand in front of the mirror, a darkened, strained reflection stares back at me. My long brunette hair is oily from weeks of being unable to wash it properly. My cheekbones are more pronounced with part of my face hollowed out due to sudden weight loss. I can still see the blue of my eyes even in the darkness, but the color is fading, just like every other part of me. The woman in the mirror is becoming less and less familiar—and one day, I fear I won't recognize her at all.

"Shit!" Nate yells.

I'm already shushing him as I race down the hall, back into the kitchen, where I find him partially bent over, wincing in pain and gripping his hand.

"I know, I know, I'm sorry," he says in a strained whisper. "I cut myself."

I want to yell at him for being loud, but instead I grab a towel and wrap it around the nasty cut on his finger.

"Are you okay?"

He nods several times.

I'm still worried about the noise. I'm always worried about the noise. It can attract biters or, worse, the burners. I call them that because all they want to do is see the world burn. They're the ones I'm scared of.

When everything went to shit, some people took it as an opportunity to let the world devolve back into a primal war of winner takes all. At first, I thought they were also infected by the virus. But they weren't. They had just lost their humanity, or maybe they never had it to begin with. Without law and order or societal norms, there's nothing they fear and nothing that's stopping them from doing whatever the hell they want. They're fueled by greed and desire. Over the past six weeks, I've seen them use Nomes as bait to draw out biters or people like me and Nate, people just trying to survive. And God knows what else the burners are using them for. It's like hell showed up on earth, and they decided someone needed to be the devil, so it may as well be them.

"Can you get the first aid kit?" Nate whispers.

Before I can respond, three loud knocks pound against the front door. My blood runs cold. This is why I'm always worried about the noise.

Chapter 4

There's a tightness in my chest as my heart sprints and panic sets in. Nate's unmoving, and his face has paled to the color of snow.

Knock. Knock. Knock.

This time the pounding is louder and harder, showing their patience is wearing thin. They're coming in here whether we let them in or not, and that's a fact we both have to process in the next few seconds. A surge of adrenaline starts to course through my body, my brain preparing me for what's next.

"Put that out!" I mouth to Nate as animatedly as I can without making any noise. He removes the smaller pot from the larger one and then slowly places a lid on it, snuffing out the fire within. Out in the halls, floorboards creak and moan, the weight of several large people shifting back and forth.

"Hello? Is anyone in there?" a deep voice calls from the other side of the door. "I have my wife and child with me. Please, let us in. We need help." The man's words come out robotic, like he's reading them from a script. It's a trap. Most everything in this world is a trap now.

Nate mouths, *Should we?*

I shake my head and point to the heavy cast-iron pan on the counter, signaling him to grab it. He picks it up and holds it at his side as I slowly inch toward the front door. A baseball bat is leaned in the corner, and I quietly retrieve it, keeping it at my side, hidden behind my leg.

The element of surprise is out the window. They know we're in here, and hiding will only make it worse. Our best play is to calmly invite them in, making them think we're stupid enough to fall for their ruse. I nod to Nate and back away from the door so he can take my spot. We've talked about this before, about what we would do when—not if—the burners came knocking. Now we've just gotta do it. He steps forward, placing his eye against the peephole. Nate pulls his head back and shakes it. I know that means they're covering it up so we can't see how many there are.

"Have any of you been bit?" Nate asks, trying to make his voice sound calm and welcoming.

"No," the man says gruffly.

"Okay, good. I'll open the door then."

Nate's shoulders rise and fall. He looks at me and whispers, "I love you."

My lips move, but no sound escapes as I mouth, *I love you too.*

The chain lock rattles as it slides out of the slot. Nate turns several dead bolts, each one making a clicking sound as it skids back into its latch. On the last click, the door bursts open. Two men grab Nate, pinning his arms behind him and yanking the cast iron from his hand.

"Please! Don't! I'm a doctor. I can help you," Nate pleads.

"How were you going to help us with this?" one of the burners asks, holding up the pan. He swings it into Nate's stomach, causing him to keel over and cough violently while gasping for the air the burner just knocked out of him. A rage blazes through me, but I stop myself from charging at them in a fury because I know it won't do me any good. I'm outnumbered and outsized. But what I have going for me is something these two big, dumb idiots don't have at all—a brain.

A third burner walks in, larger than the other two. He trudges toward me, a sneer plastered on his face. The baseball bat is hidden just behind my leg, standing on its end. The tips of my fingers are pressed against the knob to hold it upright. I keep my eyes on the ugly one approaching. A shitty tattoo with blown-out lines is inked across his forehead. It looks like he gave it to himself. It reads SATIN in all caps, but I think he intended for it to say SATAN. He stands in front of me, looking me up and down while slowly licking his cracked lips. Like the other two, he sports long, greasy hair and a dark, unkempt beard. Whether that's from dirt and grime or it's his natural color is a mystery. His clothes are stiff, covered in a mixture of filth and dried blood, and he reeks, which is saying a lot, because no one smells good in an apocalypse. But his odor is beyond nauseating. Really, there's no excuse for it.

"Aren't you a pleasant surprise to find in a shithole like this," he says with a sinister smile.

"You must be Satin."

The puzzled look on his face tells me it went right over his head, but the burner restraining Nate chuckles at my joke, so I know at least one of them can read.

"What's so funny?" Satin asks, shooting a glare over his shoulder.

His friend stifles his laugh and says, "Nothing." They're clearly not that close.

Just as Satin turns his attention back to me, I raise the baseball bat and swing it as hard as I can into the side of his head. If it weren't attached to his body, it'd for sure be a home run. The bat cracks against his skull, blood spraying in all directions. People don't realize the head bleeds like a motherfucker. The force of the hit sends his left eye spewing out of its socket. But it doesn't go too far, as the optic nerve is still attached, leaving it dangling right in front of his face—a tetherball of sorts.

"What the fuck?" the literate burner bellows as Satin crumples to the floor.

Nate starts to squirm, struggling to free himself from his grasp, while the other burner bolts toward me, swinging the cast iron wildly. There's no skill in his combat, only strength, which will eventually tire due to how much energy he's wasting. I avoid being struck once, twice, three times. His attacks become sluggish, just as I knew they would. Skillful fighting takes more than just strength. It requires patience and calculation. I find my opening and swing at him, wielding the baseball bat like a sword. He uses the pan as a shield, but the intensity of the hit causes it to slip from his hands and crash against the wood floor. The burner sucks in air as he charges toward me, driving a shoulder right into my stomach, knocking the wind out of me.

My body slams against the floor, and the baseball bat goes skidding across it. He straddles my waist, forcing the air up and out of my lungs. His rough, grimy hands wrap around my neck, squeezing and crushing my windpipe. I gasp and flail, trying to peel back his fingers and push out his arms.

"You're gonna pay for that, bitch," he spits, baring his rotten teeth.

Nate yells something, but I can't make it out. My only focus is on getting oxygen. I hear a struggle, grunts, and loud bangs, but I don't know what's happening. All I can see is this big, dumb idiot sitting on top of me. Tears bleed from the corners of my eyes and trickle down the sides of my face. My vision starts to blur, and my body tires. I think this might be it. This is how it ends, and my last view is this uggo . . . but then I see my dad. He's crystal clear. There's the thick beard that hid his smallest smiles, his weathered skin from too much time spent working in the sun, and his tender eyes that looked at me like I was his whole world. I can hear his voice too. The words he said to me many times all those years ago echo through my mind. I thought I had forgotten them, but no, they've always been there, waiting for the moment I needed to hear them again. Some dads have tea parties with their little girls—not mine, though. He thought learning self-defense and combat training was a far better use of my time.

"Never let someone bigger than you pin you to the ground. The longer you're pinned, the more strength you give up. Act quickly and violently. Strike their most vulnerable places. Eyes. Nose. Throat. Groin. Give 'em hell, girl."

I will, Dad.

In a flash, my hand thrusts up toward his face, my index and middle fingers spread two inches apart. He doesn't see it coming until it's too late, until my uncut nails pierce his soft orbs. It feels like sticking a finger into a hard-boiled egg. If it weren't so gross, the thought of a hard-boiled egg would make me hungry. My stomach rumbles. *Never mind.*

"Ack! Fuck!" he screams, releasing the grip he had on my neck. I pull my fingers back; a clear jelly oozes out of his eyes, and his hands shoot to his face, covering them. I wheeze, trying to catch my breath and conjure the strength I need to take back control.

As he cries out in pain, I drive the palm of my hand up into his nose. It makes a crunchy noise and sends him flying backward, his head cracking against the floor. He kicks and flails, wailing like a child throwing a temper tantrum.

Propping myself up with my elbows, I meet the gaze of the other burner, the one struggling with Nate. In an instant, I'm on my feet, stomping in his direction. He wears fear like I wear a pair of scrubs, and by that, I mean he wears it well, like it was made for him. The burner releases Nate and takes a step back. If he were smart, he would run. Nate seizes the opportunity by raising his elbow and driving it into the man's stomach. Before I can join in, something grabs hold of my ankle, yanking me down on all fours. My knees and the palms of my hands smash against the floor.

"Gotcha, bitch," the blind burner spits. His free arm thrashes wildly until his hand locks onto my other ankle. I try to pull away or kick, but he has my ankles bolted in place, so I'm in the position of an awkward mountain climber exercise. I try to call for Nate, but it comes out as a raspy whisper.

Nate turns and kicks the other burner square in the chest, sending him crashing into the granite countertop. He looks to me as I struggle to free myself from the blind burner. Then Nate's gaze goes to the bloodied body lying next to me, my home run. Satin begins to twitch, coming back to consciousness. Nate's eyes dart to the screaming burner who still has me in his grip, then to the burner he sent flying into the countertop—who's now regaining his footing.

I'm sure Nate's coming up with a plan in his head, one that will end in him rising to the occasion as my knight in shining armor. It looks like he's about to charge at the burner staggering toward him, but he doesn't. Instead, Nate runs . . . right out the front door. The man I've been with for more than two years, who asked me to marry him two and a half months ago, who told me he loved me just a few minutes ago . . . gone in an instant. *Fucking great.* I knew he wasn't cut out for an apocalypse.

Using all the strength I have left, I flip myself over onto my back, twisting an ankle free from the burner's grasp in the process. I bring my knee up to my chest and kick as hard as I can right into his open, screaming mouth. A half dozen teeth shatter, shooting into the back of his throat, causing him to gag and choke on the yellow-tinted chunks of calcium.

I'm back on my feet just as the other burner changes course from bolting out the door after Nate to now charging toward me. I sprint around the island counter, reaching the stove before he gets to me. My hand grips the handle of the pot filled with boiling water and rice, and I whip it, flinging the contents right into his face. The grains of soft rice cling to his skin, causing the flesh to blister and cook.

His scream blows past his falsetto range, piercing my ears. He frantically tries to flick and scrape the bubbling rice from his skin. This is my chance to run. I pick up my baseball bat from beside the couch and grab my prepacked getaway bag from the front closet, ready to bolt out the door. But I stop suddenly, realizing I'm forgetting something . . . and I can't leave without it. I sprint down the hall into our bedroom and pull open the top drawer of the dresser. Pushing aside balled-up socks, my hand grasps the object. The memory of my dad giving it to me flashes to the front of my mind.

"Here, take this."

"No, Dad. I'm not bringing a gun to college."

"It's for your own protection."

"No, I don't need it, and it's not even legal on campus."

"Fine, then at least take this."

"What is it?"

"It's a combat knife, and with your training, it's deadlier than a gun anyway."

"I don't want a combat knife either, Dad."

"Please. For my own peace of mind. You can hide it in a drawer for all I care, but I just need to know that if the time ever comes, you have something to protect yourself with."

"Fine . . . I'll take your stupid knife."

"Thank you."

I turn the blade over in my hands a couple of times, studying it like I'm reacquainting myself with an old, reliable friend. A burner groans from the kitchen, so I know it's time to go. I bolt out of the apartment and down the stairwell, pausing before I exit the building. I can't be sure there aren't more of them waiting outside, but my guess is if there were, Nate would have run right into them already. Heavy footsteps descend the stairs, echoing off the cinder block walls. I let out a heavy sigh and push open the door, hoping there's not an ambush waiting for me on the other side.

In the courtyard, my head is on a swivel, keeping a lookout for burners and searching for any clues as to where Nate could have gone. We had a plan in place for if we ever got separated, and I hope he's following through with it. We said we'd meet at our garage in the alley, hop in his car, and drive away from whatever trouble we were in. That has to be where he's at. He wouldn't just leave me. I creep through the tight walkway between our building and the one next to it and slowly open the gate at the end. Rounding the corner to the alley, I expect to find Nate standing there, leaned up against his car, maybe even jokingly quoting *Twilight* with a "Where have you been, loca?" But he's not, and I can't believe my own eyes. Not only is Nate not here, but the garage door is wide open, and his Porsche is gone too.

"You motherfuc . . ."

Chapter 5

The loud bang of a trash can toppling over a block or two away cuts my outburst short. New plan. *Think, Casey, think. My truck.* I search my backpack and pull out the spare key that I thankfully had the foresight to throw in there. The truck was a gift from my dad when I got my license, but I rarely drive it now, only moving it around at the city's request for winter snow parking restrictions and street sweeping. It's actually been a nuisance to keep, and I don't know why I never got rid of it. Maybe deep down, I knew I'd need it one day.

I take off toward where I'm pretty sure I last left it parked, praying it's still there. It should have been in Nate's two-car garage, but he was not open to that idea. His excuse for that arrangement being, "It's a Porsche, babe. It needs room to breathe." I roll my eyes at the thought of his selfishness. He may have been charming and useful when things were normal, but clearly, he's not a good fiancé to have in the end of times, especially since he ditched me at the first sight of danger.

The street is full of abandoned vehicles, debris, and decaying bodies. I'm careful as I move, crouching and hiding behind anything I can so as not to draw attention. Sticking close to buildings, I keep my back safe from exposure to the unknown. As I round another corner, I spot my truck parked three blocks down, still sitting untouched. I know I left a full tank of gas in it, and no one can start that old hunk of rust except for me—so the only worry I have is that someone could have siphoned my fuel.

Crossing the first street, I look both ways to make sure the coast is clear. There's nothing except abandoned vehicles and shattered storefronts. It looks like a bomb was dropped right in the middle of Chicago. I pause to listen for any potential sounds of danger, like snarls and groans from a biter or just another human's voice. You can't trust anyone these days. The wind whips through the city, curving its way through hollowed-out buildings, emitting an eerie whistle unlike anything I've ever heard before.

I pass by the next two streets without a hitch, and I'm now within a hundred feet of my truck. A sense of relief washes over me—but it passes quickly at the sound of a raspy growl. A biter slinks out of the alley, cutting off the clear path to my truck. Despite the fact that its nose is mostly rotted off, it sniffs the air as it shuffles. I could wait it out, see if it wanders in the other direction, but I can't take the risk of it spotting me because it'll attract others.

Sliding my trusty knife from its sheath, I crouch as low to the ground as I can, slowly making my way toward it. The biter stops in its tracks and twists its head around wildly, smelling the air. There's clearly something it likes. I glance down at my bloodstained shirt, realizing it's me. *Shit.* I have no choice. I've gotta act now.

With my knife held out in front of me, I charge at the biter. The sound of my shoes pounding against the pavement catches its attention, and it turns to face me. The creature emits a scream just as I thrust the knife at a forty-five-degree angle up under its chin, ensuring it pierces through the cerebellum and into the brain stem. Its scream is instantly extinguished. I don't know much about these creatures, but what I do know is how to kill them, thanks to watching burners take them out on the street these past six weeks. I jerk the blade down with force, dislodging it from its skull. Black, putrid sludge oozes from the wound, remnants of blood that has long since rotted into something . . . inhuman. The creature collapses to the pavement like a sack of potatoes.

I quickly scan my surroundings, making sure its brief scream didn't attract more of them. All clear, or so it seems. I reach my truck, manually unlock it, and pull open the door. Tossing my backpack into the passenger's seat, I crawl inside, gently closing the driver-side door behind me. I haven't driven this old heap in months, and I worry it won't start.

"Come on, girl," I whisper as I stick the key in the ignition and turn it.

RGGHH. RGGGHH. RGGHHH.

The sound of grinding metal screeches from beneath the hood, but the engine doesn't turn over.

"Come on!"

Again. *RGGHH. RGGHH. RGGHH.*

"Shit!" I twist the key again and again, but it's nothing but noise.

Screams roar in the distance. Through the grimy windshield, a blur of motion about fifty yards north draws my attention. I can't quite make it out, but I know it's nothing good.

I pump the gas pedal several times and punch the dashboard with a closed fist. "Come on, you piece of shit!"

I turn the key once again, and the engine sputters and then finally comes to life.

"YES!"

I flick on the windshield wipers and let loose what remaining wiper fluid I have, washing away leaves and grime. The world before me becomes clear, and I wish it hadn't. A dozen biters zigzag down the street, all in different stages of decay. They scream as they move toward me at varying speeds, from nearly running to a slow, stumbling stagger.

I put the truck in drive and pull out onto the street, lining up the front hood ornament with the center of the hungry horde. I smash my foot down on the gas pedal, and the speedometer climbs to forty before I collide with the first biter. My truck bounces as it drives over the corpse-shaped speed bump. The bowling ball that is my vehicle continues to knock down the fleshy pins as it speeds ahead. Bodies get caught up underneath the tires and axles, reducing my momentum far more than I want them to.

"Come on. Don't give up on me now," I say as I tightly grip the steering wheel and press down even harder on the gas pedal.

One biter, instead of being run over, is kicked up onto the hood. Half of its jaw is torn off, so its tongue flaps wildly in the wind. The creature punches the windshield, but it does far more damage to its own hand than the truck. Blood and decayed flesh smear across the glass as its rotting skin gives out instantly, a bloody sack bursting over the windshield. I break free of the final group of biters and begin to accelerate again while the biter continues its attack. I need to get the damn thing off, and I need to do it now.

I slam on my brake pedal. The tires screech, and the truck comes to an abrupt halt, sending the biter flying through the air. It smashes against the pavement twenty yards ahead, a mangled splat of bone, flesh, and black sludge.

With the chaos briefly subsided, I get my bearings and plan my exit route out of the city. Major highways like 94 and 41 are going to be parking lots full of abandoned vehicles by the thousands, making passage nearly impossible. From what I can see thus far, the city streets are manageable; if I take it slow and use the sidewalks when needed, I can get out of here. Outside Chicago, I'll have to stick to back roads and small county highways to stay undetected and ensure I don't get stuck in a gridlock of abandoned vehicles. It'll add hours to the trip, but it will be much safer. And maybe, just maybe, I'll make it.

I start driving, passing through a city I don't recognize anymore. It's sad what it's become, what the world's become, and I don't know how we got here. I don't think anyone does. Whatever this is, it's clearly some sort of a virus, but unlike anything we've seen before. It sickens the brain, more so than the body. But the real question is, Where did it come from? Was it made in a lab, or has God had enough of us? Was it an accident, or was it released on purpose? And if it was the latter, by who? I'm not sure we'll ever have those answers. And even if we did, it wouldn't change anything. This is our world now.

Turning right onto a cross street, I spot a group of burners up ahead standing outside a ransacked convenience store. They yell and animatedly flail their arms in an attempt to flag me down. But I'm not stopping for anyone. One of them points his gun at me, and several others take off, trying to run in front of my truck, but I push down on the gas pedal and blow past them, flipping them off. I knew there was no way they were going to shoot at me. Bullets are too valuable, and the noise is too dangerous. They become just a blip in my rearview mirror.

As I exit the city limits, the streets become clearer, and biter and burner sightings less frequent. But if I thought the city looked bizarre, I wasn't ready for what the suburbs had in store. With more open space, more large homes to loot and explore, more wood to set on fire, the chaos is no better than in the city. Massive four-thousand-plus-square-foot homes ablaze like signal torches dotted across subdivisions. Blackened trees look like onyx scarecrows. Bodies lie in the streets, women and children fleeing as a last resort. Traffic lights are strewn across intersections, their signals all now the same black.

I'm grateful when I pass through the suburbs and the city is just a speck in the rearview mirror. I used to hate driving long distances, with only cornfields and flatlands serving as my surroundings. It was boring, but now boring is a luxury, and I love every minute of it. A field of gold is a beautiful sight compared to the mayhem I've left behind. Occasionally, I pass a few cars on the side of the road, people having crashed, run out of gas, or broken down. And there're still bodies, but they're few and far between out in the country, with land so flat, I can see all the way to the horizon. It's calming, and it's the first time I've felt calm in a very long time, even before the world ended.

After another hour on the road, my high beams light up the WELCOME TO WISCONSIN road sign, signaling that there's only another hour or so before I reach my childhood home, a place I vowed never to return to. The compound my father created was mired in the past, a place to trap things in, only allowing them to grow within the confines of the world he created. His isolationism kept him safe and alive, but it also kept him from living. I knew if I ever allowed myself to get dragged back into his world, I would only become a product of what he wanted. Rather than a life of love, helping others, excitement, and new experiences, it would be one of fear, distrust, discipline. But with the world over and no new experiences to be had—not good ones, anyway—and no one to love or help who I can't assume will try to kill me or eat me, home is exactly where I'm headed. Turns out it only took an apocalypse to bring me back.

Chapter 6

I switch my headlights off and pull the truck to the side of the road, rolling to a slow stop before I kill the engine. The sky is black, and the moon is a mere sliver, but the stars are plentiful and bright. Having lived in the city the last ten years, I actually forgot they existed.

My dad's property is off to the right, completely fenced off with a thick barbed wire coiling itself around the top of every square inch of the perimeter. I still remember installing that damn thing, and the palms of my hands hurt just thinking about it. At the far end of the property, a couple of dead biters are tangled in the barbed wire. Must have gotten snared in it and then starved to death, or someone here put them out of their misery.

I softly close the truck door behind me and sling my backpack over my shoulders. My ring slightly glimmers, catching my eye, and I stare at it for a moment before deciding to take it off and pocket it. It'll be easier to pretend Nate didn't exist, rather than having to explain to my dad that my fiancé, the one he never knew about, ditched me in the middle of an attack. If I told him, I think my dad would go out and kill him himself, if he's not dead already.

The night air is cold, so I pull up my hood and shove my hands into my pockets. My shoes crunch over loose gravel as I walk to the long steel gate at the end of the driveway. The old man's added barbed wire to the top of that too, so there's no climbing over it. I remember where he hid the spare key, and hopefully, it's still there.

Standing in front of the mailbox, I do an about-face, walking six paces forward, fifteen to the left, one back, nine to the right, seven forward, and two to the left. The numbers mean something to only my father and me. The ground is covered in rocks, all made by nature except one that sits right between my feet. It's smooth as an egg in my hands with a small crack right in the middle. I slide the two halves apart, revealing a small silver key. *Bingo.*

I lock the gate behind me and glance up at the long driveway that cuts through the flat grass and the woods beyond it. From the road, you can see a yellow-and-white, two-story farmhouse, but no one lives in there anymore. It's a dummy home, an idea of my dad's, and only used for storage. There's a three-story house nestled back in the woods, undetectable to those passing by. But I know it's back there, because I helped build it. My father's property also features a cabin, a crop field, multiple gardens, a sniper tower, and several other outdoor buildings for storage and defense purposes. I haven't been here in a decade, so who knows what else the old man has added. A plethora of backup generators and solar panels allow the whole compound to run off the grid. It's quite impressive what he and I accomplished, now that I think about all of it, and up until six weeks ago, I thought it was a waste of time. Turns out, I was very wrong.

I start up the gravel driveway, nervous to see my father again. I wonder what his reception will be. Happy and relieved to see I'm alive or upset for all the time I stayed away? For all the years we didn't have. For all the memories during my early adult years that I kept him from experiencing. I'm his only child, so every experience I withhold from him is something he'll never get back. Despite all that, I know his reception will be the former because he's my dad and time apart hasn't changed that. But still, I feel nervous as the moment approaches, or maybe it's not nerves. Maybe it's guilt or even a little bit of anger that he was right.

It's eerily quiet tonight. Not even the cicadas are buzzing. Perhaps they know the world has ended and there's no point in attracting a mate now. A lone coyote howls in the distance, but it sounds more like a cry for help than anything else.

The driveway seems to darken as I reach the thick woods at the top of it. Up around the bend, there's a clearing, and that's where my childhood home sits—well, part of my childhood. I lived in the house near the road until the age of ten. Before . . .

A twig snaps behind me, and before I have a chance to turn around, I can feel what must be the barrel of a pistol pressed against the back of my head.

"Don't move or I'll blow your head off," the man says.

I close my eyes and breathe in slowly through my nose, thinking back to this exact same scenario on this exact piece of land. I raise my hands to show that I'm not a threat. But it's a lie. He just doesn't know it. In a flash, I spin around, ducking a foot or so before grabbing the arm of the person holding the gun. I twist their wrist and pinch the nerve pocket leading to their fingers, forcing them to lose their grip. The gun drops into my free hand, and I stand tall, turning it on the person I now instantly recognize. In under seven seconds, I disassemble the pistol, ejecting the clip and removing the slide, before handing it back to him.

"Don't ever point a gun at me again, JJ," I say, pulling my hood down so he can see who I am.

He's got about eight inches on me and sports a full beard and a dark head of hair cut short.

"Oh my God!" he says, wide-eyed. "Case, you're alive!" My cousin wraps his arms around me, practically lifting my body off the ground as he squeezes me as hard as he can.

"Unfortunately," I say, not sure whether I'm referring to the state of the world or being back here, or both.

"I can't believe it. How've you been?" he says, releasing me from his embrace.

"Not great. Everyone I know is either dead or pointing guns at me."

"Yeah . . . sorry about that. I didn't realize it was you." JJ reassembles his gun and slides it back into his shoulder holster.

"Just don't let it happen again." I smirk and punch him in the shoulder.

"Oww!" he says, rubbing the spot where I hit him. "I thought for sure the city would have made you weak."

"Then you don't know nothin' about the city."

He chuckles. "I suppose I don't. And now I never will." A somber moment of silence lingers as the gravity of his statement settles in. How many millions of people have died over the last couple of months?

JJ breaks the silence. "Your dad is gonna flip when he sees you."

"Is he pissed at me?"

"Are you kidding, Casey? He's devastated. We looked for you for the first few weeks every chance we got—that is, until it became too dangerous. He figured you would have headed here when everything went to shit and that somehow, something went wrong, and you must not have made it. My God, I haven't seen him this sad since . . ." JJ trails off. "You know." He pulls his lips in and glances down at his boots.

"Yeah, well, I was safe in the city until I wasn't . . . so this wasn't my first-choice destination until it became my only option."

JJ lifts his head and cracks a smile, patting me on the shoulder. "I'm glad you're home, and I know everyone else will be glad too."

"Who's all here?"

"Actually, quite a lot of people."

"Really?" I'm surprised at this news. I figured my father would have hunkered down and limited the number of individuals he could trust to have around in a situation like this. Plus, more people means more mouths to feed, which will deplete his supplies faster. Did he soften in my absence?

"Yup. Follow me. You'll see." He beckons with his hand.

JJ and I walk side by side up the driveway and then snake through the woods on the trails my father carved. The brush isn't as tame as it once was, with branches reaching across the path toward one another, trying to entwine their limbs. JJ calls out in advance to warn me of them, but several still end up slapping me across the face. A reminder that nature is far more relentless than a city will ever be.

The real house comes into view, and it's exactly how I remember it. Three stories high with pale-yellow siding, white shutters, and a wraparound porch. It looks like a normal home, and at one point, it was. The wooden chair set beside the front door rocks slowly with the shadowy outline of a large man seated in it.

"Hey, Uncle Dale," JJ calls out. "Look who I found."

The chair stops suddenly and the shadow stands. Heavy work boots thump across the porch, boards creaking under the weight before a motion light is set off, illuminating the shadowy figure. His dark hair is speckled with gray, which continues into his thick beard. Despite being in his fifties, he's still built like a brick shithouse, complete with broad shoulders, a barrel-shaped chest, and a towering stature. I step out of the woods and into the light so he can finally see who JJ found.

His eyes immediately fill with tears, as though he has found something he thought was lost forever.

"Casey?" His voice cracks like he can barely say it.

"Hi, Dad."

Chapter 7

In stunned disbelief, my father bounds toward me, arms spread, ready for an embrace. He nearly tackles me off my feet and squeezes tight, like he's afraid I'll slip away again. I inhale his familiar scent, a mix of sawdust from his woodwork and earth from spending too much time outdoors. It smells like home.

"I thought I lost you," he whispers, the tears from his eyes transferring to my neck, where he has pressed his face deeply into the side of mine.

"Dad, I can't breathe." I barely push out the words.

"Oh, sorry," he says, setting me back down on solid ground.

I inhale the cool night air, refilling my lungs.

Dad grips my shoulders, looking down at me and studying my face. It's as though he's trying to make sure it's really me and that his eyes aren't playing tricks on him. "I can't believe you're here. I . . . I looked everywhere for you."

"I know. JJ told me." I can see the pain I caused him. It's written all over his face, clear as day. But does that make me the bad guy? Or are we closer now to even, at least in my book?

My cousin clears his throat. "I'm gonna get back to patrolling, Uncle Dale, so you two can talk. Glad you're here, Casey." He tosses me a smile.

Dad drops his hands from my shoulders. "Thanks, JJ." He nods, sending him back off into the night before his gaze returns to me. "Are you okay?"

"Yeah, Dad. I'm fine."

He folds his arms across his chest. It's that typical Dad stance, which I know will be followed by a slew of questions.

"How'd you make it here?"

"I drove." I slide the combat knife from the sheath secured to my thigh and hold it up, the blade glimmering from the spotlight. "But this helped." I smirk.

His face brightens, and he grins proudly. "Hate to say I told you so."

"No, you don't," I say, returning the knife to its sheath.

Dad smiles. "Is anyone with you?"

I let out a small sigh and shake my head. It's the truth, because no one is with me, but I won't tell him about Nate. A gust of wind sends a shiver down my spine, chilling me to the bone, and I reflexively jolt.

Dad notices and puts his arm around me, pulling me into him. "Let's get you inside," he says, guiding me up the steps of the porch. Before we enter the house, he pauses and places a finger against his lips. "Everyone's asleep."

"Who's *everyone*?" I whisper.

"Well, you saw JJ. Uncle Jimmy and Aunt Julie are here too, as well as your cousin Greg. He brought a girl with him, Molly. Elaine's here too."

I smile. "Elaine made it?"

"Of course. I made sure I got to her first."

Elaine lives a mile down the road, our closest neighbor, and she's been there since I can remember. She was like a mother to me . . . I mean, a much older mother. But she did her best to fill in the large hole in my heart. As I reflect back on all the moments she was there for me, I realize now, in my spite toward my father, I deprived Elaine of things I had no right to. A sadness wells up in me like a backed-up drain, because like my father, I haven't seen her in a long time either.

"Anyone else?" I ask, quickly trying to swallow the sadness brought on by my own guilt.

"Tessa and her mom, Meredith. They made it here too."

"Tessa's here?!" I blurt out before remembering the time of night. He nods.

That makes me smile. She and I have been friends since we were little kids, although we've lost touch ever since I went into residency. Completely my fault, not hers. The hospital became my whole life, so it's been what feels like a lifetime since we've last talked, let alone seen each other.

"Then I've got the Carter family staying out in the cabins."

"Who?"

"You'll meet them tomorrow. They're good people, and they needed help, so I took them in."

We continue into the dimly lit house, where the only light comes from the glowing embers of the fireplace set in the corner. The large open-concept living room, kitchen, and sitting area are furnished with several couches, chairs, and tables. There used to be only one of each, but he's clearly added more to accommodate the extra people. His bedroom door to the right of the living room is closed, and I wonder if it's still his or if he gave it up. On our way through the kitchen, he grabs a glass bottle of water and a granola bar.

"In case you're hungry or thirsty," Dad says, handing them to me.

I pocket the granola bar and unscrew the cap from the bottle, drinking nearly half of it in several gulps. I didn't realize until the water hit my sandpaper tongue, sitting on top of it for a brief second before absorbing in like I was a neglected houseplant, that I haven't had anything to drink since before the burners burst into Nate's place.

"Thanks." I hold up the bottle.

"No need to thank me, Casey. I'm your father. My job is to take care of you."

"I'm twenty-nine, Dad."

"I don't care if you're fifty. You'll always be my daughter, so I'll always take care of you." He picks up a lantern from the island counter and ignites it. "I'm sure you're tired, so let's get you to bed. We can talk more tomorrow, when you're well rested." The lantern provides enough of a glow to see in front of us as we walk up the stairs off the kitchen. The flame licking at the glass creates a dance of light and shadows on the walls, a macabre kaleidoscope of black and white.

I follow him down the hallway to an open side room that used to just be a sitting area but looks as though it's been converted to a bedroom with no privacy, since steps off it lead up to the third floor.

"JJ sleeps in here," Dad says.

These stairs are much narrower, so he takes them slow. "I left your room open . . . sort of," he adds as he stops in front of my bedroom door.

"What do you mean, 'sort of'?"

"You have a bunkmate, but it's just temporary until I can finish another cabin." Dad turns the handle and pushes open the door, allowing me to enter first.

"Is it Tessa?" I ask, feeling along the wall for the light switch. Once my hand finds it, I flick it on, and my childhood bedroom comes into view. It's large, around fourteen feet by twenty feet, and looks nearly the way I left it, except for the presence of a second bed pushed up against the far wall beneath the bay window.

A man lies sleeping on his side with a blanket covering his lower half. His wide, muscular back is on full display, and his hair is cut short, military-style. There's a tattoo of the Navy SEAL insignia on his shoulder. Is Dad trying to set me up? Because, wow, this guy is . . . My thoughts are cut off when he rolls over. His brawny arm covers his eyes for a moment before he pulls it from his face, revealing those vomit-green irises.

"Ughh . . . turn the lights off," he groans.

As soon as I recognize him, I see red. No fucking way. This can't be happening.

Chapter 8

"Dad, why is Blake Morrison in my bedroom?"

My father furrows his brow, his eyes darting back and forth between Blake and me. "Oh, you two already know each other?"

"Of course I know him. He's a bully, and he ruined my life."

Blake swings his legs out from under the covers, showcasing that he's only wearing a pair of boxer briefs. He sits up and rubs at his eyes, and while I can see the build, face, and stature of a nearly thirty-year-old man, my brain instantly morphs him into a fourteen-year-old creature of terror. A menace on the warpath with one goal in mind: making my life a living hell.

Seven. Thirty-one. Twelve.

I spun the lock on my burnt-orange steel locker and lifted the metal handle, expecting to find my jacket hung up on a hook, my backpack, and a small stack of textbooks—but no. Instead, dozens of canned foods spilled out, crashing to the floor and rolling in all directions. My cheeks immediately flushed, as all eyes were on me. I glanced to the left and then to the right, finding Blake Morrison, with dark hair cut short on the sides and an evil smirk. He was surrounded by his friends, and they were all pointing at me, howling with laughter.

"Hey, Head Case! This is a school, not a bunker to store your doomsday supplies," Blake teased, still laughing.

Tears built, threatening to spill out, but I sucked them back in as my hand balled up into a fist at my side. I wouldn't let him see me cry. Instead,

I closed my locker and started to stomp off—but my foot rolled over a can of corn and sent me tumbling to the floor.

"You can't even survive your own feet, Pearson," Blake hollered.

I groaned, picked myself up, and continued walking, the sound of laughter taunting me until I was out of earshot.

The adult version of my childhood bully reappears before me, sitting smugly in my bedroom.

"Who are you?" Blake smirks.

"Don't get cute with me. You know exactly who I am."

He tilts his head. "Oh, you think I'm cute?"

I roll my eyes and look to my father—my father, who should have known better than to let the enemy in. "I'm not sharing a room with him. He should be dead."

"Casey!" Dad warns. "Don't say that."

"What?" I shrug. "That was the plan, remember? In the event of an apocalypse, he"—I point to Blake—"was supposed to be on the other side of the gate, down by the road, begging me to let him in."

"Jeez, Doomsday. I don't remember you being so cruel." He tosses me a teasing grin as he gets to his feet, stretching his arms over his head and letting out a heavy yawn. Every muscle in his chiseled body flexes, from his bulgy biceps to his washboard abs. He's sure grown up into what I assume . . . is an even bigger asshole. I'd love to throw a punch right at that square jaw of his.

I narrow my eyes at Blake and flick my gaze to my father. "Dad, I don't want him here."

"Sweetheart, there's nowhere else for him to go right now, so you two just have to work it out among yourselves for the time being," he says, backing out of the room.

Before I can protest further, the door is already closing, putting an end to the conversation. I groan and turn to face Blake.

"So, how have you been?" he asks, lifting his chin in a cocky manner.

"Don't talk to me, Blake."

"I'll take that as *not so good*."

My gaze slips to his pecs, then his abs, and whoops, that's quite the bulge. *Damn it.* Why is he here? And why does he have to be so muscly and good-looking? It makes me hate him even more. Shaking my head, I toss my backpack on my bed and peel off my jacket, before throwing it in the hamper.

"Well, I'm glad you made it home, Doomsday," he says. "Your dad was really worried about you."

I whip my head around, staring at him. "You don't know anything about my dad."

"I know a lot actually, since he and I are good friends and all."

"You are not friends with my dad, Blake."

"Maybe even best friends," he adds with a smirk, clearly trying to get under my skin.

He takes a couple of slow steps toward me, his chin raised and his gaze locked on mine. I feel my heart start to race . . . fight or flight, I assume.

"And maybe one day, you and I will be friends too."

"That'll never happen," I scoff.

"Why?"

"I'm not friends with assholes."

He lifts a brow. "Good, because I'm not an asshole, so it looks like you misdiagnosed me, Dr. Pearson."

"You creep. How do you know I'm a doctor?"

"Your dad told me . . . ya know, because we're friends." He cracks a grin.

"Whatever. Just stay on your side of the room, Blake." I roll my eyes.

"Gladly." He takes a step back, pinching his nose with his thumb and pointer finger. "Ya know, just because the world ended doesn't mean your hygiene routine needed to end too."

I glance down at my bloodstained, grimy pants and T-shirt and slyly sniff myself, gagging from the stench of decay and sweat.

"There's a shower down the hall if you wanna . . ."

"Don't," I say, snapping my head up to look at him. "I built this place with my dad, so I don't need you telling me where things are."

"That may be true, but you've been gone a long time and things have changed around here. Shampoo and bodywash are in the shower, and I'll even let you use my loofah, roomie." He smiles and walks back to his bed, sitting on the edge of it.

"Gross, I'm not using your loofah." I unzip my bag and pull out an oversized T-shirt.

"Suit yourself." Blake lies down and props his hands behind his head, elbows pointed out. "Now, be a doll and kill the lights on your way out," he adds, staring up at the ceiling with a shit-eating grin on his face.

Ugh, I want to strangle him. Grumbling, I leave the room with the lights on and tiptoe down the hall to the bathroom, where I close the door behind me. I start the shower. It sputters at first, but then comes to life, blasting a steady stream of hot water. I peel off my grimy clothes, dropping them into a pile, and inspect myself in the mirror, taking note of the fresh bruises around my neck and on my chest and shoulders.

Without notice, the bathroom door starts to creak open, and I frantically grab my dirty shirt from the floor, attempting to cover myself, and thrust my foot out to stop the door from opening all the way.

"I'm in here. What the hell!?"

Blake pops his head in through the gap. "Sorry, I knocked but you didn't answer."

"That doesn't mean you can just come in." I narrow my eyes. "What is wrong with you?"

"Nothing, but I thought you'd want this," he says with a cocky smile, extending a towel through the partially open door.

I don't want to accept it, but I need it, so I begrudgingly take it from him, using it to help cover my naked body. "Get out," I say.

"Most people say thank you."

"I'm not most people."

His eyes travel the length of my body like he's examining me. "You all right?" Blake gestures to the discolored skin on my neck, shoulders, and chest.

I readjust the towel, holding it up a little higher. "I'm fine."

"You sure?"

"Just get out," I say, pushing the door into him.

He presses his lips together and meets my gaze before giving me a single nod. As he steps back, I slam the door closed, and this time, I lock it. Blake lingers on the other side, silently standing there. It's another moment or two before I hear his feet pad down the hall.

I let out a heavy sigh and turn to face the mirror again, but this time it's the gangly fifteen-year-old girl with dull brown hair and a mouth full of metal, dressed in overalls one size too big, staring back at me.

"Oh my God! What is stuck in my hair!?"

A chorus of boys laughing was the first answer I received.

"*There ya go, Doomsday. I got you something you can snack on when the world ends.*" Blake balled up the gum wrapper and threw it at my face.

"Yeah! Easy access," another boy yelled. Tears poured from my eyes as I raced toward the bathroom, holding my head in my hands to cover up the wad of pink clumped in my hair.

All I wanted to do was fit in. But Blake Morrison wouldn't allow it. I was the weirdo with the crazy dad, an easy target. Picking on me made him cool, and I wish he would have continued to just be my bully. I was used to that. I could deal with it, tolerate it, live with it. But no, he had to become something far worse. Blake fooled me once, but he won't ever fool me again.

Chapter 9

My eyes snap open, and I jolt up in bed, panting, my body drenched in a cold sweat as I try to ground myself in reality. *Where am I?* I scan my surroundings, my heart hammering in my chest. There's my bedroom door. My dresser. My desk. *Home.* I'm home. I inhale and stop short of exhaling when I remember I'm here because the world ended, and if that wasn't bad enough, I somehow got bunked up with my archnemesis . . . Blake Morrison.

My gaze goes to his bed, pushed up against the far wall under the large window. It's empty and perfectly made, military-style, with the corners tucked in, not a wrinkle to be seen.

"Loser," I scoff.

I hop out of my bed and pad across the room to Blake's, grabbing a fistful of his comforter and tossing it on the floor. I tug his sheets loose, even the fitted one, and roll them into a ball.

"Welcome to your nightmare, bitch." I grin, and yes, I am well aware that I'm being petty, but Blake made . . . well, unmade his bed years ago, when he got his kicks from tormenting me. Now I get to return the favor.

I draw open the curtains above his bed, and the sunshine seeps in, bathing the room in a pinkish-orange light. In the city, I could never open the shades. It was too dangerous, so we kept them shuttered at all times, only peeking out when there was a commotion on the street. But this . . . this is nice.

A knock startles me, and I whip around, staring cautiously at my bedroom door. With a deep exhale, I calm my nerves, reminding myself that I'm not holed up in an apartment in Chicago anymore, where a knock from a stranger could be a death sentence. It almost was yesterday.

"Come in," I yell.

The door creaks open, and a voice enters before a person. "Casey? Your dad told me you were here."

"Tessa!" I cross the room in two quick steps, throwing my arms around her. "I'm so happy to see you," I say, my face still pressed into the side of hers.

"Me too." Her voice is warm with that special type of sadness that accompanies joy, a reminder of moments missed. "It's been far too long," she adds.

Tessa's right about that. We've barely kept in touch since I started medical school, just texts here and there, and I haven't seen her in years.

"You know, you could have warned me about Blake," I tease.

"I sent a message by carrier goose. Did it not get to you?"

We laugh and let go of one another. I take a step back, examining her from head to toe—my doctor instincts kicking in. She sports a head of hay-colored hair, straight and flowing down past her shoulders. Her face is soft, giving off a girl-next-door look, thanks to her light-hazel eyes and a smattering of freckles across her nose and cheeks. She's lost weight like everyone else; however, she didn't have much to lose in the first place.

"You look good, healthy."

"Thanks, Doc. And you look like you've seen better days," Tessa says, giving me a once-over. I'm dressed in an oversized T-shirt that stops midthigh, so the bruises and cuts on my legs are visible along with the ones on my neck and face.

"Yeah, well, getting out of the city was no walk in the park, but you should see the other guys," I say with a small smile, hiding the pain and trauma of what happened behind a thin veil of humor.

She squints, clearly determining whether to question me any more, but instead tosses me a grin, deciding against forcing me to relive the details. "I can only imagine," Tessa says, plopping down on my bed and folding her legs into a pretzel. "So, what's new?" She tilts her head to the side.

I fish out a pair of black leggings from my bag, thread my legs into them, and pull them up. "You mean, like, before the world ended, or recently?"

"Obviously before. I know what you've been up to since everything went to shit. Terror, blood, fear, running, starving, filth, and worst of all . . . bunking with Blake Morrison." She smirks, fanning her arm across the room to showcase all Blake's belongings. He has more than I would expect for someone who fled during an apocalypse. There's a locked chest the width of his bed pushed up against a wall. I only know it's his because MORRISON is written in Sharpie along the side of it. The windowsill is lined with items that aren't mine, so they must be his.

"I won't argue with you on that." I pull open the top drawer of my dresser, where I find a brush and a ponytail holder. I run the bristles through the length of my hair. "Before this, my whole life was working at the hospital, sunup to sundown, but I love it . . . or *loved* it," I say, tying my hair up.

"So, this is basically a vacation for you?" She chuckles.

"First one in, like, ten years. I wish I would have picked someplace more tropical, though." I shrug and let out a laugh.

"There is a little creek that runs through this compound, and I'm sure I could find a margarita glass around here somewhere," she teases.

"All we're missing is a cute cabana boy."

"Speaking of boys, where's yours?" Tessa glances around the room as though she's searching for him. I practically flinch at the question. Tessa never met Nate, but she knew I was dating a doctor in the city from the little bit we did keep in touch. Thankfully, I wasn't into social media, and I hadn't gotten around to telling her Nate and I were engaged, so there's even less I have to explain.

I rummage around in another dresser drawer, giving myself time to think of what to say. I select a sports bra and a T-shirt before slowly closing it. Honestly, I'm embarrassed to admit that Nate ditched me—far too embarrassed to even tell Tessa. I still can't believe it myself. We were together for more than two years, and he asked me to marry him. How could you just leave the person you'd planned to spend your life with?

"We went our separate ways," I finally land on without looking at her. It's not a complete lie. We did. I just didn't know "our separate ways" would be him abandoning me in the middle of being attacked by a trio of burners.

"Oh, I'm sorry, Casey. Going through a breakup and then the world ending . . . that couldn't have been easy."

I don't correct her timeline. Instead, I nod and make an *mm-hmm* sound. "What about you? Weren't you dating someone?"

"Yeah, I was," she says, shaking her head. "But I had to kill him."

My mouth forms a muted O as I search her face for any signs of humor, waiting for a *just kidding*. But she stares back at me with a stoic look, shrugging off her statement with a quick lift of her shoulders.

"Wait, what?"

"Yeah, he turned into one of those zombie things, so I . . ." She falls silent and finishes her sentence by dragging her pointer finger across her neck.

"Jesus, Tessa! I'm so sorry." I step closer to her, kneeling on the ground and placing my hand over the one she has resting on her knee.

"Don't be." She flicks our hands up together, rejecting any need for sympathy. "I found out he was cheating a few days before the outbreak, and I was going to confront him and dump him, but I put it off, and then he turned into a zombie, so I had to kill him," Tessa says matter-of-factly, like she's sharing a recipe or giving me directions. "I'm actually glad it worked out that way, though. Otherwise, he would have denied it, then gaslit me, then tried to convince me to stay with him, and I probably would have. Then he'd be faithful for a while, and once he got comfortable, he'd cheat again. That cycle would continue until I got fed up and realized my worth.

Then I'd have to go to therapy to rebuild my confidence and deal with the trust issues he infected me with. So I think it's better that our relationship ended the way it did, and by that, I mean me decapitating him," Tessa says, picking at her fingernails.

"And you're sure he was a zombie?" I get to my feet and squint, frowning as I tuck my chin in.

She nods. "Pretty sure."

We both erupt in laughter at a situation that a mere two months ago would have been entirely psychotic, but now is seemingly normal.

The door flies open, bouncing against the wall with a thud and putting an end to our amusement. I grimace at the sight of Blake strolling into *my* bedroom. He's dressed in a dirty pair of jeans and a white T-shirt that clings to his sculpted chest and abs. A gun is nestled in a shoulder holster below his left armpit like a detective would wear beneath a suit jacket. Another pistol is tucked in a hip holster. Blake eyes me, then Tessa, and then his bed.

"Thanks for that," he says, gesturing to the mess I made of it.

"You're welcome. Didn't look up to regulation standards to me, so I figured it was best to start from scratch," I say. Tessa and I share a look of contempt toward him.

His lip snarls, and he begins remaking his bed.

"There's a ton to be done around here, so I don't appreciate you creating extra work for me."

"And I don't appreciate you at all," I say, throwing my hands on my hips.

"That sounds like a *you* problem." He briefly looks at me with squinty eyes as he moves to the other end of the bed, folding and tucking his sheets.

I hold my chin high as I walk toward him, stopping right in front of his bed. "No, it's *your* problem," I say, ruffling the tucked sheet and messing it up again.

"Should I leave you two alone?" Tessa teases.

Blake and I snap our heads in her direction and say, "No," in unison.

He groans, turning to face me. I stand a little taller and stare up at him. Being this close to Blake, I start to notice things I didn't before. The small mole above his right eyebrow. The smoothness of his lips. A thin scar emerging an inch or so from his tightly trimmed beard. And then there's an intensity he holds in his eyes that I think just might be anger. Maybe I can get him to throw a punch at me. My dad would definitely kick him out for that. I shuffle even closer to him, my bust practically touching his body. His eyes flicker, and the muscles in his neck and pecs flex. *Come on, Blake. Push me. Throw me on the ground. Touch me with those big hands. Do something. Give my dad a reason to toss you out on your ass.*

He exhales noisily and shakes his head. "Doomsday, I don't have time..."

"It's Dr. Pearson," I say with an air of authority, or at least that's what I'm trying to say it with. I cross my arms over my chest and press my lips firmly together.

Blake glances over at Tessa, as if she's going to give him any sort of support, but she's on Team Casey. Always has been, always will be.

"Casey," he lands on, not respecting my request but making a large improvement over his juvenile nickname. If I'm being honest, I don't even like being called Dr. Pearson unless I'm at the hospital; otherwise it just comes off as pompous.

"Like it or not," Blake continues, "we're going to be bunking together, so..."

Bang. Bang. Bang.

Three gunshots ring from outside, making their way up through the window and into our clustered trio. It changes all our demeanors in an instant. Dropping my arms to my side, I freeze, and my eyes widen with worry. Tessa's on her feet and standing next to me, reacting the same way. Blake turns and lunges himself across his bed to look out the window.

"God dammit!" he yells. He wastes no time, pushing past us and darting out of the room, his heavy footsteps echoing throughout the house.

Tessa and I leap onto his bed and smush our faces up against the window to try to get a look at what's going on. There's a clearing hacked through the trees, giving us a small unobstructed view of the front fence line. A lone biter is tangled up in the barbed wire, snapping his jaw and swinging his arms wildly in the air. My cousin Greg stands a mere four feet from it, firing rounds at the creature. He's either missing or only hitting limbs.

"What is he doing?" I shake my head.

"Looks like he's trying not to kill it." Tessa snickers.

I slide the window open. The screen is missing, so we're able to pop our heads out and get a better look. Suddenly, Blake appears, sprinting across the front yard toward Greg. He wields a sword in one hand, yelling, "Hold your fire."

I look to Tessa. "Where the hell did he get that thing?"

"He either picked it up on the way, or he's a master of hiding long hard things down his pants." She chuckles.

Thinking back to the night before, the image of Blake wearing only a pair of boxer briefs flashes before my eyes, as well as the bulge that took me by surprise. Part of me wants to tell Tessa that she isn't wrong, but I save that detail for myself.

With one quick swing, Blake lops the biter's head clean off. Black sludge sprays and oozes from its neck. The creature's arms and legs convulse for a few brief seconds before its body goes limp.

"What the hell were you doing!?" Blake yells, his voice carrying all the way back to the house, as clear as if he were in the room with us.

Greg's hands are animated, like he's trying to explain himself, but in a normal voice that's too quiet to hear.

"It was one zombie!" Blake continues at full volume, the conversation being served up in only a half portion for Tessa and me.

Greg continues talking with his hands, with the pistol still clutched in one of them.

"Give me that!" Blake takes the gun from him. "I don't want to hear it. How dumb can you be? Wasting ammo and making noise that could attract more of them here?"

"Pfft, if he was really worried about loud noises attracting more biters, he would shut up," I say.

"He can't do that, Casey." Tessa looks to me. "Remember, the louder he yells, the more authority he has and the bigger his penis becomes, so . . ." She flips her palms flat up, lifting them up and down to mimic a scale. "Priorities."

We laugh, while Blake continues to very loudly reprimand my younger cousin. Greg hangs his head, but I can't tell whether he's ashamed of his actions or just tired of being screamed at. My gaze returns to Blake. The muscles in his back are pumped up and flexed, stretching out his tight white T-shirt. The bloody sword is at his side, clutched in his hand.

"Blake's kinda hot when he's mad." The words tumble out of my mouth before I can stop them, and I wish I could suck them back in. Objectively, he is a very, very good-looking man, but that doesn't matter, because he's a dick.

Tessa slowly swivels her head, her eyebrow already raised. "Are you lusting after the enemy?"

"Absolutely not." I give her a light shove.

She laughs and pushes me back. "You sure about that?"

"A thousand times, yes. He's the worst."

"You're right about that. You remember that crap he pulled with you in high school?"

I crawl across his bed and get to my feet. "Which time?"

"Senior year."

I pulled into the student parking lot and hopped out of my truck. It was the first day of senior year, and I had really grown into myself over the summer—a glow-up, as some would call it. I was tan and toned from working outside in the sun on all Dad's projects. I had learned how to apply makeup and style my hair thanks to a combination of YouTube and Elaine. The braces were off, and I wore clothes my size rather than a size too big. Plus, my boobs had come in, and even if that were the only change, any high school boy would still consider it a glow-up. I didn't feel any different. I just looked different.

I remember hating that school had started up again. I dreaded it because all that meant was another year of torment from Blake and his friends. At least it would be my last before heading off to college. I couldn't help but worry, though. What would they call me this year? What cruel pranks would they play on me? Would they go out with a bang and try to top all the hazing they had done before? I was late for first period because I had had trouble getting into my locker. I thought Blake had already started his reign of terror, but it was just an old, screwy lock that I eventually got open. I was also relieved to find my locker wasn't stuffed with canned goods or dirt or garbage or rotten bananas—like he and his friends had done to me several times before.

When I finally made it to first period, there was only one desk open, and of course, it was right next to Blake Morrison. A mix of nerves and anger made my pulse race. I hadn't had a class with him since freshman year, but it looked like my luck had run out. That class had been absolute hell because Blake embarrassed me every chance he got.

I stood there, frozen at the front of the classroom, until the teacher told me to take a seat. I didn't want to, and the awkward tension in the room got Blake's attention. He lifted his head, and his mouth slightly parted, like he was surprised to see me. His eyes traveled the length of my body and then made a round trip before meeting my gaze. I'm sure I was scowling at him. But surprisingly, he didn't return it. Instead, Blake smiled. What scared me was that it seemed genuine. But what scared me even more was that I couldn't help but smile back.

I quickly change my top and glance over at Tessa, rolling my eyes as she climbs out of his bed. "How could I forget?"

"You should do it back to him, ya know, give him a taste of his own medicine." She double raises her brows and smirks. "Could be fun, or at the very least, it could help pass the time."

"No way. I'd rather dig holes or kill biters."

"Fine, maybe I'll do it for you," she adds with a coy look.

I feel a tightness in my chest, and I tug at my sports bra to give myself some room to breathe. My stomach somersaults, and my heart seems to skip a beat. I grab the glass bottle of water from my nightstand and chug the rest of it.

"You all right?" Tessa asks.

"Yeah." My head bobs as I force a tight smile. "But don't do that," I say.

"Do what?"

"Mess with Blake."

Her eyes slightly taper. "Why?"

"Because we're better than that."

"I suppose you're right." Tessa grins. "But if you change your mind, I'm not opposed to taking the low road."

I match her amused expression and say, "I'll let you know if I do," knowing full well I won't. Blake's an asshole, but he's my asshole.

Chapter 10

"Casey!" Elaine shrieks with excitement when she spots Tessa and me descending the stairs off the kitchen. She sets the knife down on the cutting board and wipes her hands on her apron as she rounds the island counter, bounding toward us as fast as she can.

Her arms are already outstretched when I reach her, and she embraces me with a warmth that feels like home. "Hi, Elaine," I say, inhaling her familiar scent, a mix of lavender and vanilla.

She rubs my back like she used to do when I was a kid, showing up at her house unannounced, mostly just to vent about my dad or anything else that was bothering me. She'd listen to me rant and serve me up dessert (always homemade) with a side of sound advice, and then we'd play cribbage.

"I missed you," Elaine whispers, and I can hear the sense of relief in her voice. Relief that I'm not one more person she has to say goodbye to earlier than she expected.

"I missed you too."

She squeezes a little tighter before letting go. "Let me take a look at ya," she says, scanning me from head to toe. A slight frown settles in when she sees the injuries on my face and neck, but she replaces it with an encouraging smile. I haven't seen her in person in a very long time, but she appears almost the same to me—just a little grayer and a little shorter.

"You must be starving," Elaine says, reaching for my hand and giving it a pat before retreating to her cutting board. "I've got sliced apples." She plops a pile of them onto a plate. "And I'm making veggie omelets."

Tessa pops an apple slice in her mouth and makes her way to the kitchen table, where JJ is seated, eating what looks to be a bowl of oatmeal.

"How was your first night, Casey?" JJ asks.

"It would have been better if I didn't have to—" I stop midsentence, cut off by the sound of the front door slamming.

"Fuck, Blake," Greg groans. His face is beet red, and his hands are balled up into fists at his sides, the muscles in his arms flexed as he drives his fingers tighter and tighter into his palms.

"Language!" Elaine scolds while cracking a fresh egg into a mixing bowl.

He mumbles, "Sorry," and flicks his head, tossing his shaggy hair out of his eyes. His anger quickly replaced by embarrassment after being scolded.

"I share your sentiment, Greg," I say, midchewing.

His brows shove together as he looks me over, trying to place me. Greg is JJ's younger brother, and I haven't seen him since I last babysat him the last summer I came home during college, so that would make my little cousin twenty years old now. Aside from putting on lean muscle and shooting up to nearly six feet tall, he doesn't look all that different than he did when he was a ten-year-old running around the compound with a Super Soaker.

"Casey?" He tilts his head to the side. It's more of a question than a statement. Greg crosses the room and gives me a quick hug. "I . . . thought you were dead."

"Nope, still alive . . . unfortunately," I say, patting him on the back.

"Well, I'm glad you are." He chuckles, and grabs a couple of apple slices from the plate. The kitchen chair scrapes across the wooden floor, screeching as Greg pulls it out and plops down next to Tessa.

"Nice shooting out there, buddy," she teases, pretending to fire at him with finger guns. He grumbles and swats her hands away.

"Stop. I get enough of that from Soldier Boy," he gripes.

"Soldier Boy?" I question.

"Yeah, Blake! That guy needs to go," Greg scoffs.

Elaine gives a stern look. "Be nice," she says, whisking the eggs into an airy golden liquid.

"I'm trying, Elaine." He bites an apple slice in half. "I'm just so sick of him. All he ever does is yell at me."

"For good reason." JJ briefly glances at his younger brother.

I hate to admit it, but JJ's right, and the only reason I hate to admit it is because that means Blake's right too.

Greg tapers his eyes. "Oh, you're taking his side. I thought we were brothers, bro."

"There are no sides. You were being reckless, so all I'm saying is that Blake had good reason to yell at you." JJ drops his spoon into his bowl, the metal clanging against the ceramic. He leans back in his chair, meeting Greg's hardened gaze.

"Reckless? I was keeping this compound safe."

Tessa and I share an amused look. These two haven't changed a bit, still at each other's throats even as adults. It's mostly because their personalities are so different. JJ's always been a quiet, no-nonsense type of guy. Greg, on the other hand, is aloof and loud, the consummate class clown. The one thing they do have in common, though, is that there isn't a mean bone in either of their bodies.

"I think we were all safe from the zombie ensnared in the barbwire fence. But what we weren't safe from was you wildly shooting at it," JJ says.

"Oh, I didn't realize there *was* a right way to kill a zombie, Mr. Expert." Greg's tone drips with sarcasm.

"You didn't kill it, though. Blake did. You wasted ammo and most likely attracted more of them our way." JJ pushes out his chair and stands, collecting his dish and bringing it to the sink.

The front door opens and closes, and in walks a woman I don't recognize, dressed in matching lululemon, complete with leggings and a cropped zip-up hoodie. She's young, maybe early twenties, sporting a full face of makeup and long, wavy red hair.

"Babe, are you okay?" she asks, and I'm not sure who she's talking to, because no one immediately acknowledges her.

"I'm fine, Molly," Greg huffs.

Molly leans over the back of his chair and wraps her arms around him, nuzzling his neck as she makes cooing noises, like a puppy burrowing its face in a bowl of food. "Are you sure? I heard what happened. I can't believe how brave you were, taking on that zombie all by yourself."

Tessa stifles a laugh by chewing on her last slice of apple, playing off the noises from her throat as though she's slightly choking.

"There's no one else in the world I'd rather spend the end of the world with than you, Pookie." Molly plants several kisses on his cheek.

He twists and pulls away from her. Whatever this is, Greg's clearly not into it.

Confused, I glance over my shoulder at Elaine and JJ.

JJ chuckles, shaking his head and drying his hands on his pants.

Elaine pours the bowl of eggs into the frying pan and grins. "Greg," she says, "why don't you introduce Molly and Casey to one another?"

The girl stands up straight and turns to me with a raised brow. "Who's Casey?"

"That would be me," I say, partially lifting a hand like I'm in a classroom.

Molly furrows her brows and presses her pouty lips together, giving me a once-over.

"I'm Greg's cousin," I add.

In a nanosecond, her face changes from a look of suspicion to one of amazement.

"Oh my God!" she squeals, racing to me. "It's so great to meet you. I'm Greg's girlfriend, Molly." I extend a hand to greet her, but she flicks it away without even looking at it and hugs me instead, pinning my arms at my sides and smushing her cheek against mine. "That basically makes us cousins-in-law," she adds.

"Oh, congrats. I didn't realize you two were engaged," I say with very little enthusiasm. I'm worried if I show too much of it, she'll squeeze me even tighter and end my life before a biter or burner can. "When did that happen?"

Tessa struggles to contain her laughter at the kitchen table. She pretends to choke even harder, waving away people who show her any concern. "Wrong tube," she wheezes out.

"We're not engaged." Greg's voice is monotone, like this isn't the first time he's had to make their relationship status clear, and instead of getting angry, he is now merely annoyed.

"Not yet, we're not," she says with a giggle.

His shoulders rise and fall as he takes a deep breath in place of responding to her.

Molly finally releases me, and she's all smiles, revealing a large mouth full of white teeth. Her bright red lips are full even when they're pulled taut.

"So, how long have you two been together?" I ask.

"Not long enough." She laughs. "But luckily, we have forever left. Ain't that right, Pookie?" When he doesn't respond, she glances over her shoulder at him and repeats, "Pookie?"

"Yeah, that's right," he says defeatedly without looking at her.

"Molly, my dear," Elaine cuts in.

"Yes," she says, looking to Elaine.

"Would you mind plucking a few heirloom tomatoes from the garden for me, please?" She dials up the sweetness with a closed-mouth smile, the dimples of her cheeks puckering to full effect. I can tell Elaine's just making this request to save Greg from whatever this is, because there's a full cutting board of already chopped vegetables for her omelets.

"Absolutely," Molly says with a nod. She skips to Greg, plants a wet kiss on his cheek, and tells him, "Miss you already," before sauntering through the living room and out the front door.

As soon as the door closes, Tessa blows out her cheeks, exploding with laughter and even some spittle.

"Stop it!" Greg throws a crumpled paper towel at her. It bounces off her head and onto the table, but does nothing to stop her delight.

"Wowwwww," I say. The word comes out breathy and elongated, matching the extent of my surprise and amusement.

Greg points a finger at me. "Don't you start too."

"I wouldn't even know where to start," I say, half smiling. "She seems very, very nice."

He groans. "Yeah, she's nice all right, but she's also incredibly annoying and extremely clingy."

"Then why are you dating her?" I cock my head.

"I'm not . . ." Greg pauses to collect himself before he gets overly animated. When he speaks again, it's in a very calm and flat voice. "We're not dating, okay."

"Really? Because she sure seems to think that you are."

"Yeah, well, I can't control what she thinks." Greg waves his hand like he's swatting at a fly.

My brows shove together in confusion. I look to Tessa for an answer, but she's still in a fit of laughter. "Were you and Molly dating at one point?" I ask.

"No," he says matter-of-factly.

"Then why would she think that to begin with?"

"We hooked up one time, okay?" He drops his head in his hands. "How was I supposed to know the world was gonna end the next day?"

I now understand why Tessa's unable to contain her laughter, because I can't either. I snort. "I'm sorry, Greg."

"I'm glad you find this so amusing." He crosses his arms over his chest, waiting for us to stop.

"You know, they say if you aren't careful during a one-night stand, you can end up living with that decision for the rest of your life," Elaine says without missing a beat. She flashes a sly smirk, further fueling our cackles.

"Come on! That's not funny," Greg whines, as though his tone will make it not so.

"Yes, it is," JJ adds from Elaine's side as he helps her with breakfast.

When we finally calm down, Tessa speaks first. "Greg, if you really don't like her, why don't you just tell her?"

"Yeah, just break up with her. Gently, of course," I add.

"I can't. She's totally obsessed with me. If I break it off with her, she'll kill me. Plus . . ." He trails off and shrugs. "You know."

"Know what?" Tessa asks.

"I mean, she's the only girl here my age who isn't family—well, besides you, Tessa. I mean, you've got nine years on me, but I could go to Cougartown." Greg wiggles his eyebrows up and down.

She gives him a disgusted look and says, "Forget what I said. I think you should stay with her."

"I agree, she's lovely," I say, backing Tessa up.

"You sure?" He looks at Tessa, trying to do his best impression of a male model.

"You better be careful, Greg, or I'll sic Blake on you," she quips.

"Pfft. I'm not afraid of Blake. He's a little bitch . . ."

"I'm a what?" Blake asks, startling us. He stands in the doorway, having quietly entered without any of us noticing his presence. Closing the door behind him, he walks in with a sword in hand. Both he and his weapon are covered in decay, remnants of the biter he slayed.

"I think you heard me—otherwise you wouldn't be asking me to repeat it."

"Oh, come on. Say it again for me then, Gregory," Blake challenges.

"Boys, there are enough things to fight beyond that fence out there, so we don't need any of that in here." Elaine's words insert themselves between the two men as she points her spatula back and forth.

"Yes, ma'am." Blake nods and looks to JJ. "You ready for our run?"

"Yup. Just gotta put my boots on."

Blake grabs a rag and wipes down the blade of his sword.

"What run?" I ask.

"Supply runs." JJ takes a seat on the steps and starts lacing up his work boots. "We do several a week," he adds.

"I wanna go," I say, lifting my chin.

"No," Blake says without missing a beat.

"Why not?"

"Because you haven't gone through training." Blake washes his hands at the sink. "And you'd be a liability." He doesn't even look at me while he scrubs at his fingernails.

My annoyance with him only continues to grow, so I reach across the counter and shut the water off. That gets his attention. Blake finally lifts his head, meeting my gaze.

"I'm not a liability, and *you* don't get to decide what I can and cannot do. So, whether you like it or not, I'm going." I turn from him and head toward the stairs, sliding past JJ. I take them two at a time, in a hurry to not be left behind.

"Where are you going?" he calls out.

"To get my shoes and jacket," I yell back.

"For what? A workout? Gardening? Because you sure as hell ain't coming with us," Blake hollers, his voice growing faint the farther I ascend.

I don't know who he thinks he is, but one thing is for sure: he won't be telling me what to do—not now, not ever. I hear the front door open and close as I reach my bedroom. Racing to the window, I see JJ and Blake walking side by side toward one of the trucks. *Damn it.*

"Wait!" I yell, hoping my voice will travel through the glass and stop them in time.

Chapter 11

I sprint around the dummy house toward Blake and JJ, who are loading the black pickup truck parked at the end of the driveway. Dad is over by the front fence line, pulling the decapitated biter loose from the barbwire. A leg tears from the body as he yanks it free and drops it into a wheelbarrow.

"Dad!" I yell.

Blake listens to whatever my dad says, so I just gotta tell him to tell Blake that I'm going with. Problem solved.

I call his name again, and this time, my dad turns back and waves a hand in the air. "Hey, sweetie. How'd you sleep?"

I come to a halt a few feet from him, a bit winded. "Fine. I want to go on a run with Blake and JJ," I say, gesturing to the truck.

Blake looks over at me and slowly shakes his head.

Dad pauses before letting out a sigh. "I don't think that's a good idea, Casey. You just got in last night, and you should rest up a few more days, get acclimated, and then you—"

"Get acclimated?" I squint, crossing my arms over my chest. "I grew up here. There's nothing for me to get acclimated to."

He tugs on the severed leg still tangled in the fence, shredding the decaying flesh against the barbs as he pulls it free. It lands in the wheelbarrow with a wet thump. Sunlight glistens off the black slime, still fresh on the limbs and body, making it shine like polished obsidian. The cool air aids in slowing the rot, but the stench is unbearable, a mixture of old blood and spoiled milk.

"Things are different now," Dad says, scanning the ground around him. "Do you see the head?"

I groan and point to a section of long grass beside the fence post, where a patch of dark, matted hair peeks out. "Over there."

Dad follows my finger and fishes the head out of the grass, picking it up by its hair. It used to be a man, most likely in his forties, but it's hard to tell now, due to the decomposition. Its eyes are sunken in, clouded white, and its mouth gapes open with a partially bitten-off tongue protruding from it. Black sludge drips from the opening in its neck. Dad sets the head in the wheelbarrow and then removes his gloves, throwing them on top of the corpse.

"Dad, I'm well aware that things are different now, but I made it here from Chicago all my own, so I'm perfectly capable of going on a supply run."

He scratches at his beard and exhales. I know he's thinking it over, and I'll be getting a *Fine, you can go* from him any second now. I mean, how could he not? I practically gave up my whole childhood prepping for this.

Blake strolls over with a shit-eating grin on his face. I can't wait to wipe it right off. "Hey, Dale. JJ and I are gonna head out."

"Me too," I say, shooting him a dirty look.

"No, you're not." Blake raises his chin, challenging me.

"Yes, I am. Isn't that right, Dad?" I smile and look to my father, waiting for a *That's right*.

JJ walks up, stopping beside Blake. He gives him a pat on the back. "Ready?"

"I am," I reply with a nod.

My cousin moves his mouth side to side, looking to Blake and then my dad for confirmation.

"No, Casey, you're not going," Dad says, letting out a sigh. "We have rules for a reason, and I can't make any exceptions." He pulls his lips in, signaling that's the end of the discussion, but it's not for me.

Blake smirks. "Told ya."

"Come on, Dad! What rules? Only big, stupid muscular men can go?"

"Hey!" JJ says, cocking his head.

"Not you. Just him." I gesture to Blake and narrow my eyes.

"You're not ready to go out on a run, Case," Dad interjects.

"What?! Of course I'm ready. You trained me for this, remember?"

I can't believe it. How could he take the word of a stranger over his own daughter?

"That was a long time ago, and I don't know what your combat skills are like now. Plus, when was the last time you even fired a gun?" He tilts his head.

I haven't shot a firearm since I was eighteen, but I'm not going to tell him that. Does he not realize what I went through yesterday to get here? Not only that, but I also got here in one piece all by myself. He's treating me like I'm fragile, like I could just shatter at any moment, but he's the one who forced me to be strong. It was the only thing he would let me be. And now he doesn't trust that I am. What was the point of all the training if I'm never going to be able to use it?

"Dad, my combat skill are fine. I literally took out three burners yesterday."

"Burners?" Blake furrows his brow. "Don't you mean *zombies*? This is exactly why you can't come. You don't even know what we're dealing with."

I step toward him, positioning myself just a foot away from his face, showing that I'm not intimidated by him in the slightest. I don't care that he's nearly a foot taller than me or that his biceps are practically the size of my thighs. I jab a finger in the center of his chest. He doesn't flinch. I don't care that it feels like I'm poking a rock right now either.

"No, I don't mean *zombies*, Blake, and I know exactly what I'm dealing with . . . a complete and utter dickhead." I thrust my finger into his chest as I say each syllable.

"I think she's talking about you, Morrison," JJ simpers.

Blake rolls his eyes and says, "Yeah, I'm aware."

"I know this area like the back of my hand. I did eight years of combat training, graduated from medical school, *and* I'm a resident doctor. So, you know what that means? I can navigate better than you, can survive just as easily as you, and if someone gets hurt, I can actually do something about it." I stare into his eyes, waiting for his response.

"Were," he says.

"What?"

"You *were* a doctor in residency. Now you're just a pain in my ass."

Rage thrums through my veins, churning inside me. My hands become fists at my sides, and it takes everything in me not to throw one at his jaw. He's the one who's a pain in the ass, not me. This is my house. I belong here. He's just . . . an intruder.

"What are you even doing here, anyway? No one wants you here, Blake."

"I was asked to be here."

"By who?" The betrayal is already seething through my body, and I have no idea who to direct it at.

"Dale," he says with a smirk.

I turn to my father, who stands by idly, letting the argument play out before him. I thought Blake just fled here. I had no idea my dad *invited* him. How could he do that to me?

"Why would you invite him to live here?" I plant myself squarely into the earth, bracing myself for whatever nonsensical reason is about to escape his mouth.

"Because . . . we're friends."

My eyes dart between Blake and my dad. So Blake wasn't lying when he said they were friends. But how? My dad's a fifty-some-year-old prepper who keeps to himself. And Blake is my age, and I assume his only hobbies are bullying and lifting weights.

"How in the hell did you become friends with him, Dad?" My eyes are so narrow, I can barely see my father.

He slides his hands into the front pockets of his jeans and rocks back on his heels. "Well, this place wasn't easy to maintain alone, Casey, and I needed help with some of the bigger projects. So I put out a for-hire ad in the paper about a year and a half ago, and Blake was the most qualified applicant. He started out as my employee, but we became fast friends."

"A year and a half!? You've been chumming it up with Blake Morrison for a year and a half?"

"What's the big deal, Pearson?" Blake asks, cocking his head to the side. "Just 'cause your dad and I have spent more time together in the past eighteen months than you and him have spent together in the last decade doesn't mean you need to—"

"Shut up, Blake!" I snap.

"Casey, don't be like that," my dad interjects. "It just worked out this way, and I didn't realize this was the same Blake from when you were kids until you mentioned it last night."

"How many Blakes do you think there are around here, Dad?" My annoyance with the both of them is building by the minute.

"Do you really expect me to remember that? The last time I heard anything about Blake was when you were thirteen," he says.

I sharply exhale. I mean, it was a long time ago, and I did stop confiding in my dad about how horrible Blake was to me, only because his answer to the problem was either talking to Blake's parents or reporting it to the school. I knew that would make it worse, so I just pretended like everything was fine, and I dealt with it on my own. Dad doesn't know that it went on for years, all the way up until I graduated high school and got out of here. So I guess I can't be mad at him for not knowing. But I can be mad at him for being the reason I left this place. The only connection I had with my dad was prepping, and I hated prepping. But it was all he cared about. It was the only thing on his mind, so it was impossible to connect with him. Now he's taking Blake's side, after he spent years training me, preparing me for this exact situation. It's bullshit, and there's no way in hell I'm letting Blake boss me around.

"Whatever. I don't care if you two are friends, but I am going on the run," I say, throwing my hands on my hips.

"No. You aren't," Blake pipes in.

"Yes. I am."

"Dale, back me up here." He looks to my father, appealing for his assistance in a matter that shouldn't concern either of them.

"Casey, I'm sorry, but like I said, we have rules in place, and everyone has to follow them."

"That's right." Blake nods. "You need to pass firearms training and hand-to-hand combat before you can go on a run."

I doubt anyone here has experienced anything close to what I went through yesterday. They have no idea what's even out there.

"I've seen more action than everyone here combined," I say, clenching my jaw.

"It's not a contest, Doomsday. Anyone can kill. It's about making sure everyone comes home safe."

I'm so sick of his smug attitude. "Everyone will come home safe," I seethe through my teeth. "Because I can handle myself just fine."

"Okay then. Come at me," Blake says, waving me toward him with a flick of his fingers.

I scrunch up my face. "What?"

"Prove it, and I'll tell you what—if you can take me down, or even come close, I'll let you come." He smirks.

"That's not even a fair fight. You're a Navy SEAL, and you're twice my size."

"Great. So we're in agreement. You aren't ready." Blake turns and starts off toward the truck. "Let's go, JJ. We've got a sweet supply run to go on."

Gripped by fury, I roll my shoulders back, dig my heels into the ground, and launch myself into a full sprint. Just as I'm about to drop my shoulder into Blake's spine, he quickly steps to the side, letting me reel forward. My own momentum causes me to topple to the ground, ungracefully somersaulting as I do so.

"Nice try, Crazy Pearson. The element of surprise is certainly a powerful asset . . . when you actually have it, that is." Blake stands over me, smiling.

He offers me a helping hand, but I swat it away. "I don't need your help." Panting, I pull myself up and get back on my feet.

"Suit yourself. Now, are you done?"

"Not even close." I square up with him, fists raised, making him think I'll attack at any second. JJ and Dad take a step back, giving us our space. I stare intensely as I circle Blake like a predator with its prey, waiting for the right moment to strike. He watches me, half-amused, but he won't be soon. I fake a low jab at his kidney, then bring my right arm around in a dramatic, overly telegraphed hook motion. Halfway through, I dive and shoot down toward his legs.

Blake doesn't bite at either punch. When I plunge forward, he merely steps back and pushes my head down, forcing me to land right on my face. Grass and dirt enter my open mouth, and I choke on the unwelcome micro forest. I spit several times, trying to get it all out, and wipe my face with the back of my forearm.

"Give it up, Casey." He leans down and pats my back twice between my shoulder blades, punctuating my defeat. But what he thinks was the sharp wrap of a period is merely a comma to me.

I roll onto my back and, with a quick sweeping motion, kick Blake's legs out from under him. His tailbone smashes into the ground before his head rocks back, following suit.

"Damn," JJ gasps.

"That's my girl," Dad says.

I flip over and mount him, pinning his arms under each of my knees. One hand hovers over his throat, while the other is cocked back, ready to strike if needed. "Yield," I say, grinning.

Blake smiles back, and then he drives his shoulders into the earth, lifts his chest, and rolls his hips. In an instant, his boots are right in front of my face before they cross in an X over my chest, pulling me back and slamming me into the ground.

He sits up and looks down at me pinned to the grass. "Not bad, Pearson. Not bad at all."

"Get off of me," I yell as I try to writhe out of his grip, but I can barely move under the weight of his legs.

"Then yield." He smirks. The green in his eyes glows with excitement at his forthcoming victory, but he's going to have to earn it.

I twist my hips back and forth, trying to roll him off me, but he's too heavy, and it just results in me slowly dry humping him while he pins me down with even more force.

Blake stares at me like a lion ready to go in for the final kill. Part of him hardens against my body, instantly changing his demeanor. The smoldering look on his face fades and his cheeks flush, betraying the truth of what he would like to do to me.

"Are you done?" he asks, trying to keep his composure.

I twist and squirm under his weight a few more times, fighting until I have nothing left to give. "I guess I better be, before you finish on my leg," I wheeze.

He coyly smiles, releasing me from his death grip. Blake stands and pulls me up with him, forcefully drawing my head into his chest. Lowering his mouth to my ear, he whispers, "Maybe next time."

His hot breath on my skin sends a wave of warmth through my body. I push off him, creating a few feet of distance. The look on his face is like that of a cat who's decided to let the mouse go, just so it can catch it again later. I groan and stomp my foot.

Blake turns and heads for the truck, tossing a cocky grin over his shoulder. "Later, Doomsday! I'll be sure to bring you back something pretty," he teases.

I reach down and pick up a clump of dirt, then hurl it at him. It doesn't reach Blake, and he doesn't even notice it.

My father wraps his arm around me and pulls me into the crux of his shoulder. "You did good, Casey. Now let's go work on making you great."

Defeated, I let out a heavy sigh and nod, knowing he's right. I am rusty, and rusty isn't going to cut it if I want to beat Blake, and right now, that's all I want to do.

Chapter 12

Leaves crunch beneath our feet as we walk the property I once called home. But I guess that's what it is again. The trees are taller, and the undergrowth is fuller. Years of the forest having been untouched have allowed it to become wild and beautiful as well as haunting and foreboding.

My father walks tall and proud, pointing out the things we built together, engendering a fondness for the times we shared while also highlighting all the new things, as if to say, *Look what I did.* There are chicken coops and several structures for geese and ducks, many of which roam free, quacking and honking. He's even installed a man-made pond out back for the ducks to swim and play in. We didn't have any of this growing up, so the old man has clearly learned a lot since I've been gone.

"Remember when we first put in all that fencing?" he asks, pointing along the edge of the property, as far as the eye can see.

"How could I forget one of my favorite childhood memories?" I look to my dad, smiling to let him know I'm joking—or half joking, at least.

"I'm sure you're glad we have them now, though."

The grim reality of what life would be like here without all the things we built and all the prepping sinks in. The fence alone is responsible for so much peace of mind. No one would ever be able to sleep safely knowing that anything out there could just wander into the house or the guest cabins. I'm not ready to concede that he was right about every single choice he made, but about this one thing . . . definitely.

"I am, Dad," I say.

He smiles back and then continues pointing out more of the new additions. The trails he added so it's easier to patrol the fence lines at night. The rainwater runoff trough and tank so that he could cycle more fresh water. The additional solar panels to help keep everything running. All the projects he had been talking about for years, the ones I had always made fun of him for, saying he would never need any of this stuff. Now, without them, we would have no power, no clean drinking water, no extra food supply, and we would be on guard twenty-four seven, fearing for our lives.

"What do you think?" he asks.

"It's impressive."

"Thanks." He beams, basking in this moment that he's been waiting decades for. I know he isn't happy about what the world has become and that we actually need all these safeguards. But I can see that part of him is glad he was prepared.

"Casey?"

"Yeah."

"How come . . . how come you never came back to visit?" His eyes show a sense of longing. The two of us spending time together back here on the property has likely brought a mixture of joy at me being in his life again and also a deep sadness. A realization of the years we didn't spend together back when the world was normal. How many of these walks exist only in the world of "what if"?

I don't have it in me to tell him the truth, because what good would it do? *Hey, Dad, guess what? I didn't come back here because I resented you for making me waste my childhood. For being the reason I relentlessly got picked on and why school was a living hell for me.* Even the one summer I did come back, after freshman year of college, all I felt was sadness. Like it was seeping up through the ground, growing roots into my body and sapping the joy right out of me. I didn't come back because all we had was prepping, and I hated that more than anything. When I left for sophomore year of college, I knew I would never return . . . not unless I absolutely had to, not unless he was right.

"Oh, you know. Life happens. I was busy. Between med school and residency, I never even had time to go to the gym or go see a movie, let alone drive all the way up to Wisconsin and back." I say it as chipper as I can, emphasizing words like *busy*, *med school*, *residency*, trying to convince us both at the same time that it's the truth so we can move on.

He doesn't answer, though, and I can tell by the disappointment on his face, he isn't buying it, but he is accepting it for now. I feel so bad for cutting him out of my life, minus short texts here and there. His texts to me were always diary-length, and I barely even read them. I was just so angry at him, and I wanted my old life completely separated from the new one I had created. Actually, I didn't want anything to do with my old life. I was ashamed of it, and I was ashamed of him—but now, I'm only ashamed of myself.

I hang my head, fighting back the tears welling up in my eyes.

"Hey." Dad moves in front of me, placing his hands on the sides of my arms and gently squeezing. "You're here now, and that's all that matters."

I nod and barely meet his gaze. I'm too guilt-ridden to look at him in this moment. To let him see what my eyes will certainly betray. I put my own feelings first, never considering what it meant to him. Cutting him out was my way of punishing my father, because I felt like that was what he had done to me. It was always about preparing for the end of the world, and there was never time to just live in it.

"Hey, Dale!" a woman's voice calls from behind me.

We break apart, and I turn to see a smiling woman tossing a final piece of clothing from her arms over a thick string hanging between two trees. Her dirty-blonde hair is pulled back into a tight ponytail and her cheeks are bright red. Whether that's from the slight cold in the air or just her natural color, it's perfectly in place for the comely, round face now approaching us.

"Hello, Helen," my dad says, as though he's just taking a stroll through his neighborhood and spotted a friend he's greeted a hundred times before.

"And who is this beautiful young lady?" she asks.

"This is my daughter, Casey."

Her face brightens even more, and her eyes develop a slight sheen to them.

"Oh, Dale! I'm so happy for you," she says, still smiling. It's clear my dad has talked a lot about me, and from her reaction, she most likely thought he was never going to see me again.

"It's great to meet you." She beams, but there's a seriousness in her eyes that tells me there's more to her than this cheery routine.

"Nice to meet you too, Helen. I think you're the most cheerful person I've met in the apocalypse," I say with a laugh.

She turns, glancing around like a thief making sure the coast is clear before she meets my gaze and lets out a heavy sigh. "Oh, I just do this for my boys," she whispers. "They kind of know what's going on, but my husband, my parents, and I have tried to shield them from most of it. So we're treating this like we're at permanent summer camp, and if it looks like I'm happy and having fun, then maybe . . ." Helen looks down at her feet, shaking her head as she searches for the words within her, before meeting my gaze—the smile has returned to where it just was. "Well, anyway, if it weren't for your father, I'm not sure I'd have a family anymore."

Before I can respond, a man comes out of one of the cabins behind her, walking toward us with a tight smile. He's around six feet tall with a bowl haircut, and he wears his lean and muscular figure like a suit he's borrowed from someone else. But what really sticks out are his eyes. It's not the color of them, as they're an unremarkable shade of brown. It's the heavy, deep-purple bags resting below them and the red veins splitting and cracking in all directions across the whites of his eyes. This man doesn't sleep . . . at least, not anymore.

"Chris, I want you to meet my daughter, Casey."

He steps to me, extending a dry, calloused hand. His eyes begin to moisten but not with sadness. They're the kind of tears that form when you stifle a yawn so as not to seem rude during a conversation. They well to capacity and tumble down his face, leaving darkened streaks across his parched skin. He doesn't even notice until his wife quickly dries them for him.

"It's nice to meet you, Casey," Chris says, shaking my hand. "Where'd you come in from?"

"Chicago."

"Wow, that must have been—"

"Hell," I say.

"Yeah." He scratches the back of his neck. "I can't even imagine."

"How did you all end up here?" I ask.

Chris stuffs his hands in his pockets, shuffling his feet. "We were headed up to Helen's parents' lake house near Tomahawk, and our car broke down over on Highway 19. We couldn't get any cell service, and I figured we were just in a dead zone. I left my family and my in-laws in the car and started walking, looking for a gas station or a nearby house. Had no idea what had happened to the world, until I stumbled upon this place. Dale told me, and then he took us in. Myself, Helen, and my boys are in one cabin, and Helen's parents are in the other." He looks to my dad, his face showing nothing but admiration and gratitude for saving them. It's a look I'm sure my father wanted to see on my face for years, instead of the irritation and resentment that were building stronger and deeper with every passing moment. Now, seeing what our work has done for these two, what my dad's unrelenting perseverance has done to keep a family whole, I can't help but see him as less of the villain and more of the hero.

The somber but gracious moment is broken by the sound of high-pitched voices and two boys no older than twelve sprinting out of the cabin. "Dad! Dad! Can we play catch now?" the one with a football tucked under his arm shouts.

I greet both of them and introduce myself. They're timid, partially hiding behind their father and mother. Their father ruffles their matching bowl haircuts and tells them to say hi, and in unison, they do. At their age, I was prepping for this, and now they're living in it. I'd call it ironic, but I really don't know what it is.

Chris takes the football from his son and tells his kids to go long. They take off running, while he steps away and launches it through the air. It lands short of the boys, most likely due to his exhaustion. He smiles and nods, telling me it was nice meeting me before joining his children.

Helen echoes his sentiment and returns to her basket of clothes that still need to be hung out to dry.

"See ya around," Dad says with a wave as we continue with our walk.

"It's great what you've done for them."

He glances over at me. "It wasn't just me. It was us."

"But I wasn't even here."

"You didn't need to be, Case. We built this place together, so everyone that's here and safe is because of what *we* did."

"I would feel good about that but Blake's here too," I say with a laugh.

Dad playfully pushes me, and then his face turns serious. "I really think you'll learn to like Blake. You two have more in common than you realize."

"Oh, does he hate himself too?" I smirk.

Dad folds his lips in and shakes his head, seeming slightly amused. "I've got one last thing to show you," he says, changing the subject and leading us toward the main house.

He might have been right about the end of the world, but he's wrong about Blake. I will never learn to like him. The only thing I might learn is how to tolerate him, and that's if I don't kill him in the meantime.

Chapter 13

Dad leads the way down into the basement, past the food storage and the holding cells, which I thought were completely unnecessary back when we were building them, but now I think they just might come in handy. Maybe I'll lock Blake up in one of them and throw away the key. I try to tamp down the smile that starts to spread across my face at the thought of Blake behind bars.

We continue through an arched doorway and a tunnel, carved deep into the earth, illuminated by the warm amber glow of incandescent lighting. Up ahead, it opens up to a large, well-lit room, one that wasn't completed when I was here. I enter behind my father, finding two people, a man and a woman with their backs to us, dressed in denim tuxedos, polishing guns at a table in the center of the room.

The walls are full of enough armaments to supply a small militia—hunting rifles, semiautomatic rifles, shotguns, handguns of all variety, and an assortment of melee weapons. There are rows of storage lockers and chests of drawers filled with what I'm sure is more of the same. Dad clears his throat and the two people turn to face us.

"Casey!" Aunt Julie says. It comes out like a question, like she can't believe I'm standing in front of her.

Uncle Jimmy smiles at the sight of me. He's a man of few words, always has been, so a smile is like having a whole conversation with him.

My aunt wipes her grease-covered hands on her jean jacket and embraces me. "We were all worried sick about you. I'm so glad you're okay," she says.

"I'm glad you both are too." I smile as she releases me.

Uncle Jimmy pats me on the back and nods, sharing the same sentiment, no words needed. Growing up, my aunt and uncle lived more than two hours from us, so we only saw them for holidays and occasional birthdays for myself, Greg, or JJ. Even when we couldn't make it to one another, my aunt Julie always sent gifts and cards in the mail, reminders that she and the family were thinking of me and my dad. They're the salt of the earth, just good, hardworking, honest people. We stand in silence for a few beats, letting the moment seep in.

"What are you two up to?" Aunt Julie finally asks.

"Casey needs to practice shooting," Dad says. "She's rusty from living in the city all these years."

"She can't be any worse than Greg," my uncle says with a smirk. When he does choose to speak his few words, it's usually a joke or a small piece of wisdom.

Aunt Julie slaps him on the shoulder. "That's your son you're talking about."

"Don't remind me." He chuckles.

She rolls her eyes, trying not to laugh along with him. Dad and I exchange a grin.

"We're gonna head out to do some shooting too," Aunt Julie says. She and Uncle Jimmy pick up their freshly polished guns, complete with suppressors to silence their gunfire. She slips a box of target ammo in the pocket of her oversized jacket.

"Sounds good. We'll meetcha out there." Dad steps out of the way to let them pass, their footsteps echoing through the bunker as they leave.

My father walks to one of the drawer chests and rummages through it, grabbing a couple of items. I can't see what they are until he returns to the table positioned in the center of the room and sets them on it.

Metal clinks against metal. He lifts his hand, revealing a stack of gold throwing stars. My fingers immediately begin to tingle at the sight of them. They were always my favorite.

"Think you still got it?" Dad raises a brow.

I pluck one from the table and flip it around in my hand, feeling the smooth, cold metal and the sharp, pointy edges. It's like having a finger I thought I'd lost sewn back on. With these, I know I'll be out on a supply run in no time, and I'll prove to my father and Blake that they were wrong about me. I'm ready, I'm prepared, and I am more than capable. I know these woods like the back of my hand, and I've been training for this since Blake was still going through puberty.

So his days of bossing me around are numbered.

"Oh yeah," I say with a smile.

Dad grins back proudly. "Well, let's go find out."

Chapter 14

Outside, my dad and I head deep into the woods, near the edge of the property line. Before we left the armory, Dad fitted me with hip and ankle holsters, so I can carry two guns on me, as well as a belt pouch that'll hold up to a dozen throwing stars. That's in addition to the thigh sheath for my trusty combat knife. I'm not used to the extra weight, so my steps are a bit staggered as my muscles get familiar to the awkward restrictions placed on them.

We enter a long field that serves as the firing range. Paper targets are tacked up on trees at the far end. An assortment of wooden dummies and archery targets lines the sides of the clearing, and two makeshift tables constructed from fallen trees mark the start of the range. My aunt and uncle are already at one of them, taking turns firing shots.

"All right, let's see what ya got," my dad says as we reach the other table. He sets his guns down and dusts his hands off.

I nod and walk to a line spray-painted white in the grass and pull a throwing star from my pouch. Taking a deep breath, I close my eyes and picture back to when I'd run up and down this dirt track, hurling stars at the wooden dummies and archery targets. I'd pretend I was a ninja, plucking the stars out of one target before I would turn and, with the flick of a wrist, send the blades into another. It was the most fun I had growing up, and that's why I practiced as much as I did. Plus, I was good at it, and it's fun to do things we excel at.

I open my eyes again and exhale, picturing Blake's face on the paper target straight ahead. In one fluid motion, I move my arm back slightly before throwing it forward and flicking my wrist at the very last second. The star whistles through the air, striking the center of the target with a hard thud.

"That's my girl," my father whispers to himself.

Energized by my accuracy, I pull out another star, repeating the process. First, picture Blake. Draw back. Throw forward. Flick my wrist. Boom. It hits right next to the previous one.

"If you could carry a thousand of those, you could take down a whole army." He laughs, patting me on the back.

"It's easy when I just picture Blake's face."

My dad's laughter fades as his mouth forms a hard line.

I glance over at him and squint. "How did he go from hired hand to best friend?"

"I wouldn't say we're best friends," Dad says, folding his arms over his brawny chest. "But we are friends. Blake's a good, hardworking man. I know he wasn't good to you in the past, but why not give him a chance to show you that he's changed? I assure you he has, because no one stays the same forever."

I twist my lips, moving them side to side, thinking back to all the horrible moments Blake caused, all the tears he made me cry, all the nights I spent in bed, feeling more alone than any young girl should. I could forgive those, if only the moments had stayed bad. It's the good ones I can't forgive.

The bell ringing signaled the end of school, but I was already out in the parking lot making my way to my truck. I tossed my backpack in the passenger seat and hopped in, ready to get home and get started on my homework and whatever prepper project Dad had in store for me. The twist of my key in the ignition created only a grinding sound, like metal wailing out in pain.

"Not again." I groaned and popped the hood, so I could see what new ailment had fallen upon the old hunk of junk. Lifting the latch, I propped

the hood up with the metal support bar and scanned the assortment of objects that I could barely name, let alone fix.

"Having car trouble?" a voice called from behind me.

I turned to see Blake approaching, armed with a smile, which felt more like a disguise. For some reason, he'd been nice to me since the school year started a few weeks prior, and by nice, I mean he hadn't picked on me or pulled any cruel pranks. I had to assume he was playing the long game that year, waiting until I let my guard down so he could hit me with some massive evil plan he had been brewing.

"No," I lied, refocusing my attention on the engine or whatever it was I was looking at.

"It looks like you are, and I can help," Blake said, joining me at my side.

I stared at him, squinting in suspicion before scanning my surroundings to make sure none of his cronies were hiding in wait, ready to slam the hood on me or whatever else they might have pulled. I noticed his smile hadn't faded and there was a kindness in his eyes—despite my hesitancy coupled with silence. He had seemed nice as of late, saying hi to me in class and nodding when we passed each other in the hall. Blake had even lent me a pencil when mine broke midway through a quiz. Maybe he had changed. Maybe, like my external glow-up, he had had an internal glow-up over the summer and decided to be kind and mature instead of . . . well . . . an asshole.

"Fine. Go ahead and help," I said with a shrug. There was hesitation in my voice, as I was still uneasy accepting his about-face.

Blake leaned over the truck's exposed interior, inspecting the different components, fiddling with some wires, checking the oil and various fluid levels.

"You know a lot about cars?" I watched him work, the muscles in his arms flexing.

"Yeah, it's kind of a hobby of mine." Blake pulled something out of place, cleaned it off, and replaced it. "Try it again," he said with a grin.

I got back in the driver seat and turned the key. Nothing.

"Hold on," he yelled from behind the propped-up sheet of metal.

I could see him moving under the crack of the hood, his large hands shifting quickly, like a magician performing the shell game. I'm not sure why his behavior had changed, but there was something about him helping me while I was in need that created a small tingle in my stomach, and when his voice called out for me to try again, my ears no longer wanted to close up in disgust. Instead, I found it rather comforting.

With another twist of the key, the roar of the engine woke the rest of the vehicle from its temporary slumber. Grateful for his efforts, I felt a smile spread across my face, and I tried to tamp it as I got out of the truck. Blake closed the hood and wiped his hands off on his jeans, leaving light smears of grease behind.

"Thanks."

"No problem." He nodded. "It just had a loose wire." His eyes skimmed over me, from my head to my toes. "But everything else looks good," Blake added, and I wasn't so sure he was still talking about my truck.

"I really appreciate it," I said, my voice coming out in a soft yet eager tone, one I didn't know I was capable of producing. Blake must have felt the same way, or at least that's what I noticed in his eyes. There was a sense of curiosity that made his green irises look less vomity and more like the first budding leaves of a tree in spring.

He shoved his hands in his pockets and glanced at his feet, his usual bravado being replaced with . . . shyness?

"I feel like I owe you for your handiwork," I said as I disappeared around the side of my truck and grabbed my backpack from the passenger seat. I quickly tried to fish money out of the front pocket before I rejoined him.

"How about ice cream instead?" he said.

I froze, my hand still buried in my bag as I let the reality of his question sink in. Slowly lifting my head, I met his gaze, seeing his faint smile and the hope in his eyes that was screaming "Please say yes."

I should have said no. I shouldn't have even given him a chance to get close to me. But for some reason, some part of me didn't want to say no. Another part of me wouldn't let me say yes either.

So instead, I landed on "Sure."

That *sure* led to me letting my guard down, which hurt me far worse than all the bullying ever did. Regardless of the circumstances or how many years have passed, I won't allow Blake to ever have the chance to hurt me like that again.

"Some people never change, Dad, and he's one of them," I say.

"You can't live with hate in your heart, Casey. It's not healthy."

"You're only saying that because *you* like him."

"No, I'm saying that because I mean it. Animosity hurts you, not the person it's directed at. It's like poison, but you're the only one consuming it."

"Why are you always taking Blake's side? You're supposed to be my dad. Not his. You're supposed to protect me. Not him."

"Casey, that's not fair—" he interrupts.

"Fair!? I'll tell you what's not fair."

My aunt and uncle have stopped shooting. Their necks crane in our direction, and they watch as I explode with anger. I don't care, though, because an audience isn't going to stop me from saying what I need to say.

"It's not fair that my childhood was simultaneously ruined both at school and at home. It's not fair that I was in fear of getting on the bus or driving to school every day because the only thing waiting for me was ridicule and humiliation. Even the closing bell didn't save me, because I had to come home to my doomsday-prepping father and perform endless manual labor. And it's sure as hell not fair that you gave me nothing to look forward to in life, because you told me every single day that the goddamn world was going to end!"

My voice stops, leaving behind a reverberation nearly as loud as a gunshot. My shoulders rise and fall, matching my small, quick breaths as I work off the built-up energy from my rant. Dad lowers his head and lets out a heavy sigh like he doesn't know what to say or how to fix this. There is no fixing this. There's no going back. There are no redos. It just is what it is. He was right. And I hate him for that, but I love him for it too. Dad uncrosses his arms and meets my gaze.

"Hit me," he says.

"What?" I step back, confused and surprised by his request, given everything I just said. "No."

"Come on." He beckons with his hands. "We can kill two birds with one stone here. You need to train anyways, so you'll be ready to go on a run, and I can see how mad and upset you are with me. So come on. Let's get that anger out. Fight me," he says, squaring up and planting his feet shoulder width apart.

"No, I'm not gonna fight you," I scoff. "You're old. It'd be, like, elder abuse."

"Hey! I am far from old." Dad bounces on his feet.

"Whatever you say." I roll my eyes. "But I'm still not gonna fight you."

"Why not?"

"Because it's weird. And just because I'm mad at you doesn't mean I wanna hurt you."

"Oh, I don't think you'll be hurting me at all." He smirks.

"I know what you're doing, Dad. Reverse psychology won't work on me," I say, shaking my head.

He lowers his boxing hands and shrugs. "Guess Blake was right about you not being ready. Such a shame because I thought I raised a fighter."

I step to him and deliver a slow hook to his side. He hops back and slaps my arm away, grinning from ear to ear. "Come on! You can do better than that. Full speed!" His feet shift like a boxer's as he works himself up with excitement.

"Okay, old man."

I let on a smile as I bounce on the balls of my feet, moving back and forth to throw off his eyes, which are following the center of my mass, waiting for a hint as to what I will do. I step in, then out, faking a left jab and following with a right. My father catches my fist in his hand and pulls me forward, sending me tumbling into the dirt.

"Dad!" I yell.

"I told you to fight me, not play around and dance. Come on!"

I'm fuming now, annoyed my skills have softened so much that I can't even engage in proper combat with a man in his fifties. I stand and start to circle him, waiting to see whether he'll make the first move, but after a minute or so, I realize he's not going to.

"Whoop his ass, Casey!" my uncle shouts. Aunt Julie claps and hoots and hollers.

I feint inside, fake a jab, and go for a swift kick, connecting the toe of my shoe with his shin.

"Ow, ow, ow." He hobbles on one leg, and I take the opportunity to rush in, dropping my shoulder at his waist and tackling him to the ground. I try to pin him, but he's too large and surprisingly fast. As we're crashing to the ground, he continues rotating while holding my waist tightly. He flips me onto my back just as he hits the dirt, ending the fight in an instant.

"A shin kick followed by tackling someone twice your size. What's going on?" Dad asks, only slightly out of breath as he gets to his feet, brushing himself off.

I peel myself from the grass and stand. "What? It worked, didn't it? I threw you off guard and got you down," I say, knowing full well I'm full of shit.

If he had been a burner, I'd be dead. The burners who broke into Nate's townhome were caught off guard because they didn't expect me to fight. I had a baseball bat, I poked someone's eyes out, I threw boiling rice water at a man's face, all because it was all I had. I was fighting from behind and out of desperation, but I need to learn how to control the fight.

He shakes his head, not buying what I'm trying to sell. And I know he won't accept it either, because he needs me to be strong and capable. "You've lost it, Casey. Everything but the muscle memory of your throwing stars is just that, a memory. You need a hell of a lot more work than I thought you did," Dad says matter-of-factly.

"Come on, I'm not that bad."

"But you're not good either, so let's start with the basics. We'll pretend you know nothing, although that won't be a stretch at this point."

"Dad!"

"I'm kidding, I'm kidding. All right, let's just—"

Gunshots ring out in the distance, followed by a bell clanging violently. Screams echo among the ringing. We freeze, looking to one another.

"Let's go!" my father yells, turning and running toward the front of the property.

"What is it!?" I call out, but there's no time to ask questions. My aunt and uncle take off, and I sprint after them, darting between trees as I block branches with my arms, many still working their way past my makeshift shield, whipping and cutting my face. I'm faster than all three of them and I quickly break through the woods, entering the clearing first.

The two young boys from earlier race past me, screaming in terror. Their father is up at the front fence line, firing rounds into an onslaught of biters. There are dozens of them, climbing up over the fence, using the biters already tangled up in the barbed wire to successfully cross it. Chris's shots are wild and uncontrolled, firing at whatever movement he sees. Bullets rip through limbs and torsos but do nothing to slow the creatures. He can't keep all of them in his sight, and one biter approaches from his side, bearing down on him with increased speed, its hunger propelling it forward at an alarming rate.

I sprint toward him, trying to get a clear shot so as not to shoot him by accident, but the biter's too close. Lunging forward, it sinks its teeth into the muscle between his shoulder and neck, tearing away flesh. Blood sprays wildly, like an overshaken soda can. He shrieks and rips himself free from the creature's bite, stumbling back a few steps. I raise my gun and fire a round into the biter's head, dropping it instantly.

Chris stares in horror as black slime pours out of the hole I put in the creature's head. He turns, looking for the origin of the shot, and finds me racing toward him. Chris doesn't move. Instead, he stands there frozen in a state of shock.

The horde of biters is rapidly approaching. Their moans and tooth gnashing fill the air like a choir of dying animals pleading to be put out of their misery. I fire rounds into several of them, dropping them like flies as bullets pierce their brains.

"Get back!" I yell as I provide cover for Chris.

But he just stands there. He looks down at his wound, the blood still flowing where the skin's been ripped away, and then he meets my gaze again. Tears pour from his eyes, which seem to be looking beyond me.

"Tell my family I love them," he says.

Before I can act or respond, he puts the barrel of the gun in his mouth and pulls the trigger. Red mist sprays up into the air, and the explosion turns to a ringing in my ears.

It feels like time stands still. I scream, or at least I think I do. I can't hear anything. I can't feel anything. Grass rises up to meet my face as my legs give out from beneath me. Unable to move, I watch the biters close in, one step at a time.

Chapter 15

"Pu . . . t . . . Pear . . ." The voice is muffled and comes in small chunks, only letters and sounds falling around me in broken fragments. The ringing in my ears hasn't dissipated, and all I see is grass and decrepit feet staggering in my direction. I feel like I've been dropped onto the beaches of Normandy, the enemy moving in to finish me off as screams and gunfire barely register.

"Push . . . it . . . Pearson." The letters pull together, forming words, but they sound miles off, far beyond the biters, who are now mere yards away. If I'm supposed to end with the world, now seems as good a day as any. I always told my dad that if it did happen, I wouldn't want to be around for it anyway.

"PUSH IT, PEARSON!" The words snap me back to reality, punctuated by a gunshot, a bullet whizzing over my body. I hear flesh being torn apart as thick, black liquid splatters all around me, creating a pit of tar. The corpse of a biter collapses onto me, pinning my body to the ground, its deadweight slumped across my torso. Its stench fills my nostrils, coating my insides. Maggots crawl through the decayed tissue, feeding off open sores and pustules. I turn my head and spew vomit, unable to hold the contents of my stomach in.

Suddenly, the biter rises, rearing back, its mouth wide open, ready to bite. But then it's pulled off and tossed to the side. My father stands over me, urgency written all over his face. He reaches down, grabs a fistful of my sweater, and yanks me onto my feet.

"We need to move!" Dad grips my arm, dragging me from the fence line, our feet pounding into the earth as we run for our lives.

As we sprint toward the house, Greg emerges from inside, charging at full speed with a sword in hand. When we're at a safe distance, I turn and watch my uncle Jimmy and aunt Julie standing side by side, firing at the biters. My uncle is calm, taking care to aim his rifle at the head or spinal column. Each shot is followed by a biter stopping dead in its tracks. My aunt does the same with her pistol, calmly unloading rounds into the wall of rotting flesh moving toward us like a dark stormfront.

Tessa emerges and runs into the action with a .22 caliber pistol in her hand. She isn't as practiced and begins firing wildly. Tessa's mom, Meredith; Molly; and Elaine stay at a distance, armed with machetes and knives, guarding the interior of the property as a last resort. One that will prove useless if it actually comes to that.

I feel the heft of the gun in my hand. It begs to be used, not for its own sake, but for everyone around me. I pull the other pistol from my ankle holster and fall back in line to fight. Looking down the sight of my gun, I aim at a biter and what's left of its face. Only a few patches of hair remain in random spots on its head. Its eyes are fogged over, and its teeth are cracked and rotten. Its face increases in size as it moves toward me, filling more of the area around the sight.

I pull the trigger and a shot rings out, popping my eardrum as the bullet rips through the biter's nose, caving it in and blowing out the back of its skull. I've seen bullet wounds in the hospital plenty of times, but this is different. The skin is weak and the bone is so brittle, allowing the velocity of the bullet to rip right through it like it was made of paper.

They just keep coming, and we keep firing, pausing only to reload. A group of biters charges toward me in a triangle formation, one at the front while the others push and jockey to get ahead, wanting to be first to rip into the standing meals all around them. I fire into the front biter's kneecap, slicing its leg in two, the lower stump planting into the ground and staying put while its body continues advancing. The biter ignores the pain, if they can even feel pain, and continues rushing forward with its right leg. As it swings the thigh of its left leg, it topples to the earth, somersaulting thanks to its momentum suddenly giving out. The biters behind it trip over the grounded body and a pileup forms, allowing me and my dad to run over and take out seven biters, execution-style. The heat from our pistol barrels sears the rotting flesh before we even pull the trigger. Buckets of black sludge and bone geyser up out of the mound, covering us from head to toe.

"There's too many!" my uncle shouts.

Aunt Julie empties her clip and searches her pockets for more ammo. A biter closes in on her, and she screams just as its head is severed from its body. Greg stands over the corpse with his sword raised, covering for his mom as she retreats. He plunges the blade into the face of every biter that nears him, like a deadly game of Whac-A-Mole. I raise my gun, aim, and pull the trigger, but it clicks instead of firing off a round. *Shit. It's empty.*

I glance around, searching for my dad. I want to ask him what to do. I need his guidance, but he's nowhere to be seen. My heart clenches up as I look across the field of bodies, wondering whether one of them might be his. There're too many of them, and we're out of ammo.

"Fall back!" I shout.

We race toward the porch, regrouping in front of it. Aunt Julie tells us she's going to get more ammo, and she sprints around the dummy house toward the main one. Elaine, Molly, and Meredith take off with her.

There are more than two dozen biters still advancing toward us. A couple of swords, knives, and ten throwing stars stand between them and us becoming their next meal.

"If we're gonna die, we're gonna die fighting," I say, looking down the line at my aunt, uncle, and cousin and then at the wall of approaching biters. Death creeps up to the front of the house like a shadow growing with the setting sun.

Suddenly, the front door of the dummy house bursts open, splinters of wood flying from the frame. My father charges down the front steps.

A massive gun the size of my leg with a drum magazine is pressed against his hip, the weight of it straining the muscles in his arms. He plants his feet in the grass and flicks the safety to full auto.

A small whir charges up, and in a flash, a hail of bullets rings out so quickly, it looks like the gun is on fire. All of us hit the deck, covering our ears.

The sound is relentless. Like the loudest chain saw you could ever imagine, buzzing out in anger as brass shells pour out of the side of the gun like a waterfall, fifty rounds per second, cascading into a growing mountain on the lawn. I look up to a firework show of carnage. Blacks and reds and greens and yellows, bursting into the air. Bodies shred to pieces. Legs, arms, guts, and heads ricochet around, dancing in the air and landing like confetti strewn to the wind.

I spot a truck driving on the road, heading into the line of fire. "Dad, stop shooting!" I yell.

He doesn't hear me, though, so I jump to my feet and grab his shoulder, startling him. The gunshots cease just as the truck pulls up. Two biters are still standing, continuing to make their way toward us. The brakes squeal as the vehicle slides to a stop.

Blake jumps out and leaps over the collapsed fence. With a machete in hand, he sprints toward the final two biters, ready to swing. My shoes kick up black sludge and wet soil as I race to beat him to the kill. He's closer to them than I am, but I have my throwing stars and something to prove. I'm not going to let him show up like some sort of action hero and get all the glory.

I pull two stars from my pouch, and when I'm sure I have the two biters dialed in at the right range, I let loose one and then the other. Just as Blake's about to bring his machete down into the skull of a biter, my first throwing star pierces its eye. The retina pops like a water balloon being tossed onto concrete, milliseconds before metal crunches through bone. Blake's arm hangs in the air, the machete held high but unmoving as he watches the two biters in front of him slink to the ground, lifeless and unmoving.

Chapter 16

"What the hell happened here?" Blake asks no one in particular while he surveys the carnage.

"I don't know," my dad answers, looking around as if the answer might come to him.

But there's no reason for any of this. It doesn't make any sense. Where did they come from, and why are there so many?

"Well . . . sucks that I missed out on all the action," Blake jests, holding his arms out at his sides like a gladiator entering an arena.

When no one responds, his face slowly morphs to mirror ours, a mix of fear and pain.

"Did I miss something?" He tilts his head.

"Chris . . . he . . ." I stop, unsure of how to share what I witnessed. "He shot himself . . . after he got bit trying to buy time for his sons to run away."

A few people who didn't see this happen gasp at the realization that someone among us didn't survive the attack. The illusion that we were safe so long as we all stayed within the fences and people patrolled on night watch is shattered.

"I . . . that's . . ." Blake trails off, realizing the error he made and unsure of what to say.

"Casey, is this what the city was like?" Tessa asks, her voice cracking as she tries to figure out whether this is something we should expect more often.

"I've never seen this many in a group," I say as I bend down and rip my throwing star from a biter's eye socket. The grass is soaked, wet with black sludge and viscera. My shoes stick to the ground as layers of gore build up on my soles. Reaching the second biter I hit, I pull the star from its forehead. Blake watches me as I wipe them against my jeans, cleaning them off.

"I don't understand why there were so many of them." Blake sounds frustrated. He continues to scan the bodies at his feet.

JJ approaches from behind, stepping over limbs and carcasses. "This probably explains that downed coach bus we saw earlier," he says.

My brows shove together. "What are you talking about?"

"There was a bus pulled off to the side of the road a couple miles up. It was a little dented but nothing that would have stopped it from driving. We decided to steer clear in case there were any biters lingering on board, but it looks like the whole bus turned and came this way after we passed by."

"That's a relief," I say, more pleased with this explanation than the alternative.

"Why would that be a relief?" Blake asks.

"Because that means this was a fluke, a one-off from a stray bus. If this was a new phenomenon, biters moving in huge herds like cattle, we'd be in trouble."

"She's right," my father chimes in.

"We should have stopped and checked it out, JJ." Blake shakes his head, disappointed in himself.

"No, you did the right thing. There were too many for just the two of you to take on," Dad says, patting Blake on the shoulder.

Elaine walks down the driveway with tears in her eyes and the folded white bedsheets my dad asked for. It's a uniform fit for a ghost.

Dad takes them from her and hangs his head for a moment before lifting it. "Blake, JJ, come help me with Chris," he says.

Chapter 17

It's quiet, minus the sounds of spoons scraping against bowls and the occasional slurp. Ten of us are seated around the dinner table, which is just two large folding tables pushed together. No one has really spoken since we sat down to eat. The only words exchanged were compliments and expressions of gratitude to Elaine for preparing homemade chicken noodle soup and fresh-baked bread. We're all still on edge, still trying to process what happened today. I don't even understand it myself. I look up from my bowl of soup and glance at each person. Blake sits across from me. His mouth is a hard line, and he drops his gaze. JJ is seated next to him, staring off at nothing, having barely touched his food.

The front door creaks open, and in walks my dad. He sighs heavily and rakes his hand through his graying hair. Aside from Chris's family, he's clearly taking it the worst of all, and I think that's because he blames himself. But he wasn't there. He didn't even see it happen. I did, and now I can't unsee it. There are some things that stick with you forever, and I think this will be one of them for me. Like my father, I can't help but blame myself, but unlike him, I could have actually done something to stop it. I should have been quicker, should have gotten to Chris before he pulled the trigger.

"How'd it go, Dale?" Uncle Jimmy asks, straightening up in his chair, positioned at the far end. Aunt Julie sits beside him, her hand resting on the table, clasped in his.

Dad crosses the living room, his footsteps slow and heavy. He stops in front of his chair at the head, positioned between Blake and me, and grips the back of it, like he needs it to stand upright.

"They're inconsolable, which is expected, and they just want to be left alone to grieve for now. But um . . . Helen wanted to thank you, Elaine, for their dinner."

Elaine nods and says, "Of course, anything they need."

"How'd the rest of the cleanup go?" he asks the table.

"We moved all the bodies to the far back-right corner of the property, and we'll start burning them tomorrow morning," Blake says.

"And Chris's body?" Elaine asks.

"He's wrapped in a sheet out in the toolshed," JJ answers, not looking at anyone in particular.

"Good, because the family would like to have some sort of a memorial for Chris, so we should try to put something together with what we have." Dad is met with nods as he pulls out his chair and takes a seat. He briefly glances at his untouched bowl of soup but doesn't reach for it. "This is the first time we've lost someone here, and I'd like to say it'll be the last time, but I don't think it will."

A heaviness falls over the room at my father's words.

"What happened today was a wake-up call for me," Dad continues. "We are not prepared to survive in a world like this, so things around here have to change, and they have to change fast."

"It was a fluke, though," JJ says, snapping out of his daze. "A coach bus full of zombies crashing a mile down the road isn't going to happen again."

Dad tightens his eyes. "You don't know that, JJ. None of us do. None of us have any idea what's out there or what else is coming our way. So the best we can do is prepare for the worst."

"And what did you have in mind?" Blake says, leaning back in his chair.

"First, we've got to beef up the fence, make it stronger, add more barbwire. I also have the supplies to add an electrical current to it." Dad looks to my uncle, an electrician of twenty years.

"I can take care of that," Uncle Jimmy says with a nod.

"Second, I know, before, only those that went out on runs had to train for combat. Not anymore. Everyone will learn how to fight."

"I can't fight," Molly says in a high-pitched voice. Her mouth gapes in disbelief, so it's clear she really does believe what she's saying, but that's only because she's never been put in a position where she was forced to fight in order to survive.

"That's what I told my dad when I was eleven," I say with a raised brow. "But I learned, and so will you."

Her mouth snaps closed, and she glances down at her lap. I can't tell whether I encouraged or discouraged her, but I was going for the former.

"There will be no exceptions," Dad says firmly. "Everyone will be trained. And we need to start doing more supply runs." His eyes dart to Blake and JJ. "What did you two find today?"

"Not much," JJ says, shaking his head.

"A case of canned goods that looked like they were left behind on purpose, since they were mostly fruit cocktail and Spam, but scavengers can't be choosers. We also found some gardening tools and winter coats and boots," Blake adds.

Elaine clears her throat. "How are we on food?"

"We'll be fine for a bit." Dad doesn't elaborate any further, which tells me there's not enough food for everyone.

"A bit? What's *a bit*? Like, a week? A month?" Greg pipes in.

"There are more mouths to feed than I had anticipated, so three months, maybe four," he says, then presses his lips firmly together.

"Which doesn't get us through winter," Blake deduces.

My dad exhales forcefully through his nose. "Correct, so we need to do more supply runs. If you're not finding much, then we'll go further out to search."

"What about medicine? Or medical supplies?" I ask, realizing no one's mentioned that. With what happened today, it's inevitable that we'll eventually need them.

"I've got first aid kits, and I'm well stocked up on vitamins and over-the-counter medications," Dad says.

"Those are all well and good, but if anyone suffers a serious injury or illness, we'll need something stronger than over-the-counter medication."

Dad meets my gaze. "Then why don't you go ahead and make a list of medical supplies, Casey, and we'll add them to the scavenge list. And that goes for everyone else too. Anything you need, make sure it gets added to the list," he says, scanning the somber faces seated around the table.

"I don't need to make a list, because I'm going with." I lift my chin, ready for Blake to challenge me.

"Not until you're trained," he says like a broken record. So predictable.

"I more than proved myself today, Blake."

He squints, moving his mouth side to side, sizing me up. "Your hand-to-hand and blade combat could use some finesse. You're quick on your feet, but when knocked down, you're slow to get up. You've got great instinct, but you move with hesitation, like you're unsure of yourself. Your marksmanship needs work too. Aim is slightly to the left, which tells me you haven't shot a firearm in a very long time. So the only thing you proved today was that you need training." Blake lifts his chin, challenging me.

"I took out a third of them today while you were out collecting cans of fruit cocktail, so I don't know what the hell you're talking about, and I don't think you do either."

"If you're so effective, Casey, then why is Chris dead?" he says, cocking his head.

My mouth parts and tears prickle behind my eyes. I can't believe he said that, and from the looks on everyone else's faces, they can't believe it either. How dare he put Chris's death on me.

"That's completely uncalled for, Blake," my dad warns.

"I think it's a fair question, Dale. Like you said, we've never had a death before." He gestures to me with judgmental eyes. "But within twenty-four hours of Casey's arrival, someone ends up dead. She's the only one that saw it, so she should explain what exactly went down. That way we can learn from it and make sure it doesn't happen again."

"Asshole," Tessa says from the other end of the table, just loud enough for everyone to hear. I'd hug her if Elaine and Meredith weren't between us.

"I think what Tessa's trying to say is that none of us were prepared for what occurred today," Dad interjects.

Tessa sits up a little straighter in her chair. "No, I said what I said."

"Anyway, I think your anger is misguided." Dad looks to Blake.

"I'm not angry. I just wanna know how it happened."

"Fine," I say, narrowing my eyes. "We heard gunshots and took off running. I got there first. Chris was too close to the fence line, and they were already breaching it. He underestimated how fast some of them can be, and then one of them lunged at him, and he got bit. I took out that biter so he could retreat. But Chris didn't. He just shot himself, and I don't understand why he did."

"Well, I think that's obvious." Blake gives me a confused look. "He didn't wanna turn into one of those things. He was probably thinking of his family, what he—or the monster he became—would do to them. That's why he blew his brains out."

I can't hide my surprise or shock at Blake's explanation. *That's what he thought. That's what they all think.* I can see Chris's face, the emptiness in his eyes. It was the look of a man who thought he had no future. His final parting words. I didn't understand them then. I just thought he was in shock. But no. He was grieving his own life. He thought there was no other way. So he pulled the trigger before he could talk himself out of it. But he'd had a chance . . . he just didn't know it. *And none of them do either.*

"What is it?" my dad asks, noticing my shocked expression.

I snap out of it, shaking my head. "Just because you get bit doesn't mean you'll turn into one of them." I make eye contact with each and every person at the table to ensure they'll hear me, and they'll remember that in case it ever happens to one of them. "That's why I call them biters and not zombies." I let out a deep sigh. "You all watch too many movies."

"How do you know they don't turn?" Blake's tone is cold.

Holding out my arm, I push my sleeve up, showing off a teeth-shaped scar engraved in my skin. "Because I got bit, and I'm still your Doomsday."

Dad grabs my hand, inspecting the scar. There's a sense of sadness mixed with relief in his eyes, like he's realizing how close he truly was to losing me. He squeezes my hand before he lets go of it.

"Maybe you have special blood, like in that zombie film with Will Smith, and you're the cure to all this," Greg says.

I roll my eyes and push my sleeve down. "Again, you all watch too many movies."

"You could be an anomaly," Blake suggests.

It's like he doesn't want this to be true, or maybe he just doesn't want me to be right.

"I'm not. I saw the same thing happen to my patients in the hospital. Some people were like me—you just feel sick, and it passes within a couple days. But there are other outcomes. You could turn into a biter or a Nome."

"A gnome, like for a garden?" Molly cuts in, tilting her head.

"No, it's spelled N-O-M-E. Stands for *no memories*. It's just what I call them, the ones that lose all their memories. They become shells of themselves, completely confused, almost like they're suffering from amnesia or late-stage dementia."

Blake swallows hard, his Adam's apple rocking up and down.

I scan the table. "Have none of you ever seen a Nome?"

No one audibly responds to my question, but several shake their heads. It's clear they've been in their own little bubble way out here in the country, and they have no idea what the world is really like now.

"Are the Nomes dangerous?" Greg asks.

"In the wrong hands, they could be."

JJ pulls his head back. "What do you mean?"

"I mean they could be easily used, trained to do things they would never do if they remembered who they were and what it means to be human. Their state of confusion also leaves them vulnerable to biters."

Blake scoffs. "We don't know if any of this is actually true."

"You can believe whatever you want, Blake, but that doesn't make what I'm telling you untrue. I saw it with my own eyes. You get bit, and you have three outcomes: Nome, biter, or nothing. Chris had a sixty-six percent chance of survival, so he didn't need to pull the trigger."

"A sixty-six percent chance?" His brows knit together. "Sounds more like thirty-three percent, because from what you described of the Nomes, that's just as bad as becoming a biter."

"Maybe. Maybe not. I've never been around a Nome for more than a few minutes, so I don't know what happens to them. I don't know if they get better or worse."

"I don't think we should tell Helen any of this," Elaine says. "At least for a little while. It'll only make it worse for them, knowing Chris had a chance to live."

"I agree. Let's keep this to ourselves for the time being." Dad pulls his lips in.

"Not for too long, though. They need to know they have a chance in case they do get bit," I add.

They both nod, and Elaine stands and starts collecting empty bowls, stacking them on top of one another before carrying them to the sink. Meredith and Aunt Julie join her in the kitchen.

I turn my attention to Blake. His head hangs slightly forward, shaking back and forth.

"What's your deal?" I ask.

He meets my gaze, and I notice his face has flushed. "Nothing."

"You've been awfully quiet. Normally you're Mr. In Charge, and now you're all clammed up. Stewing in your—"

"Maybe I'm just trying to figure things out!" His raised voice brings the room to a halt.

"Figure what out?"

"Like . . . how we had never lost a single person until you showed up here."

"Are you seriously suggesting it was my fault that fifty biters attacked this place?" My voice raises, matching his. "You're the one that drove past the bus and didn't check it out. If you had, you could have warned us, and maybe Chris would still be alive." I narrow my eyes at him.

"Oh, fuck off!" Blake stands quickly, making his chair topple over. He stomps through the kitchen and up the stairs, disappearing before I have a chance to engage with him further.

"Casey, that was uncalled for." Dad sighs.

I scoff. "What about what he said?"

"You both need to cool it. We've got enough problems here without you two at each other's throats."

I toss my napkin on the table and push my chair out. "Why don't you tell your friend that, Dad!"

He calls my name as I leave the kitchen in a huff, stomping up the stairs. I'm so sick of this. It was a mistake coming here.

I enter my bedroom and crawl into my own bed. Blake's tucked under his covers, facing the wall, pretending like he's already asleep. My anger is so unsettled from the implication he cast out in front of everyone. It was hard enough to witness what I saw today, and now I've got asshole Blake blaming me for Chris's death just because I showed up . . . at my own house. I know if I don't vent some of this anger, I won't be able to sleep. And if I can't sleep, neither will he.

"What the fuck is your problem?" I spit.

Blankets shuffle as he rolls over. "What?"

"You heard me. *What* is your problem?"

"I don't have one."

"Well, I do. You just told everyone downstairs it's my fault that Chris died. How could you say that?" I'm holding back tears as the image of Chris taking his own life plays out before me again. This is what Blake does. It's what he always does. He makes me the outsider just so he can fit in, and I'm tired of it.

"That's not what I meant. I didn't mean to put it on you. I—"

"But that's exactly what you did!"

"I . . ." Blake pauses, and for a moment, all I can hear is my heart pounding in my ears. "I've got my own stuff I'm dealing with, so it just came out wrong, that's all."

"The only thing you're dealing with is being an asshole." I roll onto my side and yank the covers up to my chin. "You haven't changed at all," I say under my breath, unsure whether he can hear me, but it doesn't matter.

"Casey . . ." A small whisper creeps over the blankets and into my ear. "Casey," he whispers again, but I ignore him.

"I know you're not asleep, and I know you can hear me. I'm sorry. That wasn't fair of me. Just like what you said back wasn't fair either. But I forgive you because I know you didn't mean it."

"That's where you're wrong, Blake. I did mean it."

"No, you didn't," he argues.

"Yes, I did."

The room falls quiet and stays that way for a while. My heart rate starts to slow as exhaustion pulls me under. Just before I drift off to slumberland, Blake whispers, "No, you didn't."

"Yes, I did," I say sluggishly.

He laughs and says, "Good night, Casey."

I softly smile as I drift off to sleep.

Chapter 18

The sound of the door creaking open rips me out of my dream state, putting me on high alert. I listen, trying to visualize the potential threat moving toward me. No noise would mean a burner, sneaking in like a mouse in search of cheese. Labored breathing and the dragging of feet would mean a biter.

A gurgled moan circulates the room and a rancid smell sears into my nostrils, making my eyes water. I bite my tongue to avoid gagging or giving away my presence.

I'll have one shot at this, one surprise attack I can execute, unarmed, to try to save my life.

I feel the air shift around me, so I know it's less than a few feet away. In an instant I roll to my other side, flinging the blankets off me as I ready my leg to swing as hard as I can and take the creature's legs out from under it. But I was wrong. The biter isn't feet away from me—it's on top of me. Already midlunge, the gaping maw of a monster closes in on my face, leaving me no time to react. Its teeth sink into my nose, and my mouth immediately fills with blood as I let out a painful, gurgled scream.

"Casey! Casey!" A hand gently shakes my shoulder, rousing me from my nightmare. "Shh. It's okay."

I turn to see Blake kneeling beside my bed, his eyes filled with concern.

"What's going on?" I ask, still confused as to what's real and what isn't.

"You had a nightmare. You were screaming and flailing in your sleep," he says, and I can't help but notice that his palm is pressed against my cheek, his fingers gently caressing my skin. I'd push him away, but it's comforting.

"Sorry," I say, unsure whether I should be embarrassed or relieved that it was a dream.

"It's okay. I'm here. You're safe with me."

I look into his eyes, and I can see the myriad of meanings behind his words, dancing around as he takes me in.

"Blake."

"Shh. It's okay. You don't have to worry."

He pushes a piece of loose hair behind my ear, and his fingers trace my cheek and chin. My heart races, and I hope it's not loud enough for him to hear it hammering in my chest.

"I'm not. I mean, not anymore," I whisper, barely able to admit how safe I feel with him.

Adrenaline courses through my veins, making me feel both nervous and relaxed, like I could fall asleep in his arms or spend the rest of the night awake, exploring every inch of him. Blake leans in a little closer, brushing a finger across my lips, which are already pushed out, searching for moisture. One more millimeter and there's no going back from—

My bedsheets are violently ripped off me, jarring me awake in a most unpleasant manner. A shiver runs through my sleeping body as it's exposed to the cold air, and I moan in protest, flailing my arms in search of the now missing warmth. I was still asleep, still dreaming. But why in the hell was I dreaming about Blake Morrison?

"Blake, give them back!" I haven't even opened my eyes to confirm he's the one who yanked them away, but I have a solid feeling.

"Rise and shine, Doomsday. We've got training to do." He lightly pats his hands all over me, playing my body like a bongo, strategically skipping over my ass. His fingers graze across a sliver of my exposed lower back, sending a tingle up my spine.

He stops his bongo solo, crosses the room, his boots clomping across the hardwood floor. The curtain hooks scrape against the rod as he throws the drapes open. I wince reflexively, expecting a flood of light to hit my eyelids, but it doesn't.

I crack one eye open and glance at the window to see that the aperture is still filled to the edges with black. The sun hasn't even risen yet. Standing in front of it, Blake pulls off his T-shirt, tossing it on his bed. My eyes skim over his well-defined shoulders and back, tracing the Navy SEAL symbol inked into his skin. I have to admit he's nice to look at . . . when he's not speaking, of course. Blake picks up a gray sweatshirt and starts to thread his arms through the sleeves.

"Like what you see?" he asks without even looking at me.

My cheeks warm in embarrassment, and I quickly snag my blankets from the floor and cocoon myself with them.

"You coming?" he asks, sounding as though he's standing right over me.

When I don't respond, he heads toward the door and calls out, "Suit yourself, Pearson," before leaving the room.

Sweet relief. My brain is quick to capitalize on the opportunity for more sleep and starts to power all my systems back down like slipping into a warm bath. Just as I drift off, a cold, wet shock rips through my body, like the paddles of a defibrillator levitating me off my bed.

"What the fuck!?" I yell, wiping water out of my eyes and gasping to catch my breath. Blake stands over me, holding a cup that I'm sure is now empty.

He grins. "Whoops, I must have tripped."

"You're dead." I spring out of bed, chasing after him. He turns and heads for the door, but before he's able to pivot and exit the room, I shove him. The plastic cup falls to the floor, bouncing a couple of times before rolling to the center of the room. I grip a handful of his shirt, and I can feel his heartbeat while I have him pressed up against the wall. My face is only a few inches away from his, and he stares back at me but doesn't say a word. It's like he's evaluating the situation. I notice his grin has tapered, replaced by a more serious look, and I don't think I like it.

In a flash, he grabs my forearm and pulls me into him, quickly spinning around and pinning me to the wall. My breath hitches as my back thuds against it, causing my lungs to lose some air. I raise my hand to shove him away, but he takes hold of my wrist, restraining it above my head.

He leans in and whispers, "Looks like our training has already begun." His hot breath brushes across my skin, stirring up a memory I've long pushed aside.

"You sure it's okay that I'm here?" I glanced over at seventeen-year-old Blake as he tossed a log on the firepit, causing the glowing embers to float in the cool night air. Even through the hoodie he was wearing, I could still see the curves of his muscular arms.

"Yeah, my dad won't be home till late," he said.

Blake had called me an hour ago, asking if I wanted to come over and have a picnic with him. I told him it was late, that picnics were a daytime thing. To which he said, "There are no rules when it comes to picnics." I couldn't help but laugh, and I raced to get ready, rushing right over to see him.

Six weeks ago, I could barely stand to look at Blake. But now, I couldn't look away. He was like a sweet craving I was trying to resist, my mouth watering at the very thought of him. Something about Blake changed the summer before senior year. He came back a totally different person—at least to me. His insults were replaced with compliments. His cruel pranks replaced with tenderness. And the wall I built around myself to keep people like him out was slowly crumbling.

Blake took a seat on the blanket he laid out for us, his shoulder pressing up against mine. Although I was cold, I felt warm next to him, and it had nothing to do with the fire dancing in front of us. My heart raced. I had noticed it beat a little faster when he was around. Blake unpacked a tote bag he carried out here, pulling out two Dr Peppers, a Tupperware container, and a sleeve of Ritz crackers.

"Would you like some charcuterie?" Blake grinned. He removed the lid, revealing a stack of Kraft singles and a mound of assorted lunch meats.

I raised a brow. "You call that charcuterie?"

"I do." He nodded, holding the container in front of me. "I even unwrapped the Kraft singles."

"Very fancy of you." I smiled and plucked out a piece of cheese and a slice of ham.

He did the same and said, "Bon appétit," before popping them in his mouth. I nibbled at mine and watched him as he snacked and stared happily at the fire. It felt like this was Blake's comfort zone, his safe space, a place that he could just be himself—out here at night, alone, beneath the stars with a flickering fire. I couldn't help but feel lucky that he wanted to share it with me.

My skin tingled like there was an electric current beneath it, begging to be touched. Before I could talk myself out of it, I reached for Blake, turning his head toward me and meeting his tender gaze. There were things I wanted more in life, but not in that moment. It was just him, the boy I'd once hated with a passion—but the hatred was gone and all that was left was passion. I pressed my lips against his, and I knew instantly that the wall I had built around myself was all but ruins now.

I shake away the memory, the one that happened so long ago, it feels like it didn't happen at all. Staring back at Blake with narrowed eyes, I lift my chin, challenging him.

"You call this training?" I say.

With my free hand I drive a closed fist into his kidney, causing him to stumble back a step, but just before he does, I hook my foot behind his ankle. He trips over it and falls backward, taking me to the floor with him. His back hits just before his neck and head snap in response, but he's unfazed. Blake stares at me with amusement as I lie on top of him.

He raises a brow. "Is that all you got?"

Before I can get a word out, he bucks me off by thrusting his hips up into me. I tumble to the side, attempting to scramble away, but he's on top of me in an instant, straddling my waist and pinning my arms above my head. I squirm and struggle to get free, but he's far too strong.

"Get off of me, Blake," I say with less conviction in my voice than I intended.

"Not unless you agree to train."

I plant my feet on the floor and lift up, trying to rear him off, but he doesn't budge and all it does is leave me out of breath.

"No," I say defiantly.

He leans down so he's inches away from my face again. "That's fine. I can sit here all day. It's rather comfortable, actually."

"What is your obsession with training me?" I groan. "Do you just need to be in control or something?"

"Not at all."

"Then what's your deal? Is this another attempt to torture me? Did you not get your fill of that in high school?"

He creases his brow. "You think I'm doing this to torture you?"

"Why else would you be doing this?" I squirm beneath him.

Blake leans in a little closer. "To keep you safe, Doomsday."

In an instant, he releases his hands and gets to his feet, leaving me lying on the floor, staring up at him.

"I don't need you to keep me safe, Blake," I call out as he heads for the door.

Pausing, he glances over his shoulder at me. "I know you don't, but I want to."

I give him a confused look, but he leaves the room without another word, which disappoints me because there are things I want to do to him too. Like fight him. Yell at him. Punish him for all the years he made my life miserable. I don't care how much time has passed; there are some things you never get over, and Blake's one of them.

Determined, I rise to my feet and quickly change into clothes I can kick his ass in. A pair of leggings, tennis shoes, and a long-sleeve athletic top should do the trick. As they say, if you can't beat 'em, join 'em and then beat their ass later . . . or something like that.

The house is dark and quiet as I make my way through the hall and down two flights of stairs. No one's awake yet, and I wouldn't be either if it weren't for stupid Blake. My dad said everyone has to train, so why am I the only one being woken up for this? Clearly, Blake's just enjoying his favorite pastime . . . torturing me. Well, two can play at that game.

Out on the porch, I find Blake standing at the bottom of the steps with a shit-eating grin on his face. He presses a button on his watch and says, "One minute and five seconds."

I walk slowly toward him, squinting. "What are you keeping time for?"

"Oh, just wanted to see how long it would take you to wise up and realize that I'm right about you needing training. Looks like it didn't take long at all." He smirks.

I cock my head. "I'm only here to kick your ass."

"Good, because that's exactly what I want you to do."

"What? Why?" I ask, caught off guard by his answer.

"Because that would mean I trained you right."

I roll my eyes and throw my hands on my hips. "Whatever. What are we doing and why are we doing it so early? The sun hasn't even risen yet." I gesture to the horizon, where a streak of red and yellow light stretches across it, the sun just now starting its ascent.

The air is still and quiet, peaceful, like the earth forgot the world ended or perhaps it's just moved on without us. I look back at Blake. He hasn't taken his eyes off me, and he appears almost amused by my frustration.

"What?" I grumble.

"Nothing. I'm just waiting on you to be done complaining so we can get to work."

"I'm not complaining." I let out an irritated sigh. "Let's get this over with."

"All right, we'll start with a run. You're in good shape, overall. I can see the remnants of strong muscles, and you've kept yourself lean," he says as his eyes glide up and down my body.

I stand a little taller and fiddle with my hands because I don't know what to do with them. Should I place them back on my hips? Or do I clasp them in front of or behind me?

"Stop examining me."

"I gotta know what I'm working with, and I'm guessing your leanness has more to do with a lack of sleep and calories than it has to do with exercise."

I narrow my eyes. "Some of us worked for a living, you meathead."

He ignores my quip and focuses on stretching his legs, pulling one foot up behind him and holding it there. I cross my arms over my chest and watch him do his little stretches.

Blake grins. "I'm going to run two miles, and you're going to follow and enjoy the view. In the beginning, you're gonna fall way behind, but if we do this twice a day, soon enough you'll be able to at least watch me cross the finish line."

I scoff and roll my eyes. He's an arrogant ass, but he's not entirely wrong. I haven't really exercised since I started med school. There was never time for it, but now I've got all the time in the world, and unfortunately, I get to spend it with Blake.

"I think you might be underestimating me," I say, taking a couple of slow steps toward him.

"I don't think so."

Before I can jab back, he's already darting away from me.

I take off in a dead sprint, trying to catch up, and it's not long before we're neck and neck. Maybe Mr. G.I. Joe isn't as fast as he thinks he is, and it's him who's in need of training.

He swivels his head to look at me as I run alongside him, a casual look on his face that shows no signs of exertion. It quickly changes to amusement. "Oof, big mistake, Pearson. I said two miles, not a hundred meters," Blake says with a chuckle.

I used all my energy just to catch up to him, and now I'm already sucking wind, and my side is starting to hurt. The taste of iron builds up in my saliva, and my legs start to feel heavy, slowing me from a sprint to a jog, and then to a regular walk as I attempt to catch my breath.

"At that pace, I'll see ya in about twenty-four to twenty-eight minutes, Doomsday," Blake calls over his shoulder as he continues on, his speed never changing.

I force myself to take off in a run again but it doesn't last long, and then I'm back to walking. Ugh. This is so embarrassing. Blake is completely out of sight now, having disappeared into the woods through the trails. I pick up my pace again, holding it for a few minutes, and then I'm right back to dragging ass.

When I finally emerge from the trails, I know quite a bit of time has passed, but I'm not sure how long. The sun is a ball of fire situated above the horizon now. The birds are awake, chirping and singing in nearby trees. I press my hand against the side of my abdomen, staving off the continuous pain from a running cramp. It's a reminder of how poor my cardiovascular endurance is. That and my inability to breathe.

Rounding the side of the house, I find Blake staring at his watch, monitoring the time with a full glass of water in one hand. I'm sucking air, practically hunched over as I reach him, and he's not even sweating. How annoying.

He thrusts the water toward me. "Nice work."

I assume he's being sarcastic, but I don't have the energy to think of a clever remark right now, so I take the glass and chug it down in between breaths. I keep a close eye on him over the rim, waiting for an insult to leave those smooth lips of his.

"Twenty-four minutes, just as I predicted," he says, tapping the face of his watch. *There it is.* "It's slow, but that's okay." Blake gives me a strong pat on the shoulder. "The point is to grow into tomorrow, not dwell on today."

"Thanks," is all I can manage. I'm still trying to fill my lungs with enough air to breathe. When I finish my water, I turn and sluggishly start up the porch steps.

"Where are you going?" he asks.

"Back to bed."

Just as I reach the top of the stairs, the front door opens and out walk Tessa, Aunt Julie, Elaine, Meredith, Greg, and Molly, all dressed in athletic attire. Tessa stretches her arms over her head and yawns so wide, her eyes tear. Most of the rest of them are rubbing at their faces, trying to wake themselves up, but Elaine is the only one who looks lively and ready to go.

"That was just a warm-up, Doomsday. Time for group training," Blake says in a cheerful voice, relishing in my anguish, not even bothering to hide it.

I groan and let my head fall back in frustration.

"You're up early." Elaine smiles at me.

"Not by choice." I shoot a glare at Blake. "My roommate wouldn't let me sleep."

He gives me a confused expression. "I could've sworn you were awake, Casey. My mistake."

I shake my head and reluctantly walk back down the steps. The rest of the group gathers around, waiting for Blake to tell us what we're doing.

"Why am I the only guy in this group training sesh?" Greg glances at each of us, wrinkling his forehead.

"You know why," Blake says.

Molly holds on to Greg's arm and stands on her tippy-toes to kiss his cheek. "I can't wait to wrestle with you, Pookie."

He tries to shrug her off, but her grip is far too strong, so he acquiesces to her affection instead.

"This isn't wrestling. This is combat training, and it's serious." Blake lifts his chin. "Now, everyone, line up."

I huff and do as he says, taking my place next to Tessa.

"The key to dealing with an enemy is to remain calm and remember to always fall back on your training. Right now, you have none."

"I do," Greg argues.

Blake eyes him momentarily. "Like I said, right now you have none. But when I'm done with you, you will." He paces back and forth in front of us, his arms behind his back, one hand gripping the wrist of the other arm.

Tessa leans over and whispers, "This is probably his sexual fantasy—to role-play as a drill instructor."

"Can you imagine him in bed?" I whisper back. *"The key to sex is penetration; right now you have none, but when I'm done with you, you will."*

Tessa bursts out laughing.

"What's so funny over there?" Blake looks to us as we try to contain our amusement.

"Nothing," I say, before pressing my lips firmly together to contain my laughter. Blake's gaze lingers on me with an intensity I haven't noticed before. Did he hear what I said? Does he think I picture him in bed? Because I don't. Well, aside from that weird dream I had this morning. But that's just a subconscious thing, probably from all the stress. My palms start to feel clammy, and my heart rate increases at the thought of him thinking that I do picture us in bed. But I can't. I couldn't even picture him picking me up, my legs wrapping tightly around his waist while he grabs my ass, my fingernails raking across his broad back . . . it's unfathomable. I shake the thought away.

"We're going to start with the basics of hand-to-hand combat," Blake says, continuing to pace. "This is a last resort if you're disarmed or caught off guard without a weapon, which will happen at some point. Would someone care to come up and demonstrate an exercise with me?" He scans the group, waiting for a volunteer.

"What's he gonna do? Beat the shit out of Elaine to teach the group?" I whisper to Tessa. She cups her mouth to hold back laughter.

"Casey!" Blake points at me. "How about you come on up?"

I give Tessa a strained look.

"Looks like he's going to beat the shit out of *you* to teach the rest of us," she says with a laugh.

Blake beckons by curling his finger.

I let out a sigh and make my way to the front. It's quiet, save for the grass crunching beneath my feet as the group waits on bated breath for the spectacle that's about to take place. I take my place a few feet from Blake and wait for his instructions.

"Thank you for volunteering, Casey." He smirks.

"I didn't volunteer. You . . ."

"Let's give Casey a round of applause, everyone!" Blake turns to the group and starts clapping. In response, clapping begins but in off beats with muted slaps.

"Go, Casey," Elaine cheers. She's the only one displaying any sort of enthusiasm, but I think it's because she's just happy to be doing something different from gardening and cooking.

"All right, so for this first exercise, I want Casey here to try and take me to the ground. She doesn't have to pin me, she doesn't have to get me to tap out, she just needs to make my feet leave—"

I drop my shoulder into Blake's side while he's still explaining the instructions and drive through the tackle, taking him to the ground.

"Ufff," he moans, hitting the hard dirt.

There's a mix of muted laughter and gasps as I lie on top of him, grinning.

"You didn't wait for my go-ahead," he says.

I climb off Blake's muscular torso and get to my feet. "Is that what usually happens in combat? Does the enemy call out *I'm ready*?" I chuckle.

Blake stands and brushes off the grass and dirt clinging to his pants, staring at me tight-lipped. "What I meant to say was well done, Pearson. The element of surprise is a powerful tool indeed."

He comes across like a mix between a game show host and a karate instructor, clearly trying to hide his anger and embarrassment. I already know my next bout with him will not be so easy.

"Since you seem to have successfully completed challenge number one, why don't we move on to the next?" Blake smirks.

"Why don't we." I smile back.

"This time, I want you to get me to tap out, in any way you can."

"Any way I can?" I raise a brow, inviting him to reconsider his choice of words.

"Any way you can."

Blake takes a step back, squaring up with me. I get into position, a slight crouch with my arms out in front. He nods and furls his fingers, inviting me to attack. This time he's more than ready for me. I can see the determination in his eyes, and I know that, head-on, I stand no chance. His size and strength will make short work of me. The fight will be over before it begins.

I fake low and then come up quickly like I'm going to throw a punch with the plan to dive low again as soon as he rises to counter the hit, but he doesn't move. He doesn't even flinch. It's like he's in my head. I back off and try again, erratically switching between fake jabs, lunges, and side steps, but none of it works. Blake remains stoic, watching my core, realizing that I can't move if the rest of my body doesn't move with me. He and my dad must have been training together. I'm going to have to let him counter my first attack, but what position sets me up best for my own retaliation?

Think, Casey. I try to recall everything Dad taught me, but I'm drawing a blank, and it's because Blake is staring at me. Did he just wink? I think he winked at me. Oh yeah, he's inside my head. But he's not gonna stay there.

I fake a jab and shoot low, knowing that Blake will likely jump back and press me down into the ground face-first, neutralizing my efforts and leaving me exposed. Just as I suspect, when I dive low, his legs pop back and his weight shifts forward, his hands shooting at me, ready to drive me into the ground—but at the last second, I sidestep, letting his own momentum take him down. In an instant, I'm on top of him, wrapping my arm around his throat and using my opposite hand to pull back as hard as I can. He's in a choke hold, so he should be tapping out in less than thirty seconds. Maybe I should count down for him . . .

Suddenly, I'm floating in the air, or at least it feels that way. Blake starts to stand, and I wrap my legs around his waist so I won't fall off. He's on his feet again with ease, as if I'm not even on his back choking him out.

"Come on, Casey. Kill him," Tessa yells.

"Tessa! This is training," her mother chides her.

Blake grabs my arm with one hand and flails his other backward, getting a hold of my other arm. In one quick motion he bucks forward and yanks, sending me flying and tumbling to the ground.

Standing over me, he smiles down, still catching his breath from my choke hold.

"Not bad, Doomsday." Blake extends a hand to me.

I swat it away and pull myself up.

"Again," I say, turning to face him while sucking wind. My back aches from hitting the ground, but I ignore the pain. I'll deal with that later, after I beat Blake.

"You sure you wanna do that?" He tilts his head, giving me an amused look.

"Oh yeah. Let's go, boat boy."

He furrows his brow. "Boat boy?"

"You know, because of the navy and, like, boats and stuff . . . shut up," I say. I'm flustered and already sore. I'm beyond tired too, because he woke me up before the crack of dawn.

"You got this, Casey," Tessa yells. "Not the trash talk, though, but we'll work on that later."

"Okay, come and get it." Blake grins. He crouches a little, beckoning me with both hands. *Oh, I'll get it, Blake. I'll get it so hard.* Tessa's right—I should stop with the trash talk, both internal and external. *Just focus on taking him down.*

I steal a couple of deep breaths and charge forward. This time I don't bother to try to fake him out. I run straight at him, fully erect and upright. He's so confused that he just absorbs my body crashing into him. Rather than a full-on attack, it looks like the most aggressive hug anyone's ever given.

Blake glances down at me in surprise as I'm wrapped in his arms. "What was that?"

"This," I say, raising my leg and kneeing him right in the dick.

He sinks to his knees, moaning. His hands go straight to his crotch, holding it as he sucks in air. Several people gasp. Tessa claps and cheers.

"I'll get some ice," Elaine calls out as she scurries to the house.

"Don't waste the ice on Blake's nuts!" Tessa yells, but Elaine either doesn't hear her or ignores the request.

"I think you're the one that needs the training," I say with a smirk.

My expression quickly fades as I'm pulled to the ground by Blake's massive hands. He lies across me, putting the bulk of his weight on my chest, sapping me of any air. I try to free my arms from under him, but it's no use. All my strength and energy are gone.

"Get . . . off . . . me," I wheeze with the little oxygen I have left.

"Say please," he whispers. His hot breath enters my ear, making the tiny hairs rise to meet it.

"Plee . . ." I gasp for air.

"Sorry. What was that?"

"Pleeeease."

In a flash, all the air in the world seems to rush into my lungs at once as Blake crawls off me. He grabs my hand, and with one fell swoop, I'm shot back up onto my feet. Doubling over, I pant and cough.

Blake pats me on the back and says, "You'll be all right."

He adds, "Everyone, another round of applause for Casey!" His words evoke the same tepid and bewildered response from the group.

I stand up straight, still breathless, and smack my hand onto his shoulder.

Blake flinches, turning to me with a fixed gaze.

"I almost had you," I say.

"*Almost* is the key word."

"One day, your ass will be mine, Blake."

He simpers. "I can't wait." Before I can respond, he leans into me and whispers, "But until then, you're still not ready."

Chapter 19

The flames from the burn pit flicker and shake as they consume what's left of Chris. His funeral, if you could call it that, was hours ago, and like all funerals, it wasn't really for him. Funerals are for the living because the dead don't give a damn. His family wanted a burial, but others were worried about contamination, fearing the infection could spread to the drinking water or crops.

I've been sitting out here alone for a while now in this old, rickety lawn chair because I can't seem to pull myself away from the fire. A reminder of a simpler time. I slap my hand against my forearm, squashing a mosquito midbite. I flick the crushed bug into the grass, leaving behind a droplet of smeared blood. It's quiet tonight, like nature is giving Chris a moment of silence. But the silence is soon interrupted by boots squelching over damp grass, growing louder as they approach.

Dad appears at my side, pulling up a lawn chair and plopping it down next to me. He exhales sharply as he takes a seat, staring at the flames, which create dancing shadows across his tired face.

"How're you doing, Casey?"

"Fine," I say.

Dad tilts his head and looks to me. "How are you really doing?"

I exhale and turn to meet his gaze. "I'm surviving." There's nothing in my voice. It's as though a robot is speaking, not a human with thoughts and feelings.

Dad reaches over, resting his hand on mine as it grips the arm of my chair. "I'm sorry. I know this must have brought up some bad memories for you."

He's right about that. I think that's why I'm death-gripping the arms of this chair and why I haven't moved in hours. It feels like the past is pulling me back, forcing me to relive a painful memory I thought I had stored in a box and locked away. I glance back at the fire and blink and it's 2006 again.

A teddy bear I got when I was six was tucked under my arm, just like I was tucked under the covers, lying in bed. My eyes were shut tight as I tried to fall into a dream—but sleep wouldn't come. The sound of shattering glass made me sit up in bed. A door creaked open from somewhere in the house. Then there were footsteps—heavy ones, and more than one pair.

My mom called out, "Hello?" I slid out of bed and tiptoed to my partially open bedroom door. "Dale?" my mom said, clearly hoping that my dad had returned home early from an emergency plumbing-service call and the noise was just him being clumsy in the dark.

Dressed in a set of pink pajamas, I quietly walked down the hall, pausing at the staircase to listen. Someone else was in the house, someone other than my mother and me. I took the steps slow, careful to avoid the ones I knew creaked and moaned. Mom screamed, and I froze in place. My heart pounded so hard I thought I could hear it. I thought whoever was in the house could hear it. There was a loud noise in the kitchen, followed by boots squeaking against the tile floor. I crept slowly and stopped in front of the swinging door that led to the kitchen.

"We're not going to hurt you," said a male voice.

"Casey, get out of the house. Run!" Mom screamed.

A mix of grunts and groans and banging followed. I was confused. I wanted to see what was happening, but Mom told me to run, and I was supposed to listen to Mom.

"Casey, run!" she yelled again, but this time it came out strained.

"Dude, let's go," another voice said, less deep than the first one.

I didn't listen to Mom. Instead, I pushed open the door, and as I did, I watched a man dressed in black plunge a kitchen knife into my mother over and over and over again. My eyes swam with tears and my hands flew to my mouth, muffling a scream. The man in black shoved her to the floor. She coughed and red liquid sprayed from her mouth.

The other man yelled in horror, "What the fuck!" before taking off out the splintered back door. The man with the knife followed, his boots crunching over broken glass.

"Mom," I said, my voice cracking with sadness.

"Casey," Mom gasped.

I rushed to her side and cried, asking her what I should do. Her light-blue top was now painted red. She reached up, stretching out her hand and grabbing a dish towel hanging from the oven door above her.

"Call . . . the . . . police," she said just above a whisper as she pressed the cloth against her stained red shirt.

I ran to the cordless phone on the countertop and dialed 9-1-1, but it made no sound. Putting it back on the receiver, I picked it up again and redialed. It was silent.

"The phone doesn't work!" I said in a panic.

Mom shut her eyes tight and pressed her lips together, forming a strained, tight smile or maybe a vacuum seal to hold in the despair.

"Where's yours and Dad's cell phone?" I asked, desperately thinking of other options.

She slowly shook her head. "Your dad . . . took it with him."

I cried and asked what I should do. When she didn't answer, I begged her to tell me, yelling, "Please, please, please," over and over.

Finally, she spoke, but it felt like it was for my sake rather than her own. "Casey . . . go to the neighbor's house. It's a little over a mile down the road, the way we take to school. Run as fast as you can and tell them to call the police." Mom's words came out slow, like she was pushing them out, using all her energy to utter them.

"Can't you come with me?"

She coughed up more blood. It splattered in small flecks across her face. "No, but I'll be right here . . . waiting for you."

The tears came so fast, it felt like I was underwater. "You promise?"

"Yes, Case . . . Now go."

I nodded and wiped the tears away. I had to be brave for her. She called, "I love you," as I raced out the front door.

"I love you too, Mom," I said, and then I took off down the long driveway, heading toward the neighbor's house. I ran as fast as I could. My throat burned as I sucked in cold air. My lungs screamed but I screamed right back. I knew I couldn't stop, no matter how much I couldn't breathe, no matter how tired I was, no matter how badly my muscles ached. I had to keep moving. There were no cars on the road that night. It was just ten-year-old me and a dark country back road.

Finally, the neighbor's house came into view. No lights were on, and I worried no one would be home or maybe they were fast asleep and wouldn't bother answering. I pounded on the front door until my hands hurt. A porch light flicked on.

"Who is it?" an older woman yelled from inside the house, fear in her voice.

"Casey Pearson," I cried.

A lock clicked and the door pulled open. On the other side stood Elaine. I didn't know her name then, but I learned it that night. "Oh my God, sweetheart, come in. What's wrong?" she asked, ushering me inside.

By the time an ambulance arrived, it was too late. Mom was gone, and everything changed after that, including my father.

"Casey," my dad says, snapping me back to the present. I blink once, twice, and the past fades away, replaced by the flickering flames in the burn pit.

"I'm fine, Dad, really," I say, but the tears in my eyes tell him the opposite.

"It wasn't your fault, sweetheart."

He's told me that before—many times, actually. But it doesn't matter, because I don't believe it. The guilt from that night lives inside me like a tumor too risky to operate on, so you just have to learn to carry on with it. I could have run faster. I could have helped fight back.

Tears fall from my dad's eyes, and he doesn't have to say what's on his mind for me to know what he's thinking. "It wasn't your fault either."

He sits quietly for a moment, chewing on my words. I'm sure he'll spit them right back out, because he can't not blame himself, and the feeling is mutual. I guess I really am my father's daughter.

"I think back to that night nearly every day, all the things I wish I would have done differently. I should have left the cell phone behind, but your mother insisted I take it, just to be safe. Those were her words. I should have sent one of my employees to take care of that emergency call, but I figured I was up anyway." He shakes his head as he speaks.

"The only people to blame are the men that broke into our house. They killed Mom, not you," I say, lifting my chin, wishing I could believe my own words. *They are* responsible for killing her, but I'm the one who didn't save her.

"It was my job to keep you and your mother safe, and I failed at that." He pulls his lips in and inhales through his nose.

"You have kept me safe, and look at how many people you're keeping safe right now." I wave my arm back toward the main house and cabins. "You've more than done your job, Dad." I flip my hand over and squeeze his.

He nods and tears escape the corners of his eyes, streaking his face. They fall slowly, having to trudge through an untraveled path. I haven't seen my father cry since the night my mother was murdered. After that, he held it all in to be strong for me. The light from the fire makes his tears glint. Seeing his grief on full display swells the guilt inside me. But this shame isn't because of what I failed to do for my mom; it's because of what I *did* do to my dad.

"I lied to you," I say, meeting his gaze.

"About what?"

"My reason for staying away. I didn't not come back because I was too busy or didn't have the time. It was because I resented you. I hated my childhood. I hated all the work you made me do. I hated that I was teased for the life you made us live. I hated you because of all of this." I fan my hands out in front of me. "I just hated you so much."

"I know, Casey, and I'm sorry." He pats my hand. "When your mom died, my world ended. So, for me, it's felt like I've been surviving the end of times for twenty-plus years." His voice cracks.

"I wish I would have been there for all of them, Dad, and I'm so sorry I wasn't."

"Don't be. I took enough from you, and I wish I could give it all back, especially your childhood." He shakes his head.

"Technically, I do kind of have my childhood back."

A confused expression settles on his face.

"You know, because I'm back at home, working on all your super-fun projects, and even Blake is here, making my life a living hell again. It feels like I never left," I say with a shrug and a smile.

Dad chuckles.

From behind us, someone clears their throat. Dad and I wipe at our tears and straighten in our chairs. Like father, like daughter.

"Hey, Dale," Blake says, standing just off to the side dressed in a gray hoodie and a pair of jeans.

"Speak of the devil," I say, looking him up and down. I tighten my eyes, wondering what he's up to now. Whatever it is, I'm sure it'll somehow involve messing with me. He just can't help himself.

"Hello to you too, Casey." He softly smiles, further raising my suspicions.

"What's up, Blake?" Dad asks.

"I hate to bring this up, given the timing and all." Blake looks over to the still-burning funeral pyre. "But according to the schedule, Chris was supposed to be on night watch." None of us wants to admit it, but night watch is too important to go unassigned, even though it means erasing Chris from our lives sooner than might be okay. "I just wanted to let you know that I can take it."

"You're going on a run tomorrow, though."

I perk up, leaning forward in my chair. "I'll do it."

"You're not ready to go on a run," Blake says, cocking his head.

"No, I'll do night watch."

"You're not read—" he starts, but I cut him off.

"Shut up, Blake. It's literally walking around the property that I'm more familiar with than you. How can I not be ready for that?"

"There's more to it than just walking around," he says, rocking back on his heels. I swear he just likes to challenge me. If I said the sky was blue, Blake would argue that it depends on the day—which is true, but still.

"I literally disarmed JJ while he was on night patrol, so I'm sure I'll be fine."

Blake looks to my dad, who reacts by raising his brows and shrugging with one shoulder. His way of saying, *She has a point.*

"Fine," he says. "I'll show you what you need to do."

I cross my arms over my chest. "I don't need you to show me how to walk my own property."

"Dale."

I grumble. I still don't understand how they can possibly be friends. Blake has nothing in common with anyone, except maybe Satan.

"Casey, just let him show you."

I stand corrected. What they have in common is they're always in agreement regarding what's best for me. Which is incredibly annoying.

"I don't need a chaperone."

"Then no night watch for you," Dad says, taking his side once again. He looks to Blake. "Is there anyone else that wants to volunteer?"

Blake taps a finger on his chin like he's mulling it over. "Everyone else is asleep. It was a rough day, what with clearing the bodies, repairing the fence, and obviously, the funeral. But I'm sure Greg would if we asked. He's always trying to prove himself, so I'll go see if he's up for it," he says, turning.

"Fine." I stand from my chair dramatically and start marching toward the house. "Let's go, Blake."

I pause and glance back, noticing he's not following me. Instead, he stands there with a tickled look on his face.

"Blake, are you coming, or do you need to ask my dad for permission?"

My father belly laughs.

"Oh, I'm coming." He jogs to catch up with me.

"You two have fun."

"We won't," I yell back, shooting a glare at Blake.

Chapter 20

I haven't gotten used to the added weight of the armaments on my body. A gun on one hip, another on my ankle, a pouch of throwing stars around my waist, and a combat knife holstered on my thigh. It still causes me to waddle a bit, as I have to swing my arms out wider to avoid hitting the pistol. I probably look like a rookie cop on her beat.

Blake follows every step I take as he watches over me like a driving instructor with a teen behind the wheel. "Make sure you are looking out past the fence for approaching danger, not just in front of you."

"Kind of would defeat the purpose of going out on night watch if I didn't *watch*," I say, not looking back at him.

"What was that?"

"I said, *Good idea, sir*." I flash a jeering smile back at him.

It's been like this the entire time: Blake giving me instructions that even a grade-schooler could have figured out on their own, and me smiling and politely accepting his wisdom, hoping that the faster he thinks he has taught me everything, the faster he'll leave. But he continues along with me, never relenting in his instruction.

"Okay, now turn right up here at the fence line."

I stop dead in my tracks so abruptly that he runs into me. "Do you see something!?" he asks in an excited whisper.

"Are you kidding me?" I turn around to face him, hands on my hips as I raise my brows.

"Kidding about what?"

"Did you just tell me to 'turn right' when we came to the corner of the fence? Like, as in, when the fence on my left met up with the fence in front of me to form a corner. You thought I needed to be told to turn right, the only way I can go, otherwise I'd run right into a barbed wire fence?"

Blake opens his mouth and then closes it quickly, looking behind me as he points at the fence. "I was just making sure. You can't be too careful, and there's nothing wrong with double-checking—"

"That I know not to run into things?"

"It's just important to walk the actual property line and keep an eye out for weak spots. Some people think glancing up and down the fence line is good enough. It's not. When it comes to keeping people safe, we don't cut corners."

I can guess who he is referring to—Greg—but I can also guess that after yesterday's attack, no one is going to be slacking on security anymore.

"Also, you're gonna want to walk the perimeter every ninety minutes, but you don't have to walk the fence line beyond the woods. Just keep to the outside of them and pause to listen for any sound or movement. You can keep watch up in the sniper tower as well, but there's no substitute for boots on the ground. I personally like to patrol every hour, but it's up to you." He walks out in front of me, shining his flashlight beyond the fence, making a show to be extra vigilant in his search for any dangers.

"Looks clear out here, so let me show you the sniper tower."

"I don't need you to *show* me the sniper tower. My dad and I added that to the original house a long time ago." I take off without waiting for him to respond. He might be the expert when it comes to recon and combat, but he doesn't need to be a tour guide to my own childhood.

His footsteps are quick behind me. The beam of his flashlight swings wildly across the grass, spanning back and forth with each step. "You don't have to be so difficult," he says when he catches up to me. "I'm just trying to help you."

"I don't need your help, and stop trying to act like you know this place better than anyone else, like we're all little helpless lambs without Blake watching over his flock."

"Fine, Pearson, lead the way."

"That's it? No arguing, no fighting? Just *fine*?" I shine the flashlight in his face to see whether he's messing with me.

"Jesus," he says, shielding his eyes with his hand. "Watch where you're pointing that thing."

"I wanted to see if you had that shit-eating grin on your face."

"Nope, no grin at all. I'm giving you what you want and following your lead."

"I don't like this."

He blurts out a laugh that echoes across the open field. "I can't win. If I fight with you, I'm an asshole. If I agree with you, you don't like it."

"A Blake Morrison that isn't putting up a fight or making things difficult is a sneaky Blake Morrison, waiting to do something far more sinister later."

"Wow, that's really what you think of me?"

I put my hand on his shoulder, looking at him like a parent would a child. "It's not what I think. It's just who you are."

He frowns but quickly looks away, bucking my hand off him and continuing toward the sniper tower. We walk in silence for a bit.

"I liked what you said to your dad tonight," Blake says, peering over at me.

My face hardens as I shoot him an accusatory look. "What!? You were eavesdropping on us?"

"No—not on purpose. I was already walking up, and I could hear voices, but I didn't think anything of it. Then as I got closer, I could hear what you two were saying, and it didn't seem appropriate to interrupt, given how personal it was."

"But it was appropriate to just listen to the whole thing?" I trudge forward, trying to create more distance between us, but he keeps up and just keeps talking.

"No, it wasn't like that. It was one of those things where I was waiting for a minute or two to see if you guys were almost done, but then you kept talking, and I just froze . . ."

I eye him suspiciously, thinking back to the conversation, racking my brain for every little nugget that I wouldn't have said to Blake—not by choice, anyway. "You're a Hearing Tom. Like a Peeping Tom, but much worse."

"That's not worse."

"It is to me," I say, raising my chin.

"I only brought it up because . . . I . . . I didn't know about your mom—"

"Don't," I say, cutting him off before he can even go down a path that I really don't want to, especially with him. The last thing I want from Blake is sympathy. He never cared to learn anything about me all those years he spent ridiculing me. And even the brief period when he was kind, he ended up weaponizing the vulnerability I did show him against me.

We make the rest of our walk to the sniper tower in silence, the only sound coming from the crunching of our boots on the slightly frosted grass. The old house, the one we used to live in as a family, now feels like a corpse left out in the desert. All the insides have been picked away, leaving behind the shell of something that used to be warm and safe. The path up to the top contains four flights of stairs, which become tighter as the tower extends out of the house into its own structure, a narrow column with a square room at the top. Windows cover all four walls, each equipped with a quick push release to create a ready aperture when needed for sniping. Yet another addition to the property that I originally laughed at but now I'm thankful is here.

"I know you don't want me to bring it up, but I just . . . I get it. I lost my mom too, right before I moved to Wisconsin. It's actually why we moved. My dad and I couldn't stand to be in the same house anymore, not without her in it. We wanted a fresh, new start in a new place that didn't have a permanent cloud of death hanging over it."

Blake looks out one of the tower windows, as though he can still see that cloud in the distance, like no matter how far away they ran, it was always close by.

"I'm sorry to hear that," I say, letting out a strained sigh.

I don't know how to react or why he's telling me this. On some level, I think he's being genuine. But on another, it feels like a trap, another attempt at luring me back in so he can hurt me again.

"How'd she die?" The words tumble out of my mouth, and I'm not sure why I even ask. Maybe it's because it feels like he wants to talk to me about it, or at least talk to someone about it. Blake always seemed like he carried extra weight with him. I always thought it was his asshole attitude weighing him down, but perhaps I was wrong.

"Cancer," he says, turning to me. The slight sheen of tears in his eyes glistens from the moonlight.

"Sorry."

He pulls his lips in and says, "Thanks."

"Was it sudden?"

"Yes and no." He shrugs. "Sorry, that doesn't make any sense."

I place my hand on his arm. Blake looks down at the touch before meeting my gaze. "No, it does make sense. Loss happens in an instant, but it lasts a lifetime."

He nods in agreement. "A piece of my heart aches. It always does. Sometimes the pain is sharp and debilitating. Other times, it's a dull twinge I've learned to live with." We stand in silence for a couple of minutes, exchanging glances with the night sky and one another.

"Anyway." He smiles, trying to shake off the weight of the moment. "Back to night-watch training. As you can see, this"—he holds out his arms and rotates in a circle—"is the sniper tower."

"I would have never guessed."

He ignores my sarcasm and continues with his lesson. "Your dad and I made some changes." Blake walks to a small table and picks up a massive black spotlight. "This is your best friend up here. It has a million lumens of brightness, equivalent to a hundred thousand candles." He moseys over to one of the corners and places the handle in a metal bracket that extends and swivels. "We installed these in each corner in case you need to have your hands free to shoot. Originally, we wanted to get the spotlights like prisons have up in the towers and mount them on the outside, but they're crazy expensive and hard to get."

"I bet." I chuckle, amused at his excitement.

He lets on a grin. "Speaking of shooting." Blake gestures to the three wooden chests sitting beneath the base of the windows. "We custom-made these to house the guns."

"Smart." I smile as he continues speaking.

"It's mostly long rifles with scopes. They're the most practical for up here. But there are also a few handguns and a shotgun in case you're ever overrun and need to blast your way out of here." He's like a kid showing off a collection of his favorite toys. His enthusiasm is infectious, and I can see now why he and my dad get along so well.

"So, that's pretty much it. Patrol every ninety minutes and then you chill up here the rest of the time. Some nights, if somebody can't sleep, they'll come hang with whoever's on night watch, but yeah, I think you get the gist." He shrugs.

"I do."

"You good on your own for the rest of the night?"

"I think I can manage."

"All right. Well, you know where I am if any emergencies pop up," Blake says, walking to the top of the stairs, ready to descend into the main house. He stops before his foot drops onto the top step and gives me a final glance. "Good night, Casey."

"It will be now that you're leaving," I say, not letting him think he's won me over just because we share a similar painful past.

"Right," he says with a look of disappointment on his face as he turns and disappears out of sight. "Just try not to get us all killed," he calls up the stairs.

I smile at his parting remark.

Chapter 21

It's my third time walking the property, and I'm doing exactly as Blake said, sticking close to the fence line. I don't want to give him another excuse to say I'm not ready to go on a run. I point the flashlight ahead of me, illuminating the path so I don't trip over a fallen branch or uneven ground. It's been quiet, save for some coyotes howling in the distance. The stars are hidden behind the clouds and the moon is barely visible, with just a sliver of it peeking out.

At the corner of the fence line, I think back to Blake's super-important training. "Oh no. What do I do?" I mock, waving my hands in the air. "Thankfully, Blake equipped me with all the right knowledge." I roll my eyes and turn right, avoiding running into the fence.

What was his deal tonight? I mean, the eavesdropping and trying to be authoritative are typical Blake traits. But what was up with him telling me about his mom? He's never confided in me about anything, even when we did get close. So why now? Did he feel he had to after overhearing my conversation with Dad? Or was it so I'd put my sword down? Figuratively and kind of literally. Or did he tell me so it'd absolve him from how much of an asshole he was to me? Because it doesn't. He treated me horribly from ages thirteen to eighteen, and his mom dying isn't an excuse. Trauma makes you either a hero or a villain. He chose the latter, deciding to inflict his pain on others because he didn't want to be the only one who felt it. My mom died too, but I wasn't anyone's monster as a result. So he doesn't get a pass for that.

Something rustles in the long grass, startling me, and I quickly shine my flashlight toward it. A possum emerges, sniffing around before bolting back where it came from. I sigh with relief and keep walking, my mind returning to Blake, and I'm not sure why. Maybe because tonight reminded me of when he and I were friends, or a little more than friends. It didn't last long, though. He earned my trust, made me fall for him, and then turned back into the monster he always was.

A branch snaps to the left, somewhere within the thick forest. I scan the tree line, searching for the origin of the noise.

"Hello?" I call out.

Nothing stirs. I linger for a moment or two, just to be sure, and then I carry on. Only a few more hours until I'm relieved of my duties, and I can finally go to sleep in my warm bed. I yawn so big that my eyes tear up. A stick cracks under the weight of something stepping on it. I scramble to point the flashlight in the direction of where the sound came, but it slips from my hands, swirling a beam of light as it hits the dewy grass.

"Shit," I say, bending down to pick it up.

I take a hit from the side, and I'm sent crashing to the ground with a thud. I open my mouth to scream, but a hand covers my lips, stifling it. Struggling against the person on top of me, I buck and elbow and kick, and then I roll onto my back so I can see what I'm dealing with. *Of course.*

"What the fuck are you doing?" The words come out muffled.

Blake grins and removes his hand. "Testing your reflexes. If I was a zombie, I'd have bitten you already."

"Bullshit. Biters don't hide and do sneak attacks. And what are you doing out here anyway?" I cock my head.

"I couldn't sleep with you on night watch. It's like having no patrol at all." He chuckles.

"You're such a dick."

"Only with you." The moonlight catches his verdant eyes, making them glow.

I throw my head back into the grass, surprised at his admission. "What?"

"I mean, no, I'm not," he says nonchalantly, trying to play it off.

"You're being really weird." I squirm beneath him. "Can you please get off?"

He starts to crawl off but stops suddenly, shifting back into place like we're tethered to one another. Our eyes meet and a silence stretches between us as his body is pressed against mine. It should feel heavy, but for some reason, it feels like it's part of me, and I'm used to the weight, the pressure.

"Blake," I say, "what are you—"

Cutting me off midsentence, he lowers his head and plants his lips on mine, taking me by surprise. My first instinct is to push him off or slap him across the face. But I don't, and what surprises me even more is I close my eyes and kiss him right back. Deepening it, I pull him into me, my fingers combing through the short hair at the nape of his neck. His lips are unexpectedly soft, shifting in sync with mine like it's a routine we've rehearsed before, and we both know all the moves. My heart beats faster and faster, and my skin turns hot, like a fire's been ignited inside my body. I slip my tongue through the seam of his lips and find his, massaging it. He purrs and rolls away, pulling me with him. As I straddle his torso, his hands grip my hips, and he hardens beneath me.

Oh God. I'm kissing Blake Morrison. *I'm kissing Blake Morrison.* I told myself I wouldn't let this happen, not again, not with him—but it feels so good, and I can't help myself. So I push the thought away, and I kiss him harder, biting at his lip, making him moan. A memory comes flooding to the front of my mind, one I can't push aside.

The night at Blake's house party started out fine. I was nervous just being there, because it was the first time we were hanging out with other people, and I was the only person not drinking, but no one noticed, or maybe they didn't care. My Solo cup was filled with apple juice I'd found in the fridge rather than beer from the keg someone had their older brother buy for them. Blake and I had been friendly for three months at that point, and I was enjoying every second of it. Maybe it was because I wasn't being teased and bullied anymore, or maybe it was because I was happy for once. Every day, I had something to look forward to . . . and it was him.

I was seated next to Blake on the living room couch. A pop song blared from a broken speaker that rattled every time the bass hit. Classmates huddled near the keg, while others stood around a folding table, where a competitive game of beer pong played out. The house phone rang, and Blake yelled to turn the music down.

He answered on the fourth ring, after the party had quieted. I remember he didn't say much. Whoever was on the other end of the line did most of the talking. His face changed, anger and sorrow flashing across it. He thanked the person for calling and then set the phone back down on the receiver. The music resumed, blaring through the shaky speaker, and everything went back to normal—except for Blake. I asked him who called. He said no one. I asked if he was okay. He said he was fine. I didn't believe him.

"Let's go talk," I said, standing from the couch and reaching for his hand, trying to pull him with me.

Blake looked up at me for a moment, as though deciding what his next move would be, like he was at a fork in the road and there was no going back and trying the other path once he started down one. He shook his head ever so slightly, as though he was about to deliver bad news in response to a question that hadn't been asked. Blake flicked my hand away, chugged the rest of his beer, and got to his feet. He stumbled over to the keg, where he refilled his cup, gulping the whole thing down in under three seconds before refilling it once more. It was the fuel he needed for whatever fire he was about to start.

Blake staggered back over to me, but his eyes were different—mean. The kindness I had become so accustomed to over the last three months was snuffed out in an instant. Something in him had changed.

"Are you sure you're okay?" I whispered.

Blake put distance between us, sizing me up before tightening his eyes and laughing, even though nothing was funny. "Why are you even here, Doomsday? Don't you have a well to dig or canned goods to sort?"

I drew my head back at the mention of the nickname he hadn't called me the entire school year. I couldn't believe what I was hearing, but I assumed it was a combination of whatever news he got on the phone and the alcohol.

"Blake, you're drunk." I took a step toward him, placing my hand on his shoulder. "Let's get you to bed."

He shrugged me off. "Did you hear that, everyone?" The music lowered and all eyes were on us, like we were center stage and a spotlight had just been shined on Blake and me. I hated every second of it. "Head Case Pearson is trying to take me to bed!"

The party erupted with laughter, and several people joined in, hurling insults and comments at me. I felt sick to my stomach. My heart hammered in my chest, and my skin began to perspire, sweat gathering at my hairline.

"Blake, why are you acting like this?" I said in a low voice, hoping only he would hear me and it would snap him out of whatever this was. "I thought we were . . . friends." I didn't want to say girlfriend and boyfriend or in a relationship, because we had never put a label on it. But I felt like we were more.

"Friends?" He cackled, slapping his knee to punctuate how funny he found it. His face turned serious, his eyes dark and cold. "I could never be friends with a freak like you."

Some of the guys egged Blake on, high-fiving him and hooting and hollering while he continued to taunt and mock me. My bottom lip trembled, and my eyes welled with tears. I didn't want him to see me cry, to see how much he was hurting me, so I darted out of the house before a sob could tear through me. A quarter mile away down the road, I could still hear their laughter. My heart ached, and I thought it might have snapped right in half. Blake's interest in me, all the time we had spent together, had just been one big, cruel joke. And he had finally gotten to the punch line.

The memory makes me jerk away. Blake's eyes shoot open, and confusion takes hold of his face. "What's wrong?"

"Why'd you do that?"

"Do what?"

"Kiss me. Why'd you kiss me, Blake?"

His brows shove together. "Because I wanted to, because I like—"

"Stop!" I say, unpeeling myself from him. I dust the grass clippings off my clothes, collect my flashlight, and start walking.

"Wait," Blake yells. He catches up to me and grips my shoulder, turning me to face him.

I shrug him off and point the flashlight right at his face.

"Jesus," he says, holding up his hand to block the bright light.

I lower it and narrow my eyes. "I know what you're up to."

He jerks his head back. "I'm not up to anything. I swear." Blake tries to reach for my hand, but I yank it away.

"Yeah right. You're up to the same shit you did in high school, but I'm not falling for it this time. I'm not falling for you." I turn and stomp toward the house.

"Casey," he yells.

I ignore him. I should have ignored him from the very beginning. He's too easy to fall for.

Without warning, I'm spun around again, standing face-to-face with Blake. He leans in and kisses me, but this time, I pull away. For good measure, I swing an open hand through the air, slapping him as hard as I can across the cheek. Stunned, he lets his jaw go slack, and his eyes expand.

I point a finger at him, thrusting it into his chest. "Don't you ever fucking touch me again, Blake."

Turning on my heel, I storm off just as tears begin to prickle behind my eyes. It takes everything in me not to look back, but I know if I do, I'll be right under his spell again.

Chapter 22

My lungs scream for air as I slow my pace from a run to a jog to a full-on stop, nearly keeling over. Sweat trickles down my back, sending a chill up my spine, thanks to the cool air. Glancing up at the sky, I take solace in the fact that the sun is hidden somewhere in the clouds, refusing to make an appearance today. Good, because I don't want to see it. It feels like there's a cloud hanging over my head anyway, so it's nice to see its gloomy friends up there. I plop down on the grass and stretch my legs out in front of me, reaching for my toes.

"I think I'm dying," Tessa pants as she rounds the corner of the house, sluggishly jogging toward the front yard, where I'm seated. As soon as she reaches me, she collapses onto her back, splaying her arms and legs out as if making a snow angel.

"Why did I agree to do this?" she says, still out of breath.

"Because it got you out of having to help can vegetables."

"Oh, yeah. That's right." She nods. "Not sure I made the right choice, though." Tessa lifts her head, looking around. "Where's Molly?"

Before I can answer, she comes speed-walking toward us from around the dummy house, carrying three canteens. She's dressed in different clothes from the ones she started the run in.

"Great, you two are back," Molly calls out. "I went up and showered and got us some water," she says, handing us each a canteen.

"I'm sorry, what? You had time to shower, dress, and get us water before we even finished?" Tessa cocks her head.

"Well, I was in cross-country back at school." She takes a seat in the grass beside me. "So two miles is nothing for me. Takes about twelve minutes."

"It's sure as hell something for me, and by *something*, I mean *absolute torture*." Tessa chugs from her canteen.

I unscrew the cap from my own and take a long drink.

"Hey, look—the guys are back," Molly says, all giddy, pointing down at the road, where the truck is pulling up to the gate. JJ hops out and unlocks it, then pushes it open so the truck can pass through.

Tires crunch over gravel as it drives up and stops off to the side of us. Blake shuts the engine off and steps out of the vehicle. I groan internally at the sight of him. I was hoping he wouldn't come back at all. It was nice waking up late in my room alone, since he was already out on a scavenge run. Blake starts toward us with his hands slipped in his pockets, trying to appear all casual. I look away, pretending I don't even notice his arrival, or care.

"Casey," he says in a soft voice.

I busy myself by plucking a dead dandelion from the grass and twirling it between my fingers.

When I don't acknowledge him, he continues. "I got you something."

Ugh. Why can't he just pretend I don't exist? That's what I'm trying to do with him. But no, he can't let me be. Tessa's brows knit together, signaling her confusion. I didn't tell her what happened between me and Blake last night, because I want to forget about it, act as though it never happened.

He won't leave until I respond, so I look up at him with narrowed eyes. "I didn't ask you to get me anything."

"I know," he says with a small shrug. "It's a gift."

"I don't want any gifts from you." I tighten my eyes even more, making them become slits so I can barely see him and his stupid chiseled jaw.

Blake smiles and pulls a bag of Sour Patch Kids from his coat pocket. "But it's your favorite candy."

At first, I wonder how he knows that, but then a memory pops into my head, one I had forgotten or maybe chosen not to remember. We had gone to the movies together to see a horror film, and at concessions, he asked me what my favorite candy was. I told him Sour Patch Kids, so he selected those and a box of Reese's Pieces for himself, his favorite. "They're kind of like you in a way," I said. "First you were sour. Now you're sweet."

He grinned momentarily before it tapered, his face turning serious. "I'm sorry about the sour part," he said.

I smiled and waved it off. "Without the sour, the sweet wouldn't be as satisfying."

It sounded cute then. But now that I think about it, it's really not. I gave him a pass for how he treated me, basically gaslighting myself. How naive of me. Then again, that's what happens when you're young, dumb, and in . . . fatuated with someone.

Blake shakes the bag in front of my face, pulling me from my thoughts. I glare up at him.

"They *were* my favorite. Back when I was seventeen, Blake. I can't stand them now," I say, jutting my chin.

"Can I have them?" Tessa asks.

"No." I shoot a glare at her too.

"Really?" Blake raises a brow. "You hate them now?"

"That's right," I say with a firm nod. My mouth instantly betrays me, watering at the thought of one of those sour, sugary gummies touching my tongue. I swallow the excess saliva before it dribbles out from my lips.

He begrudgingly repockets the candy. "Fine. Well, if you change your mind, you know where to find me."

"I won't," I say without missing a beat.

Blake's mouth forms a hard line, and his shoulders slump as he turns and heads toward the house. I wish he'd head for the road instead.

"Greg!" Molly calls as he marches past us, carrying a cardboard box of items collected on the scavenge run. "Did you get me anything?" she practically sings with excitement.

Greg shoots her an annoyed glance and says, "No," and then keeps on walking.

Molly tucks her chin in. Her eyes develop a sheen, but she takes a couple of quick deep breaths, making it instantly disappear. It's not right what Greg's doing to her, and I really can't stand to watch her get hurt. She deserves to know, and the sooner the better.

"Greg doesn't like you," I say without thinking. The truth comes out like projectile vomit all at once, and I'm not sure whether I'm telling her this for her sake or for mine.

I wish someone would have told me the truth back when Blake was playing the same games with me. It would have saved me a lot of heartbreak and humiliation, so really, I'm doing what's best for her in the long run.

Molly whips her head in my direction, eyes wide. "What?"

"Casey," Tessa says through clenched teeth, almost like a warning, or in utter confusion as to why I'm telling Molly this.

"He doesn't," I say matter-of-factly. The truth is a Band-Aid that just needs to be ripped off. "You were supposed to be a one-night stand. That's it. But the world ended, so here you are. If things were normal, Greg would have ghosted you, but he can't because you're both stuck living at my father's compound." I gesture with my hands, sweeping them in front of me. "He's stringing you along because he can't avoid you. Plus, you're his only option, and if he had another, it wouldn't be you."

The moisture in Molly's eyes resurfaces, but this time she's not able to make it disappear. Tears spill over, streaming down her face.

"I know it's hard to hear, but I can tell you from experience, it's better to be alone than to be with the wrong person." I fold my lips and nod, hoping she'll understand where I'm coming from and will be grateful that I told her rather than angry at the messenger.

Molly starts to sob, and before I can try to console her, she's on her feet, bolting toward the house.

"Casey, what the hell was that?" Tessa asks, staring at me with wild eyes.

"Molly deserves to know the truth, and the longer Greg strings her along for, the more she'll get hurt in the end." I pluck another dandelion from the grass and blow the pappi, sending them into the wind.

Tessa squints, studying my face. "Is there something going on with you?"

"No," I say, tossing the stem aside.

"Come on." She pats her hand against my leg. "It's me. You can tell me anything."

I sigh, debating whether I want to reveal what happened between Blake and me. I was hoping to just forget about it, but I can't seem to.

"Blake kissed me last night."

Her mouth parts with surprise and then clamps closed. "Well . . . that explains the sour mood."

"I guess." I shrug, picking at the grass.

"How the hell did that even happen, and when?" Tessa tilts her head.

"Last night, while I was patrolling. He decided to sneak out and scare me in the middle of my shift and then he just . . . kissed me."

"Oh my God, that creep! And what did you do?"

I swallow hard, not wanting to tell her that I initially kissed him back and it got a little hot and heavy. I still don't know why I did. Maybe it was the adrenaline from being on my first night watch, and then him jumping out of the woods and scaring me amplified it even more. That must have been it.

"I slapped him," I lie. Technically, it's not a whole lie. I did slap Blake, but that was after I'd straddled his body and made out with him.

"Good." Tessa laughs. "So, that's what his little gift was about?"

"Yeah, he's trying to get back on my good side so he can suck me back in, make me like him again, and then pull the rug out from underneath me just like he did back in high school." I shake my head.

"Maybe," Tessa says.

My brows shove together. "What do you mean, *maybe*?"

"I mean . . ." She pauses and glances around. "Maybe Blake is doing exactly what you're saying, or maybe he's changed."

"Yeah, right," I scoff. "Once an asshole, always an asshole."

"But that happened, like, fourteen years ago, and you were both teenagers."

I tighten my eyes, staring back at her. I don't understand where this is coming from, but it feels like betrayal. Is she trying to play devil's advocate or, better yet, Blake's advocate? I may have been wrong about the apocalypse, but I'm not wrong about him.

"Whose side are you on, Tessa?" I purse my lips.

"Yours, Casey. I'm always on your side, but I'm just saying."

"Well, don't," I warn.

Tessa puts her hand up, palm facing out. "Okay, okay, sorry." She lowers it and fiddles with her fingernails.

"I'm going to shower," I say, getting to my feet. I can't do this conversation. First my dad is defending Blake, and now Tessa. Am I living in the Twilight Zone, or am I the only one who can see him for who he really is? An asshole. And Tessa literally called him that the other day, so I don't understand where she's coming from.

"Are we good?" Tessa asks as I start to walk away.

I look back and nod. "Yeah, we're good." I don't want to fight with her.

We are good, but I'm not. I really don't know what I am. Confused? Angry? Upset? All the above? Him kissing me last night brought up so many unresolved feelings, ones I thought I had dealt with. But maybe I hadn't. It seems they've been simmering under the surface, waiting to be stirred back up. This world, or what's left of it, is hard enough to live in as it is. So I just need to forget about Blake and focus on surviving.

Inside the house, I kick off my shoes and have started to head upstairs when a loud crash in the house stops me in my tracks. I sprint to where the sound came from, the first-floor bathroom, and rap my knuckles against the door.

"Is everything all right in there?" I call out, unsure of who I'm even asking.

There's no response. I knock several more times and then listen for movement, but there is none. I reach for the knob and turn it. Thankfully, it's unlocked.

"It's me, Casey. I'm coming in," I say before pushing open the door.

My eyes go wide at the sight of her lying unconscious on the tile floor, a small amount of blood pooling around her head. I scream for help as I rush to her side.

Chapter 23

"How did no one know Elaine is diabetic?" I ask the table.

JJ, Blake, Dad, Uncle Jimmy, and Greg exchange looks with one another, searching for a sign that one of them knew. Someone should have, but it appears no one did.

"She never said anything, ever. You know how Elaine is. She doesn't complain because she never wants to burden anyone," Dad says.

He's not wrong, but still she should have told us, because the situation is far worse now that we're behind it rather than in front of it. She's been rationing her insulin more than is medically safe to do, and she's probably been doing it for a while. Even with the rationing, she'll be out soon.

"We have to get her insulin. If we don't, she'll die," I say, emphasizing the final two words. It isn't for dramatic effect but rather to have it sink into people's minds that if we aren't willing to put our lives on the line for what Elaine needs, then she'll lose hers.

"We've checked all the pharmacies in the area. They were the first places we hit early on, but there's nothing left," Blake says.

"It's true," JJ adds. "In fact, most all of the prescription drugs were already picked clean by the time we scavenged them."

Blake lowers his head and shakes it, appearing disappointed in his inability to protect one of his own.

"What about hospitals?" I ask.

"We haven't searched those," JJ says.

"Hospitals keep tons of prescription meds. They have their own pharmacies. That's our next move," I say confidently, leaving no room for argument.

But that doesn't mean one doesn't come.

My father sighs heavily, and I know he's about to disagree with me. "Casey, the hospitals are crawling with biters. It's far too dangerous, and we just can't take that risk."

"Dad, did you not hear me? If we don't get her insulin, she's going to die."

"And how many people might end up dying trying to get it for her?"

The room goes silent. My dad's words hang in the air like a fog too dense to see through. Everyone's minds are racing with permutations as to how a hospital run could turn out. One dead? Two? Three? Four? The worst-case scenario for doing the right thing makes the math uneven, cosmically weighing out whose life is worth more.

"Might," I say, cutting through everyone's thoughts, grounding them back on what we need to do.

My dad has a look of confusion on his face from my one-word response. "Might?" he confirms.

"You asked how many people *might* end up dead. Elaine doesn't have *might*. Elaine has *definite*, an absolute outcome in her future. People might get hurt or die trying to get her medicine, sure, but that risk is there on every run anyway. If we don't do this, then there's no chance for her to survive, and you may as well start digging her grave now. So think about that before you say no." My eyes are unblinking as I scan the table, waiting for someone to challenge me.

"I hear you, Casey. I really do, and I know you aren't wrong, but the risk is far too great. We don't even know if the hospital will have insulin—and then, let's say we do find some, how much will we find? Enough to keep her healthy for a month? Six months? A year? Elaine wouldn't want us to take the risk, especially if it could end up costing someone their life. So the answer is no." My dad pounds his fist against the table, punctuating the end of his speech.

The room falls silent again as we look around at one another, waiting to see whether anyone will challenge my dad's declaration. I just need one person to be on my side. But as time drags on, it's clear to me that they're either too afraid to challenge the man who's keeping them all safe or too afraid to put their lives on the line for another. Either way, I have no support, and neither does Elaine. But I don't need it.

"Fine." I stand, glaring at each of them. "I'll go by myself."

My gaze lingers on Blake because I'm sure he's about to challenge me, declare that I need more training, that I'm a liability, or that I'll only get myself killed, but he doesn't.

Instead, he nods and stands.

"I'll go with you."

I'm surprised, but in a good way. My face relaxes, my expression replaced, I suspect, by a look of gratitude, one I share only with Blake as I tune out the rest of the people in the room.

My father rises from his chair, puffing out his chest and lifting his chin. "No! I won't allow it. Casey, I can't—"

"Dad! Enough!" I yell. He freezes in place, and the whites of his eyes show. "I know you want to keep me safe, and I know you're afraid of losing me, but don't let that fear cloud your judgment or stop you from doing the right thing." I walk over to him, pressing my hand against his chest, feeling his beating heart. "If Mom were here, what would she do, Dad?"

Looking up into my father's eyes, I can see a sadness, not in the loss that already happened, and not for fear of losing me, but a sadness with himself, for even suggesting that we don't try and save Elaine. He presses his lips firmly together and lets his head fall forward. "Okay. I'll go, but I need you to stay here."

I shake my head and step back. "No, I'm going."

"She's right, Dale." Blake takes his place beside me. "She's the only one who knows her way around the hospital, and she knows what we're looking for. It'll be quicker and safer if she comes with."

My dad closes his eyes and exhales, shaking his head as he tries to think of a way to change what needs to be done. But in the end, he knows this is the best chance we have.

"When do we need to go?" Blake asks.

"Tomorrow," I say. "She only has enough insulin for two more days. If the first hospital is a bust, then at least it gives us another day to search another."

"Fine, then the six of us will prep to go tomorrow," Dad says, giving in.

"We shouldn't all go," Blake argues. "We need people to stay back in case something like what happened the other day happens again."

"Well, I'm not staying back," my dad says.

"Me neither." Greg stands.

Soon the whole room has declined to stay back, finding the courage that I wish had been there minutes ago.

"Two of us should stay back, so let's figure out who," Blake says.

"We can draw straws," Dad suggests. "That's the only fair way of deciding."

Uncle Jimmy gets up from his chair and heads into the kitchen to get them.

"I'm not drawing straws," I say, making my stance clear.

"Fine. The rest of us will then." Dad nods, a look of sadness taking over his face.

Uncle Jimmy returns. Five straws stick out of his closed fist, the tops all even while the bottoms are hidden within his hand. "Shortest two stay back."

"I'll go first." Blake steps forward and selects a straw, grabbing it by the tip and slowly pulling it out of the bunch. It's nearly as big as my uncle's fist, and it has to be the biggest straw he could hold and still conceal.

One by one everyone else goes. As the straws get smaller and smaller, it becomes harder to tell who is staying back. My uncle pulls the final one, and the three shortest hold theirs out side by side, with the smallest two belonging to my dad and my uncle.

"No, I'm not staying," Dad says, whipping his straw to the ground.

"Yes, you are. Those were the rules. Plus . . ." I wait for him to look at me so I can make sure my point sinks in. "You're the best person to stay back. You know the layout of the property better than anyone. You know where all the weapons are and how to use every single one of them. And if it wasn't for your little Rambo moment the other day, we'd all be dead."

I can see his chest swell as he begins to nod, psyching himself up for a fate he didn't want. "Fine. I'll hold down the fort."

JJ, noticing Uncle Jimmy isn't happy about this arrangement either, steps to his father, placing a hand on his shoulder. "We'll be good, Dad, and I can make sure Greg comes back in one piece too, if you'd like."

They both laugh. "Dealer's choice," my uncle teases.

"What the hell?" Greg chides, interrupting their brief moment of humor.

"I'm just kidding, son. Besides, zombies like brains, so I don't need to worry about you out there at all." Uncle Jimmy splats a hand on his shoulder.

"Aww, thanks, Dad." Greg smiles, the joke going right over his head.

JJ and I exchange a grin.

Blake steps to my dad like a junior soldier in front of a superior, hands behind his back, at ease, while his shoulders are pinned, and his chin is angled slightly up. "I won't let anything happen to Casey. You have my word, Dale."

The display of machismo when I was the only one who was willing to go in the first place forces my eyes to roll in the back of my head.

"I won't let anything happen to myself, Blake," I sneer, ending his moment of gallantry.

Chapter 24

"How many do you see?" Greg asks.

Blake looks through a pair of binoculars, scanning the back entrance of the Meadow Crest hospital. The three of us wait, our backs pressed up against the side of the truck.

"I count six. Two near the dumpsters, two at the doors, and two by the med bay," Blake says, continuing to observe their movements through the lenses.

On our drive in, we noticed a large number of biters near the hospital's front entrance and decided to enter from the back, parking the truck far enough away to not make too much noise, but also not so far that we couldn't make a quick getaway if needed.

"I don't love four versus six," JJ says, looking around the area for possible approach paths.

"Me neither," Blake adds. "But they seem to be pretty docile right now, and if we sneak up on them, I can take out two by myself. If you can do the same, JJ, then that leaves the last two for Casey and Greg."

"Yeah, I can get two of them quick enough with my knife." JJ nods.

"Casey, Greg, does that work for you?" Blake looks to us.

I shake my head. "Let me take a pair. I can get them from a distance with my throwing stars. Less risk on that front. Greg and JJ can tag-team the last two."

"You sure?" Blake puts down the binoculars, gauging my sureness. "If you miss and they make a bunch of noise, we could be overrun in seconds."

I stare right back at him, not flinching in my response. "I won't miss."

He nods, turning to the group. In a low whisper, he says, "All right, I've got the two by the med bay. Greg and JJ, go for the ones by the dumpsters. Casey, the back entrance is yours. Follow my lead until we split, and then look for my signal. We'll strike at the same time, understood?"

Everyone bobs their heads in agreement. Unsheathing our weapons, we ready ourselves for the attack. Blake moves first, walking around the truck in a low crouch. His arms are out in front of him as if he were holding a gun, but instead it's a sword, pointed at the ready. We follow behind in a single-file line, trying to make as little noise as possible as we travel across the concrete parking lot. On his signal, we split off in three separate paths, closing in on our respective targets. Once in position, we wait, all eyes on Blake for the go-ahead.

From where I'm crouched, I could hit my two biters right now with my throwing stars, even if it is a bit far. I ready one in my throwing hand and one in my other palm so I can grab the second star and fling it less than a second later. I hold my breath, watching Blake as I try not to blink for fear of missing his mark. He flicks his hand forward, signaling us to move.

I wait a couple of seconds, knowing that if I throw too quickly, my biters will collapse and make noise before the other three have time to reach their targets. Blake reaches the first biter, and he shoves his sword up under its chin, piercing its skull. My head's on a swivel as I rotate it to watch JJ and Greg both lunging forward, weapons ready to plunge down into the skulls of the two unknowing monsters. I turn my focus back on the biters in front of me and begin running, letting loose the first star when I'm confident I'm in range to not miss. It rips through the throat of the first biter, the creature dropping to its knees before crumpling over. I switch the other star into my throwing hand and send it flying at the second biter. I follow the shining piece of steel as it glides through the air, but the biter drops down at the last second and starts to eat the other biter I just put out of its misery. The star crashes through the glass panel on the door, shattering it. *Shit.*

The biter lifts its head, pausing its meal, and looks around in confusion, unsure of what just happened. Then it spots me.

Staggering to its feet, it has a look of disbelief on its decrepit face, like it can't believe its luck in finding such a delicious thing to eat. Its eyes go wide as it starts to run toward me. I frantically go for the zipper on my pouch, ripping on the tab, but it's stuck. I yank on it over and over, but the damn thing won't budge. If I use my gun, the run's over, because the noise will bring every one of them to us. I pull out my Glock and level it at the biter, holding steady as a last resort. With my other hand, I unsheathe my knife, readying it. The biter opens its mouth and starts to emit a high-pitched scream. *"It's over if it screams anyway,"* I whisper to myself.

I don't have a choice. It's too far away. I have to pull the trigger.

The biter's mouth snaps closed, and it tumbles over midrun, smashing into the ground and sliding a few feet to a dead stop, chunks of skin peeling away. A large knife protrudes from the side of its head, and black blood oozes, seeping into the cracked concrete. Blake extracts the blade that saved the run from being a total waste.

As he strolls toward me, I'm already anticipating the verbal lashing I'll receive for almost blowing the whole operation.

"I don't know what happened," I say, stammering over my words. "It ducked at the last second, and my star would have hit dead-on if . . ."

"Shhh, easy." Blake flaps his hands, gesturing for me to stay calm. "That's why we work in teams. Shit happens."

"But . . . I . . . I promised I wouldn't miss."

"There are no guarantees in battle, Casey." He slaps me on the back, jolting me forward and shaking me out of my worry. "Come on. We're just getting started, and I need your head in the game because you're our guide now."

"Okay," I say with a nod, grateful for his understanding and encouragement. We head for the back entrance, continuing on with the plan.

I push through the rotating glass doors and find the space is eerily familiar, instantly bringing me back to the night I escaped the hospital in Chicago. It's not the same one, but in a way, they all feel the same. The floor is coated in streaks of rotted black and brown, substances that look like the combination of every fluid the body is capable of producing. There are bodies everywhere, many of which were regular humans, killed and eaten by biters. Their corpses are devoid of soft organs. Stomachs and rib cages are ripped open and hollow, now acting as homes for maggots and insects feeding on the remaining scraps of bone and putrid sinew.

The buzz of flies mixes with the humming of the track lighting, still softly glowing, thanks to backup generators that are likely running on solar panels. Hospital beds and gurneys are toppled on their sides in the halls with loose papers and clipboards scattered everywhere.

Blake starts off first, taking the lead to check for any danger, but he suddenly freezes, standing in the middle of the hall like a statue that has been commissioned as a decor piece. The three of us exchange looks, unsure of what to do.

JJ approaches Blake and puts his hand on his shoulder. "Hey man, you all right?"

Blake jumps slightly, quickly looking to JJ. "Yeah, I'm fine. Let's go."

As stressful and terrifying as this scavenge run is, this should be nothing compared to what he did in the SEALs, so I don't understand why this has him so spooked.

A whisper comes up from behind me. "Hey, Casey."

I turn to see Greg apprehensively waiting for me. "Yeah?" I say.

"Before we head in, just in case one of us dies, I have a question for you."

I can only imagine what this could be about, but I'm sure it doesn't need to happen here. "Is now really the right time?"

His eyes look up and to the right before he levels to me. "Probably not, but it might be the only time."

I sigh. "Okay . . . what is it?"

"Did you tell Molly she was supposed to be just a one-night stand?"

"Yes," I say without hesitation.

His eyebrows burrow toward the center of his forehead. "What? Why?"

"Because you already should've told her. Stringing her along because you're afraid to hurt her feelings or because you have no other options is wrong, and it's not fair to her."

"Well, now she won't talk to me."

"I thought that's what you wanted."

"I did. But . . ." He scratches his head, sheepishly looking at the floor. "Now I kinda like her. Is that love?"

I sigh heavily. I really don't have time for this. "Look, Greg, we can talk about this later. Right now, let's just focus on staying alive."

"Fine. But this isn't over." He points at me, emphasizing that he means business.

"I just said we could talk about it later. That means it's not over."

"Oh . . . okay. Cool." He smiles.

I shake my head, wondering how many college classes he actually attended, or if a healthy regimen of booze, weed, and variations of Molly rotted his brain. Tabling our conversation, we head deeper into the lobby. The odor coming from the putrefied corpses becomes unbearable, and Greg starts to gag behind me, loudly dry heaving. I turn and grab his face, pinching his nose and covering his mouth.

"Stop that," I yell in a whisper.

"I can't. It's so gross." He gags again, so I pull my hand away, not wanting vomit spewed all over me.

"If you need to throw up, just get it over with quietly. But no coughing and no dry heaving."

Greg gags again and nods, rushing over to a nearby corpse. He sticks his face near its rotting body and takes in a whiff so deeply, it makes him barf into its open cavity. *Fucking gross.*

After a minute, he gives a thumbs-up, wipes his face with his sleeve, and rejoins us.

Near the front desk, a placard on the wall indicates the different areas of the hospital.

"Look," I say, pointing to the sign. "The ICU is on the third floor. That's our best bet for finding the biggest meds repository. Let's find the stairwell and head on up."

Down the hall, a small green sign tucked up in the corner indicates a stairwell. We're making our way toward it when Greg blurts out, "Hey, wait. This says there's a cafeteria here."

"You can wait until we get back to the house to get a snack," Blake snaps at him.

"No, not to eat now. Although I am kinda hungry after throwing up. But we should stock up on food and bring it back." The group is collectively impressed with Greg's quick thinking. We smile like proud parents who just watched their child score a touchdown for the first time in peewee football.

"Fine, let's split up. One duo can grab extra supplies, while the other two go for the insulin," JJ says.

Blake nods in agreement.

"Okay, Greg, follow me." JJ pats him on the shoulder. "We'll head to the cafeteria."

"Whoa, whoa, whoa, I'm not going with Blake," I say. "JJ can come with me to the ICU and keep watch while I search for the meds."

"I'm not going with him either," Greg argues. "Besides, Casey, Blake can watch your six better than anyone. He was a Navy SEAL, after all."

"Stop talking about me like I'm some infectious virus," Blake grumbles.

"Well, you are." I smirk.

"Rock, paper, scissors for it?" Greg holds out his hand in a fist over his other palm.

"Seriously?" Blake huffs.

"Deal," I say, holding my fist out. "On *shoot*?"

Greg raises a brow. "Of course. Best of three?"

"I'm not a heathen. Obviously, best of three," I say, pounding my fist down into my cupped palm.

My punishment for losing to Greg is crouched in front of me, scanning every inch of the hallway on the third floor. His steps are silent, and he moves with a swiftness and surety of purpose that one can't help but be impressed with. When Blake deems this section of hallway safe, he motions for me to join him.

"All good?" I ask.

"Yeah, for now." He slowly moves along the hallway, following the signage directing us to the ICU. "I'm really glad, by the way," Blake whispers.

"Glad about what?"

"That you changed your mind."

"Changed my mind?" I ask, confusion twisting my face.

"When you won RPS, you picked me to go with you. I am the best guy for the job, so that was smart on your part." Blake pats me on the shoulder.

"I didn't win. I lost. That's why I'm with you."

"Feels like a win to me," he says with a smirk.

"That makes one of us. Now, shut up and keep your eyes peeled instead of on me." I spin my finger in circles at him, his body turning around in response.

The situation up on the third floor is even worse than ground level. The ICU likely had some of the first people turn into biters, and the scenery before me reflects that in the most gruesome way. Bodies are piled on top of one another, more densely packed and further decayed than before. Some at the bottom of the piles have turned into rotting sludge, their essence seeping across the floor in a yellowish pus, moistening the black death streaks marking the halls. Most of the bodies look like carved turkeys after a Thanksgiving meal, small pieces of graying meat loosely hanging from bone. The hallway appears to have a dark cloud suspended in the air as what has to be hundreds of thousands of flies buzz about for the remaining morsels of food.

"It looks like we're about to walk into hell," Blake whispers back to me.

"That's cuz we are."

Pushing through the haze of insects, mouths closed tight to avoid inhaling any flies, we scan the edges of the hall, checking every room we pass to ensure no biters are waiting in ambush. Halfway down the hall, we both jolt back in panic at movement from one of the bodies on the floor. It's a biter, but it's so weak and decayed, it can't even stand. Its legs are nothing but bone, covered in scratches and bite marks. It lifts its head, its eyes bouncing back and forth, widening with excitement. The creature reaches its arm out, planting a hand on the ground as it tries to pull itself forward, but the bone gives out, and its skull smacks down against its arm. With a look of desperation, it begins gnawing at its own skin, chewing the dried flesh like a piece of jerky that's been left out in the sun.

As we continue, we notice half a dozen or more biters like this one, too weak to move.

"What's wrong with them?" Blake asks, crouched down in front of one that's trying to eat the bones of a nearby corpse.

"They're starving," I say, looking at the caved-in face of another biter, which is essentially just a skull with rotting eyeballs.

Near the biter, a body wearing a white doctor's coat is leaned up against the wall. I reach into its pocket and fish around.

"Are you robbing the dead now?" Blake asks, staring at my hand with a look of shame.

I pull out a name badge with a barcode on the back, the laminate still glistening in the dim light.

"No, just borrowing. If the backup generators are keeping the reserve power running, then the pharmacy will still be locked." I hold up the badge. "And this will open it."

"Good thinking, Pearson."

"I know." I stand and begin moving down the hall with more confidence, since the area seems clear of any biters capable of doing us harm.

At the nurses' station in the middle of the floor, a body is draped over the desk, arms hanging down to the ground with only the bones left in place. I hop over it and open the drawers along the wall, pulling out untouched supplies. Gauze, tongue depressors, disposable gloves, iodine, and a half dozen other items.

"Come here." I wave Blake over. "Turn around." Unzipping his backpack, I stuff everything inside it until his pack is so full, it becomes difficult to zip closed.

"What's in there?"

"First aid supplies, pain meds, disinfectant."

"Good find," he says, readjusting the bag on his shoulders to account for the increased weight.

"All right, we're almost to the pharmacy room. Follow me." I take the lead again, heading down the hall. I can finally see the med room. A badge scanner is mounted outside it, and I take off at a jog, passing by the final few rooms.

Suddenly, I'm slammed into the wall. A shriek pierces right into my ear as two hands dig at my sides, fingers pressing hard as they try to puncture my skin. I whip my head around just in time to see the open maw of a biter, closing in on my nose, ready to rip it clean off my face. I stifle my own scream.

A flash of metal fills the open hole, Blake's knife stabbing down through its skull and into its mouth. The biter slinks to the ground, its jaw still chomping up and down like a set of windup teeth.

"Jesus fucking Christ." I wipe the saliva from my face and try not to think too hard on whether I just pissed myself.

"You're welcome." Blake smiles, pulling the knife from the creature's head.

"Yeah, yeah, yeah." I wave off his heroics, even though he did just save my life.

He faces me in a huff, squinting. "Are you gonna stay mad at me for forever?" Blake snaps.

"No . . . just until you die. Or I die. Actually, if you would have just let that thing kill me, I would have been done being mad at you."

"You're impossible." He shakes his head in frustration.

I ignore him and swipe the badge across the reader. We've got more important things to focus on than feelings. The small light turns from red to green, and the lock clicks out of place as I push the door open. This time, I let Blake take the lead, scanning the room to make sure it's safe to enter.

"Clear," he whispers, gently pulling me in and closing the door behind us.

"You should stay out in the hall," I say.

"Why?"

"In case there are more biters like the one that just attacked me. We don't want to be surprised when we try and make a quick exit, nor do I want to get trapped in here. There's only one way out."

He starts to open his mouth like he's going to argue with me, but instead he nods and heads out into the hall, pulling the door closed behind him.

I make a beeline to the refrigerated cabinet, hoping it's still working off the generator reserve. A wave of cool air hits my face, and glistening in front of me like crystals are more than twenty-five bottles of insulin, safe and intact. I grab all of them, stuffing them into my backpack, careful not to break them. I scan the room, noticing the shelves are mostly still stocked and untouched since the world ended. Dozens and dozens of bottles of antibiotics, cholesterol and blood pressure medications, stronger painkillers, muscle relaxers, liver and gastrointestinal medications—you name it, it's here, waiting to be plucked like a ripe apple from a tree.

"This is a gold mine," I whisper to myself, grabbing everything in sight.

Once my bag is stuffed full, I open the door, expecting to find Blake standing guard, but he's nowhere to be seen. I frantically glance around, hoping to lay eyes on him.

"Blake!" I yell in a whisper. "Blake!"

I jog down the hall on my tiptoes, trying not to make any noise as I look into each room I pass. My head darts from left to right in panicked jerks. Room after room, each one is empty, and I begin to worry even more, contemplating the worst. I skid to a stop, twisting backward as I gaze into an ICU room behind me on the left. Standing just inside the doorframe, staring into it, is Blake, his back covered with the bulging rucksack.

"Blake!" I whisper, trying to get his attention.

At first, I think I hear him respond in a low grunt, not saying any words, instead just making a sound to let me know he heard me. But his body doesn't move, and the grunt turns into a moan, steady and longer than the first one. I creep behind Blake and peer around him, finally seeing what it is he's staring at.

In the middle of the room, a biter sways back and forth, emaciated to the point its ribs are showing, and its skin hangs loose on its bones like all the muscle has melted away. It's barely able to stand as it inches toward Blake. The biter's arms are stretched out in front like a mummy, trying to keep its balance.

"Blake, let's go," I whisper to him.

He doesn't respond. What the hell is his problem? Why is he just staring at this thing, frozen in time, like when we first entered the hospital?

"Blake! What the fuck are you doing? We've gotta go." *Still nothing.*

I reach forward and yank on the bag slung over his shoulders, but his body is rigid, promptly snapping back into place. I try to move around him, but he fills the doorframe. The biter is now less than six feet away from him, so I yank on him again.

"BLAKE!" I scream at the top of my lungs, filling the entire floor of the hospital with my voice, hoping that'll snap him back to reality. His head rattles, and he glances back at me, finding the source of the scream, only to see me pointing behind him, a look of horror on my face.

He turns just as the biter lunges at him, using its last bit of strength to reach for his body. Blake raises his arm in front of his face, shielding himself. The biter sinks its teeth right into his arm; blood secretes from his flesh, dripping off his elbow and onto the floor.

My eyes nearly split at the corners. *No. No. No. No. No. This can't be happening...*

Chapter 25

With knife in hand and Blake now out of the doorframe, there's space for me to get to the biter, although . . . it's too late. I lunge forward, forcing the blade up underneath its chin. It pushes through the soft, decaying flesh, crunching past cartilage, and punctures the brain stem. The creature instantly goes rigid. I jerk the knife down and shove the biter back, black sludge pouring out of the new hole I created as its body splats against the floor.

"What the fuck, Blake!?" I grab his shoulder, spinning him to face me. "What did you do?"

He's just as stiff as the biter and stands there motionless. It's like he's looking right through me. Tears fall from the corners of his unblinking green eyes, trickling down his blanched skin. I shake him, trying to get him to respond, but he doesn't.

The sleeve below his elbow is stained red. Blood streams down his hand and fingers, dripping onto the white tile, forming a small puddle. *Shit!* I riffle through the rucksack hung on his shoulder, fishing out cotton pads, a half-empty bottle of rubbing alcohol, and a bandage wrap.

"Blake," I say, taking his arm in my hand. He doesn't resist my help, and I'm not sure he even realizes I'm helping him, because he doesn't respond to my touch. I carefully roll up his sleeve, inspecting the wound. A fractured blood moon outlined with deep craters is engraved into his skin, one half displayed on either side of his forearm where the biter sank its teeth. It's in the exact same spot as my bite. I unscrew the rubbing alcohol and generously pour it onto the wound. It should burn, but Blake doesn't flinch. Covering the torn and frayed flesh with several bandages, I press the cotton tightly against the lesions to slow the bleeding.

"You're gonna be okay, Blake," I say, wrapping his forearm with a roll of bandage.

He's still in shock, and I need to pull him out of it—otherwise, we're not going to make it out of here alive. I need him to be present, to be with me. I tear the dressing with my teeth, toss the roll aside, and push his sleeve down. After returning the first aid supplies to his bag, I reclose it. A low growl comes from somewhere in the hospital, followed by shuffling feet. My heart pounds against my tightening rib cage. We have to get out of here. All the noise and commotion attracted more of them—and who knows how many more that actually is?

"Blake," I say in a strained whisper, snapping my fingers in front of his face several times to no response. "Blake, come on!" I grip his shoulder and shake it as hard as I can.

My patience is worn thin due to what sounds like a horde of biters heading our way. Their raspy growls start to fill the hall right outside this room. *Bang. Bang. Bang.* A series of gunshots fire off in the distance. They sound like they're coming from another floor or outside the hospital. JJ and Greg must be in deep shit too. *Damn it, Blake!* Without thinking, I raise my hand and swing, cracking him right across the face. Surprisingly, it fails to pull him out of his shocked state.

I need to get him to snap out of this. My hands fly to the back of his neck, and I pull him into me. Standing on my tippy-toes, I close my eyes and press my lips to his, passionately moving them, kissing him to hopefully bring him back to me. At first his lips are cold, but then they start to warm against mine, pulsating as though his heart has begun to beat through them. I draw my head back and look up at him, hoping he's here with me again.

Blake blinks several times and then winces, gripping his bandaged arm. "Ahh," he groans.

My hands cup the sides of his face, forcing him to look me in the eye, so he'll hear me. "Blake, we have to get out of here."

He tries to shake his head. "Just go without me."

"No, I'm not leaving you."

"I deserve to be left behind," he says, defeated.

The grunts and groans grow louder. My pulse races and the hairs on the back of my neck stand up straight. They're getting closer, and if we don't get out of here, we'll be cornered in this room.

I press my lips against his, this time with more force, giving him enough to want more, to come with me, to fight. "Let's go!" I say, staring into his eyes. "Together."

His face flushes, like he's conflicted on whether to stay or to go with me. I don't have time for this, so I clutch his lacerated forearm and squeeze until he cries out in pain—and then I yank him as I take off out of the hospital room and into the hall. To the right, the way we came in, there are dozens of decaying biters staggering in our direction, snarling and snapping their jaws. Only fifteen yards separate them from us. *Fuck.*

I swivel my head in the other direction, spotting an elevator at the end of the hall. With the hospital running only on backup generators, there's no way it works. I glance back at the horde of rotting creatures closing in on us, realizing I don't have a choice.

"Come on," I say to Blake, pulling him with me.

We sprint down the hall toward the elevator, zigzagging to avoid tipped-over hospital beds, putrefied corpses, and random debris scattered about. I leap over a severed torso that's been gutted and ripped apart.

At the elevator, I unsheathe my knife and jab it into the crack where the doors meet. "Blake, help me."

He grips the handle of the knife and twists it, creating a gap big enough for me to slip my hands through and start to try to force it open. Blake uses the weight of his body to crank one door back in its slot. Returning my knife to its sheath, I peer into the elevator shaft.

"Oh good, it's on the first floor," I say as Blake forces the other door all the way open.

"How are we going to get down?" He furrows his brow. "We could break a leg jumping two stories."

He's right. But we don't have any other option. The biters are gaining on us, and they seem to be moving faster than usual. Perhaps the thought of actually having a fresh meal rather than cannibalizing one another has motivated them. Blake appears both confused and shocked, like he's still grappling with the bite while also trying to work out how it happened. My gaze goes to his belt, followed by my hands, swiftly undoing it.

"What are you doing?"

I don't have time to explain, so I just keep moving, slipping the belt from the loops of his jeans. With the buckle clutched in my hand, I lasso it toward the elevator cable; with a flick of my wrist, it curves around it and returns to me. Catching the other end midair, I thread it through the buckle and pull it tight, ensuring it'll hold.

"Here," I say, handing it to him. "Go."

He shakes his head. "No, you go first."

"It's gotta be you, Blake."

I slip my backpack off and remove my shirt, sliding it up over my head.

He swallows hard, his eyes lingering on my cleavage and exposed midriff.

"Blake, focus," I say.

He quickly snaps his attention to my face.

"My shirt won't hold you or provide enough resistance on the cables. You go first with the belt, and I'll follow. But I'll need you to try and catch me or at least soften my landing."

I slip my bag on my back and look over my shoulder. They're less than ten yards away.

"Go!" I say, panicked.

He nods, grips the belt, and jumps into the shaft. The leather squeals as it skids down the cable, stopping only when his boots thud against the top of the elevator. Blake thrusts his boot against the ceiling panel, busting it out.

He raises his arms above his head, looking up at me. "Come on, Casey."

Gripping one sleeve, I lasso the sweater around the cable just like I did with the belt and catch the other sleeve with my opposite hand, looping it around itself. Closing my eyes, I yank it tight and take a couple of deep breaths, readying myself. Something grazes the back of my neck, giving me the motivation to leap. I scream, my hands gripping the sweater as I slide down the cable too fast. It feels like I'm free-falling. My boots hit hard against the elevator, but not as hard as they would have if it weren't for Blake.

His arms are wrapped around me tightly, having caught my body to slow my descent. He lifts my chin with his hand, and I finally open my eyes, meeting his.

"I got you," Blake says.

Before I can respond, a loud bang startles me, and the elevator shakes as something splats against it. I nearly lose my footing, but Blake holds me a little tighter. Lying a few feet from us, a biter writhes on its back, its legs snapped beneath the weight of its fall, its intestines spilling out from its torso. Blake grabs my hand, leading me toward the knocked-out ceiling panel, our passage into the empty elevator.

"Go," he says, gripping both of my hands.

I nod several times, putting all my trust in him. He lowers me down into the elevator. Another body slams against the top of it, causing the whole thing to rock and his grip to give out. But I land on my feet.

"Hurry!" I call up to him as I unsheathe my knife and plunge it into the crack where the doors meet. Blake climbs down, dropping to his feet just as another biter smashes into the elevator, spraying rotten blood onto us. I twist my knife, creating a gap large enough for Blake to slip his hands in, one on top of the other, prying the doors apart.

Biters continue to fall into the shaft, splatting against the ceiling above us. Each crash sounds like a gunshot.

We pass through the open elevator doors and are back on the first floor of the hospital. It's surprisingly quiet, but that doesn't mean it'll stay that way.

"Come on," I say, holding my knife out in front of me, keeping my eyes peeled in all directions.

Blake and I move with haste toward the exit, dodging the wreckage and rotting corpses to avoid drawing any more attention to ourselves. A biter squawks in the distance, and we keep going, sticking close to one another.

"Are you okay?" I whisper to Blake.

He glances over at me with fearful eyes and nods. I've never seen him scared before, and for some reason, all I want to do is be the one who makes him fearless. Up ahead, an exit sign glows a reddish hue. It's our way out of this hellhole.

I accelerate my pace, pushing myself harder to reach the door first. I throw it open, and the sun's bright rays enter my eyes all at once, forcing me to squint and look away. Blake crosses the threshold and slams the door closed behind him. We suck in big gulps of air, trying to catch our breath while scanning the back lot.

A high-pitched screech steals our attention. JJ and Greg push a gurney and a laundry canvas cart, each piled high with food and supplies across the parking lot. One of the wheels squeaks every few seconds or so, finally quieting when they reach the truck bed.

The door we just came through bursts open behind us. Dozens of biters spill out.

"Blake, go," I say, shoving him forward.

I'm on his heels, screaming for JJ and Greg.

They pause loading supplies and look to us. Realizing what we're up against, they each grab an end of the gurney and toss the whole thing into the truck bed, followed by the laundry cart. Greg closes the tailgate and races around the side, hopping in the front. JJ pulls the back passenger door open and gets into the driver's seat, starting the engine.

"Come on," I say, pushing myself to run faster. Blake lags a little behind me, and I fear he'll stop altogether, so I slow down to ensure I'm in lockstep with him. I won't leave him behind, and I won't let him stay behind either.

I reach the truck first and climb in, moving to the opposite side so Blake has room to jump in.

"Hurry!" Greg's voice is full of panic.

Blake practically vaults into the vehicle.

"Go! Go! Go!" he yells, yanking the door closed behind him, snapping off a biter's arm in it. JJ slams his foot on the gas pedal. Tires squeal as we peel out of the lot.

Greg turns back in his seat, raising a brow. "What the hell were you two doing in there?"

I look down at myself, realizing I'm only wearing a sports bra on top because my shirt is hanging from an elevator cable.

I roll my eyes. "We were trying to get out alive."

"Right," Greg teases, double raising his brows.

Blake stares blankly.

"Dude, what's up with you?" Greg asks, noticing how quiet he is.

When he doesn't answer, I do. "Blake got bit."

JJ's eyes grow wide in the reflection of the rearview mirror. "What? How?"

Greg's mouth parts, but no words come out.

"It doesn't matter how it happened," I say, because I honestly don't know how it did.

Blake is quiet, his knee nervously bouncing up and down as he stares ahead at nothing in particular. It's like he's making a plan of his own and deciding whether to act on it.

Greg presses his lips firmly together and shakes his head in dismay, facing forward once again. JJ's attention is laser-focused on the road as he swerves around biters and abandoned vehicles.

A gust of air whips through the truck, thanks to Blake flinging open his door. He attempts to jump out of the moving vehicle, but I lunge at him and jerk him back.

"Blake! Stop!" I tug on his arm with one hand and grab a fistful of his shirt with the other.

JJ yells at him to close the door, while Greg spins around and tries to help me keep him inside.

"You have a chance, Blake. It's not over yet!" I shout, hoping I'll talk some sense into him.

I leap across his body and seize hold of the door handle, yanking on it as hard as I can. It slams closed, putting an end to the whipping wind. Blake's shoulders slump in defeat, and he lets his head fall forward.

I'm breathless and annoyed. "What the hell was that?"

"What?" He slowly looks to me with narrowed eyes. "You want me dead anyway."

"Not like this, I don't."

Without a thought, he lunges at the door again, propelling it open.

"Jesus fucking Christ!" JJ yells.

I grip his shoulder and pull back, drawing him into his seat. I'm not doing this again, so I climb on top of him, straddling my legs around his waist, while Greg tugs the door closed and lets out an exasperated sigh. Throwing my arms around Blake, I hold him tight and bury my face between his neck and shoulder.

"If you jump, then I'm coming with you," I whisper into his ear.

He doesn't say anything. All I can hear are his labored breaths and his pounding heart.

"Get a room," Greg quips from the front seat, pretending to dry heave.

"Shut up, Greg. I'm trying to make sure Blake doesn't kill himself."

"Yeah, okay . . ."

I tune everything out except Blake, paying close attention to how his body responds. His heart rate randomly increases. It could be a symptom of the virus. His skin feels hot against my cheek. Another possible symptom. However, the hard bulge pressing into my crotch is definitely not from the virus. Tears prickle at my eyes, and I shut them tight, squeezing them away. All I wanted was Blake out of my life, but now that it's a possibility, I don't want it anymore. At least not like this. Not this way. As we drive, the tension in Blake's body starts to ease. He practically melts into me, his muscles relaxing and his head dropping onto my shoulder.

"Are you good now?" I whisper, just loud enough for him to hear.

"I think so," he says.

"You're not gonna jump?"

His head slightly shakes against mine. "No."

"Promise?"

"Yeah."

"What happened back there?" I ask, my fingers brushing against the nape of his neck. "It was like you were somewhere else entirely."

"I don't know," he says. "But thanks for bringing me back."

"What the fuck!?" JJ shouts. The engine revs, and the truck accelerates.

I scramble off Blake so I can see what's got him in a tizzy. "What? What is it?" I ask, leaning between the passenger's and driver's seats to get a glimpse through the windshield.

Up ahead, a plume of black smoke looms over my dad's property, just above the tree line. A vehicle I don't recognize sits parked at the end of the driveway, right in front of the gate. I slip the pistol from my holster, double-checking that it's fully loaded before spinning the cylinder and flicking it back into place. Greg pumps his shotgun.

"What is that?" JJ points a finger.

"What's what?" Blake asks, snapping out of his daze. He leans forward, pressing up against me.

I squint, following JJ's finger. It takes a moment for it to come into view clear enough to know what I'm looking at, what's lying in the road. When it does, my jaw drops.

"It's a body."

Chapter 26

The tires skid to a stop, kicking up brown dust. We pile out of the vehicle, running toward the unfamiliar truck parked up against the gate. A large rug has been thrown on top of the barbed wire, crushing it down to provide safe passage over. My eyes go to the body. It's not anyone we recognize, and it's not a biter either. It's a man. He's filthy. Maybe in his forties, with a scraggly, dark beard and a buzzed haircut. There's a gunshot wound right through the center of his head. He was dead in an instant, his eyes left propped open, staring up at the sky.

The source of the smoke is none other than my truck, the one that survived so many evenings parked overnight on the streets of Chicago, accumulating new paint colors, thanks to dents and scrapes, while the pigeons used it as a restroom. More than once, it had its windows smashed in, thieves hoping to find something of value but deciding to leave behind my collection of 2000s-pop mix CDs. Apparently, our definitions of *value* differed somewhat. But Old Blue has finally met her end here on the front lawn. The paint has been taken over by a spread of thick black soot, pluming from the burning tires and the seats' upholstery.

JJ unlocks the property gate and pushes it open. Behind the truck, strewn across the grass, is a more alarming and disturbing scene than the blazing pyre of metal.

"Oh my God," I yell, running past the fire.

Three bodies are splayed out in the grass, their blood staining the lawn for yards in every direction. Some is even caked onto the side of the blue paint of their cover position, boiling over and baking in the heat of the fire.

We inspect the bodies, checking to see whether we can aid anyone who's been hurt, not knowing immediately who it could be or how this happened.

"Who is it!?" Greg yells frantically.

"I . . . I don't know," I say, flipping one of them over so I can see their face. They're riddled with bullet holes, small circles of red that blemish the front of their clothes in more places than they could probably feel. Their mouths are slack, making their final screams permanent. I don't recognize a single one of them. But I do recognize the way they dress and, even more so, the way they smell. The mixture of body odor, decay, and fluids from unspeakable activities, mixed into a cocktail of filth and evil that gags the lungs. They're burners.

A blur of motion catches in my periphery. Uncle Jimmy sprints down the lawn with a fire extinguisher in hand. He pulls the pin and sprays a dense white foam onto the flames consuming my truck. In a few seconds, the fire's out, replaced by light wisps of steam from the frothy retardant. It's like the spirit of the fire is vacating this plane, off to create destruction elsewhere.

My father treks down the driveway with a gun in hand, scanning from side to side as though he's unsure the area is safe yet.

"Is everyone all right?" I ask as he approaches.

"Oh, we're just fine. Can't say the same for these fellas." My dad gestures to the men on the ground with his gun, like he's more than ready to fire a few more rounds into them.

"What the hell happened?" JJ asks, a look of concern on his face.

"They showed up about forty-five minutes after y'all left. Parked their truck at the gate and tried sneaking in by throwin' that rug over the barbwire. Luckily, Jimmy spotted them, and we armed ourselves and unloaded on them before they could even make it to the dummy house."

Greg looks down at the bodies. "Who are they?"

"I don't know who they were, but they're dead now." Dad spits at them.

"They're burners," I say.

"What?" they all respond at once.

"Burners. Piece-of-shit humans who were pieces of shit before the world ended, but now they get to be bigger pieces of shit because there's no one to stop them. Ya know, burners?" I look back and forth between their faces.

"Why not just call them pieces of shit?" Greg tilts his head.

"It doesn't really have a nice ring to it," I say.

"We've never seen anyone like these guys before." JJ pulls his lips in.

"Well, they were all over Chicago, and they're a hundred times more dangerous than any biter. For a while there, I actually thought they were infected too, like a crazed biter that just wanted to cause violence but still had somewhat of a functioning brain. But I realized it was even worse than I had imagined. There's nothing wrong with these people—not medically, anyway. They're just evil."

"The good news is, that was Chicago. I think we're pretty safe way out here since no one lives near your dad for miles," Greg chimes in.

"He's right," Blake says, finally joining the conversation. He holds his arm down low at his side. "We haven't run into anyone like that on our scavenges," he adds.

"Maybe that was true, but it's not anymore."

"But then why are they here now?" JJ asks.

"The big cities are picked over, so—"

"They'll be searching," Blake says, finishing my sentence.

"Exactly, and with winter coming, they'll be desperate. There are tons of summer homes all over rural Wisconsin that are likely just sitting there, wide open for the taking. There's also freshwater lakes, and most people probably went south because of the weather. That makes this a prime area for the worst of them."

"They must have been watching the place," Dad says, looking out beyond the road, searching the horizon. "It can't be a coincidence that they hit not long after four of our people left."

"No, I'm sure it wasn't." Uncle Jimmy stands alongside my dad.

"We need to fortify the perimeter even more then. Our fences were meant to keep out biters, not a bunch of determined humans with weapons." Dad exhales sharply through his nose.

"I'll get started on adding the electric current to the fence along the road," Uncle Jimmy says.

"Good." My dad nods. "And I've got plenty of barbed wire and sheet metal. We should be able to build the fence up a bit higher as well as add a few traps. It's gonna be a lot of work but—"

"We don't have a choice," I interject.

"No . . . we don't." Dad shakes his head and stares at the ground. I'm sure he's losing himself in thought. Playing out all the awful scenarios that could befall each and every one of us, given the attack and the new threat. But now isn't the time for him to worry. It's time for us to act.

"Hey," Dad says, looking at the four of us. "How'd the run go? Find any insulin?" His face is excited; he's hoping to hear the only good answer that we could possibly give.

We exchange uncomfortable glances, a somber silence filling the space between us as we decide who will be the first to speak, unsure of how to deliver the mixture of news we need to share. In the time this takes to play out, my dad's and uncle's faces have already turned to disappointment, assuming the worst when we aren't quick to answer.

"We did," I finally say, watching as the two men in front of me light back up with joy.

"That's amazing! How much?"

"Not sure exactly, as I don't know Elaine's prescribed dosage, but I would say at least eight months' worth."

"That buys us a lot of time to find her more," Uncle Jimmy says, nodding as he proudly pats his boys on the shoulder. "You did a good thing."

Dad studies our faces, realizing there's more to our story. "Then why do you all look like someone took a piss in your cereal this morning?"

We can't hide the reality of what happened to Blake. I step forward to tell them the bad news, but Blake steps around me, pushing past my shoulder. He pulls his sleeve up over his wound and holds it out for them to see. "This is why."

Their faces run through a gauntlet of emotions, from surprise to horror, to worry.

"What happened?" Dad asks. His eyes swim with tears, and his lip trembles slightly, as though Blake's fate has already been sealed.

"I got bit," he says, stating the obvious.

"How?" Dad pries, needing to know the circumstances that led to it.

"There was a biter in one of the rooms I missed. Casey and I were making our exit, and it lunged at her. There was no time to react, so I pushed her out of the way, and then this happened." He flicks his head at the wound and gives me a fleeting look.

I squint but quickly relax my eyes so no one notices. Blake's lying about what happened, and I don't know why, but I decide not to say anything . . . for now.

"Blake," my father says in a strained whisper, his voice cracking as he looks at his second-in-command like a wounded puppy.

"Dale." Blake grabs the back of my dad's neck and tugs at him slightly, jarring him from the sudden force. "I'm gonna be fine. Casey says I have a sixty-six percent chance of not turning into a biter. The odds are in my favor, so there's no need to get ahead of ourselves." He lets go of him and walks away from all of us, stopping to turn back once. He opens his mouth like he's about to say something profound or kind, but at the last second, he changes his mind and continues walking.

"Where're you going?" I call out.

"Down to the holding cells."

"You don't need to do that yet," Dad says. He looks to me, double-checking his instructions. "Right, Casey?"

"Blake, you still have twenty-plus hours before there's even a possibility of turning into a Nome, so you don't have to rush down there. Not yet, anyway," I yell.

"Get yourself cleaned up, have a nice warm meal, and then you can head down there tonight, buddy." Dad nods.

Blake seems to be debating whether it's even worth the bother. It's almost like being in limbo, knowing he has to go down there eventually. He finally seems to agree, walking back toward us. "Fine, I'll help you guys clean up this mess, then I'll do all that."

Given that his fate is the one hanging in the balance, no one argues with his plan for the evening.

"I'm gonna run this insulin up to Elaine," I say, already heading to the house as a murmur of encouragement swirls around me, sending me off for the immediate medical need.

I glance back and watch Blake. My heart skips a beat at what he's going through. I know it all too well. He'll start feeling sick at the twelve-hour mark, and then hopefully, he'll share the same fate I did. Blake leans down, grabs the legs of a burner, and starts dragging it through the grass. JJ joins him, picking up the other half by its arms—the two of them hoisting the body into the air as it hangs like a slack tightrope.

"Where should we bury them?" JJ asks, looking to either my dad or his.

"We're not," my dad says without missing a beat. "They don't deserve a burial."

Uncle Jimmy and Dad jointly pick up another body, lifting it.

"They wanted to see the world burn . . . well, they can be the kindling." Dad punctuates his hatred for them by spitting at the corpse.

Chapter 27

My teeth clamp down, ripping through the perfectly crisp yet tender flesh. Golden liquid trapped in the embryotic dome erupts in my mouth, dribbling down my chin. Bacon, egg, and cheese toast is an incredible treat, and it was afforded to Blake this morning since it might be his last breakfast with his memories intact. As his dedicated guard, I too am reaping the rewards.

"You know you don't have to sit down here and watch me." Blake stares through the bars of his cell, a slight look of disgust on his face, likely from the way I'm unabashedly eating with reckless abandon.

"I know. But I want to," I answer with a mouth full of food.

"Well . . . thanks. That's actually really—"

"Especially since my dad is treating you like you're on death row with these decadent meals. He has Elaine making you all the best stuff in reserve. I mean, look at this." I hold up another slice of toast topped with bacon and an over-easy egg, smothered in melted cheese, and speckled with salt and pepper. "This is a masterpiece." I dive in for another bite, as big as my mouth is capable of.

"I'm glad you're enjoying yourself at my expense."

I nod along with my heavy chewing. "Mm-hmm."

Blake gets to his feet and crosses his cell. Gripping his hands around the bars, he leans his forehead against the cold metal, eyeing me suspiciously with a raised brow. His face is flushed, sweat dripping from his hairline. He looks terrible, and I'm sure feels that way too, but he hasn't complained once.

"Or maybe," Blake says, "you're hoping I turn into one of those monsters, and you just wanna be here for the show."

"Nah. I'm actually hoping you lose your memories."

"What? Why?" He jerks his head back.

"So you'll forget how much of an asshole you are." I smile up at him, trying to make my dimpled cheeks as prominent as possible.

He chuckles and looks down at his watch, noting the time and doing a quick calculation based on when he was bitten. "It looks like you'll only have to wait about twenty more minutes to see if your wish comes true."

I notice the worry lines on his face, and my smile fades. My jocular attitude and attempts to keep the situation light are waning in their efficacy as the nearness of his fate is beginning to take hold. His bright eyes have seemed to dull, darting in random patterns, likely in lockstep with the frantic swirling of his thoughts. I set my plate down and wipe my hands and face with a napkin, composing myself.

"Are you scared?" I ask in a serious tone. I know I am, but I don't say that part out loud.

I can tell by his expression that he wants to answer no. He wants to play tough and act like this is nothing compared to what he's been through in his life. But not even he can fake it through the gravity of what might happen next. "Yeah," he says just above a whisper, like he doesn't want me to hear it.

"Don't be. I'm sure you'll be fine."

"Why's that?"

"Because only the good die young, so you're gonna live forever."

He stares at me; his face is unmoving. He starts to lightly cough, holding it in his throat, but soon the coughing breaks free. His mouth opens, and he erupts in a full, deep laugh as he takes some comfort in my wit.

Blake sits on his cot and finally starts eating. His runny yolk has congealed, but he doesn't seem to care. He checks his watch several times in between bites. I can't take my eyes off him because I'm scared, and deep down, I'm worried I'm gonna lose him. I study his face and eyes as they go through the torturous uncertainty. He meets my gaze every few seconds. There's a fear in his eyes that I wish I could cure for him, but not everything can be fixed.

As much as I've joked about a negative outcome befalling him, I do hope he has the same good fortune I did. I glance down at my own scar from when I was bitten, realizing I didn't go through any of the same agony of waiting that Blake is because I didn't know any better. I thought a deranged patient, hopped up on meds or in a fugue state, bit me, and that was that. What he's experiencing is far worse. We only fear what we're uncertain of, and right now, that's Blake's future. His life hangs in the balance.

"You know at the hospital, when I froze?" he says, pulling me from my thoughts.

I lift my head and watch him stare off at the side wall of his cell. It's the same look he had in the hospital, and it's like he's standing right back where he was.

"I couldn't forget . . . even if I wanted to," I say.

Blake shakes his head, and tears run down his reddened cheeks. Suddenly, he slaps himself with both hands at the same time, blowing out a heavy stream of air.

"I knew him," he admits.

I stand and walk to his cell, passing my arms through the bars, letting them hang down on their own. "Who?" I ask, not fully following what he's saying.

"The biter. The one that bit me."

"What do you mean you *knew* him?"

Blake stares into my eyes with such an intense gaze, it's like he wants me to see into his soul, so he doesn't have to say it himself. "He was my friend. We were in the SEALs together. His name was Grant, and he saved my ass more than once, and vice versa. You can't really get closer than a bond like that." I can see from the look on his face that these moments of life and death, someone else putting themselves on the line for you, are playing out in the theater of his mind.

He tightly presses his eyes shut, as though he's trying to squeeze the memories out, not wanting to relive something so painful. Blake wipes away the tears and glances up at the ceiling, inhaling and exhaling deeply. "Grant was in town visiting. We'd gone out drinking to blow off some steam. The next day, he was feeling like shit. I chalked it up to him being hungover, since I wasn't much better off myself. I told him to just take it easy, pound some fluids, and I'd get us something nice and greasy to soak up the aftermath of the booze. But his hangover wouldn't go away, even into the next day, and then things started getting really weird. His memory was starting to go to shit, and I don't mean like he was blackout the night before, which he was, and couldn't remember how we got home, but I mean . . . he couldn't remember my name, or his. I panicked, and I took him to the hospital."

"That was the right move," I say.

"Yeah." He turns to the far wall of the cell, his back facing me. "Well, maybe not." Blake pounds his fist against the cinder block, holding it there. I can see his arm begin to shake, like he's trying to push right through it, letting free the guilt trapped inside him.

"I was waiting in the lobby. The doctors said they needed to run some tests, but something was off. Nurses and doctors started rushing in and out. At first, they just seemed hurried and busy, but then their urgency morphed into fear, and I knew something big was going down. That's when I saw my first one. A patient stumbled out of the double doors covered in blood, and he looked . . ." Blake turns to me, shaking his head. His gaze falls to the ground, searching for a description for a thing that doesn't exist. "I'd never seen anything like it. Seconds later, the hospital erupted in chaos. There were screams all around me, people running for exits, some bloodied, some still untouched. More and more of those *things* came pouring out from where my friend had been taken. I figured he was dead." Blake walks to his cell door, taking my hands in his. "It wasn't until the other night at dinner, when you told us about the different outcomes, that I realized if I had known better, I could have saved him."

A new torrent of tears begins to stream down his face as he squeezes my hands. His grip is actually too much, sending pain shooting up my arms, but I'm more than happy to endure it in the moment. It all makes sense now. That's why he was so upset with me, why he stormed off during dinner. He went from thinking he had left his dead friend to thinking he might have left someone who had a chance.

"That's why I didn't want to believe you. Because believing you meant that I was a coward and selfish and evil in a way I couldn't bear to deal with. It meant that at the slightest inkling of danger, I only cared about me. It meant that I left my friend behind. I wouldn't even be standing here if it weren't for him. I'd be lying dead in a compound over in Syria, rotting in the sand with my head cut off or my legs blown halfway across the country. When danger came screaming toward us and stuck itself between Grant and me, he looked it head-on and chose my life. When the same happened in that hospital . . . I ran."

I squeeze his hands, guiding them up, hoping that his eyes will follow, and they do. "You didn't know. You couldn't possibly have known."

Blake tries to pull away, but I yank him right back, keeping him engaged. He can beat himself up for being a jerk to me, but I won't let him beat himself up for this.

"Hey, I did the same thing as you, Blake."

He cocks his head back, both confused and intrigued, unsure of how anything in my life could be equivalent to what he did.

"I worked in a hospital, remember? I was on shift the night everything went to hell, and when my patients started turning and people were dying, you know what I did?"

My eyes bounce back and forth, waiting for him to reply with the obvious answer, but he just shakes his head instead.

"I ran. I ran right out the exit and never looked back. I left every single one of my patients, every single one of my coworkers, every single person on my team. I left them to fend for themselves. And if I wouldn't have run . . . I'd be dead right now. I was lucky that I only came away with this." I lift my arm, showing him the scar again. The jagged curve of someone's teeth, like a dental mold etched into my skin that's softened over into a paler spot, a reverse tattoo, taking the color with it.

Blake holds his bite mark up next to mine. They're in nearly identical spots on our arms, and he looks between them both, the gravity of the situation sinking in.

"I know you're probably right. But I'm still not proud of what I did. I didn't even try to save him."

"Hey." I squeeze his arm to jar him out of his wallowing. "You don't have to be proud of what you did. But you do have to give yourself grace. There's no changing what happened, so you just need to be okay with it."

He stares back at me and nods, not saying anything. I'm sure he won't be able to easily forgive himself, but in a few minutes, it might not be a problem he ever has to deal with again. Blake tilts his head to the side to read the time on his watch. "Only five minutes left."

"Would you prefer to be alone for this?"

"I want you to stay."

"Okay then. I'll stay."

Silence fills the room for what feels like an eternity, the minutes melting away as slowly as an ice cube in a refrigerator, just a couple of degrees above where it could hold itself together forever. Blake takes a deep breath and closes his eyes.

"Wait," I say.

His eyes burst back open. "What!?"

"You said your friend lost his memories, right?" My fingers bounce back and forth in front of me like I'm visualizing my thoughts dancing around in my head.

"Yeah."

"So he was a Nome."

"I guess so."

"But he was a biter when you saw him in the hospital on our run." I'm pacing in front of the cell, trying to connect the dots in this scenario, more talking out loud than I am to Blake.

"I mean, obviously. That's how I got this." Blake holds up his arm, as if I need a reminder as to what happened.

"Hmmm." I start massaging my scalp, prodding my brain to work out what I think I've come to realize.

"What is it? What are you thinking?"

"I saw patients turn into Nomes, and I saw patients turn into biters, but the biters weren't Nomes, or vice versa."

"What's your point? We know that both things can happen."

"Right, but what if when a Nome is bit, they turn into a biter? No matter what. Like, the additional infection instantly overloads the system and deteriorates whatever's left, devolving them even further." I stop pacing, letting the idea settle in.

"Have you ever seen that happen before?"

"No. Anytime I would see a Nome get attacked in the city, it was always by multiple biters at once. They would be ripped apart and eaten on the spot, so they never had a chance to turn." A light bulb goes off in my head. The herd of biters that came and attacked the compound—it never made any sense to me. That many turning into biters? It's statistically impossible.

"The bus!" I yell out.

"What about the bus?" Blake isn't following, and I can tell my ramblings are more confusing than they are helpful.

"If the bus had been full of regular people and someone turned, the biter would have just attacked as many as it possibly could while all the others fled. It would be days before the survivors turned, and they'd be scattered all over the place. But"—I begin pacing again—"if the bus were attacked by multiple biters, it'd be just as chaotic with people fleeing and dying. Still impossible. Unless . . ."

I run to the cell and grip the bars, pressing my face right in between two of them. "What if that bus was full of Nomes and only one biter? The Nomes would be so confused by the attack. They'd be trying to flee, toppling over one another, especially if the bus door was locked. Based on what happened to your friend, all the Nomes would turn into biters."

Blake tilts his head. "But how would all the Nomes get on the bus? And who was driving?"

"Someone must have been transporting them on purpose, and something went very wrong."

"Who would want a bunch of random Nomes?"

"Someone who wants bait or free labor or an army." The realities that they haven't seen out here are astounding, a mixture of a curse and a blessing. On the one hand, they haven't witnessed Nomes being used as slaves for labor and personal enjoyment or prodded around to lure others out. That also means they aren't prepared. But trouble is coming, whether we like it or not. I can feel it in my bones.

I turn to Blake, almost forgetting he's still in the room. His forehead is beading with sweat, glistening from the overhead light in the cell. He swallows hard, far too often for what is normal, as he stares down at his watch.

"Are you okay?" I soften my tone, realizing that all my hypothesizing is not doing anything to help take his mind off what might happen.

"I'm fine." He wipes the sweat away reflexively, not pulling his gaze from his watch. "I just have a headache." Blake taps the watch face, taking in deep, heavy breaths, one after another. "About a minute now."

"It's gonna be okay." I force a smile, trying to remain positive, but he still won't break from the staring contest he has going with his watch.

I return to the cell door, reaching through the bars. His hand is close enough to grab, so I draw him toward me, breaking his trance.

Blake stands up straight, hesitating, like he wants to go back to his way of doing things, but instead, he pivots his weight and comes closer, lacing his fingers through mine.

"Thank you," is all he says, and I only smile in response at first, not knowing any words that could possibly comfort him in this moment, but then it dawns on me. If I were about to lose all my memories, what is the thing I would want most?

"What's your best memory?" I ask, watching as he looks at me like I asked him a pop question. A mixture of terror at revealing a response, coupled with the uncertainty of it not being the right one.

"What? Why?" he asks, clearly unsure whether this is something genuine and real between us, something that'll give him even the smallest semblance of relief prior to the numbers on his watch face switching over, or if I'm just using this moment for my own enjoyment, a private torture show for one.

"In case you lose them."

He looks down the bridge of his nose, quickly wiping away a tear that formed and was ready to fall. I can see the inner workings of him searching for the memory, the nerve endings poring through his hard drive like two fingers dancing along the contents of a filing cabinet.

"So I can remind you of your favorite one."

A smile slowly spreads across his face, a sense of relief relaxing the veins near his temples. "That's easy," he says.

"What is it?" I ask.

"It's you."

The warmth of excitement from the increased blood flow is making him glow in a nervous hue, and I can't tell if it's because he's anticipating his own teasing punch line or if it's because he's letting his true feelings show.

"Wow," I say in minor shock of his admission. "I didn't realize there was a fourth outcome from the infection."

"Huh?" His face instantly loses its glow, a coal removed from the fire, thrown into a frigid lake. "What do you mean?" His tone is now clinical, like a patient asking a doctor the definition of a medical term.

"Growing new organs. It would be an incredible medical anomaly, but I guess it's possible, since you just grew a heart."

He shakes his head, but the smile on his face betrays any sense of anger or annoyance. "Oh, come on. I already had a heart."

"Where?" I tease, reaching through the bar and poking at his hard pecs.

He laughs and grabs my hand, taking it in his. He looks down at me with the laser focus of someone being cross-examined in court. "I'm serious, Casey. And you'd better remind me if I forget."

I don't question the veracity of his statement and instead agree, not wanting to deny his potentially final conscious request. "I will."

He releases my hand and lets his body fall back into the wall, slinking down to the floor, wrapping his arms around his knees. My brows knit together with worry. I crouch, watching him.

Blake takes a deep breath through his nose, his lips shifting in such small movements that I can't make out what he's saying, but by the rhythm and pattern, I can guess he's counting. And then he stops. His forehead falls between his knees, and he goes still.

"Blake?" I say, needing to know whether he's okay. "Blake?"

Finally, he lifts his head from its resting spot and leans it back against the wall, rolling his head up and down like he's giving himself a scalp massage. He pushes off the cinder block and stands, looking around the cell like he's getting his bearings. When his gaze lands on me, his face twists up, not out of fear or shock, but out of curiosity.

"Blake?" I reach my hand through the bars, stretching it as far as I can, my fingers spread wide, trying to claw the air for just an extra inch. He takes my hand in his, shaking it up and down like we're associates in a boardroom.

"Blake, are you all right?"

"Who are you?" he asks.

My heart plummets down into my stomach, splashing acid everywhere as a burn begins to radiate throughout my core. I let go of his hand and stumble back in shock.

"Where am I?" he asks, peering up at the ceiling and turning in circles, his steps choppy and frantic. I can sense that panic is about to set in. I've seen this with many dementia patients or people coming out of heavy narcotics, and despite how heartbroken I am, I need to be there for him, to keep him calm. His entire life just changed for the worse, and I'm gutted that it happened to coincide with me realizing that I actually care about him.

"What am I doing in here!?" He looks like a fish trying to frantically find its way out of an aquarium, swimming beneath the water of my tears.

"I'm so sorry, Blake," I whisper as I wipe my tears away, not wanting to worry him any more than he probably is.

I walk to his cell, calling out his name until he settles down enough to focus on me and what I'm trying to tell him.

"I'm so, so sorry, Blake," I say, unable to hold back my sadness any longer.

"Who's Blake?" he asks.

I reach my hands out and he grabs them reflexively, holding me by the wrists like he isn't sure what to do with these "things" that just entered his space. I glance down at my feet. My tears sit atop the concrete floor, unable to penetrate the uniform, smooth surface, no different from the effect they have on the husk of the man standing before me.

Blake lets go of my wrists and collapses to the floor. A burst of laughter erupts from his mouth and rocks through me, like a sound wave sent from a bullhorn. He rocks back and forth, grabbing his sides, chuckling even louder.

"You fucking dick!"

"You should have seen your face!" He points at me, howling in amusement.

I look around for something to throw at him. Spotting my breakfast plate, I grab the hash brown patty from it and tomahawk it through the bars, hitting him square in the face. Pieces fly around the cell and a grease spot now glistens on his slightly reddened skin, but it does little to stop his fit of joy.

"By the way, Pearson, I accept your apology." He's still beaming, tickled with joy at his prank.

I squeeze my eyes tight, shaking my head in tiny tremors. "I wasn't apologizing to you for anything. I was apologizing for your situation."

"That's not how I took it." He relaxes into a smug state of bliss, as if every word of this exchange is like a drop of honey hitting his tongue.

"Whatever." I turn on my heel and head for the door, no longer feeling the need to watch over him . . . at least for now.

"Where are you going?" he calls out, the coolness of his voice now replaced with a mix of genuine curiosity and concern that his plaything is leaving early.

"To inform everyone that you're not a Nome but that you are, in fact, still an asshole."

Chapter 28

Pushing the door open at the top of the stairs, I find everyone either seated or mulling around the kitchen and living room, waiting for news on Blake. All heads swivel in my direction at the sound of my arrival.

My dad immediately rises from his chair, taking a step toward me, his eyes full of worry. "How is he?"

"I've got some good news and some bad news," I say, letting out a sigh. "Good news, he didn't become a Nome. Bad news, he's still a dick."

A sense of relief washes over the room, with a few people stifling laughs.

"Casey!" Elaine chides, holding back a small smile.

Dad gives me a stern look, but it fades away just as quickly as it appeared.

"What? Blake literally pretended to lose his memory. Who does that?" I roll my eyes.

Greg and JJ burst out laughing and high-five one another, sharing the same sentiment over Blake's antics.

"Classic," Greg says, still chuckling.

"So he's in the clear now?" Elaine tilts her head to the side, her eyes practically pleading with me to say yes.

"Not yet. In another twelve hours or so, we'll find out if he turns into . . . one of those monsters."

"I'd argue he already is one," Tessa calls from the couch. It garners a mix of laughs and disappointing looks. Her mother swats her leg, clearly unamused.

"Oww," Tessa groans in response.

I force a tight smile, finding both the humor and the sadness in the situation. I really don't know what the odds are either way. Was I one of the lucky ones? Will Blake be just as lucky? Only time will tell. I walk to Elaine, who's washing dishes at the sink. The color in her face has returned, and she looks so much better.

"How are you doing?" I ask in a low voice.

I haven't had much of a chance to check in on her after we got back from the hospital run, aside from administering her insulin. There are tears in her eyes, but they're not sad ones. They're grateful ones. Elaine wipes her hands on a towel and takes mine in hers, patting the top of it.

"More than fine, sweetie. You saved my life."

I smile softly, knowing it's all I ever wanted to do. I wasn't able to save my own mother's life, but to save Elaine's feels restorative in a way—like the guilt I've carried for far too long is starting to fade.

"Just returning the favor," I say, full well meaning it. Elaine was there for me after my mother passed, in ways no one else could be. She might not have saved my life. But she saved me. Elaine smiles and squeezes my hand, knowing exactly what I mean.

My dad clears his throat, addressing the room. "We should get back to work," he says, his voice deep and commanding. "This place needs to be a fortress, because we can't survive if we're not safe." Dad slowly scans the room, and he's met with nods all around. Everyone knows what's at stake.

As much as he's spent his life and a huge chunk of mine preparing for the end of the world, there are some things you can never truly be ready for. This is one of them.

"Do you think there's more people out there like the ones that showed up yesterday?" Helen asks. I haven't seen her since Chris's funeral. She and her family have kept to themselves, locked away in their cabins, dealing with the grief of losing a husband, a father, a son-in-law.

She hugs her boys, sitting quietly on either side of her, a little tighter. I don't know her well at all, having only spoken to her a few minutes. But I can see she's different now that she's lost her husband. That's what death does. It changes you.

Dad looks to me and nods, his way of saying *Go ahead, speak up*. I want to lie to her, especially with her kids in the room and that terrified look plastered on her face. But I can't. Lying won't protect her or her children. If anything, it'll put them in harm's way. They have to know so they can be prepared.

"There's more out there just like them. Whether they show up here or not isn't a question of if. It's a question of when."

Helen's chest deflates as she lets all the air out of her lungs, making room for the answer I gave, which she most definitely didn't want to hear. But it's the one she needed to hear.

"We have to prepare for the worst if we want the best outcome," my dad says. "Any questions?"

Tessa gets to her feet and shakes her head, crossing the room to me. "You all right?" she whispers.

I nod in response. I think the seriousness of my words and flatness in my tone have her worried. But I'm not worried about me. I'm worried about Blake. I let out a small sigh, hoping in twelve hours, he'll be the same asshole he's always been.

"I don't have a question, but I do have an announcement," Greg says, standing from the couch.

"Okayyyy." Dad's voice is full of hesitation as he draws the word out into three syllables. He knows it's never a good idea to give Greg the floor.

Tessa and I exchange an amused glance, and she bumps her shoulder into me. Whatever this is, it isn't going to be serious, but maybe that's what we need right now. A little Greg palate cleanser for the shit show we're in.

"Molly," he says, turning to face her. She's seated in the sofa chair, wearing a scowl, purposefully looking away from him.

"I know you've heard some rumors recently from some gossipers"—Greg shoots a glare in my direction—"about me thinking you're only a one-night stand. And I'll admit I did think that, but only because I was scared, scared to love someone and scared to let someone into my heart." He places a hand against his chest. "Yesterday when Blake was savagely bit, I had an epiphany about us. I wasn't scared to love you, Molly. I was scared to lose you."

Molly slowly turns her head, his words pulling her to meet his gaze. She's still wearing the scowl, but it's fading ever so slightly as her eyes begin to develop a sheen.

"And I realized I'd rather be full of fear with you by my side than the bravest man in the whole world without you. You're not my one-night stand." Greg plants one knee on the floor. His hand disappears into the pocket of his jeans, re-emerging a moment later with a massive diamond ring. Pinched between his thumb and finger, he extends it to her. "Molly Ronan, will you be my forever-night stand?"

Aunt Julie gasps, while Tessa and I try to stifle our laughter. JJ doesn't look impressed, but he grins. Most everyone else is shocked by this odd and very sudden declaration of love.

"There's no way she says yes to that," Tessa whispers.

"Absolutely not," I whisper back.

Molly leaps from her chair, jumping into Greg's arms. "Yes! Yes! Yes! A thousand times, yes!" she squeals.

He lifts her off the floor, planting kisses on her cheeks and neck. The room erupts in a slow, confused clap as Greg sets her back down and slides the diamond ring, which looks a size too big, onto her slender finger. She admires it for a moment before kissing him. His hands run up and down her body. Hers do the same to his as they suck face, moaning through their sloppy, wet kisses.

"Oh God," I say, averting my eyes.

"Gross," Tessa adds.

"Greg, that's enough!" Aunt Julie yells.

The newly engaged couple separates from one another, panting and out of breath from their make-out session.

"Sorry, Mom. I can't help myself around my fiancéeee," Greg says, extending the pronunciation of the word as he double raises his brows at Molly.

"OMG, I'm a fiancée," she squeals with excitement.

Aunt Julie and Uncle Jimmy peel themselves from their seats to congratulate Greg and Molly.

"And you're my family," Molly says as she hugs my aunt and uncle. She and Greg continue making the rounds, embracing each and every person.

"Congrats," I say when Greg reaches me.

"Thanks. It would have never happened without you, cuz," he says, patting me on the back.

"I am not taking responsibility for this."

"Where the hell did you get that rock, Greg?" Tessa chimes in. Her eyes keep darting to Molly's hand and what has to be a three-carat diamond on her finger. The light seeping through the window catches it, making it glint.

"Found it on a doctor's corpse at the hospital after I vomited. Couldn't let it go to waste."

Shocked, my mouth parts, but it shouldn't, because nothing Greg does should surprise me. "That's disgusting," is all I can say.

"No, Casey. It's love." He tilts his head and smirks. "And honestly, it felt meant to be. Kismet, as they say. When I was in that hospital, I couldn't stop thinking about Molly. Everything reminded me of her."

"Really?" I arch a brow. "We're talking about the same hospital? The one full of dead, decaying, maggot-covered bodies and brain-eating biters."

"That's right." He nods. "Everything reminded me of her. That annoying generator noise. Molly. The squeaky wheel on the gurney JJ and I snagged. Molly. The flickering lights in the cafeteria that gave me a splitting headache. Molly. So when I saw that ring, I was like . . . that's for Molly."

"Wow," Tessa says, trying to contain her laughter. "That's really special."

"I thought so too. Thanks, Tessa." Greg doesn't pick up on her sarcasm.

I feel a tap on my shoulder, and I glance over it to find my dad with his lips pressed firmly together. He holds out his wrist, noting the time and that it's passing us by.

We don't need to speak to know what we're both thinking. We've got two countdowns. One ends less than twelve hours from now. That one's for Blake. The other . . . we have no idea how long that countdown will go on for. Could end tomorrow. Could end a month from now. More burners will come. They want to see the whole world burn. That includes my father's compound, and the only way to stave off the flames is to be ready for the fire.

I meet Dad's gaze and nod, confirming that we're on the exact same page for once.

Chapter 29

"Casey! Casey!" A loud whisper finds its way into my ear canal, crawling up into my brain and behind my eyes. The pale-yellow light of the basement creeps its way in, waking me. I find myself lying on a thin mattress that provided little to no support during the night, and my back is making that evident as I sit up, using my elbows to shift my hips backward. I stretch my arms into the air, working the stiffness out of my body before placing my hands on the floor. The cold concrete bites at my soft palms, zapping me into a state of alertness.

"Did you sleep down here?" Blake's voice pulls me up even further as I acclimate to my environment, remembering that I fell asleep on the basement floor, instead of in my room. I stand and stretch even more, hoping the pain I'm feeling will go away, but it holds fast, throbbing in dull waves.

"Yeah." My voice cracks as I reach my arms up toward the ceiling yet again, spreading my fingers as wide as they'll go.

"Why?" Blake's tone is a mixture of confusion and anticipation, as if he's hoping for a certain response but expecting another.

I take a second to respond, not sure of the answer myself. "I just figured . . . you wouldn't wanna be alone."

"You didn't have to do that," he says out loud, but I can hear through his words the true sentiment, which is that he's glad I did.

"I know."

"You could've had our room all to yourself. Hell, you could've even pushed our beds together and made one big mega bed. Slept like a queen." Blake is staring off as though he is daydreaming about the idea of getting a good night's rest in a massive bed himself.

"Came up with that idea pretty quickly. Is that what you used to do before I showed up?" I cross my arms, waiting for his response.

He shakes his head, laughing a bit before answering. "No, I got used to a tiny single bed in the military. Anything bigger is just wasted on me."

"Well, it wouldn't have been the same without you in it, and by that, I mean miserable and . . ." I force a laugh as my voice trails off and silence replaces my tired banter. We both know we're putting off talking about the elephant in the room, the inevitable deadline fast approaching.

"How're you feeling?" The doctor side of me kicks in, wanting to assess his health changes from yesterday to gauge the direction he's heading in. I'm not sure if there are any actual indicators as to whether a person is going to change into a biter, but it's worth trying to find out. I mean, we really don't know anything, minus my theory on Nomes auto changing into biters when bitten. Even that, I want to keep to us because I don't know for sure, and there's no sense in scaring everyone else. It could be something we deal with a long way down the road, but right now, I'm only focused on today and Blake.

"Fine. I mean, I feel off. I'm sweating bullets, as if I were sitting in a sauna rather than in a cold basement." He tugs on his T-shirt to air it out. "And I've got a splitting headache, but other than that, I feel great. Plus, I'm not a biter, so I can't really complain now, can I?"

I pull my lips into a tight smile and nod, trying to remain positive and encouraging of the current situation. But I can see how red his face is, the sweat beads forming on his forehead and throughout his buzzed hair, like drops of dew on the morning grass. The veins near his temples are even more prominent than before. They're pulsating, his body trying to feed blood to his brain, quelling the headache that won't subside. He gets to his feet and stretches his arms over his head before bringing them back down to his sides.

"It's not long now, is it?" he asks, looking to me with a solemn face.

Blake surrendered his watch to me last night, unable to deal with the torture of constantly checking the time ticking away, creeping in on his binary fate.

I glance down at his watch hanging loosely around my wrist, a couple of sizes too big. The numbers tell me there're less than ten minutes before the story of Blake's life either adds a new, harrowing chapter or comes to an abrupt halt.

"No . . . not long," I say, keeping my voice calm.

He nods in response, biting down on his lip as he closes his eyes and lets out a heavy sigh.

"By the way . . ." I add.

He snaps his eyes open in response.

"If you pretend to turn into a biter, I'm just gonna shoot you in the face. No hesitation whatsoever." I lift my shirt, showing off the pistol tucked in the waistband of my pants. "So no jokes this time."

"Oh, really?" Blake walks to his cell door, slipping his arms through the metal bars and letting them rest there. He never takes his eyes off me. "You think you could do that? You think you have the stones to just shoot me." He snaps his fingers, loud and quick. "Just like that."

"How do you think I got so good with my throwing stars?"

Blake cocks his head to the side, waiting for my answer.

"I pictured your face on the target. That's why I never miss."

He can't help but smile. "Wow. All those years of practice, and you were thinking of me the whole time." He cups his hands together, tucking them under his chin, batting his eyelashes.

"Thinking of killing you, yes." My voice is stern, not letting his charm get the upper hand.

"Still counts." He shrugs slightly. "I was in your thoughts."

I walk to the cell, ready to swat at one of his arms or give it a slight tug, just to mess with him, but the closer I get, the more I can see how badly he's holding up.

"Blake, are you sure you're all right?" Sweat drips down his skin, collecting on the tip of his nose and his chin before falling to the floor in large droplets.

"Yeah." He coughs out his answer and uses the sleeve of his shirt to wipe his brow. It's only dry for a second before sweat seeps from his pores again, making his forehead look like a clear night sky speckled with countless glistening lights dazzling their brilliance against one another. He focuses on me, ignoring the effects of whatever's going on inside him. It's clear from the look he's giving me that my face is revealing words I've left unspoken.

"You look worried," Blake says.

He's not wrong. I am worried, and as much as I want to remain optimistic that he'll be fine, assure myself that the worst thing that could happen isn't the thing that's going to happen, I know there are no guarantees. I don't know what his odds are, so I have to assume he has just as good of odds to turn as he does to stay who he is. It's out of my hands, though, and that's the hardest thing to accept, especially as a doctor. I can recall many times staring at the face of a dying patient, knowing their time was coming to an end and having to answer the question every dying patient asks. *Am I going to be okay?* Almost always, we both know the true answer, but that doesn't mean it's the right one. The right answer is to smile, take their hand, and tell them that they're going to be fine.

I swallow hard and blink several times to keep myself from tearing up. "I'm not worried, Blake, because you're going to be fine," I say, forcing the corners of my mouth up just enough to hopefully convince him that I truly believe it.

He smiles, but I know he's not buying it. I'm sure, as a SEAL, he had to watch people die and deliver the same spiel that I gave my patients. Blake clears his throat before he speaks. "In case I turn—"

"You won't," I cut him off.

"In case I do," he powers through, ignoring my objection, "I really want you to know how sorry I am . . . for everything." Blake lowers his head, shaking it for a second before meeting my gaze. I know what he's doing. I've seen it before. It's akin to a deathbed confession. Asking for forgiveness or apologizing for all the wrongs one has accumulated over their lifetime. A final catharsis that's often more for their own sake than that of those around them. Still, I appreciate him saying it with such conviction.

"I know you are." I step toward him, taking his hands in mine and squeezing gently to doubly confirm I believe him. "It's fine, Blake. Really."

He pulls away again. "No, it's not. I need you to know that I never wanted to be your monster. I was just so angry at the world, and I took it out on you. After my mom passed . . ." He pauses, glancing up at the ceiling, like he's trying to see her up there. "After my mom passed, my dad turned to alcohol, and the alcohol made him turn to me. But not in a loving way. There was nothing loving about him when he was drinking. It made him cruel and violent and angry. He was my monster, and then, like these goddamn biters, he turned me into one too." Tears trickle down his cheeks, and he hangs his head, wiping them away with his T-shirt.

"At one point, the summer after junior year, he turned back into my dad, the man I knew before my mom passed. He got sober and so did I, in a way. I didn't have that anger and resentment inside of my body poisoning me anymore. When I started senior year, I was happy, so there was nothing to take out on anyone. I put down my swords, and I got to know you. The more I got to know you, the more I realized I didn't hate you at all."

"Yes, you did, Blake," I say matter-of-factly. "I get you want to apologize, but let's not rewrite history."

"I'm not rewriting it, Casey. I'm telling you the side you never knew about."

I give him a crooked look. "What didn't I know?"

"The night of the party," he says, tilting his head. "I got a call from the sheriff. My dad had been picked up for a DUI. He relapsed, and I knew right then and there that everything was going to go back to the way it was. He'd be my monster again, and I would inevitably be yours. But I couldn't have you close to me because I needed to protect you from him and from me, especially since I had fallen for you."

"You never fell for me, Blake." Tears start to build, and I take a couple of quick deep breaths, holding them in.

His hands grip the bars of the cell, and he bobs his head up and down, signaling that it's the truth.

"Yes, I did, and that's why I had to push you away. I needed you to hate me so much that you'd stay away from me for good, because I didn't trust myself to stay away from you."

I believe what he's saying, but I hate him for making me love him, and I hate him even more for making me hate him. We were basically kids, and I'm sure he had the best of intentions, even though I don't agree with them. But what he endured, between the loss of his mom and his father's downward spiral, I can't imagine. I understand the pain of watching a parent struggle with the loss of the person they loved most in this world. I witnessed my own father swallow his sorrow and put on a brave face for me, knowing that I was grieving too. His grief was masked by a hyperfixation on preparing for the worst-case scenario—the end of the world. Despite hating what my childhood became after my mom passed, I can't imagine my dad not having been there to protect me, guide me, and love me—the only way he knew how. I want to forgive Blake and absolve him of his guilt. If I were on the outside looking in, I would. It would be easy to rationalize his actions with his circumstances, to see and understand exactly how it all played out. But I'm not on the outside. I'm in here with him.

My lip trembles. "You shouldn't have done that, Blake."

"Done what?"

"Made me hate you."

"Why?" he asks.

Blake stares at me with so much intensity, it feels like he could burst right through the steel bars separating us.

"Because you succeeded."

He lowers his head and turns away from me. "It's the one thing I wish I would have failed at," Blake says, his shoulders slumping forward. He rubs at his face like he's trying to wake himself up from a bad dream.

I fall silent, letting the words hang heavy in the air. Although I'm standing still, my heart starts to pound, beating faster and faster, like it could shoot right out of my chest, splat onto the concrete floor for Blake to see. It's as though it's trying to speak louder than my brain, trying to be the voice inside me that cuts through it all.

"Well, you're failing now," I say softly.

His breath hitches and the air in the room all but evaporates. The moment feels frozen, like an entity in the sky hit pause on a remote, stretching out time to allow it to process what's happening. The air slowly returns, passing through Blake's nose via a sniffle. He turns and stands taller, as though a burden has been lifted from his shoulders, making him lighten.

"Blake," I whisper, not wanting to ruin whatever this is. Maybe it's a preamble or maybe it's closure. It may even be both. If my words are small and meek enough, perhaps I can avoid having this moment come crashing down on us. "I don't hate you anymore."

He's unable to hide the growing smile spreading across his face. "So, does that mean you like me?"

"Let's not get ahead of ourselves," I say with a laugh.

He grins, unable to take his eyes off me, until reality dawns on him, the ticking countdown. Blake clears his throat, his face turning serious. "How much time is left?" he asks before twisting his mouth to one side.

"Oh, you're in the clear," I say nonchalantly, as if sharing the weather forecast with him.

"What?" The word comes out breathy and quick, having left his mouth faster than his lips and tongue had time to form a thought. He rushes to the cell door, seizing the bars like a caged animal ready to burst out. "Are you serious?"

"Yup." I nod.

"Since when?"

I glance down at the watch, pretending like I'm calculating the delta of time. "Uhhh, about twenty minutes, give or take." I smirk.

"So I didn't need to confess any of that?"

"Nope, you could have kept all that to yourself," I say, stretching my arms up over my head. I clasp my hands together as I arch my back. Cracking my sternum, I let out a sigh of relief at the sound of my vertebrae crunching.

The confused look on his face tells me he's rapidly contemplating his decision, balancing the raw vulnerability with the catharsis of the lessened guilt. I reach into my pocket and retrieve the metal key to Blake's cell. Inserting it into the keyhole, I pause and lock eyes with him.

"So, Blake, I guess there's just one last thing I want to know."

"What's that?"

"Are you still my monster?"

A small grin starts to grow at the edges of his mouth, barely curling his lips, not even lifting his cheeks high enough to squeeze against his eyes. "Always," he says.

I give the key a heavy twist and pull open the cell door, gazing up at him through my lashes. He's not the same man who went into that cell, at least not to me. Blake's eyes bounce rapidly from side to side, scanning my face, searching for a shared feeling that he knows was there once before. I know it's there too, and I don't think it ever left. It was just camouflaged with hate and resentment. The rush of joy and anticipation, mixed with a new level of understanding, lures his lips to mine like a magnet that's finally found its counterpart.

We breathe in one another as we kiss, like we could suck the life out of each other, but even then, it feels like we'd have another one to live.

I unlock our lips, gliding my cheek along his and then biting the bottom of his earlobe. He moans, and his hands firmly cup my ass.

"I want you," I whisper, hot, heavy breath in his ear.

It's true. I want nothing more in this moment than for Blake to take me. Even if the whole world were burning around me, I would stand in that fire and welcome the scalding heat if this was the last pleasure I felt. I bring my lips back to his, parting my mouth as our tongues pick up right where they left off, swirling in a vortex of anticipated escalation.

"I thought you . . . told me . . . never to . . . touch you . . . again." A couple of words at a time sneak out between the less-than-one-second intervals we're able to stay apart.

"Forget what I said." I grab his shirt, twisting the fabric in my hands, and pull him even tighter into my body. "Touch me everywhere, Blake," I say when my mouth is free to speak the things my heart has been screaming.

For a brief moment everything stands still, our heavy breathing is the only sound in the room, our shoulders rising and falling in slow motion, and then in a flash, he's pulling my shirt up over my head, unable to wait any longer. We've waited long enough. Our mouths collide again, and our labored breaths are the soundtrack that plays as he unclasps my bra, letting it fall to the floor. As I melt into him, I can't help but be frustrated with Blake for messing everything up back in high school. If he had just leaned on me rather than pushing me away, we could have had this moment long ago, and then a thousand more of them.

Blake pauses only to look at me, to really take me in. He can't help but smile as his eyes scan my body. I tug off his shirt. I knew what was under there, but now it's mine. Blake pulls me into him, his hot skin pressed up against mine as he ravages me, unable to get enough. He squeezes my breast, his grip hard due to his strength and longing. I moan from the pressure and find his lips again, kissing and sucking, while my hand ventures down his rigid abs and beneath the elastic band of his joggers. He's rock hard, and it makes me grin, because I know it's for me.

"God, I want you so fucking bad, Casey," he says, breathless.

"I want you too. I want all of you," I say in between kisses.

The palm of his hand slides past my pubic bone, curving under, two fingers disappearing inside me. He's found a new place to touch, and fuck, it feels good. Once the source of my torment, Blake swings violently from the man who once ruined me to the man I now want to ruin me.

He undoes my pants and slides them down my thighs, eager to see and explore more of me. Sinking to his knees, he kisses my most sensitive area through the cotton fabric of my underwear, licking and biting. He's only teasing me, and I'm already breathless. The anticipation is killing me. It's more dangerous than anything I've ever faced. Because if I don't get it, I might just die.

Blake looks up at me, an intensity burning in his eyes.

"Do you like me yet?" He smiles, still teasing.

"I'm getting there," I say, biting my lip while my hands run through his hair.

Blake slides my underwear down my legs, so I'm on full display for him, and I can tell from the look in his eyes he likes what he sees. He licks his lips and meets my gaze again.

"Let's get you all the way there then," he says, burying his face into my center. The pleasure is immediate, rocking through my entire body. Every nerve is firing on all cylinders.

I assumed Blake wouldn't be shy, that he would be happy to take charge and be full of passion, but I never assumed he would be this attentive to my needs, playing and teasing with the care and grace of a longtime lover instead of a one-night fuck. He's touching parts of me that I thought were untouchable, and none of them are on my body.

The way his tongue moves, I think he wants me to more than like him. It flicks and licks and swirls, nearly making me scream. I start to quiver, my legs becoming weak with the buildup of desire and the coming release. Oh fuck, I don't think I could ever hate Blake again after this, no matter what he did.

I can't take it anymore, yet all I want is more. I lean forward, resting my weight on his face as he cranes his neck back, devouring me without hesitation. My breath turns to rhythmic moans, faster and faster, Blake's tongue answering with more pressure and more speed. My hand grabs the back of his head for support, clawing at his short hair as I rock gently on him.

Blake is unrelenting, and I have to pull his face away. He looks up at me, just as pleased with himself as I am with him. "So, do you like me?"

I grab him, pulling him up to me. "You know I do," I say. "Now make me love you."

He spins me around and presses me into the door of his cell. My hands grip the bars as I arch my back, lifting my ass and standing on my tiptoes, creating the easiest path for him. I need to feel him inside me. I need the fullness of him to occupy every inch of me.

Without looking back, I feel a hand gently grip around my throat, elongating it as Blake leaves wet kisses down my neck and shoulders.

"I'll do anything you want me to, Casey."

I lean my head back, twisting it to find his lips and kiss him as he guides himself into me, filling me with the pressure I've been aching for. He doesn't have to ask me if I love him. He knows I do. He can feel it in the way my body reacts to his, my heart beating a little faster when he's around. He can see it in my eyes, the way they linger on him, not really wanting to look away even when I'm mad at him.

I step back, pushing him out of me and guide us to the floor. I want to see his face, to get lost in his eyes, to kiss him while I can barely breathe, because he makes me breathless. I straddle Blake, making him moan as I swallow the length of him. My lips find his again. It's like finding air underneath water. We breathe each other in as we rock back and forth, melting together, becoming one.

We don't stop until every muscle in our bodies gives out. I collapse on top of Blake, laying my chest on his as he wraps his arms around me. His heart races, beating through him into me, syncing with the rhythm of my own. Right now, it doesn't feel like the world ended, because mine is lying in my arms.

Chapter 30

I hear my name. It's faint, coming from somewhere in the distance. *"Casey!"* it says again, louder this time. Then there are footsteps, tapping across pavement. A door clicks nearby, and I realize I'm half-awake, half in a dream. My eyes shoot open, and my surroundings come into view—the partially open cell door, the stainless-steel bars stretched floor to ceiling, and a pair of strong arms wrapped around me. His warm skin is pressed against mine as he spoons me from behind, purring into my ear, still asleep.

The door creaks open. *Shit. Shit. Shit.* I scramble, attempting to dress, but there's no time, so I tug the sheet up to cover my breasts and nudge Blake, waking him. He rubs at his eyes and groans.

"Oh my God!" Tessa says, standing outside the open cell, her jaw slack, eyes bugged out.

I feel my cheeks flush, and I wish I could hide—but it's too late. Blake pulls himself into a seated position, and his pecs push against my bare back, sending a tingle up and down my spine.

"You're sleeping with the enemy!" Tessa exclaims.

My eyes widen, matching her shocked expression. I have a strong desire to run away, but I can't because doing so would tug the sheet off either Blake or me.

"You were on monster watch?" She gestures to us, sitting naked with only the thin sheet providing cover. "How the hell did this happen?" Her voice comes out all screechy.

I don't know what to say or how to answer her question, but I need her to be quiet because I don't want someone else coming down here and finding Blake and me in this compromising position. I press my pointer finger to my lips and shush her.

"Sorry," she says, relaxing the muscles in her face. "I'm just . . . wow." Tessa blinks several times, while I pull the sheet a little tighter around my chest. "I wasn't expecting this."

I glance over at Blake. The corner of his lips lifts as he tilts his head, his way of saying he didn't expect this either. And I'm right there with him. I mean, up until yesterday, I wanted to kill Blake. But somehow my desire to murder him morphed into hot, end-of-the-world, there's-no-going-back sex. Funny how that happens.

Tessa taps her finger against her chin and stares up at the ceiling. "Actually, maybe I was expecting this," she says, lowering her chin.

"What?" I ask, bewildered. "How? Why?"

I mean, I know how it appears. It looks like *I* was expecting this, or perhaps planning for it, because I told everyone to stay away. I told them to wait for either me or both me and Blake to come up after we found out whether he turned. He didn't want anyone down here if/when he changed, including me, but I couldn't do that . . . stay away, that is. When he fell asleep, I didn't leave, and I made myself a little makeshift bed so I'd be down here in the wee hours of the morning to ensure he didn't have to face the unknown alone. The bed was for sleeping, not sex, but apparently, it had a dual purpose.

"Well, it was obvious you liked Blake," Tessa says.

"No, it wasn't, and no, I didn't."

"You did a little." He dances the pads of his fingers across my back. I jerk my shoulder into him.

"Right?" Tessa says, placing a hand on her hip. "And from the glimpse I got of Blake's . . . *package*, I assume you might love him now."

"Do you?" Blake cheekily smiles. He's enjoying this far too much.

"Oh my God. Both of you stop." I lean forward, covering my face with my hands in an attempt to hide from their questions.

Beneath the sheet, Blake's hand grazes across my thigh, settling and gripping the inside of it. His fingers brush along my most sensitive skin. I bite down on my lip to stop myself from moaning and asking for more. Even more wouldn't be enough. There's something about his touch. It reaches every part of my body, even if it's just a light brush across a sliver of my skin. I've never felt that before. I've never felt someone touch all of me with a single stroke. My heart starts to beat so fast, it's like it's a continuous hum. I let my hands fall to my lap and I sit up straight, looking as nonchalant as I can, despite what's happening beneath the sheet.

"Why are you smiling like that?" Tessa eyes me suspiciously.

I give a blank stare and elbow Blake in his abdomen. He stifles a laugh and friskily squeezes my side. He knows exactly what he's doing to me.

"I'm not even smiling," I lie, trying to keep my mouth in a straight line. "And what are you doing down here?" My head tilts to the left, amplifying my subject-changing question. "No one was supposed to come down here."

"Oh yeah. I forgot about that." Tessa shrugs. "Although I realize now why that rule was in place." She double raises her brow and smirks.

I roll my eyes. "It was not in place for that. This"—I gesture to Blake and me—"just happened. It wasn't planned."

"Sure," she teases, unable to contain her amused smile. "Anyway . . . ummm." Tessa pauses for a second like she doesn't want to say what she came down here to tell us.

"What is it?" I ask.

"There's someone here to see you, and he says he's your fiancé."

My eyes grow impossibly wide. It feels like they could split at the corners. *Fiancé? How is that possible?* There's an immediate tightness in my chest, constricting my lungs, making it hard to breathe, to process this news.

"Nate's here?" I ask, barely getting the words out.

My stomach drops as though a trapdoor has suddenly opened up beneath it. I notice Blake's touch is gone, or maybe I can't feel him anymore. No, that's not it. His skin is no longer pressed up against mine, his hand has retreated from my thigh, and his posture's now rigid.

"Yeah." Tessa nods. "But he insists we call him Dr. Warner." Her eyes practically roll.

"You have a fiancé?" Blake asks, the question coming out strained.

I force myself to meet his gaze. Staring at him with my mouth slightly parted, I try to explain, but the words are tangled up in my throat. I don't know how to answer him. The longer I sit here not explaining, not answering, the more his face changes from a look of disbelief into one of betrayal and hurt.

"I thought you told me you two broke up?" Tessa cuts in, coming to my aid.

My eyes dart back and forth between the two of them.

"I . . . yeah. We did . . . in a way . . . break up," I say, locking on with Blake again.

I can't believe it. How could Nate be here? And why? He ditched me back in the city, so why would he ever come looking for me? Why risk coming all the way up here?

Blake's eyes are unblinking. "What do you mean by that?" The words come out sharp, and he practically clicks his tongue.

I don't know what to say to him. I can't tell them Nate ditched me in the city and almost got me killed, because he's here now—and actually, now that I think about it, he wouldn't come here if he had intentionally left me behind. *Right?* Did I misinterpret his actions? I remember back to the moments before Nate fled out of the apartment. I was tied up with one burner, while another was regaining his footing. Nate had scanned his surroundings, and I remember thinking he was coming up with a plan to get us out of there. Maybe he took off because he was trying to draw the burners away from me, but they didn't go after him. Maybe he ran into more trouble. Maybe he tried to get his Porsche ready for us to flee but it was stolen by other burners. Nate and I were together for years and were planning to get married. You don't just run away from that at the first sign of trouble.

"We got separated back in the city," I say. "And I thought he was long gone or dead."

Underneath the sheet, Blake shuffles on his boxer briefs and then stands, pulling on a pair of jeans and a long-sleeve T-shirt. I glance up at him, waiting for a reaction, but he doesn't give me one. He leaves the cell and starts off toward the door. Tessa awkwardly steps aside, letting him pass by.

"Where are you going?" I call out.

Blake pauses and briefly glances back at me, his mouth half grimacing and half smirking.

"To meet your stupid fiancé."

Chapter 31

Tessa trails behind as I race to catch up with Blake outside. My face is hot to the touch, and my breath is labored from throwing on my clothes and sprinting after Blake before he can make it to Nate. But I'm too late. Out front, Nate stands in a circle with half my family surrounding him. Dad, Aunt Julie, and Elaine are full of smiles. JJ and Uncle Jimmy wear neutral expressions, as though they're still assessing what to make of this new arrival. Blake enters the circle with his chin raised and eyes slightly tapered.

"Better get over there before your boyfriends meet," Tessa says with a chuckle.

I whip my head toward her. "They're not my boyfriends. Well, I guess Nate is my fiancé. But Blake . . . I'm not sure what we are. Even less so now."

"Enemies with benefits," she teases.

"Stop." I crack a small smile and lightly shove her. She's wrong about one part—I no longer view him as the enemy. The boy I was able to find something amazing in all those years ago finally came back to me, and it only took the world ending for it to happen. But just as we acknowledged our feelings for one another in the most intimate way possible . . . a wrench was thrown into our rekindling.

My gaze goes back to Nate and Blake, standing across from one another. Nate's back is to me, but even so, I can see he's clearly been through hell. His clothes are stained, full of filth. The skin on his arms and the back of his neck are covered in either more filth or scrapes and bruises. He's lost weight, mainly muscle, and his hair's cut short, which is just as surprising as his sudden appearance here, since his hair has always been his most prized possession.

I notice Dad's lips are moving as he gestures to Blake and then to Nate, clearly introducing them. Nate, none the wiser, extends a hand. If he knew what Blake did to me with that hand this morning, he'd for sure be throwing a fist instead. A jolt of electricity flashes through my body just thinking about it. I shake away the thought and blow out a gust of air, readying myself to face this head-on.

Tessa slaps a hand on my shoulder, startling me. "You might want to go and run interference before Blake and Nate get to talking about their common interests—you know, things or people they like to do." She raises a brow, grinning.

"Oh God."

I immediately start off toward them, almost in a daze, because I still can't believe Nate's here. This is all too much, and I'm worried about what Blake may say or do. I take several deep breaths as I walk, trying to calm myself. I've just gotta play it cool, and then I've gotta figure out what the hell happened back in the city.

Blake's gaze veers around Nate, locking onto me as I approach. He wears an expression that's both sultry and brooding, like he's upset but he doesn't want to be. I can barely look at him, yet I also can't look away.

Seemingly sensing my presence or noticing that Blake's fixated on something behind him, Nate twists his head, glancing over his shoulder. I can't believe he's alive and that he made it all the way here. I thought he was dead, and I'm honestly so glad he's not. Even if he did ditch me, I would never want that for him. Nate's mouth parts at the sight of me. I smile, my lips moving and twitching in all directions, as I'm not sure what reaction I'm supposed to have, especially with Blake watching. While I'm happy to see the man who got down on one knee and asked me to marry him, my body is still yearning for the touch of someone else. Nate turns on his heel and takes off in a sprint toward me. He doesn't stop until I'm wrapped up in his arms and my feet are lifting off the ground.

"I can't believe it," he says. "I missed you so much." He kisses the side of my head through his words and squeezes me tight, like he's afraid I'll slip—or pull—away.

Although I'm wrapped in Nate's embrace, my eyes are on Blake, who stands fifteen yards away wearing a pained expression. I don't tell Nate I missed him too. I can't bring myself to say it because I didn't, not with how he left. But maybe I was wrong. Maybe I should have missed him.

"What happened?" I whisper.

"What do you mean?"

"Nate . . . you ditched me. You left me behind." My voice cracks.

He lets go of me, allowing my feet to touch the earth again. He takes a step back, his hands resting on my shoulders and eyes frantically searching mine like he's looking for something he thought was long gone.

"No, Casey, I would never." Nate adamantly shakes his head. "I went through hell trying to get to you."

His hands cup my face so I'm forced to look at him, forced to take in his appearance. Bruises in various hues from yellows to purples stretch across his neck. His left eye is black and blue, and up close, I can see how jagged his hair is, cut longer in some places and shorter in others, like he clipped it in the dark with a pair of rusty scissors. He's clearly not lying about going through hell to get to me, but what happened before that? Why'd he run, and why didn't he wait for me? That's what I need to know.

"But you left me, and then I couldn't find you," I say, trying to maintain my strength.

"No, you have it all wrong. Yes, I ran, but I did that so they would chase after me. I figured they would, but they didn't. By the time I realized they weren't following me, I was already outside, so I went to the Porsche like we always talked about, and I waited for you. But then I heard more of them closing in on me, so I hopped in my car and drove around the block, staying out of sight until the coast was clear. When I came back, you were gone. I even went up to the apartment to check, and then I stayed in the area for days looking for you until I remembered your truck. I didn't know where it was parked, but I figured you had to have made it to it. And the only place you'd go outside the city was here." Nate brushes a finger across my cheek. "When I was a hundred percent certain you weren't in Chicago anymore, I came looking for you, praying, wishing, hoping you would be here." He folds his lips in, blinking several times. "And you were." Nate lets his head fall forward momentarily before lifting it. "All the horrible things I went through in order to get to you . . ." He looks at me with a fixed gaze, a sheen coating his eyes. "I would do them all again, because I love you so much, Casey."

I stare into the eyes of the man who didn't give up on me, didn't abandon me, and even risked his own life to make sure I was safe. What I thought was Nate fleeing at the first sign of trouble, ditching me to save his own ass, was actually him trying to protect me. I was the one who abandoned him, left him sick with worry as he searched for me. He fought his way out of Chicago all the way up here in the middle of nowhere Wisconsin, while I was content, enjoying safety and shelter. I even slept with someone else because I thought Nate had left me. How could I have done that? What kind of person does that make me? I feel so guilty, so sick to my stomach. I'm the bad guy in all this, not him.

Nate leans in and plants a hard kiss on my lips, his hands raking through my hair. My heart feels unsteady, as though it doesn't know where it belongs. It's breaking and mending at the same time. It breaks for Blake, but part of it feels like it's being restored, healed. I kiss Nate back, forcing pressure and movement through my lips, only enough for him not to ask any questions about what I've been up to.

"Nate," Blake calls out.

Startled, I pull away and wipe at my mouth. My dad and Blake approach, stopping a few feet from us.

Nate turns to face him, thrusting his jaw forward. "It's Dr. Warner."

"Right," Blake says, curling his upper lip. "We should talk sleeping arrangements since it appears you'll be staying." He narrows his eyes ever so slightly, but I notice it, and I also notice when they flick to me.

"Yes, that's the plan." Nate nods. He reaches for my hand and smiles as he threads his fingers through mine.

In response, Blake huffs through his nose, making his nostrils flare.

"Good," my dad cuts in. "So I'm sure you noticed from the little tour I gave you that space is tight. Right now, Blake and Casey are sharing a room. But I was thinking"—Dad splats a hand on Blake's shoulder—"that you'd probably want to move to another room now that Nate's here. The dummy house *is* heated, so we can make arrangements there."

Blake's eyes tighten. "I'm perfectly fine staying in Casey's room."

Dad lowers his voice, talking through the side of his mouth. "I was suggesting it so they could have some privacy."

"That's very kind of you, Dale," Nate says. "And that would be lovely."

Blake clenches his jaw.

"No, Blake should stay," I interrupt, quickly glancing at him. I notice the corner of his lips perk up, his eyes brighten a shade, and he relaxes the muscles in his face.

Nate's brows shove together, and I know he's about to argue with me, so I continue before he can get a word in.

"Blake's still recovering from a bite, so he should be comfortable and around other people, in case there's . . . any complications. You never know, especially with a virus this novel, how differently people can react to it, even when it seems to have run its course," I say, pulling the words completely out of my ass. I don't want to hurt Blake, but I also don't want to hurt Nate. However, I know someone's eventually going to get hurt. In the meantime, I just need to smooth things over, until I can figure out what to do with the two of them.

Despite the look of suspicion on Nate's face (because he is a doctor, after all) and his eyes darting between Blake and me, he simply nods, most likely not having the energy to argue and not wanting to ruffle any feathers. Blake softly smiles, though it fades just as fast as it appeared, like lightning flashing across the sky.

"All right then," my dad says, clasping his hands together. "We'll table this until Blake is feeling one hundred percent."

Blake doesn't move or give my dad any sort of reaction. He just stands there staring at me, but I can't fully meet his gaze. Maybe it's the guilt I feel from learning that Nate didn't ditch me at all. Or maybe it's because I don't trust myself to only look at him.

Dad pats Nate on the shoulder. "It looks like you could use a hot shower and a warm meal, son."

"That's exactly what I could use." Nate grins.

Blake's Adam's apple slowly rocks up and down the length of his neck, like he's being forced to consume something he doesn't want to. I get it. Life is sometimes hard to swallow.

Closing my bedroom door behind me, I let out a heavy sigh before turning to face Nate in more ways than one. Immediately, his lips are pressed hard against mine, hungry for another kiss. He wastes no time, his hands finding their way to my breasts, squeezing them, then sliding down my lower back and grabbing my ass. His fingers slip between my skin and the waistband of my pants. Even though I'm kissing Nate, all I can think about is Blake. I pull away, breathless, looking everywhere but at him.

"What? What's wrong?" he asks, confusion taking over his face.

My mouth parts slightly to answer him, but no words come out, because I don't know which ones I should tell him. If I had known Nate never intended to ditch me, that he only ran to lure the burners away so I could escape, then Blake and I would have never happened.

But I didn't, and I didn't realize he was out there risking his life trying to get here to me. Knowing that changes everything. I mean, it has to. We were engaged. We had planned to spend forever together. We were working so hard to build a life that we would one day be able to live in. Honestly, it's a miracle Nate made it to me, and it feels weird to throw that away. But for some reason, I can't go right back to the way things were with Nate. I need time to get over Blake before I can be with my fiancé again . . . I just can't tell Nate that's the reason I'm pushing him away.

I inhale through my nose, nearly gagging on the smell of decay and rot Nate's secreting. I'm not sure how I didn't notice the odor before. The hair on his head, along with the new hair on his face, is caked in dried blood and grime. His skin is covered in the same, giving it a muddy color peppered with fresh scrapes and scabs that have crusted over.

"Casey," he says, impatient for my response.

I scrunch up my nose and cover it with my hand. "It's just . . . you smell really bad."

He glances down at his clothes, covered in ten days of filth. Tugging on the collar of his T-shirt, he sniffs it and retches.

"Sorry," he says. "Is there really a shower here?"

"There really is." I smile.

"Oh, thank God." Nate sighs with relief.

I pick up the stack of folded clothes from my bed and extend it toward him. "Here. They're my dad's. Bathroom's at the end of the hall." I hold the door open for him and gesture to the left. "Towels and washcloths are beneath the sink."

Nate nods and leaves the room, pausing once to glance over his shoulder. He waggles his brows. "Want to join me?"

"Oh, I would, but we're not supposed to waste water," I say awkwardly.

"Right." He tilts his head. "Maybe when I get back then." He winks and continues on, looking back at me once more when he turns to shut the bathroom door.

With him out of sight, I let the tension in my face melt away, allowing my smile to fade. I close my bedroom door behind me and sigh with relief because I'm finally alone, and maybe—just maybe—I'll be able to think this through. My eyes land on Blake's perfectly made bed, and I can't help but imagine him and me in it, so I avert my gaze to my own bed. But it's not mine anymore; it's mine and Nate's, and I'm not sure how I feel about that. I know how I should feel, but knowing those feelings and having those feelings are two very different things.

I close my eyes, wishing I could just forget about this morning, wipe it completely from my brain. I was with Nate for two years. We lived together. We were engaged, and Blake wasn't even a factor. Once in a while, Blake would cross my mind, but the only thought I'd have about him was *I hope he's suffering.* Or I'd use the image of him as motivation to get through something really tough—like passing the MCAT, interviewing for residency, dealing with a difficult patient. My spite for Blake was highly motivating.

But that's not the case anymore. He's lodged in my brain—the same way food and sleep and oxygen are, wired into it as a need, not a want. I don't know how that happened in such a short time. I didn't think it was possible. Somehow, the hours I spent loving Blake are just as significant as the years I spent loving Nate. Then again, maybe that's all this is supposed to be, powerful and fleeting, a reminder that love doesn't have to be forever to be real.

My eyes spring open at the sound of my bedroom door creaking. I whip around to find Blake closing it behind him. Neither of us says a word. I mean, what really is there to say. I can't tell him what he wants to hear, and there's nothing he can say that would change my mind. My heart . . . he doesn't have to change that, because he has it—at least for right now. But I learned to love him, and I'll learn to unlove him too.

Without warning, Blake crosses the room, and his hands cup the sides of my face as he pulls me in for a kiss. Not just any kiss. It's the kind you get lost in even though you know your way. It's the kind that awakens every part of you, even though you feel like you're in a dream. And it's the kind you thank God for, even if you don't believe he exists.

As much as I want this, I know I shouldn't.

"I can't," I say, withdrawing from him.

Blake's mouth barely parts, his lips still swollen from our kiss. A look of betrayal washes over him like I've stabbed him in the back or, better yet, the heart.

"What do you mean, you can't?" His eyes frantically search mine.

"Nate's here."

That should be the end of it, but I know it won't be because it doesn't feel like a good enough reason—not with how fast my heart is beating or the way it's pumping blood to every part of me he's touched.

His brows shove together, and he recoils his head. "So, that means we're done?"

"Did we really ever start, Blake?"

He looks away, unable to answer the question that pained me to even ask in the first place. Two years versus a few hours . . . that's what I keep reminding myself. Time. Because that's what matters. It's all we have until we don't have it anymore. Blake had all the time in the world to be with me. He just waited until the world ended, and even then, it was only because he had no other choice. Nate chose me, whereas Blake chose me after every other choice was made for him.

"Tell me you don't love me."

It's not a demand. It's a challenge, one I'm not up for.

"No," I say, blinking away the brewing tears.

"Why not?"

"Because I don't wanna lie to you."

In an instant, his lips are on mine again, begging and pleading for me to tell him the truth.

"I want you so bad, Casey. And not right now—forever," he says in between breaths.

"Blake, stop." I pull away again, even though not a single part of me wants to.

"Stop what?" he says breathless.

"Stop making this so hard."

"If it's hard for you to tell me this is over, then you know it's not the right decision."

"I don't know that, and neither do you."

He takes a step toward me, grazing a finger across my cheek. "Without you, my world ends."

"The world already ended, Blake."

"Only for a little bit, until you came back into it."

Without warning, tears fall. They're too fast and too sudden for me to stop them. Before I can speak, the bedroom door is opening. Blake and I separate from one another. He walks to his dresser, pretending to rummage through it, while I wipe away the tears.

"Training starts in twenty minutes," Blake says.

I turn to find Nate standing in the center of the room with a towel wrapped around his waist, his eyes darting between the two of us.

"What's training?" Nate asks, slightly squinting.

I blink away the rest of the tears, hoping he doesn't notice.

"Combat training, buddy." Blake smirks. "And everyone has to do it."

Chapter 32

"All right, everyone, get lined up now! We have a lot to cover, and we're burnin' daylight, so double-time, let's go!" Blake yells out as he paces in front of us, his hands clasped behind his back.

His demeanor and tone are disconnected, like he's in front of a group of new recruits he's never met before. "We're going to pair up and do this activity with a partner. Yes, you will be fighting. Yes, you might get hurt. But the goal is, by the end of this, you won't be so susceptible to being hurt when you don't know your attacker."

The group mills about, small murmurs spreading as people start looking around for who they'll partner with. Nate bumps his shoulder into me with a smile on his face, an unspoken assumption that, of course, we'll pair up.

"Nate!" Blake yells. "Since this is your first time, you'll be with me."

Oh God. He's gonna kill him. I shoot daggers at Blake, warning him with my eyes that he better not do anything stupid. Hurting Nate won't make him go away, and it also won't magically bring us back together. If anything, it'll royally piss me off. But Blake doesn't see my warning, because he's locked in on Nate.

"Uhh, sure, Blake." Nate weaves his way to the front. "And it's Dr. Warner, by the way."

A large smile spreads across Blake's face as he drops a heavy hand onto Nate's shoulder. "That's good, because you might need a doctor after this." The group giggles to themselves, though Nate appears confused, unsure whether Blake's just joking around or serious. He raises his shoulders and puffs out his chest, but even all inflated, he's still smaller than Blake.

"Everyone else, finish finding your partners."

Tessa and I pair up. Molly stands beside Greg, holding his hand. Elaine wraps her arm around Aunt Julie. Tessa's mom takes her spot next to Helen. And Helen's boys partner up with one another. We all wait for further instructions.

The crisp, cold air cuts its way through the fabric of my clothes, sending a shiver down my spine. The sun is dull, trying to fight its way through a covering of clouds. The light shines a pallid yellow gray, making the world look like it's part of a low-budget student film. With the state of it, that's exactly how it feels. Blake stands at the front, hands on his hips as he surveys the crowd.

"To start, I want you to take your opponent to the ground. Keep it clean . . . mostly. But remember if you take it too easy on your partner, you aren't helping them learn or grow."

I turn to Tessa and shake my head, letting her know I'm taking it easy, regardless of Blake's instructions, which feel like are more for him and Nate than any of us. A way for him to hurt Nate, while also being absolved of it. But he better not.

"I'm going to sit this one out," Elaine says, walking over to a lawn chair and taking a seat. Meredith, Helen, and Aunt Julie echo her sentiment and join her.

"Suit yourself," Blake says. "Everyone else. Fight!"

Tessa turns and comes at me slowly. We grapple, like two Greco-Roman wrestlers locked in combat, our arms wrapped around each other's head and arms, circling in what will look to the group like a stalemate. But we're more so just holding each other so I can focus on Blake.

"I think Mr. Enemy with Benefits is going to kill your fiancé," Tessa whispers.

"I know, and then I'm going to kill him."

Blake bounces on his feet, not moving toward Nate, who has no idea how outmatched he is. After a few moments, Nate runs at Blake with reckless abandon, trying to drive his shoulder into him with a tackle, but Blake easily sidesteps him, tripping him with one leg while he shoves his shoulder hard, sending him barrel-rolling into the grass.

"It's like David and Goliath, but David doesn't have his trusty slingshot." Tessa looks on with a mixture of horror and amusement.

Nate peels himself out of the dirt, brushing loose grass off his clothes as he bobs his head, realizing this won't be as easy as he thought. He charges again, this time being mindful of Blake dodging out of the way. Nate jukes at the last second and tries to shove him backward, but Blake grabs his outstretched arms and dips underneath him, carrying Nate and then standing and flipping him in the air. Nate lands flat on his back, the wind getting knocked out of him.

"Oh God." I flinch.

Tessa slaps me lightly on the cheek, startling me.

"What?"

"How are you in a love triangle during an apocalypse? I can't even find a boyfriend, and you have two men."

"I don't have two men. And you had a boyfriend. But you killed him, remember?"

"Oh yeah," she says. "But it looks like we're both gonna have dead partners if those two keep fighting."

"Should I stop it?"

"Not yet. It's kinda hot." Tessa laughs.

Blake now has Nate in a headlock. I roll my eyes at his childish behavior.

"Blake's really going in on him," she adds, raising her brows.

"I think he's trying to kill Nate so I'll be with him."

"What?"

I nod. "He said he wants to be with me."

"When?"

"This morning during . . ." I trail off. "And right after Nate showed up."

"Ow! Ow! Ow!" Nate screams, stealing our attention.

Blake twists Nate's arm behind his back, pulling it up high enough that with a small bit of pressure, it looks like he could rip it clean off.

"Uncle! Uncle!" Nate yells.

Blake lets his arm go and shoves him away, sending Nate reeling into the grass. He turns and looks at me, a big shit-eating grin across his face as he gives a quick wink.

I shake my head and press my lips firmly together, not impressed by this macho behavior.

Nate uses Blake's lapse in vigilance to his advantage, charging into him from the side and lifting him off his feet before spiking him into the ground. *Oh, great.* Nate's picked up on the macho behavior too. What is it with men?

The fighting stops for a brief second with Nate on top of Blake, trying to keep him pinned to the ground. Blake's face turns a deep shade of red, his anger surfacing like a crimson mask.

"Oh no," is all I have time to say to myself before Nate's world is turned upside down, quite literally.

Blake whips his legs up in an X over Nate's chest, the same as he did to me when we first sparred, and sends him smashing backward into the ground, but unlike with me, he doesn't stop there. He stands and grabs Nate's legs, lifting them high into the air as he hooks Nate's knees over his shoulders, grabbing him by the waist and curling his body back upright. It looks like Nate is sitting in a Blake-shaped chair. He drives Nate back to the cold hard earth, body-slamming him like a stunt from the WWE. When he hits the ground, a loud snap reverberates through all of us, sending a chill down my spine. It's the only noise we hear before a rush of pain screams out of Nate's mouth.

"Ack! My shoulder!" He writhes in agony, pounding the dirt with his good arm. His injured shoulder is rolled up off his collar, dislocated from the joint.

"Holy shit," Tessa says.

I'm already fuming as I race to Nate's side. "What the hell, Blake!?" I glare up at him, and his face briefly changes, his eyes flickering with the same venom that coursed through them all those years ago at the party, right before he stabbed me in the heart. Has the venom always been there? Maybe he hasn't changed at all. Maybe he's the same old jerk and his true self surfaces whenever he doesn't get his way. My heart pounds against my rib cage. Has Blake fooled me again?

"What? We were just horse playing."

"Tessa, hold Nate still on his side and put pressure into him with your knees so he can't shift away from me." She nods and races over to assist.

"Sorry, Nate," she says, pushing up against him as he winces.

"It's Dr. Warner." His words come out breathy and shrieky.

Tessa shoves him even harder, annoyed by his response. A slight smirk appears on her face as he grimaces.

I snap my fingers in Nate's face to get his attention. "You know what I have to do, and you know it's gonna hurt."

"I know! I know!" Nate yells. "Just do it."

I nod to Tessa, signaling her to hold steady, and then I grab his shoulder and upper arm. "All right. On three. One. Two . . ."

Nate's shoulder pops into place. "Ack! Fuck." His rapid breathing starts to even out at the relief of being put back together again.

I stand and turn to Blake, shoving him as hard as I can. It sends him stumbling back a few steps. "What is your fucking problem!?"

"It was an accident," Blake says, shrugging it off like it's no big deal.

I narrow my eyes and take a step closer to him. He's full of shit. He did it on purpose.

"Yeah, and so were we," I whisper, only loud enough for him to hear me.

I don't know why I say it. Actually, I do. I want to hurt him because he thinks it's okay to hurt others, purely for his own enjoyment or to prove himself. His face turns downward, displaying the pain he feels from my words, which cut a little too deep. His green eyes mist over, and he lowers his head. Without another word, Blake walks away—but this time, I don't feel bad for him.

Chapter 33

The water from the shower pulses against the back of my head, massaging my thoughts, which are all over the place. I don't know what to think anymore. As mad as I am at Blake, the feelings I have for him are still there, and I'm just waiting for them to subside. But I think I really convinced him they were gone, which should make it easier to get over him. At least, I hope so. That way I can get back to building a future with Nate.

"Casey," a voice calls from the other side of the shower curtain, startling me. I didn't hear anyone come in, and I could have sworn I locked the door. The only movement in the room is steam swirling in the air and water gushing from the showerhead.

"I'm sorry for earlier," Blake says. "I didn't mean to hurt your . . . fiancé."

My breath hitches at the mere thought of him being close enough to touch. I don't say anything. He sharply exhales and the room grows silent again, minus the sound of moving water. It's like he's waiting for me to say more, begging me to utter the words he so badly needs to hear. But I can't bring myself to say them. This isn't about harboring hatred for the boy he used to be; this is about his actions now, as a man. I can see he's grown, evolved, because the old Blake would have never apologized.

"I'm leaving," he adds when I don't respond.

Immediately, my heart races, hammering inside my chest. My breaths turn short and fast, like I'm trying to catch them, and a spell of dizziness washes over me. He can't be serious. I whip open the shower curtain, locking eyes with Blake while the water continues to rain down on my wet, naked body. He holds my gaze, never looking away for an instant. I kind of want him to look at me, to take me all in, but he doesn't.

"No, you're not," I say, jutting my chin.

"I am, Casey. I'm on patrol tonight, but I plan to tell everyone tomorrow, and then I'll leave the following day. That'll give me time to wrap everything up here and figure out my next steps."

"You don't have to leave." I practically choke on the sentence as a sob threatens to tag along with it. Tears fall from my eyes, mixing with the water from the shower, camouflaging my sadness.

"I do," he says with a nod. "Besides, isn't that what you wanted? For me to get the hell out of here?" He forces the corner of his lips up, adding a lightness to his words. He's trying to make it look like he's not hurt. But he's not fooling me. I can see it in his eyes. I can hear it in his words. It's practically written all over him.

"You know I don't want that."

"It looks like neither of us are getting what we want, then." Blake shrugs.

"So, what? You're just going to leave . . . and go where?" My eyes plead with him to be reasonable. If he could hear the beating of my own heart, he'd know it was pleading with him too. "There's nowhere to go, Blake."

"Nowhere is better than here."

"Stop with the melodramatics," I scoff. "Why can't we just be friends?"

"I don't wanna be your friend." He drops eye contact, staring at his boots.

I want to stop his pain, take away his sadness, but that means I'd have to give it to Nate. Am I even making the right choice? Should my loyalty stay with Nate just because we were together before the world ended, just because I had more time with him? I really don't know. I just wish things could be different.

"So, if you can't have me the way you want me, then you don't want me in your life at all? Is that right?"

He bites down on his lower lip, letting his teeth graze across it. "Yeah, I guess it is."

"That's selfish and petty and stupid," I spit.

"It just might be. But I can't watch you love someone else. It'd be like watching the world end all over again, and I don't think I'd survive a second doomsday," he says with a small chuckle.

His joke doesn't land. It doesn't land at all.

"I hate you," I say, my lip trembling.

Blake stares back at me, like he's trying to call my bluff, but I hold strong. Finally, he reaches up with his hand and grabs the top of the shower curtain, sliding it closed and separating us from one another again.

"Take care, Casey," he says, and then he leaves the room, closing the door behind him.

Chapter 34

I awake in my bedroom, and it feels emptier than it should, the air taking on a thinness that only comes when you're truly alone. Rolling over, I notice Blake's bed is made, with his navy rucksack stuffed full and closed up, sinking his mattress slightly. He really meant what he said. He's actually leaving.

I peel myself from my sheets and walk over to the packed-up piece of luggage, if you can call it that. I prod and poke at it, hoping that it's nothing but air, a prank he has schemed that will end with the bag deflating and him jumping out from somewhere yelling, *Gotcha!* But the heavy lump barely moves, the tightly packed clothes and miscellaneous objects having no room for play within their canvas prison.

A sense of sadness and dread continues to swell inside me, filling my chest even more than the overstuffed object. I made the decision, though, so I can only blame myself for how I'm feeling. I chose Nate over Blake. Two years of history with my existing fiancé, the man who came back for me in spite of my ditching him, or one night of lust with the man I hated for more than a decade, who's leaving me the first time things don't go his way. Nate is the safe choice, the easy one, the right one. But if he is, then why does it hurt so much? I guess that's life. Sometimes it just hurts.

My bedroom door creaks open, and I spin around, a smile already on my face, anticipating it's Blake, coming to tell me that he's changed his mind, that he'll stay. But no. It's not him. It's Nate. My smile fades but not all the way, because I don't let it. He's the one I chose when the world was whole, so he's the one I'll stay with through the end of it.

"Hey," I say, trying to make my voice sound light and airy.

"Morning, babe." He smiles. "Wanna come take a walk with me? I have an errand I need to run."

"An errand?"

"To my car. I left it parked about a mile up the road. I didn't know what kind of reception I would receive when I arrived. Hell, I didn't even know if you would be here or if I had the right address. So I left it hidden off the side of the road in case I needed to make a quick exit." He steps forward, still smiling as he draws me into him, his hands wrapping around my waist. "But now that I'm here to stay, I figured I should go and get it. Plus, I've got some supplies in the trunk, mostly nonperishable foods, toiletries, and extra clothes."

"Yeah, sure," I say with a nod. "Just let me get dressed quick."

"Perfect," he purrs, before kissing me on the lips.

Nate and I head down the driveway, walking side by side. I haven't seen Blake yet, but I want to, and I can't help desperately searching for him. Nate doesn't seem to notice as he occasionally glances over at me, offering tight smiles. Or maybe he does notice. Maybe he realizes something's off, but he just can't pinpoint it.

Finally, I spot Blake, deep in a hug with my father over in the clearing to the right of the property. The fabric of their shirts wrinkling under the pressure of their hands as they pull each other so tight, it looks like they might morph into one. After what feels like too long, they release one another, their faces flushed red as tears well up in their eyes.

I can't believe it. He's actually leaving. My heart aches, and I hate him for doing this to me, to my dad, to all of us. It's all so stupid and petty. Where would Blake even go? For someone who's so pragmatic about survival, this is a foolish decision, made from emotion rather than reason. He's risking his own life because he can't stand to see me with Nate.

But I bet he's not telling my dad or anyone else that. I wonder what story he's giving them. I rubberneck, watching Blake for as long as I can until we pass by. He doesn't seem to notice, and I glance back once just to be sure, but he doesn't even look at me.

At the front gate, Nate pulls a key from his back pocket and inserts it into the padlock holding the chain in place. He removes it, letting it slink to the ground, before repocketing the key.

"Where did you get that?" I ask, pointing to his pocket.

"Oh, I told one of the older ladies in the kitchen that I needed to pull my car in, and they gave me this key."

I nod silently as Nate forces open the gate just wide enough for us to pass through.

"Ladies first." He bows and gestures to the open road beyond the dirt path.

Outside the property, I find myself staring at the county highway that seemingly goes on forever in both directions. The sun peeks out from a couple of fluffy clouds in the sky, and birds flutter above, chirping and squeaking. Way out here, it doesn't even look like the world ended. The chain rattles against the gate, pulling me from my thoughts. I turn around, watching Nate fiddle with the lock and then Dad and Blake. They part ways, walking in opposite directions, their heads slightly tilted down.

"Casey? Are you all right?" Nate asks.

"Yeah. I'm fine. Let's go."

"This way," he says, turning left.

I nod and follow, in step with him.

The highway is empty for the entire walk. Not a single biter or creature of any kind in sight. The black asphalt is starting to crack, and the shoulder is becoming overgrown with vegetation as small vines and grass work their way across the road, plotting to meet up with their brethren on the other side. I can imagine years from now, after many Wisconsin winters have expanded the cracks in the highway with the freezing and expanding of water, the flora and fauna will take this all back, and a path of green will replace this intruding line that nature never welcomed in the first place.

"Here it is!" Nate excitedly calls out as he runs to his car.

"That's your hiding place?" I laugh.

Nate's Porsche is barely off the shoulder of the highway. A single loose branch is leaned up against the tires on one side.

"Well, yeah. I mean, what did you want me to do? Pull it off into the woods, cover it in branches and leaves? It would ruin the paint job."

"Not sure that matters anymore," I say, rolling my eyes.

Nate pulls the single branch away and hops in the car, firing up the engine. He rolls down his window and says, "Hop on in," patting the front passenger seat with his hand.

I sink down into the low-profile vehicle and fasten my seat belt.

"Ready?" Nate slips on a pair of Gucci aviators and gives me a cheesy smile.

Before I can say anything, he pulls out and makes a U-turn. He revs the engine, and the tires squeal as he quickly accelerates. It jolts me back in my seat, making my stomach feel like it dropped and I lost it back on the road.

"Where are you going? Did you already get turned around, city boy? The house is back that way." I chuckle, pointing my thumb over my shoulder and waiting for him to stop abruptly to correct his mistake.

"I know," is all he says, staring straight ahead at the road, his hands gripping the steering wheel.

"What? Then where are you going?" My tone is a mixture of confusion and panic.

Nate has no idea what's around this area, so where else could he be driving us to?

"We're leaving."

My eyes search his profile, looking for any sign that he's just messing with me, trying to pull my leg before he brings the car to a stop, but there is none. He just continues staring forward, looking like a man on a mission.

"Nate, turn the car around." My tone is calm yet firm.

He ignores me, revving the engine as he increases the car's speed even more, the trees flying by in a blur of green along the sides of the road.

"Nate! Turn the fucking car around right now!" I slam my hands into the dashboard, popping open the glove box.

"No, Casey! There's nothing to go back to."

"What? What are you talking about?"

"I had to make a deal."

My heart drops into the pit of my stomach, splashing acid all around as the gravity of the situation sinks in.

"What did you do?"

"They were going to kill me. I had no choice."

"What did you fucking do!?" I scream, causing Nate to recoil into himself.

"They were gonna kill me, Casey. So I made a deal. I told them about your father's compound, that they'd be safe, and they'd have supplies for years. They said if I showed them where it was and I helped them get inside, then they'd let me and you go."

"You did what?" I'm seeing red right now, and my breaths come out fast and hard. I can't believe him. I can't fucking believe him. I should have known something was off just by the fact that Nate showed up with all his limbs still intact. He's not cut out for an apocalypse, so of course he made a fucking deal to save his own ass.

"It was the only way. Did you not hear me? They were going to kill me!"

"Where are they?"

"Where are who?" he asks.

"You know who! The fucking burners! The ones you made a goddamn deal with. Where are they?" I slap at Nate's arms, wanting to take my rage out on him in ways he could never imagine.

"They're probably heading into the compound as we speak." His voice is soft, delivering the death blow as calmly as he can.

"Stop the car, RIGHT NOW!"

"No! We aren't going back." The knuckles on his hands are white from how tightly he's gripping the steering wheel.

"Yes, we are."

I lunge across the center console and grab the steering wheel, trying to turn it hard to the left. Nate steadies it, bringing the car back under control after it drifts briefly in the road. He screams at me to stop, but I don't. I grab for it again, but this time he throws a hard, sharp elbow directly into my eye.

"Knock it off, Casey! You're gonna kill us both," he yells.

My head slams into the window as I'm sent reeling back from the blow. Searing pain shoots up into my skull and travels down my spine. A massive headache instantly roars its way into existence, clouding my vision.

Nate snaps his head back and forth, looking over at me while still keeping his eyes on the road. I'm not sure whether he's checking on me out of concern or checking to make sure I won't attack him.

"You motherfucker!" I lunge across the center console again, but this time not at the steering wheel—at Nate. My fingers are outstretched and curled, like a pair of talons ready to lay waste to the skin on his face. I claw and scratch at his cheek, ear, and eyes, trying to distract him from his driving.

"Ack! Casey! Stop it! I can't see!"

His reflexes kick in, and he lets go of the wheel, grabbing at my hands to try to stop me. But I've already abandoned his face and quickly grip the now-free steering wheel, whipping it hard to the left. The tires let out a violent squeal, burned rubber instantly filling the cabin with a rotten stench. We shoot across the road like a rocket, onto the shoulder and into the grass. Nate slams on the brakes but it's too late. The tires lock up on the soft soil, careening us toward a mighty oak tree, the Porsche no longer in anyone's control. The sounds of metal crunching and glass shattering are the last things I remember before everything goes black.

Chapter 35

My ears are ringing, a high-pitched whistle that drowns out any other noise. Slowly, my eyes flutter open as the scene before me begins to reveal itself, piece by piece. The canvas of the deflated airbag, dangling down at my feet, flecks of red staining it in too many places to count. The cracked windshield spiderwebbed in all directions, making it impossible to see what's on the other side. Twinkling diamonds litter the car like a freshly fallen snow, dazzling brilliantly against the red leather interior.

The side of my face feels like a pincushion, with dozens of needles sticking out in all directions. The pads of my fingers gently find the sources of pain. I bring my hand to my line of sight, seeing it's now coated in sticky red, like I've just finished eating a rack of ribs.

I try moving my extremities and am relieved, realizing my legs work just fine. Undoing my safety belt, I climb out of the totaled vehicle. The hood of Nate's Porsche is wrapped tightly around a tree, the small German sports car being no match for the towering arboreal giant. Steam rises from the warped hot metal, drops of fluid splashing onto the ground. I stagger, nearly tumbling over, but grip the car door to steady myself for a moment.

Nate is passed out on the steering column, the deflated airbag hanging below him like a bib. Small droplets of blood have already begun to dry on his forehead.

KSSHH!!! BEEP. *"Dr. Warner? Paging Dr. Warner!"* A man's voice emits from somewhere in the car.

Static is cut by a quick beep, followed by more static. A muffled voice comes through again.

"Dr. Warner, if you can hear me, you're free to go. We're starting our approach to the compound now. Thanks for leaving the gate open. Enjoy that girl of yours and steer clear. Ya hear? Because there won't be another deal on the table the next time we run into each other." A deep laugh erupts before static takes over and the line clicks dead.

I dive into the back seat and scramble for the source of the noise, finding a small black walkie-talkie underneath the driver's seat.

"You son of a bitch," I spit at his unconscious body, and a part of me hopes he didn't survive the accident. I try the radio, hoping I can delay the attack of whoever is on the other line, but after a dozen attempts, I give up, realizing they probably shut it off to move incognito.

I turn to run back toward the house. Unfortunately, thanks to Nate driving in the opposite direction, we're now even farther from the compound. It only takes a few steps of attempting to jog before I realize the damage the accident has inflicted. While my legs are intact and not bleeding, my deeply bruised shins make themselves known in a violent and agonizing way, pain shooting through my bones with each step.

"Fuck," I yell.

I hear the creaking of metal hinges and the crunching of glass just before "Casey!" is let out into the void.

Nate leans against the back corner of his Porsche, staggering in place. His shoulder looks to be dislocated again, and there's an unnatural bend in his right ankle, likely an unclean fracture that won't heal properly without surgery.

"Casey!" he calls again, struggling to keep himself vertical as he attempts to move toward me. "Where are you going?"

Nate's hand slips off the car and his ankle snaps beneath him, dropping him instantly to the ground. He screams out in agony.

I narrow my eyes. "I'm going to save my family."

His painful cries morph into a twisted laugh as he shakes his head in disapproval. "You'll die trying."

"I'd rather die with them today than spend the rest of my life with you."

"God, you are more useless and stupid than I thought you were. I knew I made the right decision leaving you behind." He cracks a wide smile, revealing bloodstained teeth, relishing in his confession.

Piece of shit. I turn my back on Nate and start walking, refusing to give him the satisfaction of my anger.

"Say hi to your dead dad for me, you fucking biiiitch!" Nate screams. The words reach a part of me I can't ignore, spinning me around. My hand instinctively slips into my holster as I find one of my throwing stars and send it flying through the air, right into Nate's shoulder.

"Ackk!" he yelps as he looks at the steel object lodged in his body, blood trickling down his shirt. His hand goes to it, trying to remove the star, but the pain is far too great for him to pull it out himself.

I start to turn and walk away, but stop and face him again, smirking.

"Whoops. Don't wanna forget that," I say, sauntering over to Nate. I squat down in front of him and grip the throwing star, giving it a small twist before yanking it from his flesh. He screams again, grasping at the wound the second it's free of the blade. Blood pours more freely from the unblocked hole.

"Thanks for holding on to it for me." I smile and stare into his eyes, seeing him for the man he truly is—and by that, I mean no man at all.

He spits a spray of blood at my face, chuckling and crying at the same time.

"That's not very nice, Nate."

"It's Dr. Warner, ya cunt." He cracks a grin.

I stand, looking down at the crumpled piece of shit before me, him and the car. Letting out a heavy sigh, I strike my knee into his forehead, smashing his skull into the metal of the bumper. His eyes instantly roll up into his head as he slumps to the ground.

"You're right, Nate. I am a cunt."

I've never understood why that word was ever considered an insult. To me, it's a compliment. It's one of the strongest organs there is. It creates life, it makes men stupid, and it bleeds every month—yet it doesn't die. I can't say Nate will have the same fate, though. Blood trickles from the back of his head and seeps out of the wound in his shoulder, staining his shirt red. I feel around in my front pocket and pull out the engagement ring he slipped on my finger months ago. With his return, I've been carrying it with me, debating whether to wear it again. I'm glad I didn't now, and I toss it in his lap.

A barrage of gunshots echoes in the ether, miles away, but it feels like it pierced right through me. I turn, leaving Nate slumped against the back of his precious Porsche, and take off at a full sprint, ignoring the pain in my shins.

Chapter 36

I reach the compound, winded and sucking air, nearly keeling over. The front gate has been smashed off its hinges. Multiple unfamiliar trucks litter the lawn, with gunshots ringing out from all directions. One vehicle is on fire and several bodies lay splayed out on the grass, guns at their sides and arms kicked up in strange positions, as if permanently frozen in midrun.

The soil is spattered with blood, and I can't help but be reminded of the similar scene a few days back. But this is on a much larger scale. Screams pierce the air, and there are flashes of movement at the top of the property, but it's too hard to decipher who is who. It feels like that first night everything went to hell at the hospital, but this time, I'm prepared.

Surveying the mayhem, I decide approaching across the front lawn leaves me too exposed, so I creep along the fence line, making my way into the woods, through the thick foliage, staying low and quiet, while using the brush as cover.

I still can't believe Nate sold us out. If he was worried about the burners killing him, why didn't he just tell us so we could have planned our own attack and beefed up our defenses? I already know the answer, though. Nate is a coward who only thinks about himself. Even if there were a way that he could have saved everyone here without betraying their trust, he wouldn't have cared, so long as numero uno was taken care of. I should have made sure he was dead before I left him on the side of the road. But a slow, painful death is what he deserves. Besides, if he's such a great doctor, then he should be able to patch himself up. I shake Nate from my thoughts and focus on my surroundings.

Snaking and weaving through the woods, I'm able to quickly and quietly get to the other side of the property without detection. A lifetime of familiarity with the nature here keeps me safe in ways I never would have thought. Near the edge of the tree line, I stop and scan the area, planning my next move. I have no idea how many burners are here. It could be five, it could be fifty, but I'm guessing, based on the number of gunshots I heard, what I saw coming in, and the scouting party they sent the other day, there are at least fifteen to twenty of them.

Ten throwing stars, a knife, and some hand-to-hand combat skills aren't going to help me take a dozen-plus armed attackers. I edge my way out of the tree line to try to get a glimpse of the sniper tower, but suddenly I'm yanked backward, and the strong tug of something at the middle of my shirt pulls me deeper into the woods. I hold my breath, fumbling quickly for my own knife as I anticipate a burner's blade slashing across my throat or a bullet leaping from one side of my skull to the other. Instead, I'm twisted around, and two arms wrap around me, squeezing me in a tight embrace. The breath I was holding is forced out by the pressure. I bring the knife in my hand down to my side, instead of plunging into the body in front of me. Because it's Tessa. Over her shoulder, I see Molly, looking on with abject horror.

"Oh my God. I'm so glad you two are okay." I squeeze Tessa back, trying to reassure Molly with my eyes that everything is going to be okay, even though I have no idea the severity of what's going on. She starts to cry and runs to us, joining in on our hug.

I can feel her head shaking against my shoulder as she burrows it into me. "Hey, it's gonna be okay. We're gonna be okay," I say, pulling away from both of them. There's no time for us to fall apart.

"Greg was up there on watch when they stormed the property." She wipes at her tears, pointing through the trees off toward the sniper tower.

"I saw two men go up there. He's probably . . . he's probably . . ." Molly cries harder.

I grab the sides of her arms. "Fine. He's probably fine." I let go of her as she calms herself and look to Tessa. "Now, tell me what happened."

"We were both out in the back garden picking vegetables for Elaine when we heard gunshots. A dozen or so men rushed the front lawn from the old house, so we ran into the woods. I didn't even think to go get my . . ." Tessa drops her face into her hands, inhaling several deep breaths.

"Hey, you did the right thing. What were you guys gonna do? Scare them off with your garden shears and spades? They would have killed you or worse. But now, we have the element of surprise. We can fight back."

"What is happening?" Molly's voice croaks.

"Nate set us up. Sold this place out just so he could save his own ass."

"Why?" Tessa and Molly say in unison.

"Burners took him captive after he ditched me in Chicago, and the only thing he could do to get them to let him go was offer this place up on a silver platter."

"Ditched?" Tessa squints.

I pull my lips in and nod, shame coating my face.

"Fucking slimeball." Tessa spits on the ground. "I knew I never liked that guy."

"Where's Nate now?" Molly asks, fear filling her eyes, like Nate's some kind of boogeyman who'll jump out at any moment.

"He's either dead or dying."

"Looks like we both killed our boyfriends," Tessa says with the smallest smile, trying to find humor in the darkest of times. That's when we need it most. It's easy to laugh when you're happy. I smile back and reach for her hand, squeezing it.

"So, what are we supposed to do?" Molly asks, her eyes darting all over the place.

"We're going to kill these assholes. That's what." I stand tall, projecting confidence to my newly recruited sisters-in-arms.

"With what? Your throwing stars and a knife?" Tessa gestures to the only weapons currently on any of us.

A devilish grin creeps across my face. "No. Follow me."

I lead the girls through the woods to a secret place my dad and I marked off. Certain grooves in the bark of trees are the only guideposts along the way. The spot is covered by a dead log and years' worth of leaves and decaying vegetation. I start pulling everything off, and Molly and Tessa quickly join in. Underneath it all is a single piece of plywood. We bend down and lift it, flipping it over to reveal the top of a large green chest, previously the lodging for all the components of an over-the-shoulder rocket-propelled grenade launcher. I never got to see it, but I also never believed my dad when he told me the chest was just for storage and had arrived empty. I unlatch the lid and toss it open, revealing the contents.

"Holy shit!" Tessa clasps her hands over her mouth, realizing how much noise she made in her excitement. "Holy shit!" she repeats, but this time in a whisper.

Molly's eyes widen. "That's a lot of guns."

"It sure is," I say, looking like a proud parent showing off the report card of their favorite child. "Think we can go in and save some people now?"

"Hell yeah!" the girls say in unison.

Chapter 37

"Everyone locked and loaded?" I eye Tessa and Molly, one on either side of me. We look like something out of *The Matrix*, the scene where Neo and Trinity walk through the metal detectors, their entire bodies covered in various guns, blades, explosives, and ammunition. I can't even recall how many times I watched that movie with my dad, and I smile at the memory.

Each of us has at least four pistols, a semi-machine gun, a combat knife, two flashbangs, and all the necessary ammunition to participate in a shoot-out for the better part of an hour. I also gave Tessa the one grenade my dad bought off the black market a long time ago. "I'm not even sure if it actually works, and hopefully you don't have to use it, but if you get in a spot where . . . ya know."

"I know," is all she said in response.

"I'm ready," Molly whispers at my side.

"Let's do this." Tessa pats my back, giving my shoulder a small squeeze of reassurance.

"We need to go in quiet. We are severely outnumbered, and we have to assume they're all armed and may have hostages. First thing we do is take out anyone patrolling the area. We don't want any stragglers getting the drop on us from behind, and if we get made, then . . . well, we're gonna be in for one hell of a firefight." I am drawing out a map of the property in the dirt with a stick, talking through the plan one last time before we make our move.

"What about Greg?" Molly chimes in, her voice laced with concern.

"That's next. After the approach is clear, we need to take the sniper tower back. If they have someone up there watching, we'll never make it to the house. So, we . . ."

"You said Greg was probably fine." Tears well up in Molly's eyes, and her lower lip starts to quiver.

"I said *if*. *If* they have someone up there. We need to plan for everything."

She nods and lets me get back to it.

"Okay, so then we make a break for the sniper tower and secure it. Molly, you can stay up there with Greg and provide supporting fire as needed. Tessa, you'll come with me, and we'll head for the main house. Any questions?" My eyes dart back and forth, watching as both of them shake their heads. "All right, follow me, and stay low."

The gunfire has ceased for several minutes now as we make our way back through the woods, which tells me the burners are settled in, thinking they have control of the place and everyone in it. I poke my head out of the tree line, scanning in every direction, looking for the slightest bit of movement. When I see none, I wave the girls on behind me, and we quickly slink along the trees, staying low to the ground as we move toward the house. When the brush opens up, I spot the first burner, a lone man pacing back and forth, watching the north and west approaches to the house. He has a single shotgun in his hands and holds it pointed at the ground, a relaxed grip indicating he doesn't expect any danger.

"Stay here," I whisper as I get into position.

I count out the number of steps he takes before he does his about-face, the same number each time and always at the same speed, like a human metronome, assigned to a single strip of earth. When he plants his weight and pivots his foot, I follow his shirt up to where it stops, drawing an imaginary bull's-eye on the back of his neck. This time, I picture Nate's smug face. I step forward, my body rustling the leaves of the bushes around me. At the sudden sound, he stops and spins around, his eyes going wide as my figure emerges, moving toward him. The man raises a brow and lifts his gun. *Too slow.* My arm shoots out, my wrist snapping at the last second as the throwing star cuts through the air like a Frisbee, planting itself right into his Adam's apple. He drops the gun and his hands shoot up to his neck. Gurgling violently, his mouth sprays red with each successive cough. Blood pours from his throat like red wine from a bottle. *I could really use a drink right now.*

I sprint at him, bringing myself within a few feet before I leap into the air, my right leg lifted. I plant the bottom of my thick-soled boot into his throat, sending the throwing star deeper and severing the spinal cord. The force of my kick sends his body toppling over backward. I use my knife to fish the throwing star out of his neck, prying back and turning his head into something that looks more like the lid of a can after the can opener has gone most of the way around.

I hear gagging behind me, and I turn to see Molly almost throwing up her breakfast at the sight before her.

Tessa is smiling, nodding in approval. "Bad . . . ass," she whispers.

I smile back and motion for them to follow me again. It's eerily quiet. If I had shown up now, I wouldn't even have suspected anything was wrong. But the air still smells of gunpowder, smoke, and blood. The tension of fear and terror are palpable as we move in closer to our target.

The dummy house is a little more fortified, with two men standing at the visible corners of the building and another patrolling from the front to the back of the house in the same steady rhythm as the previous burner.

We duck low, backing into the woods for the cover we need to plan our next attack. "Tessa, Molly, you need to shoot the two guys at the corners. I'll take the one patrolling when he comes back to this side of the house. If we time it out right, we can drop all three at the same time," I say, directing them to each of their targets.

"But we'll make noise," Molly protests.

"We don't have a choice. They have their backs to the house, and they're not gonna turn around."

"Unless . . ." Tessa starts rummaging around in the leaves, feeling her way with her hands before she comes up with a rock the size of a tennis ball. "We distract them."

I collect the rock, feeling its heft. I look at the house and decide that a well-timed throw through the window could provide a brief second for an attack. "That could work. But if they don't bite . . ."

"I know," Tessa says, "but we have to try."

I nod in response and get myself situated, determining the force I'll need to use in order to hurl the stone right through the glass. My heart rate accelerates and sweat builds on my brow. If I screw this up, or they look for the source of the throw instead of turning to the glass, that'll be the end of all of us. The weight of this burden feels thousands of times heavier than the rock in my hand.

I look at both of my girls, giving them one last chance to back out, save themselves from the possibility of a swift death at the hands of some crazed lunatics. I wouldn't blame either of them, not in this moment, but they stare at me with a steely confidence in their eyes, gripping the handles of their knives even tighter. *They're ready.*

I suck in a deep breath and tune everything out as I gaze at the reflection of the sun glinting off the glass-pane window. I cup the rock in my hand and tell myself this is no different from my throwing stars. Nice and easy. The brush around me rustles softly as I let the stone loose. It arches through the air, appearing to hang above us for an eternity, the anticipation of its path keeping it from flying faster. Then, like a marionette having its strings cut, it plummets down, smashing through the window. Glass particles shatter into the house and tumble onto the porch.

The two burners turn to the window, just as we hoped they would, and then we run—Tessa at the man on the left and Molly the one on the right. Midsprint, the other burner comes around the side of the house, but I'm ready, catching him in the throat at the same time that the two girls leap into the air, snatching the men from behind and plunging their knives into their soft, fleshy necks. They sweep the blades across in a swift slash, painting the sides of the house a deep crimson.

I sigh with relief, tears nearly welling up and falling from my eyes as I look at my two girls, still safe and unharmed. They turn to me, blood covering the blades of their knives. Tessa is smiling, but Molly is trembling and looks like she's just seen a ghost. The knife slips from her hand, falling into the grass.

"Molly?" I place a hand on her shoulder.

"I've never killed anyone," she says, her voice shaking like she's just come out of a cold plunge.

"Oh, I . . . uh . . ." I look to Tessa for support, but she shrugs, mouthing, *I don't know.*

"If we don't kill these guys, they'll kill Greg." I stare at Molly, hoping that truth breaks through the shocked state she's in.

She lifts her head, her eyes burrowing a hole in the fabric of time and space. That was all she needed to hear. If the kill is for Greg, it's fine, which kind of worries me a little, but we'll deal with that later. She plucks her knife from the ground, spinning the blade between her fingers.

"Let's go," she says, charging in her fiancé's direction.

PKOWWWWW!

A shot rings out from the sniper tower, kicking up grass and earth as it just misses Molly's head.

I grab a fistful of her shirt, yanking her back to the ground so fast, she loses her footing and falls right on her ass. Kicking at the grass with her heels, she tries to move for cover.

"Holy shit! Holy shit! I almost just had my head blown off!" she says, bug-eyed and all panicky.

"You can't just go running ahead. That'll get you killed. We have no idea how many there are or where they all are. They were smart enough to occupy the sniper tower and use it as a lookout." I peek my head around the side of the house, spotting a man in the tower with his gun aimed right down at us. I jerk my head back just as another shot rings out. "Shit, he's trained on us."

I rack my brain trying to think of the best way to approach. The point of the tower was a perfect 360 view of the property, precisely so someone *couldn't* sneak up on it. The only way to make it is a full-on sprint, having the girls provide cover fire, and even then, my odds are low. But with that tower occupied, everyone is at risk.

"Okay. There's no way to sneak up on him, so I'm just gonna have to make a run for it."

"Casey, no! You'll get shot," Tessa says, grabbing my shoulder and giving it a shake, as though she can work some sense into me.

"I have to try. If you two can provide cover fire, I might be able to make it."

"Casey, I want to save Greg more than anything, but I can't let you do this," Molly says, lowering her head.

"I'm going whether you guys provide cover fire or not. You can either help me, or you can let him have free rein on me. It's up to you." I turn back to the corner of the house and lay eyes on the dead burner at my feet. "Help me lift him up. I have an idea."

The girls look at me with confusion that morphs into disgust as they put their hands on the burner's corpse, his blood-soaked clothes already stiffening in the cool air.

"Okay. I'm gonna push him out past the house, into the line of sight for the shooter. Once he shoots, I'll take off running. You two, wait one second and then start firing at the sniper tower. If you can hit the guy from here, that'll be amazing, but even so, just keep shooting nice and steady till I make it to the dummy house. Never give him a chance to feel comfortable enough to poke his head out and take another shot. Understood?"

They both nod reluctantly, still not wanting me to go through with this.

"The second I'm inside, get back behind your cover." I look to where I can guess the shooter is—X-ray vision of my imagination allows me to paint the grimace on his visage as he squints one eye down his sight.

With all my might, I push the corpse out into the open. The crack of the rifle rings out. Just as the bullet rips through the soft flesh of his fellow burner, I take off at a dead sprint, kicking up grass behind me. I glance up to see the man reloading for another shot, his eyes going wide as I present him an easy piece of prey, right out in the open. Behind me, gunfire begins to call out in a steady and even thump, bullets splitting wood and shattering glass. The burner drops to the floor, avoiding the incoming rounds. I bear down on my goal, running harder and faster than I ever have in my life. My heart is pumping blood so quickly I can hear it sloshing around in my ears, and then everything is quiet. I don't have time to look back, but I realize Tessa and Molly are out of bullets, and they're both reloading at the same time.

Fuck.

The burner pokes his head just above the window line, noticing he has a brief opening. My brain is scrambling, screaming at every muscle in my body to search for cover and hide, but the nearest safe haven is the building ahead. I glance up just in time to see the burner leveling the rifle at me. I cut hard to the left, then back to the right, then I fake to the left and dart farther to the right. Zigzagging erratically, I pray that he's not a very good shot.

PKOOWW!

Before the gunshot can stop echoing through the ether, a searing pain erupts from my ear as a high-pitched whistle passes by in a millisecond. I stumble forward but don't lose my footing, and I'm back up at full speed just as the girls' chorus of shots starts up again, carrying me into the old house relatively unscathed.

Leaning against a wall, I suck wind at a rate I never have before. My ear stings, and I reach up and touch it. The contact from my own skin burns, and I pull my hand away. Blood covers the pads of my fingertips, and the only thought running through my head is how one inch would have ended my life.

I creep through the house, unsure whether the burner in the tower has any support down below, but all the way up to the last narrow staircase is clear. The sound of old boards creaking under my weight guides me along the way.

If he only has his long rifle, then he won't be able to do much once I charge in, but something tells me he has a smaller firearm or a knife ready and waiting. With my pistol drawn and pointed up at the top of the landing, I slowly skulk up the stairs, keeping the gun tight to my chest so my arms don't breach the frame first. I debate tossing one of my two flashbangs up into the room, but it feels like a waste for potentially one target—plus, I have no idea what's waiting for us in the main house.

Three stairs from the top, an explosion rings out from my left, wood splintering from the wall across my face. I hit the deck immediately, waiting for another shot to come. He's scared, and he's given away his position. I decide to hurl one of my throwing stars into the ceiling, creating a quick, albeit very weak, distraction. I plant my foot on one of the stairs and leap forward, turning to my left as I crash onto the tower floor. Lying flat on my side, I raise my pistol and fire wildly at the only figure I can see standing in the room. Two gunshots ring out in response as my gun clicks empty, and I close my eyes, thinking this is it. But the room is silent, the smell of gunpowder hanging heavy in the air.

I open my eyes to see the burner lying still, both our bodies on our sides as we're locked in a staring contest that he couldn't possibly lose. Blood pours out of the holes in his shirt, soaking into the fibers of the floorboards. I can't seem to move, all my energy having been spent on the sprint here and the ensuing firefight. It isn't until I hear Molly scream that I remember why I ran up here in the first place.

"GREG!" Footsteps clamber behind me.

A hand rolls me onto my back. "Are you hurt?" Tessa asks.

I shake my head. She smiles and reaches for my hand, heaving me onto my feet.

Greg is lying on the floor, his hands tied behind his back. He looks to be out cold, the imprint of a rifle butt raised up on his forehead. Molly is in a panic, trying to rouse him. He stirs slightly, moaning out of his forced slumber.

I cut the ties around his wrists, freeing him.

"Greg? How're you doing?" I ask while Molly and I help him sit up. Feeling his pulse, I check to see how his eyes are responding to the light in the room. His heart rate is slow but rising rapidly.

Greg winces, closing his eyes as he touches the raised bump on his forehead. "What happened?"

"Looks like you got knocked out cold with the butt of a rifle," I say.

"Who did it? Was it Blake? I swear to God . . ." he starts to seethe.

"What? No, we're under attack."

The second the final word leaves my mouth, Greg's eyes pop open. Fighting through the pain, he's on his feet in a second, and that's when he sees the burner, bleeding out on the floor a mere six feet away from him.

"What the fuck? Who is that!?" He points at the corpse. "Where's JJ? Where's Mom and Dad?" He heads for the door, but I reach out and grab his shirt, heaving him back.

"Greg, easy. I know this is a lot. But we need you to stay here with Molly."

"No way. I'm going to find my family." He pushes me aside, but Tessa jumps in front of the doorframe, blocking his exit.

"Greg! Listen to her. We need you to stay up here." Tessa shoves his chest with both hands, forcing him back a step.

He sighs heavily and shakes the fog out of his head.

"We can't lose this tower again. It was a miracle I even got up here in the first place. You need to stay here, protect the tower, shoot any burners you see, and provide cover fire as needed. Got it?" I can see he's struggling, unable to be okay with just staying put while his family's in danger. "Please," I add.

Molly steps forward and squeezes him as hard as she can, tears running down her cheeks as she tries to crawl inside his body—her affection for Greg wanting nothing more than for them to fuse into one being. "Greg, we need to do this, for our family."

He looks down at her glistening wide eyes, and within the endless depths of the love behind them, he must see the reassurance he needs. He picks Molly up and squeezes her so hard her back cracks a few times. She giggles as Greg gently sets her down. He turns and salutes me. "Consider the tower secure and your six covered, ma'am."

I chuckle, patting him on the shoulder. "Thanks, sir."

We exchange tights smiles and firm nods, and then Tessa and I take our leave, heading toward the main house. This time, with the safety and security of friendly eyes watching from above.

The three bodies are still lying outside where we left them. Even in the cool weather, flies are accumulating in a fury, excited by the newly found food. A hatching place for their larvae, which will become an all-you-can-eat buffet for the maggots that'll turn them into nothing but bones. *Exactly what they deserve.*

A scream cuts through the woods, emanating from where the small cabins are. It sounds like a woman, but the scream isn't for her; it's something otherworldly, a sound I've never heard before. Two quick gunshots ring out, and then the scream magnifies in volume, a hundredfold over what it just was. Neither of us needs to see the two small bodies lying limp in the grass to know exactly what just happened. Another cry pierces the air before a man yells. A gunshot rings out and the world is silent once again. A lineage lying upon the earth, the only place it will ever exist again, erased in seconds.

Tessa looks at me, tears pouring out of her in silent streams as she motions toward the sound, as if to ask, *Should we go do something?* I shake my head and bite hard into my tongue, trying to channel my focus on the here and now, the pain grounding me to a spot on the porch. I tell myself, *There's nothing you can do for them now,* over and over.

I motion with my hands for us to scout around the house, and we check the windows for any signs of burners and meet back where we started.

"Where do you think they all are?" Tessa asks.

"I don't know. They have to be around here, though. Where would everyone else be?"

We slink into the house; the kitchen looks as though a bomb went off. Tables are overturned; plates and utensils are shattered and strewn across the floor. Our boots crunch over the fragments as we try to avoid them without success.

We hear a loud bump from the master bedroom. Muffled cries escape from under the door. Immediately we both plant our backs to the wall on either side of it, moving slowly, listening for any other sounds. More muffled cries are followed by bumping on the floor, but no voices, and no footsteps.

I bring my gun up and point to the door handle, signaling for Tessa to grab it. I hold up three fingers and rhythmically bring them down.

Three.

Two.

One.

Tessa pushes the door in as I swing my gun around the frame, scanning the room from left to right, top to bottom, in seconds. But there are no burners in here, and then we see the source of the noise.

Tied up in the corner, back-to-back, with gags in their mouths, are Elaine and my aunt. Julie's in bad shape, blood running down her head, like she put up a fight and was beaten for it.

Tessa and I race to them, quickly removing their gags and untying their hands.

"Are you two okay?"

"Julie's hurt," Elaine answers in a whisper, coughing from the dryness of her mouth.

"Let me see," I say, turning my attention to my aunt, inspecting the top of her head. It's a bloody mess, but I find the source of it, a nasty open gash a few inches in length sliced across it, like the skin split due to a heavy blow. I examine her eyes, noticing they're not responding well. She's clearly concussed.

"Where's my mom?" Tessa asks.

Elaine shakes her head and points toward the bed, her eyes swimming with tears.

Confused, Tessa rises slowly, approaching the bed as though a creature is ready to crawl out from under it and drag her into the darkness. Then I see the look on her face change.

"Mom!" She can't help herself, yelling the word as she rushes around the side of the mattress and drops to her knees.

I follow, my heart breaking at the sight. Tessa's mom lies on the ground, a small pool of blood beneath her head, her hair matted and wet from the sticky liquid.

"Oh my God! Mom!" Tessa shakes her, trying to make her respond.

Grabbing Tessa's shoulders, I pull her off. "Easy. We don't know how hurt she is, so don't shake her, okay?" Tessa nods and slides to the floor, leaning her back against the bed.

I place my fingers gently on Meredith's neck, checking for a pulse. After a few seconds, my heart nearly stops, a mirror of what my fingers are feeling. Panic settles in, but I keep it deep within, not wanting to alarm Tessa. I hold my fingers in place, keeping up the ruse that I'm counting out her heart rate, the sadness welling up so strongly inside me that I'm not sure how I'll be able to tell her that she'll never speak to her mother again.

But suddenly, a tiny bit of pressure makes her skin rise up into the pads of my fingers, sinking back down for nearly two seconds, and then rising again. *Oh, thank God.* I turn to Tessa, nodding in quick bursts. "She's okay. Her pulse is very faint, but it's there."

Tessa dives onto her mother, holding her in her arms and brushing the hair out of her face. Aunt Julie and Elaine stand over us, tears in their eyes and hands covering their mouths.

"Where's everyone else?"

"I don't know. Dale and Jimmy ran out into the yard shooting when the men showed up, but I didn't see anyone else," Elaine explains.

Aunt Julie cries from the pain of her wound and from the unknown of whether her children and her husband are alive and well.

I know it's not a consolation for the rest who are missing, but I tell her, "Greg is safe, by the way. He's up in the sniper tower with Molly. They have the lookout secured, and they're watching down on us."

Her wet, crumpled face, saturated with blood, lights up. "Like guardian angels."

"Yeah," I say, thinking we're gonna need more of those if we're going to survive this. "Are you two gonna be okay in here? Tessa and I need to go find the others." I turn to see Tessa staring up at me, a torrent of sadness and worry spilling out of her as she shakes her head.

"I can't leave my mom," she cries.

As much as I want her to come with me and finish this, I know, in this state, she won't be any good anyway, which puts us both at risk.

"Okay. Stay then. Keep everyone in here safe."

"I'll come with you." Aunt Julie takes a sudden step forward but nearly topples over, catching herself on the bedpost. Elaine steadies her and helps her sit.

"No, Aunt Julie. You're too injured. Just stay here."

My aunt slumps her shoulders and slowly nods. She doesn't want to agree with me, but she also knows it's for the best.

"Are you all going to be fine in here?" I ask the room.

"The real question is, Are you going to be fine out there?" Elaine says, reaching for my hand. She holds it and pats it with her other.

I take a deep breath and exhale at the prospect of facing this on my own, but somewhere deep inside me, I sense I will be. It might be pure delusion, but I can still feel it.

"Yeah," I say.

"I know you will. You were the strongest little girl I ever met, and now you're the strongest woman I've ever known." Elaine gives me an encouraging nod and lets go of my hand.

I smile and tell them to take care of each other before leaving the room and making my way back out into the kitchen.

I debate whether to check upstairs or downstairs first. Upstairs is noisier; the stairs creak more and there are a lot of corners, but I have windows I can jump out of if needed, and there's more light. Downstairs has the armory and it's quiet, but it also leaves me trapped.

I decide the armory is the spot my dad or Uncle Jimmy likely would have gone to, not wanting the burners to take it over, so I descend into the depths of the house, keeping my noise to a minimum.

The closer I get to the bottom of the steps, the louder a pair of voices become. I recognize neither of them, and I slowly poke my head around the corner, hoping to get a glimpse of the scene before being noticed.

Two men stand near the entrance to the tunnel leading back to the armory, chatting it up like they're on watch duty at a mall. Scanning the rest of the room, I see one of the cell doors is closed, bloody handprints stained across several of the bars. My stomach drops as I wonder who's locked in there, and whether they're alive.

I grab two of my throwing stars, tried and true for taking down people quietly, and palm them. After a deep breath, I emerge around the corner, hurling the objects one after the other into the burners. The first one strikes the man on the right directly in his open mouth. A second before, he had started laughing at a joke the other burner told, and now the glint of silver disappears into the blackness of his throat before a stream of blood begins to pour out of him. He chokes, his body trying to dislodge the object from his throat, his tongue flailing as he grabs at his neck. The burner heaves up air, only accelerating his choking on his own blood.

The other burner takes the star directly in the chin. My aim was a little high and now he looks like a member of the Mursi Tribe, the glinting, pointed disc jutting from his face as he lets out an agonizing scream.

With my knife in hand, I sprint at him, my sudden movement catching his eye. He's bewildered by my presence and the searing pain I've inflicted and almost forgets to respond. His expression changes from a glare of surprise to one of anger. Stamping his feet, he tries to rip out the object from the bone. At the last second, he snaps to attention and raises his weapon, pointing it at me. I have too long of a distance to close, my outstretched arm with knife in hand is still two full body lengths away from making contact with his skin, and I have no choice but to throw it at him. It flips over on itself, tumbling through the air like a gymnast, before the handle smacks into his forehead, sending him reeling back. The blade clangs against the concrete floor.

The burner brings his gun back up, but the second of time I bought myself allows me to slide forward. Dipping below the gun, I punch him directly in the balls. His hands involuntarily grab for them as he lets the gun drop to his side, the shoulder strap stopping it from hitting the ground. I sweep the back of his leg, making his kneecaps smash into the floor and his arms splay out, catching himself on all fours. Jumping onto him, I plant both of my feet on his back, riding his spine to the ground like a skateboard. His chin ornament drives into the concrete, and a muffled scream emits from his sealed mouth. I raise my boot and stomp his head. The structure caves and cracks, like an egg that's been dropped onto the floor. A pool of red spills out, the yolk having been released from the shell.

"Casey!?" a familiar voice exclaims.

Chapter 38

A million questions run through my mind as I paw at the bars, touching his hands, reaching through to his face. There's a light returning to his eyes, a flicker that nearly extinguished. He probably thought he would never see me again, and he may have even prepared for the end. But death didn't arrive—well, not for him—and instead my presence is pulling him back into a world he wants to be in, and one he wants to fight for.

"I'm so happy to see you," Blake says.

"Are you hurt?" I'm trying to look him over, but I can only take in pieces of him through the door, like his bloody hands. "Where's the blood coming from?" I ask.

He smirks, looking down at them himself, as if seeing it for the first time. "Nah. This isn't mine. One of them got too close to my cell door and decided to start talking nasty about what they were gonna do to Julie, Elaine, and Meredith, so I grabbed the back of his head and smashed his face into the bars . . . a couple times, actually."

When he says their names, a certain dread sets into his face, harsh lines of concern digging into his forehead. "Where is everyone? Are they okay?"

"Greg and Molly are up in the sniper tower keeping watch. Julie's a little banged up. Tessa and Elaine are fine. Meredith . . ." I pause, realizing that I don't actually know the truth about Meredith, other than that she's alive for now. "Is gonna be okay."

Blake inhales deeply through his nose, digesting everyone's status, and then the scream I heard before we entered the house comes rushing back into my brain. It comes in slowly at first, in fragments, like it's breaking through the barrier I created to focus on the moment at hand, but it wants out. It needs to be heard.

"The Carter family," I say. Blake looks to me, waiting for me continue, but he can read it on my face. The somber tone that we once held between us in this very spot, as we awaited his fate, has returned. The fate of an entire family already sealed. He reaches for my hand, squeezing it.

"I haven't found my dad or JJ or Uncle Jimmy yet. Do you know where they are?"

I almost flinch, waiting for him to answer.

"I overheard the two that were keeping watch. They said something about making them dig it themselves."

"The burn pit . . . past the fence." I turn to run back up the stairs, the image of my family members already lying in shallow graves, dirt being tossed on their bloodied and lifeless bodies, is plastered across my mind, like the burn-in of a once static image on a TV.

"Casey!" Blake's voice stops me dead in my tracks. "Uhhh," he says, rattling the cell door.

"Right!"

A quick trip to the armory has Blake and me fully stocked up with weaponry, the two of us ready to take on the world, or what's left of it. The burners must have thought the weaponry they had on them was enough for the job, since they left my dad's arsenal untouched, possibly saving it for another day. Big mistake, though. They should have made that day this one.

Through the woods out near the burn pit, we can hear yelling, harsh bursts of directives aimed at a few men who are hunched down, their arms swinging in a rhythmic scooping motion, elbows rising with the handles of the shovels, before striking into the earth.

A small plume of smoke grows from a newly set fire. They're using the corpses we already burned, biters and evil men just like them, as kindling. Their charred bodies are already sapped of fuel, so the fire is small and pallid, barely rising a foot off the pile.

No less than a dozen burners stand around the helpless diggers in a semicircle, throwing clumps of dirt and scorched body parts at them while they work.

"There's too many of them. We don't stand a chance," I whisper to Blake.

I try to shake the thought of defeat from my mind, but the situation feels so hopeless, so oppressively unwinnable. I hear a shout and look back just in time to see the butt of a rifle connect with the spine of one of the diggers. Their body collapses to the ground as a puff of dirt rises into the air, lifting the laughter of the men toward us. Between the dirt-caked boots standing tightly together, I see the wiry, speckled-gray bristles of a beard, rising up off the ground as its owner gets back to their feet.

"Dad," I say to myself, my rage only being held in check by my own sense of helplessness.

A hand grabs my shoulder as a cheek presses against the side of my head, his chin resting gently on my shoulder.

"We can do this," Blake says. "I've faced worse odds in the SEALs. These clowns probably have no training, and they're too comfortable, thinking they have this place under control. A quick burst from that SMG you have there, and you could injure nearly all of them before they even realize what's happening."

I nod, keeping my eyes on the burners.

"Here's the plan. You lay down a volley aimed at the five or six guys on the left over there." He points over my shoulder, and my eyes follow the line of his arm. "That way you don't risk hitting any of your family. Worst-case scenario, you injure one or two of them, and they all run in a panic, scrambling to find the source of the gunfire, giving Dale, Jimmy, and JJ time to either flee or grab a weapon and fight. Meanwhile, I strike from the wings, velociraptor-style."

"Clever girl." I smile, picturing Blake emerging from the thick brush of woods, the fire in his green eyes turning them into a searing yellow as he unleashes hell.

"Exactly."

"What's the best-case scenario?"

"Huh?"

"You said worst case, but you didn't tell me the best case."

"Oh, best case, you kill all of them on the spot and it becomes two versus ten instead of what it is now. Any more questions?"

"What are you gonna do? Don't I need to know your part of the plan?"

Blake squats down to the forest floor, using some of the still moist blood on his hands to make a paste out of the soil, turning it into a thick red-brown sludge. He closes his eyes and smears it all over his face. His eyes pop back open, the whites standing out like keys on a piano against his camouflaged skin.

"Don't worry about me, Doomsday." Blake smiles and disappears into the woods without another word.

That's exactly what I'm going to give these burners . . . their very own doomsday.

The wind shifts, blowing smoke from the fire in my direction. The stench is like a backyard barbecue where the grill master opted to char up some expired, rotten meat. Boiling pus and decay mix with hair and fabric remaining on the bodies, creating a fragrance that a full diaper would be envious of. I lift my shirt collar up over my nose, semi-blocking the smell to avoid gagging and giving away my cover.

I have no idea whether Blake is ready or in position. When am I supposed to shoot? Will he give me a signal? Or will I just know? Will the bond that ties us together manifest itself in a physical response, something to say, *We can do this, Casey*?

"All right, enough! They look plenty deep," one burner yells. His face is disfigured, as though it's been melted away by acid or scalding water. He forces my family to rise and stand at the foot of each of their freshly dug graves.

"Turn around and face away from the holes," he yells.

"You gonna shoot us now?" my father asks, a proud defiance in his voice.

"HA! Shoot you? Where would the fun be in that?" The man snaps his fingers and holds his hand out to his side. Another burner places a stick with a lit piece of cloth, flaming at the end, into his open hand. "We're gonna burn you alive. Let your screams sink into our brains so we can replay them again and again in our minds. It'll help us sleep at night, like a lullaby for a baby." He arches back, letting out a roar of laughter. The rest of his compatriots join in. The lead burner goes quiet and raises his leg, kicking my father in the chest. The force sends him flying back into the open grave. I gasp, covering my mouth with my hand, adrenaline surging through my body.

He points the tip of the flaming stick into the hole, while another burner comes to his side, carrying a canister of liquid.

Fuck this.

I flick the safety off and point the gun at the fifth burner in from the left and let my finger sink back into the trigger. The gun whirs to life in a flash, four bullets ripping into the burner in under a second before I start panning to the left. Twenty-six more bullets divide themselves among the remaining four men, blood spraying in every direction as the scene devolves into chaos.

The five men I shot at are either writhing on the ground or lying completely still, no longer a part of the equation. The other seven have turned to the woods, firing wildly in hopes of hitting me. I anticipated this response and took cover behind one of the many oak trees in the forest. No bullet will be able to penetrate the three feet of solid wood, at least from their current positions.

"Cowards! Get in there! Kill whatever motherfucker did this!" I hear a burner yell out, and I can guess who—that ugly, nasty one.

I spot another substantial piece of cover and dart through the woods, changing my location. As I'm running, I look out at the scene and see JJ and Jimmy struggling with the men who were standing in front of them, wrestling for control of their firearms.

Where the hell is Blake?

A heavy rustling of branches and snapping of twigs begins to encircle me as the burners enter the woods. My position of safety is quickly becoming compromised.

Shit. Shit. Shit. I'm gonna be surrounded. Where the fuck is Blake?

A large branch snaps just on the other side of the tree I'm hiding behind, and I poke my head around the corner, my gun at the ready. I lean without taking a step, afraid of the underbrush giving away my position.

My hair is yanked back hard, almost pulling me off my feet as I'm spun around. His rank mixture of grime, BO, and rotten breath hits me in the face like a fistful of raw sewage.

"Peekaboo," he says, smiling with a knife pressed to my throat. "Boys! I found herrugggghhhhkk—"

Hacking and slurping sounds escape his mouth as blood pools and spills out, trickling down his chin. Blake has one hand over the man's forehead; the other has plunged a knife deep into his throat, angled up into the brain. He slowly withdraws the blade and puts a finger to his lips, tapping it a few times as he lowers the body to the ground. Before I can speak, he's gone, back into the cover of the forest.

Two burners come around the trail, guns at the ready, answering the call of their newly deceased friend. When they see me, sinister, salivating smiles cross their faces, and then they look to the ground. Their grins curve downward with the movement of their heads, the corpse coming into view for them. His throat looks like a programmed fountain at a mall or airport, weaker and weaker torrents of blood pumping out at even intervals.

"What the hell?" one of them says just as a flash of black appears from behind a tree. Blake slides across the dry foliage, and his knife glistens between the first burner's legs, the fabric of his pants soaking in an upside-down V like he's just wet himself. The burner falls to his knees as Blake pops back to his feet, grabbing the second man by his hair and plunging the knife into the side of his neck. He pushes it in farther, dragging it up and down to rip through flesh and tendon, the burner's head now looking like a PEZ dispenser. The first burner is still on his knees, frozen, eyes wide and mouth agape, but no sound is being emitted.

I point to the man as if to say, *What about him?*

Blake shakes his head. "I severed his femoral artery. He'll be dead in less than thirty seconds." He disappears again, a wisp in the air like the last breaths of the men he just encountered. *Jesus, he's like a super-sadistic Batman.*

In the distance, I hear the symphony of Blake's destruction, a crescendo working in tandem, the strings section wailing out, screaming their final notes. Then a new sound joins the fray.

"Enough with the games!" A loud voice shakes through the woods. "Come out now, or we burn all three of them alive!"

Blake returns to my side without a sound. He and I can see the burn pit through the trees. My dad, Jimmy, and JJ are all kneeling with their hands placed against the back of their heads, a burner standing behind each of them. The leader paces back and forth in front of them, the gas canister swinging at his side.

"What do we do?" I ask, frantic and scared.

"Surrender."

"Surrender!? Are you joking?"

"Trust me," Blake says, putting his hands up and walking out of the woods.

I shake my head in disbelief. He gave up so easily after all that show of skill and bravado. For what? A few more dead burners? I follow him, hands up, trusting he has a plan and will get us out of this.

"Ahhh, there you are. Mr. G.I. Joe himself, ripping my men apart. Now, walk over . . ." The ugly burner gasps when his eyes land on me.

"What do we have here? Aren't you a pretty little thing left behind in this ugly world? Toss all your weapons on the ground, and please don't pretend like you each only have one gun. I can see your clothes bulging everywhere, and if I have to come search you, then . . . well, I'll just kill you on the spot."

I look to Blake, and he nods, confirming that I should follow the orders. He lobs me a small wink, and it instantly makes me feel calm and better about the situation. We pitch our guns out into the grass, creating a small cache of firepower until the leader seems satisfied that we've given up all our weapons.

"You see, I was going to just kill you and then burn these three, but how about a little trade instead? If you"—he points at Blake—"burn the three of them . . ." He waves his hand to JJ, my dad, and Uncle Jimmy. "I'll let you kill yourself, fast and easy . . . *and* I'll let the girl live. She can"—he licks his lips before flicking his tongue in and out of his mouth like a lizard—"join us."

Blake looks to me and then the faces of my family.

"That's the best offer you're gonna get, soldier, and the clock is ticking." The leader glances down at his wrist, pretending to count down the seconds on a watch that isn't there. "Five . . . four . . . three . . . two . . ."

"Okay! I'll do it. I'll do it," Blake says, shuffling toward them, his head and shoulders sunken down as he avoids making eye contact with me.

"Blake, no! You can't trust them!" I start to run at him, but the leader draws a pistol from his side, cocking it and pointing it directly at me.

"Ah, ah, ah . . . let's not be too eager. Trust me, you'll have plenty of time to play later." He looks me up and down, taking me in again before his lust turns to surprise. "Wait a minute. I know you. You're that little bitch from Chicago. You did this to me!" He slaps his palm into his own face, fingers wide as he slowly drags it across the topography of his features. "You ruined my fucking face!"

"To be fair, it wasn't good to begin with," I quip, not allowing him to rattle me.

The other three burners stifle laughs as their leader glares at them before leveling his attention back on me. "Oh, I'm gonna enjoy the future that's in store for you. I can picture it now. Night after night, piece by piece, the horrors that will come your way. You'll be wishing I'd just kill you, take you out of your misery, but I won't. You'll come to look at this ruined face as the most beautiful thing in the world, and you'll beg it for salvation." He turns to Blake, pointing the gun at him. "But a deal's a deal, so the girl shall live. Forever, if I can help it."

"I'm sorry, Casey. But I can't watch you die." Blake continues walking toward JJ, the gas canister lifted up to his chest. JJ hangs his head, his shoulders tightening.

"That's a good boy. Now, you sit tight here, my angel, and enjoy the show." The leader walks back behind my father, firing the pistol into the air right next to his ear. Dad instinctively cups his ear, the drum likely shattered.

The leader presses the muzzle of the pistol into his hand, searing a red ring into the skin. My father shouts at the pain.

"Stop it!" I yell, my voice crackling with rage.

"Stop? Oh, we're just getting started." He fires off a round near Blake's feet, the earth kicking up around him. "Quit stalling, pretty boy, and do it or the deal's off."

Blake lifts the canister over JJ's head and starts to tilt it. "Sorry, man. Just picture my face on the men behind you."

"Huh?" JJ responds, confused by his statement.

My hand moves down to my tried-and-true beauties at my side, all along, as Blake's words sink in. He whips the gas canister forward, hitting the burner standing behind JJ square in the nose. It sends him toppling back into the open grave.

Blake leaps to his left, his knife outstretched as the burner behind my uncle Jimmy turns his gun on him and fires off a shot, ripping through the top layer of flesh on Blake's left arm, just before the blade of the knife disappears into the man's temple. I stand and throw one star at the man positioned behind my father. The silver disk spins like a buzz saw, ripping into the bridge of his nose as two of the prongs poke out both of his eyes at once. The other star I hurl at the leader with more venom and force than I've put behind any throw I've made in my life. But the extra force doesn't have the desired effect, as it leaves my hand a split second later, causing it to veer slightly down and to the left, lodging into his collarbone. He screams out, a fit of rage and pain causing him to drop his gun. My father, realizing the opportunity, grabs for the weapon, but the leader recovers too quickly and crushes Dad's hand beneath his boot.

"I'll kill you all," he yells out, kneeing my father in the face.

I sprint toward the deformed object of my hatred, hoping to tackle him back into the grave before he has time to get control of the gun, but the distance is too great, and within a second, I'm staring down the barrel of a pistol.

"Such a waste," the leader says, eyeing my living body one last time. "Oh well." He thumbs back the hammer and squeezes the trigger.

The world around me freezes. The burst of flame from the gun becomes the sun, everything else in the vicinity around it sucked in by its gravity. The bullet spirals out of the weapon, a satellite launched into orbit by rocket fuel. The leader's eyes are red, reflecting the fire from the burn pit, channeling through his body, into the object in his hand. But the pull of gravity is even stronger from another celestial body. The full beard, buzzed hair, and broad shoulders, diving to intercept the missile in flight.

And then time starts back up.

Chapter 39

"Dad!" I scream, running toward him, forgetting that there's still a man with a gun pointed at me. My only concern is for my father, and I don't care if I die right now, trying to get to him.

The leader looks down at the large body at his feet, blood already staining his white shirt. Dad gasps for air, covering the wound with his hand to put pressure on it and slow the bleeding.

"Looks like Daddy's heroics were all for nothing," the burner says, smiling. He kicks my father hard in the side with enough force to break his ribs. "And now I get to kill you while you watch your father bleed out. Payback's a bitc—"

Blake plunges his knife into the unscathed-yet-still-ugly side of the burner's face, the steel sliding just below the surface of the skin along his forehead. The blade slices down, filleting the flesh off like the scales of a fish. With one clean swipe, the burner's nose and cheek separate from his skull, falling off like a half mask.

He screams, his one eye permanently bulged without the skin around it. The hollowed nose and lipless mouth give him the appearance of a bloodied skeleton. The pain is so intense, the burner tries to bring his own gun to his head and end it all, but Blake strikes it from his hand. He shoves him into the grave that my father dug before kicking burning embers into the hole. JJ runs over with the gas canister that Blake used to save him and pours the remaining contents into the grave.

Flames leap from the earth, like the mouth of hell itself has opened up. The fire almost licks the gas canister in JJ's hands, and he recoils quickly from the blast of heat. Horrifying screams of agony emit from the inferno, as the burner's hands flail at the sides of the grave, clawing at the soil he'll soon call home.

There's no time to relish this moment, because the man who gave up nearly everything to raise me in a way that would make sure I was protected may have given up the last thing he had to offer.

"Dad, no! Don't close your eyes! You're gonna be okay," I say, grazing my hand through his hair, in an attempt to calm him, while pressing down on his own hand to help put pressure on his injury. "Get me towels! Get me something! Anything! We need to stop the bleeding!" I'm screaming to everyone, to anyone.

JJ takes off running toward the house, while Blake sinks to his knees on the other side of my father, helping to put pressure on the wound, which won't stop bleeding.

"Dale," Blake says, "I need you to hang in there. You're the toughest sonofabitch I know, and a little old thing like a bullet isn't gonna take you down. Right?" He's saying all the right words, but his conviction tells me he knows the same truth that I do.

My dad looks up at Blake, cracking a grin. "Yeah, buddy. That's right." Tears fall onto my father's shirt, and I glance over, realizing they're coming from Blake. He squeezes my and my dad's hands as they're piled on top of one another, all trying to do the same thing—keep him alive, keep him with us.

"Sweetheart." My dad's gaze lands on me. His voice croaks, faint and weak, the smell of iron coming from his mouth.

"Dad," I say, swallowing the sob that threatens to pour out. "Hold on just a little longer. I can save you."

"You already did," he says.

I can see the look of acceptance in his eyes, the look that a patient gives me after I have told them that final sweet lie. That everything is going to be fine. The look that says, *I'm okay with this*. I know he's drifting away from me, but I don't want him to.

"I can't do this without you, Dad. Please, you have to stay." My tears fall fast and hard, a torrential downpour of sadness. My lips stick together from the excess saliva mixing with the salty pain.

"You can. I know you can." He smiles, lifting his other hand to brush away the hairs clinging to my cheeks.

I shake my head defiantly, saying *no* over and over again.

"I'm sorry for ruining your childhood." He coughs a fine mist of blood mixed with his saliva. Speckles of red quickly stain his cheeks and beard.

"You didn't." I squeeze his hand and press down harder, willing him to stay alive, to stay with me. I feel the pressure from Blake doing the same.

"I did. I know I did. But . . . I just." He coughs again, even more blood coming out, this time thick enough to emerge as full drops. "I just wanted you to realize that even when it feels like the world has ended, yours doesn't have to."

Tears fall from my eyes, dripping onto his shirt, getting lost in the sea of red. "I love you, Dad."

"I love you too, Case."

His eyes swing to Blake. "Take care of my girl," he says.

Blake nods and whispers, "I will. I promise."

Dad's gaze returns to me, and he cups my face with his hand, gently stroking my cheek with his thumb. My body shakes with grief, but I'm trying to hold still and strong, so he will too.

"Your mother would be so proud of you," he says, barely getting the words out.

His hand slips from my face and falls to the grass, his eyes staring up at the sky.

The sob rips through me, and I throw myself across my father's chest, hugging him as tight as I can, willing him to come back.

Chapter 40

I pause for a moment, catching my breath as I lean against the old shovel to keep myself upright. My arms are weak, almost like noodles, barely doing what my brain tells them to. The palms of my hands are raw, blistered and torn open. But I don't feel the pain, because it pales in comparison to the anguish inside me. It's all consuming. My eyes go to the horizon just as the sun starts to dip below. The sky is a mosaic of pinks and oranges, splashed in every direction. It's as though Dad painted it on his way up there, leaving something beautiful in his wake—a final lesson from him. *Just because the world ended doesn't mean yours has to end too.*

I shake out my tired hands and get back to work, gripping the handle of the shovel and tossing another spade of loose soil into the hole I dug myself. My father lies at the bottom of it, wrapped tightly in the blanket he and my mother used to share. Everyone wanted to help. They insisted. But no, this was my hole to dig, and it's my hole to fill. Dad would have wanted it that way, just him and me, like it always used to be. So I keep shoveling, even when I want to stop, because Pearsons don't quit until the job's done. A cry starts deep in my gut, climbing upward as it grows. It stretches my esophagus, pushing its way out of me. I have no more tears left. I've either cried them all out or my body is too dehydrated to make more.

"Are we almost done yet, Dad?" I whisper through a sob, wishing and hoping he'd answer me, even if to tell me, *No, Casey. We're just getting started.* Because that's truly what I wish. I wish we were just getting started, and I know now that was the point of everything my dad did, everything he had us do. The time we spent prepping and working and all the blood, sweat, and tears we shed. None of it was for the end. It was for a beginning. My father didn't prepare me for the end of the world. He prepared me to start a new one. And I just wish he were a part of it.

The final spade of soil falls onto his grave, and I pat the blade against it several times, flattening out the dirt, wanting to keep him safe and secure in there. I chose this spot beneath the apple tree, the same one he and I used to sit under eating our sandwiches on a break or ice cream after a long day of hard work. I figured this is where he'd want to be if he couldn't be here with me.

The grass crunches behind me, and I turn quickly to find Blake approaching, a solemn look plastered on his face. I know it matches mine.

"Hey," he says.

"Hi," I say, leaning the shovel up against the tree and dusting my hands off on my damp shirt.

He pulls his hand from behind his back. Clutched in it are two ice cream Drumsticks, the same kind my dad and I used to enjoy after a long day of work. I'm surprised. I didn't think any of those were left in the world. The wrapper crinkles as he extends one to me.

"Your dad was saving these," Blake says. "And I thought you might like to have one with me." His eyes are glossy, but he holds in his grief.

"You thought right." I take it from him and grab a seat in the grass beside my father's grave.

Blake hesitates for a moment, like he's waiting for me to tell him to go away or that I want to be alone. But I don't. I smile up at him and pat the earth beside me. He takes a seat, pressing his shoulder into mine, leaving not even a centimeter between us. We unwrap our Drumsticks and bite into the chocolate coating, sinking our teeth into the vanilla ice cream trapped beneath it. It doesn't taste as sweet as it used to, but

I don't think it's the ice cream that's lacking flavor. It was the moments I shared with my dad that made it sweet.

Blake puts his arm around me, pulling me into him. I lean my head against his shoulder, licking at my ice cream cone while staring out at the sunset. Every ending precedes a new beginning, and there'll be plenty of sweet moments ahead, regardless of the ones that have already passed.

"No matter what this new world throws at us, we're gonna be okay," Blake says.

I lift my head and look to him, taking in those bright-green eyes, the same ones I used to imagine spiking a shovel through. Now I can't imagine them any other way than staring back at me.

"I know, Blake. Dad made sure of that."

A tear falls from the corner of his eye, and he holds me a little tighter. I lean in, planting my ice cream–coated lips against his. They're extra sweet, and they might just be the sweetest thing I've ever tasted.

Epilogue

Six months later

"You look beautiful, Molly," I say as I watch her twirl in front of the full-length mirror. It's cracked in multiple places, fissures running to and fro on the surface, making it look like there are multiple versions of her. But it works nonetheless. She's adorned in an all-white dress, the lower half billowing out as her momentum fills the fabric with air.

"Thanks, Casey," she says, pausing her twirl and looking to me with an unsure sadness in her eyes. "Are you sure you're okay with me wearing this?"

"Of course." I smile. "It was just gathering dust in a dresser. Plus, she would have wanted it to be put to good use." It's my mother's wedding dress, and my dad kept it all these years, safely locked away in his bedroom closet.

"But what about you and Blake, if . . . ya know? Wouldn't you wanna wear it?" Molly asks.

"Well, we were enemies first, then lovers, then enemies again, and now lovers. So we're due to switch back to enemies very soon," I say with a laugh. "So don't worry about us. This is your day."

"That's right, Molly, so enjoy it, because tomorrow, it's back to training and surviving the end of the world," Tessa says as she swipes an old Maybelline blush across her cheeks.

I pat her shoulder as she gets to her feet and stands beside me.

"Thank you both for standing up with me." Molly beams at us, tears in her eyes. We grab her hand and squeeze it, creating a little sisterhood circle of our own.

Tessa and I have donned old dresses I found in the back of my closet. A sequined one I bought my senior year, when I thought Blake would ask me to homecoming. It was unworn until today. And a pink bridesmaid's dress from a wedding I stood up in my freshman year of college. We look rather ridiculous, but it doesn't matter.

A knock on the door interrupts us. "Can I come in?" Blake's voice calls from the other side, instantly giving me butterflies.

"Of course!" Molly blurts out, excited for someone else to see her in the dress.

Blake walks in wearing his navy dress attire. It was the only formal outfit he could find, but he wears it well, and it appears I like a man in uniform.

"Molly, you look beautiful!" he says, giving her a hug.

"Thanks, Blake."

He turns to Tessa and me, all smiles. "And so do both of you."

"Don't lie to me, Blake," Tessa says, trying to flatten out her puffy, pink dress. "I look like a cake topper for a little girl's birthday party."

"But a beautiful cake topper," I tease.

Blake smiles and steps to me, kissing my cheek and resting his hand on my waist to pull me into him. "And you look like you should be on top of something else," he whispers, biting the tip of my earlobe. I giggle, giving him a smoldering look as I pull away.

"You two are disgustingly cute," Tessa says with a smirk.

"Yeah, you're like a younger Greg and me, our puppy love growing into a full dog." Molly cups her hands together over her heart.

I furrow my brow. "I'm, like, a decade older than you, and I've known Blake since I was thirteen."

"Love works in mysterious ways." She beams.

"We're all set out there," Blake says with an amused look on his face. "Are you ready, Molly?"

She nods, the ringlets in her hair bouncing like springs. "I've been ready since that first night I spent with Greg, when he brought me back to his dorm and—"

"All right, let's get you hitched then," I interrupt before she goes into more detail.

Outside on the front lawn, people are seated in a hodgepodge of chairs, overturned buckets, and stumps set up in rows. Several carpet runners serve as the aisle, with red and white rose petals strewn over them. Aunt Julie stands at the end of the passage of rugs, under a makeshift altar made of two-by-fours and adorned with wildflowers. She has tears in her eyes as she holds her head high, waiting to officiate this special occasion. Greg stands to the right of her, dressed in one of my dad's old suits. It's a size too big, but with his raised shoulders and puffed-out chest, it's barely noticeable.

Over the last six months, we've taken in a dozen people, so there are many new faces gathered before us. After our successful mission to the hospital, we got a little bolder with our scavenge runs, confident that we could handle ourselves, even in places filled with biters. We explored more hospitals, gated homes, and government buildings, but the jackpot was a secured warehouse. We found enough grains and canned goods to feed everyone here for years. So when we discovered stragglers in need of saving, we welcomed them into the fold.

We've built several new cabins, made the dummy house livable again, and fortified our perimeter even more, raising the height of the barbed wire and adding a day shift for patrolling. We vowed to never allow an attack like we suffered to befall us again, or at least we'll do everything in our power to stop it from happening again.

Standing off to the side from Aunt Julie is Terrance with a harmonica in hand, ready to play the wedding procession down the aisle. He's a large man in his late fifties with dark skin, a barrel-size chest, and a thick beard. Terrance is one of the new faces who joined us during a scavenging raid. Near the end of a run, we were loading up the truck, and in a moment of brief silence, we heard a sound that none of us had heard in a very long time. Music. Sitting on the roof of a house with a rifle resting on his lap was Terrance, playing his harmonica without a care in the world. He had barricaded the first floor of the house, coming and going through a second-story window with the use of a rope ladder he could retract back into itself with a hidden pull cord. Blake and I struck up a conversation with him, like neighbors greeting one another while out on a walk. We got along well, and it felt like the old normal. He's been with us ever since. Terrance is one tough sonofabitch, but not the toughest sonofabitch I've ever known. He reminds me a lot of my dad, and I think the two of them would have been fast friends.

"Don't you clean up nice," a voice calls from behind me. I turn to see Elaine, smiling from ear to ear.

"Same to you," I say, pointing at her floral dress, which she made out of an old sheet. We embrace one another in a tight hug.

"All those months ago. Greg avoiding her like the plague. Did you ever think this day would come?" she asks.

I turn back to look at Molly, hiding behind a tree out of Greg's sight, a grin plastered across her face. I haven't seen someone that happy since . . . maybe ever. And despite everything, her bubbly nature and optimism for this fallen world have never faltered.

"Yes. Yes, I did," I say with a smile.

"May I walk you to your seat, madam?" JJ asks, arm extended with his elbow bent, waiting for Elaine's hand.

"Aren't you about to walk up the aisle? You can't be seen so soon," Elaine protests.

"I don't think it's that formal of a crowd." JJ smirks.

Greg starts fist-bumping Terrance as he goads him into playing some tunes before the ceremony starts. Terrance obliges and begins performing "Bad to the Bone" on his harmonica.

Elaine lets out a heavy sigh. "At least there will be an open bar at the reception." She chuckles as JJ escorts her to her seat.

"Pssst," I hear someone say.

I spin around to find Molly waving me over. I quickly sprint across the grass, hoping she's not getting cold feet.

"Hey, everything okay? Are you ready?" I ask, finding her with her back leaned up against the tree.

"Mm-hmm." She nods, her lips pulled in, tears beginning to form across her eyes.

"What's wrong?"

"Nothing. It's just . . . when I pictured this day, I thought my mom would be sitting in the front row, my brother and sister both standing up with me. And my dad would walk me down the aisle and give me away." A tear escapes her eye and I swiftly dab it dry, saving her makeup from streaking.

"I know, Molly," I say, resting my hand on her arm. "I know it more than anyone, but it doesn't make it any better and it doesn't make it suck any less. Just because this day isn't what you pictured doesn't mean it can't be wonderful. It's different, yes, but different doesn't mean bad. There are so many people here that love you dearly, and none more than that big goof up there waiting for you."

Molly pokes her head around the tree to get a glimpse of Greg and starts giggling upon seeing him dancing and singing the lyrics to the song "Don't Worry, Be Happy." She looks back at me with a smile on her face.

"Sometimes the family you're born with can't always be there. But the family you pick up along the way can be. So let's celebrate that and the two of you becoming a family of your own." I tilt my head, returning the smile.

Molly lunges forward, drawing me into her before I have a chance to react. It's reminiscent of the first hug we ever shared.

"Thanks, Case," she whispers into my ear. "I'm ready."

Signaling Terrance to start the actual wedding music, I join Tessa, JJ, and Blake at the end of the aisle.

"She didn't get cold feet, did she?" Tessa asks.

"No, her feet are scalding hot," I joke.

As the music begins, Tessa and JJ link arms and start off down the aisle. Blake nods to me as we stand side by side, waiting for our turn.

Sloane slips out from her chair in the last row and brushes past me, saying, "I'm going to check on the food and make sure the reception is all set back at the house." She's a couple of years older than I am, with a striking appearance, thanks to her long dark, wavy hair and light-green eyes. Sloane joined us about seven weeks ago, after her car hit a patch of ice and skidded off the road two miles down. She fit in almost immediately, thanks to her willingness to help with anything and everything. Her military background made her a valuable asset right from the beginning. She took night shifts, learned how to patrol, went on scavenge runs, and helped to train others on combat and weaponry. She was lucky to have stumbled upon this place, and we've been lucky to have her.

"No, no, sit," I say, waving a hand and gesturing to her chair. "We'll worry about that after the ceremony."

She gives me a strained look. "But shouldn't the reception be ready for Molly and Greg after the ceremony?"

"Yes, and it will be. Just relax."

Sloane tightly smiles and retakes her seat, even though I know she doesn't want to. She's a lot like me in that way, unable to sit still, because there's always something that can be done. I got that from my dad, and I wonder whether her dad was the same way. I smile back and thread my arm through Blake's, ready to walk down the aisle with him.

"Hello, my dear," he whispers.

"What did you have in mind?" I raise a brow.

"Huh?" His face is confused.

"Sniper tower, cab of the truck, tree house. What would you like me on top of?"

Blake smirks. "Definitely a tower, but not the sniper variety."

"Tower? Let's not go overboard."

"Seems to do the trick for you." He winks, making me laugh.

My eyes veer back to Tessa and JJ, realizing they're more than halfway to Greg, so we missed our mark. "Whoops. We're up," I say, tugging him forward.

He grins at me and mouths *I love you* as we walk down the aisle.

I smile back and mouth *I love you too*, just before we part ways. Blake and Greg hug. Blake gives him an extra pat on the back, then takes his spot on JJ's other side.

With everyone in place, I nod to Terrance once more. The familiar music begins and everyone instinctively stands, turning toward the end of the aisle.

Molly is as beautiful as any bride I've ever seen, apocalypse be damned. The universe must think so too, given the perfect weather and songbirds singing from nearby trees. The sun illuminates her from behind, and for a moment all I can see is the dress radiating light, and I can't help but wonder whether Molly doesn't have more than just my uncle Jimmy walking her down the aisle.

Greg has tears running down his face, with a smile so wide his lips might burst. Uncle Jimmy steps forward and whispers to Greg. A message only for a father's and son's ears. He kisses Molly on the cheek, hands her off to Greg, and takes a seat in the front row.

"Dearly beloved, we are gathered here on this glorious afternoon to join in marriage . . . ," Aunt Julie says, sticking to the traditions we all tried to remember, but none of us had ever officiated a wedding before, so she's winging it.

I look out into the crowd, noting the smiling faces, caught up in the moment, as most wedding attendees are prone to be. The majority of them haven't known Greg and Molly for more than a few months, but they're honored to be a part of their special day anyway. Because a day like this offers all of us hope that we can love and be loved even in the darkest times. The world may have ended, but our humanity is endless.

I look to the road beyond the fence, stretching for miles and . . .

What the hell is that? I squint to get a better view.

A semitruck drives down the highway, its white metal siding glinting in the sun as a plume of black smoke bursts from the exhaust pipe. A working vehicle driving on the road has happened a few times, like in Sloane's case before she crashed, but a semitruck? *Never.*

I try to get Blake's attention without ruining the moment, but he's on the other side of JJ, and he's just as enthralled with the ceremony as everyone else.

Suddenly, the truck slows. My heart pounds as I watch it, hoping it's nothing. But then several men appear on top of the trailer, having climbed up the back of it. They get in a line, seemingly facing us, pulling items out of backpacks slung over their shoulders One of them drops down on his belly, while another man places something large and black in front of him. It takes me a moment to realize what it is . . . but when I do, my eyes go wide. It's a sniper rifle.

"If anyone has any objections, speak now or forever hold your peace," Aunt Julie says, scanning the crowd.

It's quiet for only a split second, until I scream, "RUNNNNNN!" just as bullets rip through the air, hitting the ground around us.

Acknowledgments

I never thought I would write a book like this, and that's because this book doesn't fit within one genre—or even two. *Dating After the End of the World* is a little bit of everything, and it was a passion project for me. I wanted to challenge myself. I wanted to write something different, something that blurred the lines of genre, something that made you laugh and cry, made your heart pound for one reason or another, something that was adventurous and thrilling and horrifying, something that had heart and humor.

So the first person I want to thank is the one who allowed me to write this weird story, my editor, Anh Schluep. When Anh asked if I wanted to do another book with Montlake and then asked what ideas I had for it, I pitched this one. If you read *It's a Date (Again)*, my first romance novel, you know this novel is nothing like that. After I pitched the concept for *Dating After the End of The World*, I said, "I know it's weird, but I'm really excited about it." To which Anh replied, "If you're excited about it, then we're excited about it." So thank you, Anh, for believing in my unhinged postapocalyptic, enemies-to-lovers zombie story and for also letting me run absolutely wild with it.

Thank you to Lindsey Faber for your wonderful editorial insights and for tag-teaming this book with Anh to make it so much better. Speaking of teams, thank you to the entire team at Montlake for all your support and all your hard work.

Thank you to my readers for supporting me across genres, no matter whether I'm writing thrillers, romance, speculative fiction, horror, or whatever this book happens to be. Writing saved me in more ways than one, so really, *you* saved me, and I can't thank you enough for that. Special shout-out to my silly gaggle of geese, a.k.a. my Facebook reader group, Jeneva Rose's Convention of Readers. If you're not a part of the group, you should join us. It's a fun, positive little slice of the internet!

Thank you to my dad, who not only demanded a zombie book but in many ways inspired aspects of this novel. Growing up, my dad was a bit of a doomsday prepper—not a good one, though. He mostly just bought lots of canned goods, which were super fun to haul in and then eventually be forced to eat because they were set to expire. So, thanks for that, Dad.

Thank you to my first readers, and by that, I mean those who read an early version of this book and delivered a nice balance of compliments and critiques, so I had the motivation and guidance to polish it into what it is now. Thank you to Delaney Starr, Cristina Montero (sorry, I didn't change Nate to Kevin, but just imagine that's his name), Bri Becker, Kent Willetts, Andrea Willetts, Austin Nerge, and James Nerge.

And finally, thank you to my husband, Drew. This book wouldn't have been possible without you. Actually, none of them would have been possible without you. You believed in me when I didn't believe in myself, and you encouraged me when I wanted to quit. I'll be by your side until the world ends—and then I'll be a little behind you in an effort to sacrifice myself for your well-being. Just kidding. It's because I'm a slow runner . . . still counts as a sacrifice, though.

About the Author

Photo © 2022 Katharine Hannah

Jeneva Rose is the *New York Times* and Amazon #1 bestselling author of several novels, including the multimillion-copy bestseller *The Perfect Marriage*. Her work has been translated into more than two dozen languages and optioned for film and TV. She lives in Wisconsin with her husband, Drew, and her English bulldogs, Winston and Phyllis. For more information, visit www.jenevarose.com.